Trouble

Jesse Kellerman

W F HOWES LTD

This large print edition published in 2007 by
W F Howes Ltd
Unit 4, Rearsby Business Park, Gaddesby Lane,
Rearsby, Leicester LE7 4YH

First publish   dom in 2007

1   Kellerman, Jesse   1 2

Trouble / Jesse
Kellerman

LP

1780140

The right of Jesse Kellerman to be identified as
the author of this work has been asserted by him
in accordance with the Copyright, Designs and
Patents Act, 1988.

A CIP catalogue record for this book is available
from the British Library

ISBN 978 1 84632 076 7

Typeset by Palimpsest Book Production Limited,
Grangemouth, Stirlingshire
Printed and bound in Great Britain
by Antony Rowe Ltd, Chippenham, Wilts.

Trouble

ALSO BY JESSE KELLERMAN
FROM CLIPPER LARGE PRINT

Sunstroke

To Gavri

She spread a salve to soothe his aches
He suffered from its bitter taste

THE BOOK OF ODD THOUGHTS, 5:7

PART I

SURGERY

CHAPTER 1

J onah Stem heard a scream.

He was walking to Times Square at two forty-five in the morning to buy new shoes. The staid, sturdy Rockport Walkers that had survived two years of theoretical medicine had finally succumbed to its uncontrollably runny realities. Befouled beyond repair, they made a squishing noise and left a trail, like overgrown snails. Salient among the novel qualities they had come to possess was the stink of human shit.

Shoes were shoes. Their destruction didn't bother Jonah per se, except that it acutely underscored his own incompetence – something he didn't need to be reminded of these days, with people lining up to do it for him.

For this mess, as he did generally, Jonah blamed himself. He knew the rules; he'd read the Book, heard it from the Ghosts of Third Year Past. Once your day was over, the only safe strategy was OTD – Out the Door – ASAP. If you lingered and got caught, you were SOL. Particularly on surgery. Surgeons – surgical residents, rather – didn't especially care that your day had been over for twenty minutes. (Attendings didn't especially care about you at all.) When they needed you, you went. The best way to avoid being needed, then, was to get out of the building supersonic fast.

Instead he'd dawdled. He had twelve weeks here; it paid to take the time to learn his way around. Asking too many questions – even innocuous ones like *Where are we meeting* or *Where's the bathroom* – made you look unprepared. It primed the pump for getting pimped, because while the Gods of Surgery might forget your name, forget that you had other obligations, forget that you were a person with a beating heart and an independent will, They always, *always* remembered your weaknesses. They took note of who copped to ignorance, and on that person They pounced, eager to impart Their full-tilt no-holds-barred balls-to-the-wall medical education until he sobbed and sniveled like a little pants-wetting baby girl.

Jonah liked hospitals at that hour, the alleged end of the workday, when patients finished their early dinners and settled in for TV and Toradol and complaining. Midtown–St Agatha's – a thrumming snuffleupagus of sterile linoleum, wheelchairs, high-rising paperwork, hypo-allergenic pillowcases, accident victims, cancer victims, moans, kidney stones, sample closets, graywater mop buckets, insurance fraud, viruses, bacteria, prions, fractures,

4

lesions, lacerations, nociceptors firing and relaxing – took a breath. A place like St Aggie's was never truly silent, but like all large medical institutions, it seemed to hiccup at around six thirty P.M., granting an illusion of peace; an idea of what peace might be, if you weren't imprisoned in a goddamned hospital.

He meandered varicose corridors, shucking the stickiness, the soreness, the self-pity. He was here to learn. He was going to be a doctor; he spent years toiling to earn the right to be so abused. He had taken college courses and review courses. He had spent hours glued to books, had bushwhacked the MCAT and pummeled the Boards. All to get here. Finishing work feeling like a used condom was a *privilege*. Who cares about the antiseptic smell; the harsh, bluish lights; the overenthusiastic pastels, like chunks of Miami air-dropped smack in the middle of Manhattan. He felt better, and then there were fingers snapping in his face.

'Hello. Are you there.'

This was how they were. You accepted it or you dropped out. You found ways to cope. You imagined yourself in a different milieu – say, at a party – where you had the asshole in question beat by at least thirty yards.

You totted up your victories. One: hygiene. Residents didn't get out much, and this one in particular suffered from excess cerumen production, which two years ago Jonah would have called by its more descriptive, real-world name:

5

a Colossal Avalanche of Earwax. Advantage, Stem.

Two: style. The resident's spreading waistline had succumbed to an infestation of beepers and PDAs, phones and Blackberries, making him look like Batman minus the pointy ears and award-winning physique. Advantage, Stem.

Three: charm. Obviously, he had that locked up; look at the guy, poking him in the arm and ordering him downstairs with that imperious smirk, advantage, St—

'Stop staring at me like you're deaf.' The resident's badge bounced as he gesticulated. His name was BENDERKING DEVON PGY-2. He had a hare-lip, currently twisted into a sneer. 'I know you can hear me.'

'Sorry.'

'We need hands.'

Jonah loved that. The rest of his body, including his brain, was irrelevant.

His shift was long done; he didn't belong to Benderking's team; he needed to get home for his four hours of sleep. But this was his third day on the service, and he wanted to make a good impression; so he smiled and said *I'm there* and jogged along toward the OR. Unless a doctor asked you to wash his car or fellate his poodle, you did it, and you did it with love.

As they hurried downstairs, Benderking gave him the essentials: Caucasian F 37 stomach pain. After an unattended hour in the ER, the

6

nurses find her flailing around, tachycardic, hypotensive, pushing 103°, respiratory distress, distended. Eighteen months status post gastric bypass, she had experienced a weight loss of one hundred and twenty-five pounds plus. Like setting a person down after a twenty-year piggyback ride.

Through the double doors and there she was: loose skin flapping, the skin she no longer fit, a drab pink wedding dress she could not remove.

The room was madness, everyone running to prep as they waited for the surgeon, pausing only to engage in the choicest OR pastime: yelling at the medical student. Jonah fetched a gown and gloves, and the scrub nurse yelled *you contaminated it, get another*, even though the items were still sealed and sterile, as though he was uniquely, grotesquely infectious. He shuffled to and from the supply room, dutifully shlepping another gown, another pair of gloves.

Into this squall sailed a gray-haired, gray-skinned, epicene man in his sixties: Gerard 'The Slice' Detaglia. He wiggled his pianist's hands and said, 'Shall we dance?'

Scrub-in. Detaglia buffed each side of each finger with five strokes from a Betadine sponge. This behavior – carried out with a priest's solemnity – marked him as decidedly old school; surgeons under forty favored instead a quicker but equally effective chemical rub. But Jonah wasn't going to make the same mistake as yesterday, when he'd used the rub while the surgeon sponged, and the

7

rest of the team shot him a look of horror, and he instantly gleaned that he'd screwed up.

They were everywhere, these laws that nobody told you about but that ensured a beatdown when you broke them. Which you did. You couldn't help breaking them. *Nobody had told you about them.*

The guiding principle of medical education was that people learn best under threat of mortification.

Standing at the back of the line, waiting for his turn at the sink, Jonah reflected that there was truth to this proposition. As soon as he'd committed the scrub faux pas, a new rule – *do as the surgeon* – had automatically appeared in his brain, produced by the same mechanism that spurs skunks to spray, anemones to contract, birds to wing at the sound of a gun. He knew; and he wouldn't mess up again.

The Gods of Surgery were jealous and punishing, and he had sinned. As a third-year, he could not be expected to do much more than suture, retract, suction. Like any apprentice, his real purpose was not to help but to validate the hierarchy. As every doctor before him had suffered, so must he.

The team backed into the OR, hands elevated and dripping. The scrub nurse passed out towels to Detaglia and the residents, leaving Jonah to fend for himself. In the end he didn't have time to find one, and was still wet when they gowned and gloved him, leaving him squirmy and humid inside two layers of latex.

'Medical student.'

Another way they kept you in check, by never

using your name. Obey unthinkingly, Nonhuman. In this case, the scrub nurse was giving him the light handle covers and saying *Get on with it already*.

He obeyed.

Strangely, surgery went much faster with the stereo off. Detaglia dove through skin, fat, muscle; he commandeered his nurses like a pasha; they moved at his bidding and flirted shamelessly. After an hour of retracting, Jonah's forearms blazed with pain. *It's worth it, you're going to be a doctor, Doctor Stem, Doctor Doctor oh Doctor, Christ it hurts it hurts stop shaking everyone is looking at you.* They weren't, of course; they weren't paying any attention to him. He had to stop thinking this way. If he was going to make it through the year – *day three* – he'd have to thicken his skin. He had never been the hypersensitive sort – at least, he didn't think so – and this was the wrong time to start. He tightened his grip.

The patient's innards bulged in the wrong places, embarrassingly so, and prying her open felt intrusive, like barging into someone's bedroom before they've had a chance to pick up their underwear. As Detaglia worked, Jonah thought of the scene in *Raiders of the Lost Ark* when they spring the Door Best Left Alone and everyone within a mile turns to fondue. He forced himself to look. *Get in there, see what's going on, you can't learn unless you stare it straight in the face.* Many of his fellow students – had they bothered to listen to Benderking – would have checked out mentally

9

by now. But Jonah had a strong, almost Victorian sense of Duty, and having committed to being in the room, he intended to *be* there. It was disgusting, but that was life, sometimes you did things you didn't want to do. He was further gripped by the notion that he'd paid tuition for this, and dammit if he wasn't going to learn. He wanted to barf. He blinked. *Look.*

As he leaned forward to observe the incision, the peritoneum burst, and a blast of bloody guts spilled across the table, his chest, the floor, his—

His shoes.

He looked down. In his haste, he'd forgotten to don booties.

The Slice sighed and said, 'Oh, heck.'

The organs Jonah knew from books and labs were robust, smooth, warm. This lady's reminded him of a Brunswick stew; they resisted categorization: poking through, tearing, melting. She leaked. Shit and bile and cells, all curdling in a vile juice. The terminology Jonah used to organize the situation – acute mesenteric ischemia, bowel infarction – did not capture its true disorder, as her shocked body ceased to respect its God-given blueprint.

And she hemorrhaged. Blood slickened the floor. The circ nurse mopped like a fiend, snarling at Jonah to express her displeasure. *Medical student would you get out of the goddamned way. Medical student please lift your goddamned leg please. I'd like to pick that up medical student but I can't because you're in my goddamned way.*

He contorted to accommodate her, struggling not to lose his grip.

Worst of all was the smell; the body gave off gas like a downed zeppelin. The stench reminded him of a frathouse, Sunday morning circa ten thirty A.M. The sheepish, post-bacchanalian miasma of *seemed-like-a-good-idea-at-the-time*: putrid meat and stale flatulence, comically magnified. To prevent himself from passing out, Jonah focused on the irreparable damage done to his shoes.

It took five hours to remove eighty percent of her intestine, which came out black and kinked, like a harvest of seaweed. When Detaglia revascularized the little that remained, the tissue flushed pink, the cardinal color of life rushing to reclaim its seat. Jonah was impressed. Everyone was impressed. The Slice was known as a clutch hitter, but this was special. Assuming she did not die overnight, the patient might go on to lead a full and rewarding life. With a colostomy bag.

'Well,' said Detaglia, glancing at the red biohazard sack, heavy with guts, 'she wanted to lose weight.'

By the time Jonah had ditched his scrubs, it was half past two. Rounds began at six A.M. If he went home, he'd get at most ninety minutes of sleep before having to hop back on the subway. He should have asked for the day off but considered it gauche, not to mention spineless, to start taking liberties with his schedule after three days on the job.

The thought of being on his feet for another

eighteen hours – in those shoes – made his skin crawl. This was New York, though, capital of late-night solutions.

He hit the street.

It was hot out and he could hear traffic skating the West Side Highway. Except for the hospital, Eleventh Avenue above 50th consisted of auto dealerships proffering luxury vehicles unsuited to Manhattan life. Above the locked-down driveways of body shops, broken windows glinted scaly and blue-black, fish netted in an oil spill. Near the pile of dirt and pigeon waste that was DeWitt Clinton Park, someone had left a toilet – tank, bowl, the works – out on the sidewalk like a Dadaist sculpture. He gave it a title: *My Life Is Poop.*

The moon was stingy; the streetlights weakly flickering.

That was when he heard the scream.

Coming from 53rd Street, it had an operatic quality: a pure, shrill, hellish beauty.

Following it around the corner, he saw a woman on all fours. Behind her stood a man in a flacid overcoat several sizes too big. He seemed in no particular hurry, slumped casually against a Dumpster, watching her crawl away.

oh my God he stabbed me

Despite the pressing heat, she was dressed in a down jacket and dark stockings. She jerked like a windup toy, listing to avoid her left hand, her left arm dripping with dark black blood. Screaming and screaming and screaming. The jagged hull of an adjacent demolition site reflected her voice at unexpected angles.

please help me
                    please help me
  please help me

She looked straight at Jonah, her face incandescent with fear, striped by swinging hair, a pale sheet of need. *Help me help me.*

She was speaking to him. *Help me.*

Later he would come to understand that most people would have walked away. A few would've called the police and waited, watching from a distance. But to Jonah the situation presented itself quite differently. What he saw was the man, the woman, the moon – and he felt not only disinclined to leave but an overwhelming obligation to stay, as if the woman's voice – *help* – was in fact the voice of God, funneled and filtered and broken but no less imperative: a moment chosen for him.

And he was going to be a doctor.

He did not think.

He ran forward, waving his arms. *Hey.*

The man glanced up and immediately reconfigured himself in agitation: shifting from foot to foot, rolling his shoulders, scratching at a tangled beard and tugging gnarls of incoherent hair. He muttered to himself. Shirtless beneath the coat, its sleeves dangling past his hands, making him look childish and lost. Jonah recognized the man's state; he knew it intimately, embraced it regularly; and he felt a wash of calm. He knew what to do.

He said *Please look at me.*

The man looked at him.

Jonah said *Nobody's going to hurt you.*

I'm dying screamed the woman.

Without turning around, Jonah said to her *You're going to be okay.*

dying

dying

I'm dying

Can you do something for me? Mister? Please. Take a step back.

The man grimaced with impatience, like Jonah had jumped a cue. He sidestepped and Jonah stepped to match him.

Okay, hang on. I don't want to—

The man tried a second time to go around him, and Jonah came forward—

—listen I don't want to nobody wants to

and everything accelerated.

Hair and heat and suffocating body odor; a wrenched limb; down; the ground; and then, for the second time that night, Jonah bathed in a great deal of blood.

CHAPTER 2

'Please don't take me back to the hospital.'

'Back?'

Two EMTs stood over him. One checked his pupillary response while the other asked if he knew his name, the date, the president.

He said, 'I have a concussion.'

'You sure do, Mr Smarty-Pants.'

'Ow. *Ow.*' He jerked his elbow away.

'C'mon, honey, be good.' The EMT held up a piece of gauze, orange with iodine. Jonah relented. He couldn't see the size of the scrape, but his entire arm beat with pain. More gauze; ripping tape. Then the ambulance door opened. Red light and radio crackle. Quiet. He was alone.

He shut his eyes, and his mind filled with still lifes: the man, the woman, the moon. He wanted to sit up but could not; his head dove sideways; his balance was off.

Why's my balance off.

Interestingly, he had no trouble recalling the hydromechanics of the vestibular system. *Spatial equilibrium is produced by synchronous processing of signals from the retinae and from the movement of endolymph fluid through the semicircular canals and ampullae. Reorientation of the head causes agitation of the cilia—*

Sometime later he awoke to the sibilance of torn cloth. A large male nurse was cutting his shirt off with a pair of blunt scissors. Faces – some of which he recognized, although none of the names were there – whizzed through his peripheral vision: getting his shoes off, poking him, measuring him, strapping him, shouting, recording numbers. He had never witnessed a primary trauma survey from the bottom up, and his head began to fill with mnemonics.

ABCDE! AirwayBreathingCirculationDisability Expo—

'Goddammit stop. Stop.' He sat up, batting away the hands that were now in the process of cutting off his pants. 'Stop it, I'm fine.'

'He's awake.'

'Yes I'm awake. I'm awake. I'm fine.'

'You hit your head.'

'I'm – *will you stop cutting my pants*.' He knew what they were going to do, and so he wanted to get out of the trauma bay by any means necessary. Those fucking EMTs had brought him back to St Aggie's. It was like *Groundhog Day*. Once they established that he was stable, they'd bring in the on-call surgical team, including BENDERKING DEVON PGY-2; they'd strip his clothes off for the secondary survey; everyone he had to work with

16

tomorrow (he still believed he was coming in for work) would see him naked, a common enough nightmare that was *actually happening to him.*

After a lengthy argument, he convinced them to let him remove his own pants. By that point he was walking, steady, alert, oriented. He kept saying *I'm fine*, but they put him through the whole humiliating process: ears, nose, mouth, rectum. They wanted to send him for a CT.

I'm fine.

You hit your head.

He knew they were right. They had to check for a bleed. Part of him suspected, however, that they were prolonging their examination for kicks. Having established him as mostly okay, they had begun to make wisecracks. *Paging Doctor Asscheeks.*

They wheeled him down to Imaging. He closed his eyes, shivering as they laid him on the table. The radiology labs were kept arctic cold at all times, and the gown he was in felt terribly flimsy. He made a note to be sensitive to patients who requested additional blankets.

The tech said, 'Hey kid, I hear you got a nice, hairless tush.'

They discharged him an hour and a half later. He went back up to the trauma bay to see what had become of his shirt (gone, of course). As he gave up and decided to go home, he was accosted by a baby-faced woman in a neat pin-striped pantsuit.

17

'Hello there pardner,' she said. 'Some night.'

He accepted her card. Meredith Scott Vaccaro, Assistant District Attorney, a borough seal depicting an eagle hovering over Pilgrim and Indian.

'Call me Scottie.'

He looked at her.

'If you're feeling up to it,' she said, 'we can talk right now? We can do it here? What you say we go get you a cup of coffee. You got a cafeteria here, don't you? Take care of this quick as possible?'

He looked at her card again. The Law wanted a word with him. How'd she get here so fast? Had he done something wrong? He tried hard to remember what had happened, but the reel ran with blank frames, dark and blurry. He had been scared. He didn't know what he'd done, but it was the right thing, had to be. The woman . . . a girl, really; she had been so small. He asked if she was okay.

'Hurt. She'll survive.' Vaccaro paused. 'The gentleman, though, he I'm afraid didn't fare so hot.'

Jonah said nothing. He worried the edge of her card with his fingernail.

Vaccaro said, 'So, y'know, I'd like to get your side of the story, straighten it out ASAP. We don't need your life to be any more complicated than necessary.'

'This is a form that allows me to ask you questions. I can't talk to you without it, so if you want to give me your version of the events, you should sign it. No worries, it's very standard. Bear in mind you don't have to talk to me if you don't want to? Go ahead, read it, it's all in there. You want some coffee. Take a minute, when you're ready you initial and sign? Be right back.'

He watched her walk down the empty caf and turn into the vending machine nook. The six questions in front of him were familiar from television and movies. His right to remain silent, to consult an attorney. By initialing after each, he acknowledged understanding. Or . . . forfeiture. He tried to analyze the text but kept losing his place on the page, distracted by a dim voice: his father's. Usually low and generous, it now rose steeply. *Jonah. Don't sign it. Call me first. Jonah. DO NOT SIGN IT.*

He stopped reading and relaxed his eyes, listening to the tray conveyor belt whirr.

You had to admire lawyers for producing a document so simple, yet with the power to so thoroughgoingly screw you. Obliterate your civil rights with the stroke of a pen. He hadn't been arrested – had he? – so he had no obligation to co-operate.

But he also had no reason *not* to co-operate. He couldn't possibly hurt himself by telling his version of the events. He had nothing to hide, and he wanted to go home.

He initialed and signed.

Immediately Vaccaro strode up with two paper cups, as though she'd been watching around the corner via closed-circuit, waiting for the pen to drop.

'Great,' she said. 'Let's first you tell me in your own words what happened.'

He talked. Vaccaro took notes. One part of his brain, the part that provided commentary on itself, told him that he was babbling. He tried to stop up the flow of words, but they came tumbling out. He mixed up the order of events. Backtracked. Made it seem, he felt sickeningly sure, as though he had something to hide. A custodian arrived with a mop; two hairnetted women took their places near the cash registers. Through a picture window on the westernmost wall he could make out the Hudson, smothered in fog; premonitions of daylight on the water; the stark Jersey shore.

He mentioned that he didn't know who had called the police.

'You did,' said Vaccaro.

'I did?'

'Yup.'

Then she began to ask questions. They seemed innocent, but he had difficulty enough establishing a chronology without having to explain why he'd been out walking at that hour, what time he'd left work, whether or not he was acquainted with the woman.

'No.'

'Or her attacker?'

'No.'

'They're strangers to you.'

He nodded.

'What you did was pretty dangerous, y'know.'

'I guess.' For the first time he considered this. 'Yeah. I guess.'

'Then what made you decide to get involved?'

He thought about the woman. Her torn stockings; her jacket engulfing her. In his memory she seemed so small. His heart had grown to scoop her up.

What made him decide to get involved.

Vaccaro leaned across and offered him a tissue. 'I'm fine,' he said.

She nosed at his cup. Without noticing, he had spilled coffee all over the table. Mumbling apologies, he wiped it up, then stuffed his trembling hands in his lap.

She asked more questions. Forty minutes passed.

He said, 'I can't do this anymore.'

'All right,' she said, chewing her pen. 'Let's get you home.'

He stood. His pants, too, were coffee-stained. 'I'm not in trouble, am I?'

'I'll be in touch if I need to,' she said.

He said, 'Okay,' thinking: she didn't say *no*.

CHAPTER 3

A cop drove him home. On the way Jonah left a voicemail for his chief resident, fudging and summarizing. He called it *an accident*. He apologized, promised to make up the day, and balled up on the rear seat of the cruiser, his chin against his knee, shivering.

More images came back. The scream, the woman, her hair tossed over the side of her face. He remembered locking arms, tripping; a pile of garbage bags. He remembered a raised hand. A blade like a beak. Pushing it back. And then the warm night, warmer.

He remembered, too, the man falling away from him, folding up in the gutter, a resigned susurration, like a bottle being emptied.

'Buddy.' The cop eyed him in the rearview.

Jonah emitted something like a burp.

'You need to throw up?'

'. . . no.'

'You look like shit.'

'I need to throw up.'

They pulled over on 23rd Street. His heaves drew stares from the bag-eyed Pakistanis thronging behind a flatbed truck to offload a food cart. BAGEL

BUTTER EGG MUFFIN COFFEE TEA. Although he hadn't eaten in fourteen hours, the thought of food brought another wave of nausea. His neck was wet. He retched, spat. What had been murky and indistinct turned lurid, three-dimensional. The man grew to an impossible height; his knife lengthened into a machete. The opening of his veins brought a tidal wave, and the woman screamed loud enough to shatter stone. Worst of all, he could see where the blade had gone in: right on the carotid. Like a slaughtered steer.

He asked the policeman to drop him at Washington Square Park, got out, and took a circuitous route home, walking until his head started to clear.

The East Village slept late. Puma-clad joggers, dog-walkers in faux-fur miniskirts, streetcorner prophets praying to the newly risen sun. Stout Hispanic men – half-hidden in shadow; the anonymous cogs of the metropolis – lugged trash bags and fruit crates. Along St Mark's, graffitied shutters sealed off cafés, sushi bars, bar bars, gelato slingers, tchotchke vendors with overflowing dump bins of tube socks. Used clothing that cost more than new clothing; fetishized poverty. A smorgasbord of T-shirts bearing political slogans *du moment*; the many faces of Che; purposefully unclever catchphrases like TAKE ME DRUNK I'M HOME. Jonah's favorite was a swastika with a ⊘. He often wondered who besides NYU freshmen was green enough to accept that as a nuanced position.

Near Tompkins Square Park, a skateboarder

repeatedly attempted to jump a fire hydrant, each time coming a little closer to success and to wrecking the door of a parked Cadillac. A friend with a video camera encouraged him by displaying a crescent of thumb and forefinger: *inches*. Dew and hosewater ran scummy across the sidewalk, frothing whatever solutes lurked in the concrete. Jonah smelled the oncoming day: summer in New York. Excrement, saline, coffee grounds, fried food. The array of sensations did him good, thinned the muck in his head. Sunlight carved faces: a dejected kid dribbling a basketball; a tattooed girl using her boyfriend's cigarette to light hers; a derelict with a shit-eating grin sharing a bench with an old man in polyester pants throwing breadcrumbs to the pigeons. They all seemed to nod at him, to say *We know what you've been up to*. He hurried into his building and up its ominously canted stairwell.

In his apartment he hung his keys on the nail by the door. He didn't expect an answer to his *Hello*. Lance usually slept past noon. In the last three days they'd barely seen each other: an hour while Jonah studied and Lance got ready to head out for the night. It would probably go like that all year long, nocturne and diurne.

The shower ran brown as he scraped dirt and blood from his body; he ruined a washcloth getting it all off. The gauze on his elbow peeled back, revealing that he'd lost a patch of skin the size of a playing card. He used Band-Aids, Neosporin, and tissues to jury-rig a new bandage.

24

As he got into bed, his cell buzzed: his chief excusing him for the day. Gratefully he set his alarm for three P.M. and sank beneath the blanket. Drifting off, he saw the face of the man he'd killed, contorting and whitening and accusing as he decanted himself through a hole in his throat.

The phone rang at two.

'. . . hello?'

'Hello is Jonah Stem there.'

'. . . 's me.'

'This is Christopher Yip from the *New York Post*, I heard about your heroic act last night and I wanted to ask you a couple of questions, first how old are you and—'

'Please—' His mind was soup. 'I don't want to ans—'

'Where are you currently employed you're a medical resident is that right?'

'I do – I'm a student, not a resident. Please, I—'

'When you stepped in to fight were you aware that he had a knife and if so—'

'Excuse me, I'm hanging up.' As he did, he heard *Do you expect a rewar—*

He disconnected the phone and rolled into a pool of sweat, hoping to recapture his nap. When that failed, he put on his bathrobe and shuffled out to fix himself breakfast (lunch?), so groggy that he almost tripped over Lance, crouching in the hallway.

'Morning sunshine. I had a brainstorm last night.

It's gonna be fuckin brilliant.' Lance bit off a length of electrical tape and smeared it along the baseboards, sealing in a yard of computer cable. He crabwalked four feet and did it again.

After a year and a half of roommateship, such a scene did not surprise Jonah in the slightest. 'Okay,' he said and headed to the kitchenette, an unwalled area distinguished from the living room primarily by one's imagination.

'Last night' – bite, tape – 'Ruby and I went to the Brooklyn Museum to see *Rashomon*, which by the way is a certifiable classic, it's *whack*, have you seen it?'

'No.' Jonah pawed through the freezer until he found a package of soy burgers, one of which he threw into the microwave unadorned.

'You should. Anyway, as I'm watching it I'm realizing that the trend of the past like half-century has been to explore *multiple* perspectives, you know' – bite, tape – 'documenting subjectivity. But we've gotten totally *fragmented*. We can't focus anymore. Everywhere we go, there's these people, these ideas, these *images*, moving a hundred miles an hour, and when do we ever see, I mean *really* see? We're so ADD, look at me, I've been taking Ritalin since I was four.'

'And snorting it since you were nine.'

'Ex*act*ly.' Lance pulled the sofa out and crawled behind it. 'To vanquish this, we need to look inside, back to fuckin basics. Especially considering nine-eleven, this seems like the path that our

26

culture needs to go. It hit me like a nuclear warhead, or maybe a dirty bomb. Anyway I've been overthinking myself for months, dude, but now I see: it's all about *self*. And as I'm thinking this, the craziest shit happens, the projector breaks down. Do you believe it? *Asswipes*.'

'I'm sure you can get it on DVD.'

'It doesn't compare to the big screen, dude. No loss, though, as at that moment I understood something critical. And that is this: when the movie stopped, it *stopped*. That's the difference between film and the actual flow of time. I said to Ruby, "This here shit is an all-too-clear reminder that our chosen medium is a construct." See? It's a sand-eatingly artificial reduction of life to two hours and forty minutes. We limit ourselves, and as artists, that's not cool. Hence.' From behind the sofa rose a fistful of cable. 'Real-time cinema. I'm taking it to the next level. All me, all the time. Webcams in every room. It's going to be a whole new *genre* of inward-looking cinema, a complete network of consciousness. And I have a great name for it, too, ready? *Self*umentary. Is that dope or what?'

Jonah didn't think this was a very original idea. Lots of people had webcams. He wondered why Lance thought anyone would pick him over young women in the buff. But he knew better than to object. 'The dopest.'

In the seven years Jonah had known him, Lance DePauw had always swelled with protean ambition.

At Michigan he'd burned through several career choices (sports commentary; video game design; and, for one hilarious semester, solid-state physics), each time failing to achieve world renown before his interest expired. His best idea – a beer-delivery service called Foam Home – had seen its knockout business model buckle under the weight of Lance's decision to use all initial stock to throw Alpha Sigma Phi's biggest party since the Kennedy administration.

Jonah often got the sense that Lance had been born in the wrong era. He had a gift for throwing cash around, and would have done fine in medieval Florence, serving as patron to an impoverished sculptor; his passions trailed the zeitgeist like a banner flapping behind a propeller plane. These days, though, you were either talented or a conformist pussy, and no way would Lance content himself with the latter.

It fell to Jonah to listen, respond, humor the air castles. He had practice as a listener; he'd done it all his life. Although at present he felt too frayed to contribute much more than *Yes* and *No* and *Sounds cool.*

'You know what these camerabobs cost? Like twenty bucks. And they're good, too, for their size. Like some shit out of *Get Smart.* That show was genius. Half the things they made up, you can get at Best Buy. Plus I'll save money on film.'

The microwave beeped. Jonah dumped the patty on a paper plate and added a dot of ketchup.

Swooning with nausea, he leaned against the kitchen counter, watching his best friend run wires to the fridge, behind the fridge, *in* the fridge. He took a bite of burger, stifled a gag. 'I thought digital was blasphemy.'

'You got to take the sacred cows and machine-gun the cocksuckers,' Lance intoned. 'You think Michelangelo gave a rat's sack about tradition? Check it: this one's wireless, on-the-fly roving broadcasts. Or we can put it in your room.'

'That's really okay.'

'Yeah,' Lance said thoughtfully. 'You're right, I'm not sure if it's appropriate to shift the focus off my protagonist.'

Unable to stomach the burger, Jonah set it down. He rubbed his face. The man the woman the moon. To his great distress, they seemed to be sharpening, their colors acid-bright. There was the man, his breath a long-distance kiss, the knife. There was blood. He tried to stop thinking about it. *Be human.* Lance was watching him, still waiting for an opinion. If he opened his mouth, maybe it would go away.

'What happened to the Corner Project.' For three months, Lance had been shooting out the window, single-position shots of Avenue A and 11th that lasted three hours.

'Fuck that shit, I'm through with it.'

'You said it was like a Warhol film.'

'In terms of how much it *ate*. This is much realer.'

'I'm glad you've found your muse.'

'She found me, dude.' Lance positioned a camera above the living-room TV.

'Not in here,' Jonah said.

'It's not a camera on you, it's a camera on the room. If you happen to be *in*—'

'No.'

A moment's pout, then Lance began pulling up tape. 'Fuckin killjoy.' He slid the sofa back into place and surveyed his handiwork with satisfaction. He coiled up the excess cable and scurried down the hall to the third bedroom, designated as the editing studio. A moment later he reappeared holding an ornately carved wooden box – a souvenir of Egypt-and-Morocco, junior year – from which he fished the raw materials for a joint. 'What're you doing here? I thought you had work. Is it a legal holiday? Is it Veterans Day?' He licked paper. 'Fuck me, I have lost *all* sense of calendar.'

'I had to stay late. I got back this morning.' Jonah paused. 'I saw a woman being murdered.'

'What?'

Jonah told him. Lance's pupils expanded as though he was already high. 'Holy *shit*. This whole time I'm yadda yadda yadda, why didn't you *tell me*?'

Jonah shrugged.

'Are you *okay*? What happened to your elbow? Fuck, dude, *fuck*.'

'I'm tired. I need to do some reading, I have work tom—'

'Are you re*tarded*?' Lance waved the unlit joint. 'You should spend the day in homage to yourself.'

'I don't see anyone giving me a trophy.'

'Done and done.' And Lance ran out.

Shaking his head, Jonah went to the corner of the living room, where a card table sagged beneath a stack of dense, outsize paperbacks. Like most med students, he bowed to the fiction that knowledge increased in proportion to textbook ownership. He picked out a surgery primer at random and opened to a section on wound management.

Lance returned. 'I love the Internet,' he said.

'Did you really order me a trophy?'

'Fuck *yes* I did. I can't believe you didn't tell me about this earlier. This is a moment that deserves to be enshrined. Look into the wireless.'

'Put it away.' He flipped pages and found himself staring at the vasculature of the neck. His gut churned and he dropped the book on the floor.

'Lo, the hero is weary, but he shall overcome – and prevail.'

Jonah got up and headed for his room.

'Hang on, you're moving too fast.'

He closed the door in Lance's lens.

You can't escape me forever, Stem. I'll make a star out of you yet.

Gashed trachea, rent esophagus, major vessels misrouted, whistling blood, coughing blood, drooling blood, hissing it from nostrils and ears, a human Roman candle.

Hey, dude, you think you'll be on TV?

Why was it so much worse than surgery. Fluids were fluids; wounds were wounds. He had been operating to save her. That was it: he was a surgeon, he'd removed a man's violence. A violencectomy. He had saved a life. He was a healer.

He heard Lance give up and walk away.

The man the woman the moon.

He sat on the edge of the bed and stared at the area rug. Talking to Vaccaro had been a mistake, he decided. At the time she'd asked him to sign away his rights, he had been half out of his head. There had to be legal refuge in that. He hoped.

The *Post* would carry the story with or without his consent. His parents got the *Times*, but he couldn't count on keeping the news from them for long: Erich would find a copy of the *Post* lying around on the train; Erich would tell Kate, who would tell his mother, who would, upon recovering her composure, tell his father. If not Erich, then someone else; it was inevitable.

His mother got anxious and distant in the face of bad news; his father, analytical and directed. Jonah's usual role in this minidrama was to let them run their course, reassure them of his well-being, and field their advice before discarding it. He tended not to listen even when he knew they were right, a habit he supposed he shared with most of the world. But this was a new sort of problem. He needed help.

You have reached the home of Paula and Steven Stem.

'Hello,' he said into the machine. 'Hello hello hello hel—'

'Yonah.'

'Hi Madonna, is my mother there, please?'

'I get her.' The phone clattered down.

His parents had a policy of screening all calls, whether it was noon or midnight. He had lobbied unsuccessfully to convince them to invest in caller ID. Although far from technophobic – his father was a gadget-freak – on this point they remained firm.

What if it's important?

I pick up when I hear you, Jonah.

What if I'm in prison and they allow me three rings before they cut me off, and you never get to hear my voice, and I rot for the rest of my life?

That's a risk I'm willing to take.

He wondered if she'd make that joke now.

His mother's wryness sprung from too much education crammed into too domestic a life. She had a WASPy knack for coolly picking apart histrionics, and an equal knack for dismissing those same criticisms when she was the one losing it. Jonah didn't relish the idea of either reaction.

'My darling son, I think it's so charming that you're calling me from work. Just like your father.'

'I'm at home.'

'Then I think it's so charming that you're calling me on your day off. What a good boy.'

He had to smile. 'How are you, Mom?'

'I'm making Peking duck. It's a lot trickier than I'd've thought. You make these itsy-bitsy garnishes with scallions. In my previous life, I was not a Chinese chef.'

'You never made Peking duck for me.'

'I didn't feel the need to impress you. Besides, it would have gone unappreciated. Did you know that for two years you refused to eat anything other than macaroni and cheese? We began to worry you'd get scurvy. That was why we started buying you Flintstones vitamins, so you wouldn't end up looking like a sixteenth-century sailor.' Her knife scraped against what he guessed was the big bamboo chopping block. 'I'm so happy you called. Do you need money?'

'That's not the only reason I call you.'

'Of course not. Do you?'

'Listen, Mom—'

'Oh boy.' He heard her put down the knife. 'Is this going to be *serious*?'

'It might be.'

In the background he heard her telling Madonna to *dice these, please*; he heard the phone brushing against her bony shoulder as she wiped her hands on a gingham towel. He could see her perfectly. He did not feel up to this.

'All right, I'm all ears.'

'Are you in the den?'

'I'm in the breakfast room. Why?'

'I . . . wondered where you were.' He paused. 'I love you, Mom.'

'I love you too.' She sounded alarmed. 'What's the matter?'

Telling her was much harder than telling Lance. Midway through, he began to shake. She said nothing, her long, clear breaths filling the silences.

'Nothing happened to me,' he said. 'Understand? I am perfectly fine. Not a scratch. Mom. Tell me you understand.'

'I understand.' She swallowed. 'What did the police say?'

'It was an accident.'

'Do they know that?'

'Yes.'

'What did they say about you?'

'They didn't say anything.'

'Have you called your father?'

'You're the first person who knows. Besides Lance.'

'We should, we can conference call him. Hang on.'

He started to object but she had already moved the receiver away.

'*Mom.*' Hearing her dial, he groaned and slammed a fist into his bed.

'I'm sure he'll know what to say,' she said, coming back on over the ringing. 'To be perfectly honest I don't.'

'I was going to call him right afterward.'

'Well now we can all talk together.'

'Doctor's office.'

'Hi Laurie, it's Paula, it's important.'

While they waited he said, 'You're getting angry at me.'

'Why would I be angry at you?'

'You are,' he said, 'and it's not helping. Not at all. This is hard enough—'

'Hello?'

'Steve, it's me.'

'Laurie said it's important. I'm about to eat, what's on your mind.'

'You're eating? Why are you eating now?'

'I haven't had a moment, I've been on my feet all day.'

'It's three o'clock. If you eat now you won't be hungry for the dinner I'm making.' She sounded hysterical. *Please, Mom, please.*

'All right,' his father said, 'then I won't eat. I am putting the sandwich down. Here it goes, down on the desk. Better?'

'Excuse me,' Jonah said.

'Jonah?'

'Jonah's in trouble.'

'N— *Mom.*'

'What trouble?'

'Wait, wait, wait, wait, wait. Everybody stop talking. Mom, *I* will explain what happened, and I don't need any help, so please do *not* interrupt me.'

'Someone please tell me what's going on.'

With the fourth retelling, he was too preoccupied with managing his parents' panic to get worked up over the gory details.

'You talked to them without a lawyer?'

Here we go. 'I should have called you first. I was too tired to be rational and I wanted to set the record straight before they could think that I'd done something wrong.'

36

'You *didn't* do anything wrong,' his mother said.

'I know, which is why—'

'You could have been killed. Jonah? You could have been stabbed.'

'I wasn't.'

'What I'm concerned about,' his father said in his steady, scholarly way, 'is that you might have said something incriminating without realizing it.'

'There's nothing incriminating about what he did.'

'Fine, Paula, but I'm imagining how a prosecutor might spin it.'

'I didn't get the impression that she thought I was guilty of anything.'

'That's her job, Jonah,' said his father. 'To get you to talk.'

His mother said, 'Do they know what's going to happen next?'

'She said she'd be in touch if she needed to.'

'I'm not sure I like the way that sounds,' said his father.

'They must have a way of proving it was an accident,' his mother said. 'From the, I don't know, the position of the body. They do it all the time.'

'No witnesses,' said his father.

'The girl,' Jonah said. 'She saw it.'

'Her word is gold on this, I suppose. We should get in touch with her.'

'"We"?'

'I want you to go tomorrow – or, better yet, I can call him now – hang on.'

'Who're you calling?'

'Chip Belzer. He's an old friend.'

'He's one of the top defense attorneys in New York,' his mother said.

'I don't need a *defense attorney*.'

'Not yet you don't. Laurie—' His father put down the phone.

'This is not what I needed from this conversation,' Jonah said.

'What you need is to protect yourself.'

He started to argue, then thought better of it. Parents defended, by definition. That's what they had to be worried about. His worry, however, was a whole nother beast. His heart was tripping along at a frightening clip.

He saw it again.

STOP.

He saw it again.

stopstopstopstopstopstop

'Jonah? Are you listening to me?'

'. . . yes.'

'I asked if you knew your schedule yet.'

'For when?'

'Thanksgiving,' she said. To his mother, Thanksgiving outranked Christmas, birthdays, and anniversaries. She began planning over the summer and used it as a star by which to navigate the year's shortcomings and victories. 'You said you'd let me know when you got your call schedule.'

'Okay.'

'Do you have it?'

'It's August.'

His mother ignored this. 'Kate and Erich are bringing their nanny.'

'They brought her last year.'

'It's hard for me to get used to new people.'

'You got used to Gretchen pretty fast.'

'She's not a person, she's an angel.'

At least her sense of humor was returning, and not in a brittle way. He decided to capitalize. He told her he could run out and father a child, if that made her so happy.

'I thought you did already,' she said. 'I always assumed that I had a whole slew of illegitimate grand-progeny, running around in, oh, I don't know. *Canada.*'

'All right,' his father said. 'I spoke to Chip. He can see you, but he has a limited amount of time so you should probably get moving.'

'What – now?'

'He's at Forty-seven East Fifty-fifth between Park and Lexington. The name of the firm is Belzer and MacInnis.'

'I can't go now.'

'You have to,' said his mother.

'I told him you'd be there in a half hour. Take a cab.'

'And Jonah? Remember to tell me when you get your call schedule.'

'All *right.*' He thumbed TALK, lobbed the phone onto his bed, and began hunting for a spare pair of shoes.

CHAPTER 4

Despite two Harvard degrees and a spate of highbrow publications, Chip Belzer spoke old-timey street punk, like he'd tap-danced out of *West Side Story*. Jonah was glad they were on the same team.

In Belzer's opinion, the possibility of a formal charge was remote. To prove his point, he read the homicide statutes aloud.

'"With intent to cause the death of another person . . ." blah-dee-blue-dee-blah. Except – listen to this – except if you had "reasonable ground to believe that any other participant intended to engage in conduct likely to result in death or serious physical injury."' He set the book down. 'That includes carrying a weapon. Trust me, kiddo: they ain't wasting their time on you. Meantime, be on the safe side, say nothing.'

Jonah said, 'Do you think I did anything wrong?'

'Wrong?' Belzer appeared to consider the concept distasteful. 'As in, morally? Absolutely not. Do you?'

'No. I don't know.'

'Well, I do.' Belzer smiled. 'Look. The girl was in trouble.'

'Yes.'

'And the guy pulled a knife on you.'

'I think so.'

'You think so, or you know so.'

'We were fighting. It was dark.' Jonah paused. 'He had a knife.'

'Right. You saw it and you felt threatened. Unless you *meant* to assault him.' Belzer raised an eyebrow.

'Why would I do that?'

'Good question. You wouldn't, and you *didn't*. You're not a homicidal crackhead. You're a *medical student*. You saw a woman being killed, and your behavior was commensurate. That's appropriate force. You get me? You're as innocent as the day you were born. At least with regard to this. I dunno what you do in your free time.'

'. . . all right.'

'You're being kinda rough on yourself, don't you think?'

Jonah shrugged.

'The guy tried to kill someone. He tried to kill *you*. You should be congratulating yourself. You did good. Anyway you got to move on.'

It was hard for Jonah not to scoff. *Move on*. He bet that if he looked hard enough, he could still find flecks of dried blood on his back. And he was not a big one for moving on, especially not under duress.

But a defense attorney's job was to see behavior in discrete packets: defensible or not. He probably parceled out the same wisdom to men who had committed real crimes, stolen and raped and killed. *So you crushed her skull with a brick, kay surah surah.*

Belzer tossed the criminal-law handbook in a drawer and laced his fingers. A large gold pinkie ring glinted on his right hand. 'Your dad's a great guy, y'know that?'

'I do.'

'One of the smartest guys I know.'

'Thanks.'

'And you look like your mom.'

'Thanks again.'

'Look,' Belzer said, twiddling the ring, 'put it out of your head. Nobody ever felt better worrying about the past.'

With the publication of Friday's *Post*, however, putting it out of his head ceased to be an option.

Yo Superman!

Word got around fast.

Lookee, Superman, whyncha open this jar for me? Careful don't break it.

Hey, Superman. Mr Massive Intestinal Cyst needs X-rays. Go use your powers.

Up went the article, on bulletin boards and in bathrooms; it papered the freight elevators and the cafeteria; it had been enshrined in the locker room and pasted over fliers for talks on RECENT DEVELOPMENTS IN RENAL TRANSPLANT and FMRI IMAGING OF CONGENITAL CARDIAC LESIONS.

Everywhere Jonah went, he faced himself: the

lousy photo that Christopher Yip had dug up. It looked like the portraits they printed of murder victims – grainy, smiling, apple-cheeked – and it sent the residents on his service into gleeful fits.

Up, up, and away!

They furthermore harangued him with quotes from the text: a half-page of pap plagued by an outbreak of modifiers and crowned with a lurid, forty-point headline. In it, Jonah was variously a 'resident,' a 'third-year resident,' and a 'surgeon.'

Congratulations on your residency, Superman! Mind writing me a letter of recommendation?

Reports of his jaunt through the trauma bay rapidly built into a vivid mythology involving his rear and other standout features of his nakedness. The comic possibilities were simply *endless*.

Superdick!

Supercock!

He felt as though he'd been forced to run for office on a platform of

SUPERDOC BATTLES SICKO W/ KNIFE

Damage done, he resolved to take it in stride. When people called him Clark he stuck his arms out and whistled the wind. He hummed the theme song and pretended to tear his shirt off with flexitudinous panache. The nurses prodded his biceps. They remarked on his tight pants. He said *Wouldn't you like to find out?*

People he hadn't heard from in years e-mailed him best wishes and awkwardly put admiration. A girl from his high school doubted he remembered her (he didn't) but wanted to know if he could get together for coffee (he couldn't).

His friend Vik, rotating through medicine up at HUM, sent him a large bouquet of flowers with a card reading *your lucky these arent for your funeral you idiot.*

On Wednesday, his sister called.

'What were you *thinking*.'

'I wasn't.'

'You could've been *stabbed*.' Sometimes she sounded so much like his mother that it gave him the chills.

'I know,' he said.

'Aren't you upset? Why don't you sound upset.'

'Of course I'm upset.'

'Then why don't you sound upset?'

'I'm exhausted,' he said. Which was true. It was now Thursday, and he'd been at St Aggie's six days in a row, sixteen hours a day. His superiors hadn't explicitly ordered him to make up the missed day, but tacit expectations bore down on him like Scripture. He'd worked Saturday, Sunday, Monday. Tuesday he had call until midnight, and today he had to come in for a seminar on post-op care. He was a zombie, but anything was better than going home to the apartment – empty once Lance had left for the night – to be hounded by silence and insomnia. Irrelevancies channeling nightmares: the hiss of a braking bus, so much like a man's dying sough.

'The reporter got everything wrong. He made you older than you are.'

'I don't know where he got any of that information. Not from me.'

'He said you're from Manhattan.'

'I am.'

'Not *originally*,' she said. 'He implies that you're native.'

'Yeah. I know. He's wrong, isn't it terrible.'

'Don't be passive-aggressive, Jonah-face.'

He scrunched his eyes. 'Sorry.'

'It's okay, I still love you.'

'Thanks, Katie.'

'You go back to work. Wait, want to hear something funny? I broke the news to Gretchen today that Mommy's going to have another baby. I told her, you know how Mommy has a brother. And I pointed to your picture. Guess what she said.'

He scratched at his patient's chart. 'I give up.'

'"Unka Jonah." I thought that was very advanced.'

He smiled. 'You know what, it really is.'

'Of course, I don't think she's *grasped* the implications of having a sibling. At some point I expect the mother of all tantrums. Okay, that's it. Go back to work. Loveyou. Oh – and Jonah? Please don't get stabbed.'

One upside of the *Post* article was that it clarified for him what had happened that night. Judging by how disfigured his own biography was, Jonah

45

figured that about twenty percent of the story was accurate.

The 'crazed attacker' was Ramon 'Raymond' Iniguez, thirty-eight, an ex-teacher and resident of the Beacon House, a Hell's Kitchen facility for the mentally ill. His brother, a musician from the Bronx, declined comment. His victim, Eve Jones, thirty-one, taught dance therapy at the Beacon. The police believed that Iniguez had followed Jones after work, and while they declined to speculate about his ultimate intent, the heroic timing of etc., etc.

Whatever mockery he faced as a result of Christopher Yip's hyperbolic reportage paled next to his relief at learning that Eve Jones had been treated for her injuries and released the following morning.

Iniguez's funeral was scheduled for Saturday, August 28.

His inset picture – inky, creased – didn't match the one in Jonah's mind, although Jonah hadn't been in the best position to make a full study at the time of their introduction. The Raymond Iniguez in the photo was clean-shaven, wearing a necktie and a Yankees cap and an easy, goofy expression that made Jonah queasy. In his mind he attempted to retouch the face, replace the smile with a snarl, dry out the plump cheeks and leave them raw-boned. Eventually, he tore that section of the page out.

Eve Jones, on the other hand, squared up perfectly:

46

wrapped in her enormous jacket, matchstick legs exceeding the frame, crime-scene tape in the foreground. Wide-eyed and needy. Seeing her confirmed his protective instinct and redoubled it. As wretched as he felt, he knew he had done the right thing. She was alive.

And he noticed something else about her. Not that it mattered – although in a cosmic sense he was glad – not that it mattered; a person in trouble was a person in trouble, regardless of race or sex or creed; he was an equal-opportunity savior. But he noticed – had to notice – because he wasn't blind, after all, and he was a normal human male, and anyway the fact was ineluctable: Eve Jones was very, very pretty.

CHAPTER 5

SATURDAY, AUGUST 28, 2004.

O n the morning of Raymond Iniguez's funeral, Jonah walked to Union Square and took the crosstown Ⓛ. The car was deserted, overcooled, florid with ads for a language school in Queens that promised fluency in English and accent reduction within months. Models from 'China,' 'Ukraine,' and 'Ghana' gave thumbs-up.

If, instead of the Ⓛ, he had gotten on the ⑥, he could have ridden up to the Bronx funeral parlor where the service was being held. He'd looked it up, and had for a brief and self-indulgent moment considered going. But for what possible purpose? To stand in the back, waiting till the mourners noticed him and came to clobber him with trays of crudités? Not to mention what Belzer would say.

You went where, *kiddo?*

He had other obligations, anyhow.

At Eighth Avenue he changed to the ○ᴬ and went to Penn Station, where the Long Island Rail

Road departed for Great Neck at 9:22 A.M. He had an off-peak ten-trip ticket with four remaining. Settling into a vacant car – few people went outbound before ten on a Saturday – he swung his bag onto his lap and took out books. After a few minutes, he settled his head against the window and closed his eyes.

The train came in on time, but nobody was at the station to meet him, so he set out on foot. It was a mile and a half, and it hadn't gotten hot yet.

He passed Waldbaum's supermarket, whose size always came as a jolt when he hadn't been out of the City recently. A crafts fair had recently come and gone, its posters still nailed to the ample oaks that shaded and greened the streets. He touched the tops of mailboxes, some still wet with unburnt dew. Leaving the town center, he moved into a windless suburban silence unbroken save the flitting of finches and the yodeling of pets. Shingles and big cars; openness and shade and bosomy shrubs; a nice relief from Manhattan gray.

By ten thirty A.M. he was on the front step of an off-white ranch-style house at the end of a leafy cul-de-sac. The front yard testified to good intentions gone awry: along one side of the walkway ran a row of mismatched flowers (lavender, petunias, ranunculi) in various states of decline, while the other side was lined only midway to the house, as though encouraging visitors to step off the chipped flagstone and tramp across the lawn, which grew high in places and not at all in others. Someone here had given up. Still, summer being summer – blooming sun, sweet charred smells – the overall effect was comfortably shabby rather than desolate. In winter it looked worse. Jonah knew.

He had a key but knocked first.

The foyer was fusty and dim, with mangy orange carpeting and three soft-edged shafts of light streaming through the cutouts in the front door. In the living room, though, he noted fluffed pillows and lemony surfaces. They'd had the housekeeper in.

He followed the sound of the TV to the back room, where a middle-aged man was passed out in the easy chair: sawing wood, his face leathery and rictal. He wore baggy boxer shorts and a faded T-shirt that said FLORIDA KEYS. A pair of smudged reading glasses bracketed the top of his head, and his fingers dangled inside an empty tumbler on the floor.

His name was George Richter, and he was not related to Jonah by blood. Before Jonah started coming out to his house regularly, they had met in person twice: both times over celebratory dinners, both times more polite than honest. In some ways, Jonah knew a lot about him – how he looked asleep, for instance, or how he cried without tears – but in others, he was a complete stranger. Jonah didn't know his middle name, didn't know if George preferred the Beatles or the Stones. He didn't know how or when George had developed an affinity for liquor – rye, of all things, especially Old Overholt. Had he always drunk too much? Jonah didn't know. He wasn't about to ask George. And the only other person who could answer these questions was in no state to do so.

Jonah gingerly extricated the tumbler and took it to the kitchen, where he rinsed it out and refilled it with cold water from a pitcher in the fridge. He put on a pot of coffee. While it brewed, he sorted through the considerable pile of unopened mail on the kitchen table. A half-finished *New York Times* crossword lay buried beneath credit-card mailers post-marked Delaware. Jonah found a bitten stub of pencil and filled in a few of the unsolved clues. As the pot began to bubble, the cat slunk in and licked his ankle.

'Hello, Lazy.'

He fixed a mug with Mocha Mix and three Equals, and returned to the back room. He put the coffee and the tumbler of water on a low table near the lonely treadmill. The TV was a Zenith with rabbit ears and a wood laminate shell. Jonah switched it off.

George stirred. 'Jonah. What time is it.'

'About eleven.'

'You didn't tell me you were coming.'

'I told you.'

'I would've picked you up.' George rose and opened the curtains. Outside, the backyard flouted his neglect by flourishing. 'I thought you were coming last week.'

'I couldn't come,' Jonah said. 'I had to work, I e-mailed you.'

The cat sidled against George's bare shin, and he stooped to graze its head.

'Hannah's asleep?'

George picked up the tumbler and swirled it, as if hoping to coax liquor out of its walls. When that failed, he abandoned it for the coffee. 'Bad night. I didn't get to sleep until five.'

'Sorry to hear it,' Jonah said.

George shrugged. 'What's new with you. Are you studying – what are you studying.'

'Surgery.'

George looked confused. 'I thought it was neuroscience.'

'Neurology. That was last month. This year I go through all the specialties.'

'Rrrr. Rotations.'

'Right.' He was waiting for a question about the accident, but evidently George didn't know. Either that or he'd forgotten already, which was to be expected; he had a short memory for the inconveniences of others.

George said, 'Well, whatever you do, you'll be terrific. You're going to be a great doctor.'

If anyone would know Jonah thought.

They made breakfast. Jonah pointed out the old crossword to George, who threw it out and brought in the new one tucked under his arm. He sharpened a pencil and poured himself three fingers of booze, which Jonah regarded as a step toward scaling back. They sat in the living room and waited for Hannah to wake up, Jonah reading about fistulae and supplying George with answers.

'A beaklike shape, seven letters, R-O-S.'

'Rostrum.'

'Rost . . . rum, *exactamente*. Thank you.'

'My pleasure.' He knew all the obscure ones; puzzle writers repeated themselves, and med school had destroyed his useless-junk filter. Often he'd inadvertently memorize a fact, surprising himself later with its retrieval.

He checked his watch at one o'clock. Right about now, Raymond Iniguez was disappearing into the earth.

At two o'clock George said, 'You maybe want to go peek in on her?'

Jonah closed his book.

Upstairs, he examined himself in the bathroom mirror. Hannah liked him to look as he had in college, and while he couldn't halt the incremental effects of age – of late, he had begun to thicken in the jaw, like his father – he reordered himself as best he could, wetting his hair and moving his side part to the center. The results pleased him. Almost good enough to need his fake ID back.

He knocked on her door and heard her turn beneath many strata of blankets. She was always cold. The technical term was *neuroleptic-induced hypothermia*.

53

He called her name and, receiving no answer, entered.

The smell of perfume swept over him. The dresser – where she normally kept an assortment of body sprays that claimed to mimic pricey eaux de toilette – was bare. Packaged products sometimes aroused her suspicions. If that happened before George could get to them, they invariably met a violent end.

She hadn't redecorated since she was twelve. Posters of Janet Jackson and Johnny Depp had lost corners, disclosing swatches of unfaded wallpaper. Her Norton Anthologies; her yearbook. Scotch-taped pictures of high-school friends; the high-school softball team; the group photo taken with the governor the year they won the tri-state title. A graduation tassel thumbtacked to the door. Stacks of cassettes and drawers full of jerseys. Her trophies – too hard, too sharp – had long since been removed to the basement. By the bedside, near the ladybug phone, was a picture of her dead mother. The sole clue to a recent life was a Michigan pennant Jonah had put up last October.

'Hannah.'

She was a lump.

'You awake?'

A hand burrowed up through the sheets, followed by eyes like targets.

'Can I come over to the bed?'

She nodded.

He sat by her side. 'How you feeling?'

She coughed. 'Thirsty.' She dragged herself out of bed. She was wearing jeans and a wool sweater beneath a maroon terrycloth robe. Through a moth hole near her stomach he saw sallow, cheesy folds of skin. Her girth yo-yoed as a result of *neuroleptic-induced weight gain*.

He didn't try to touch her, but as they went downstairs, she laid a hand on his arm.

'I'm not here,' she said.

He didn't know what to make of that. He said, 'I am.'

They sat in the kitchen, out of George's earshot. She gave most of her breakfast to the cat, and Jonah asked if she wanted him to prepare something else. She shook her head. Her hair was approaching rat's nest, so he offered to brush it out. When she didn't refuse, he went back upstairs to fetch a wide-toothed comb and a bottle of baby oil.

He sat behind her, talking softly, nothing serious, doing his best to make her smile. Her moods spun like a slot machine. Sedate, like today; or remote and confounded; or splintery and distrustful. He had learned to watch for subtle shifts.

'You're all tied up,' he said, loosening a tangle. He imagined her hair as neurons gone haywire, grown out of her skull, seeking shelter in the open air from her perpetually insurrecting mind. He straightened her out, made her sleek and ordered.

By this point in his education he'd seen plenty of brains, handled them in anatomy and studied cross sections, and he knew that what afflicted her was generally thought of as *neurochemical*. Others disagreed, contending that in fact the problem was *anatomic*. Still others (fewer every year, as psychiatry grew progressively more biologized) called it *psychosocial*. And while everyone agreed that in her case it was *undifferentiated* and *chronic* and *progressive*, nobody seemed willing to come out and call it by its true name, *horrible*.

'What do you like that's on, these days? *Survivor?*'

She shrugged. 'No.'

'What then.'

'*Emeril.*'

He laughed. 'Next time I come, you can cook me dinner.'

'I'll make you fricassee,' she said, and smiled.

There she was: Hannah. Lurking in there, peeping out every so often to wave. It manhandled his heart. He rushed to take advantage of her lucidity. 'Knock-knock.'

'Who's there.'

'Interrupting cow,' he said.

'Interrupting c—'

'*Mooo.*'

She smiled.

'Knock-knock,' he said.

'Who's there.'

'Dyslexic interrupting cow.'

'Dyslexic interrupting c—'

'*Ooom.*'

They laughed together.

'My turn,' she said. 'Knock-knock.'

'Who's there.'

'Interrupting turtle.'

'Interrupting tur—'

Slowly she craned her head forward, as though emerging from a shell.

'Knock-knock,' he said.

'Wait, my turn,' she said.

'Sorry,' he said. 'I'm interrupting joke-teller.'

'Knock-knock.'

'Who's there.'

'Interrupting dyslexic turtle.'

'Interrupting dyslexic tur—'

And she retracted into her invisible shell.

They had a good laugh over that. She'd taught him the routine, back in the day.

'Tell me a joke?' she asked.

All he could think of were dirty ones he'd over-heard in the OR. He didn't think she'd find them funny. 'I'm sorta running dry,' he said.

A mistake. She iced over again, pushing away the remains of her bagel. Lazy Susan tried to get at it, but Hannah set her on the floor and shooed her out.

He began quickly to speak, to spool out tricks; did his best to amuse her and induce her to come back. She tugged skin from her lip with flawless apathy. She attacked a cuticle until it began to spot with blood. He felt an urge to shake her, and he certainly didn't want to do that, so soon he shut up and they sat there doing nothing.

Outside, a neighbor was yelling about getting charcoal.

'Your hair is okay,' he said. 'You could use a bath.'

'I took one.'

'When?'

'This morning.'

Lying or disoriented: he didn't know. She needed a shower; she often needed one, as George was embarrassed by her nudity and chafed at bathing her, leaving it to Jonah or Bernadette, the nurse who came three days a week.

'To get the oil out,' he said.

She nibbled her thumb. 'He doesn't like to.'

He glanced into the living room. George had nodded off, bottle slumped against him like a tiny, misshapen lover.

Jonah looked at her. 'Okay. Let's you and me.'

Her back was so white it was almost green. Her legs hadn't been shaved in an eternity. Her armpits. Once upon a time, her left shoulder had been slightly bigger than her right: evidence of overuse. Now they had evened out, shrunk, her musculature softened and swallowed by fat. Still, he assumed she had strength buried in there. These days he could beat her in arm wrestling but that was new.

She hunched over as he soaped her, covering her breasts in an imitation of modesty. He had no trouble remembering the moment she had become asexual to him: the first time he saw her forcibly

58

sedated. Watching her kick, and spit, and buck, and bellow, he had thought that she resembled nothing so much as a baby. Such helplessness rendered lust a perverse non sequitur, and all his desire imploded, flash-bang-gone.

Realizing this was bittersweet, because one of her chief attractions had been the way she looked up to him, and she'd always had a sort of neonatal quality: from her big fish eyes to her tendency to burrow into his body, searching out refuge and pulse. Even before getting sick, she had enabled him to feel like a provider. Used to being the baby brother, used to having his judgment second-guessed, he loved to be her hero.

They met at Michigan. Lance introduced them; his mother had been a friend of Wendy Richter's, and when Hannah returned to Ann Arbor in the fall of 1998 – a semester off – following Wendy's death from breast cancer, he took it upon himself to cheer her up by introducing her to some cool freshmen. (Later she told Jonah she'd lacked the heart to inform Lance that 'cool freshmen' was an oxymoron.) *You'll like him, he's a New Yorker, too.*

No thanks Hannah said. Displaced East Coast kids gratingly tended to stick together, and she wanted out of that scene.

No thanks Jonah said. He'd known Lance for a month by that point, and had learned enough to be skeptical of his skills as a matchmaker.

But Lance prevailed upon the both of them, and on Halloween Jonah found himself at Skeepers talking to a girl with black hair and widish shoulders, and before long they decided it was too noisy inside, and before long they were kissing, and before long they were e-mailing each other a dozen times a day, and before long his sister had declared them *an item*.

A convenient enough phrase from her outsider's perspective; but looking back, he perceived its inaccuracy. Their itemhood was more correctly an absorption, Hannah soaking into him. Shy, solitary, she preferred to concentrate on one thing at any given moment. The same singularity of purpose explained her choice of sport, pitching being an activity that compresses the world down to a point, moving along a line, with human hands for endpoints. She had the true athlete's monomania, and turned toward him with a devotion of gemlike density, so raw it sometimes stung him.

In retrospect, of course, he questioned the depth of what they'd had. They'd been young; and today he was different, rusty. Guileless Hannah; trusting; optimistic: qualities that today struck him as naïve; an amendment to his thinking caused, ironically, by watching her decay, numbering its banal tragedies. Were he to travel back in time, see her through the prism of the present . . . but he couldn't travel back in time, nobody could, and it was pointless to sit there what-iffing, so he wouldn't.

What he had loved about her: she was giving. She was humble, holding opinions without the need to impress them upon everyone. Even at her saddest, she was not without some light. Except for those shoulders, she was eminently holdable, and those he got used to. She didn't care for parties but went when he asked. She had a fantastically beautiful back, strong and smooth and caramel-colored. She would stick bottles of chocolate milk in his backpack for him to discover right when he was searching for his ID to buy a drink. She took compliments well; did not, like so many other girls, believe that to be attractive she had to speak a little bit simpler, rope in a few IQ points. She got him into running; together they would make lazy circuits of the campus. She didn't care what kind of doctor he decided to become, although when he told her he was thinking of oncology she took it as a gift – a tribute to her mother – and she cried, so happy that he was part of her life, would be part of her life forever.

By the start of his senior year they'd come up with an absolutely ironclad plan. They would move to New York so he could start medical school; she would find a job in . . . that part was never clear . . . and they would share an apartment until he finished his third year, at which point they would defy fashion and prudence, and get married.

His mother hadn't been crazy about them living together, but – lacking prudish or religious grounds on which to justify her qualms – never said more than *Aren't you a little young?* Her attitude remained a sore point, as Jonah believed that she'd never liked Hannah to begin with. As

61

evidence, he noted the haste with which she had rushed to push him back into the dating pool. *It's not healthy, Jonah. Life goes on. Kate has friends.* Eventually, he told her to stop it. With his mom, that was enough to shut her up.

It seemed incredible that he had missed the first signs: fireworks going off in his face. But what had he known? He'd been busy. First studying for med school. So much reading. So many tests. He'd been too, too busy. Too busy to speak up when, the April before graduation, she quit the team, citing an inability to focus. Shocked – but supportive – he said nothing. (And how long before then, he wondered, how many times in the first three years, how many hairline cracks.) Too busy to see a problem when she began to withdraw, stopped going out with friends, didn't want to go to the movies. She was too tired to run; they stopped running. Once or twice he arrived at the house on Greenwood she shared with four teammates to find her heaped on her bed, bawling into a pillow. (Or maybe more than once or twice, maybe more than that, maybe.) After recovering, resetting herself, she would write it off as residual depression about her mother, and – too busy to consider other possibilities, accepting her at her word – he said nothing.

That summer, 2002, they moved back to New York and took a cramped fifth-floor walk-up on East 103rd, within walking distance of the hospital. The exigencies of school left him no time even to unpack, but Hannah assured him she would do it all. She intended to get the place in order; with his help, she made a list of all the stuff you forget you need until you need it: Brillo pads, Q-tips, lightbulbs, hangers, paper plates, batteries, a screwdriver, a bathmat, vinegar. She talked about going to the Bed Bath & Beyond on 60th and First. She hoped they delivered.

She never did any of it. Not wanting to inaugurate their life together by fighting – too busy – he said nothing.

She did not get a job, spending hours staring glassy-eyed at the classifieds or craigslist. She did not call up friends. She did not go to the gym. She complained of fatigue. She would read the same words over and over and over; they had lots of paperbacks dog-eared on page three. She forgot things. She did not brush her teeth for days, then a week, then weeks; she developed a bad cavity but never bothered to find a dentist. She was skittish, labile, weepy, unpredictable. She sobbed that he would stop loving her and he – befuddled, unprovoked, distracted by reams of niggling anatomical detail, chalking her outbursts up to weather or boredom or anomie or PMS – gave her a kiss and a hug and said nothing. He told himself that she was stressed about being unemployed; pressuring her would make it worse. He said nothing. Nothing at all, nothing for months, though she continued to crumble. He would get up at night to go to the bathroom and discover her standing by the window, mumbling. He thought she was sleepwalking; he said nothing.

Hindsight made him into a fool. But there had been no breakpoint, no howling neon arrow; life provides few exclamation marks. He stood by as she boiled by degrees.

Not until December, when he came home from a late night in the HUM library and found their bookshelf emptied, Hannah in a pool of confetti, did he understand.

I took out the sharp letters.

He stood in the entryway, snow-speckled backpack still on his shoulder.

They're dangerous.

He picked up his copy of *Evolutionary Analysis.* Deep scratches marred the cover, so that it read *olu ionar nal sis*

Hannah, trembling, smiling joylessly, said *They can cut you.*

He calmed her down and ran her a bath. He pocketed her Lady Bics, settled her into the water, and said *I'll be right back.*

He went through her phone until he found George's work number.

Something's wrong.

And George said – in way that suggested he'd been expecting this call – *I'll be there in an hour.*

He brought her back to Great Neck. Two weeks later, George came home from the market and heard water running upstairs. She stood in the shower, letting it blast her square in her chest, her clothing clinging to her like so many drowned rats. Her shoes on. She was screaming, afraid of everything, accusing the air. She attacked him with a half-empty bottle of shampoo. She put her fist through the glass shelf underneath the mirror, requiring twenty-six stitches near her wrist.

Despite having a test the next day, Jonah took a car service out to Nassau University Medical Center, where George greeted him with a handshake. There was no anger in his face, no *Why didn't you speak up* or *How could you do this to my daughter*. Instead Jonah saw the same haggard acceptance he'd heard over the phone, as though George considered this disaster – this inversion of the universe – about as novel as sand at the beach. And Jonah, who had always believed Hannah's mother had died of breast cancer – because that was what she had told him – said *You've been here before*.

George nodded.

With Wendy.

George nodded again.

Jonah said nothing. He did not ask what, ultimately, had happened to Wendy – but he knew that it sure as fucking life wasn't breast cancer. He sat in a hard plastic waiting-room chair, listening to the hospital sounds that were growing familiar to him, pages and beeps and squeaky rubber wheels, and with a supreme effort, went over his conversations with Hannah on the subject of her mother, a re-examination yielding the distinct impression – rewriting history, or knowing? – that her reluctance to talk about her death sprung not from pain but from fear that he would leave her if he knew. He looked at George, toeing the clean floor with his balmorals, and understood that he had been sold a false bill of goods.

A month later he illegally sublet the walk-up and moved in with Lance. Living in the Village would mean a forty-minute commute, but Jonah had no intention of staying uptown, much less in the apartment. It only took a few hours to get his possessions in order: most were still boxed. He left them that way for another month, at which point he realized that he was in for the long haul, and began to unpack.

A year and a half later he was here, in that same upstairs bathroom. The supports for the glass shelf had been removed, leaving two caulked-over holes in the tile below the mirror. A year and a half; a dateless time; an aging time; a time of starvation and of gluttony; of caretaking and suspended animation; of off-peak ten-trip tickets and crossword puzzles and denial and regret and futility, most of all futility, the refuge provided by routine. He had not gotten over it because he had no idea what that meant. She was still alive. She was naked. He soaped her back. He wet her hair.

At quarter after five George ordered a pizza. While Jonah ate, he wondered if the Iniguez funeral party was coming to a raucous head. They weren't Irish or anything, they probably had a home filled with dark nosegays of Catholic fatalism. He didn't want to think about it.

At six he got up to leave. George said *No no no, I'll drive you.* Jonah declined. He needed the fresh air, needed to stretch his legs. Most of all he needed to be away. For this he hated himself.

'You don't want to leave her alone for too long,' Jonah said.

George scoffed. 'Five minutes.'

As they drove, George said, 'Have you given any thought to what I asked you.'

'What's that.'

'I've been doing some poking around. I found a package. It's a cruise. I asked you about it last time.'

'I don't remember.' He remembered perfectly well.

'The week of Christmas. A full Christmas dinner is included. The Caribbean. They make stops. Islands and things.'

'Sounds like fun.'

George nodded. 'So what do you think.'

'I think it sounds like fun.'

George glanced at him, and when he said no more, said, 'It would be a huge help to me. You could sleep in the basement. You know the bed down there.'

Jonah nodded once. 'Mm-hm.'

'You're out here enough as it is.' George looked at him again. 'Bernadette can come during the day. You'd be in charge at night.'

'That's my vacation time.'

'You told me, and I understand that.'

'I was hoping to get away myself.'

'You still can. It's just the week.'

'Right, so—'

'You told me your vacation was two weeks.'

'I – okay, but—'

'So you'd have one week here and one to yourself. You can go away for New Year's.'

'Why can't she come with you?'

'You know the answer to that as well as I do.'

'I honestly don't see the problem.'

'It's a *ship*, Jonah.'

'I'm sure they have doctors on board.'

'That's not the point.' George shook his head. 'I need a *break*.'

Jonah said nothing.

'I don't ask you for much.'

Jonah said nothing.

'If it were up to me, I'd have Bernadette in the whole time. It'd never fly, you know that.'

'What about Reese.' Hannah's aunt – her mother's sister – lived in Ohio.

'She and Lewis are taking the kids to visit his parents in Delray Beach.'

'There must be someone else free.'

George said, 'She asked for you, Jonah.'

Guilt is malleable; it is enterprising. It seeks a level; it glues together unrelated events, giving the appearance of causality. A dead man; a sick girl. Jonah's guilt engine, already smoking, burned hotter.

And it was true, wasn't it, that George didn't ask him for much.

He had never asked him to start coming out in the first place. He'd never asked Jonah to put the coffee on, to untangle Hannah, to pick up the occasional bouquet of flowers. Of his own accord, he had started doing these things, and they had become truths. If every day he came obligated ten more, he had only himself to blame: he had fixed the exchange rate.

They arrived at the station. 'I can pay you,' George said.

'You don't need to pay me.' Jonah zipped up his bag. 'I'll think about it.'

'Give me a call.'

'Okay.' He wasn't saying *yes*.

'Let me know soon, we have to book the tickets.'

'I'll call you.' He was saying *yes*.

George put a hand on his shoulder. 'You're a lifesaver.'

'I'll give you a call.'

Light summer rain fell, the sourceless mist that somehow manages to leave the City dirtier than before, turning manholes to matte pennies and ferrying downwind whiffs of garbage. Though it was after eight, most shops were open. The counterlady from Bar Racuda lingered outside on a smoking break. Beneath a frowny-face umbrella, a man wearing fake eyelashes waved to attract a cab, pausing to wink at Jonah as he trudged up Avenue A.

Hello world he thought. *Must be going. Till tomorrow.*

He ducked into a bodega, grabbed a bag of pretzels, and stepped up to the bulletproof booth. The clerk rang him up without taking his eyes off a black-and-white TV set showing the Red Sox-A's game.

'What happened to the Yankees?' Jonah asked.

'Rain ow.' The clerk dropped a nickel, bent to get it, and when he came back up he was Raymond Iniguez.

Jonah reeled backward, wiping a row of peanut-butter jars to the floor and slamming against the freezer case.

'*Heya.*' The clerk was on his feet. 'Whassa matta wih you? You stupeh?' The clerk was Korean and in his sixties. 'You go to break something.'

'I'm sorry,' Jonah said and rushed out.

He stopped on the corner, stooping, licked by the humidity, digging his nails into his palms. Unreasonable. Out of control. If he could transmogrify that guy into Raymond Iniguez, he could do it to anybody.

He peered into the bodega. The clerk had gone back to his TV. No harm done.

Then relax. *Relax.*

As he stepped into his building, the door whacked a tall brown paper parcel bearing his name and a return address in Bismarck. For an instant he strangled on the notion that it was a bomb sent by Raymond from beyond the grave or arranged by a vengeful family member. It would blow off his arms, smear him along the walls like raspberry jam *will you chill out for god's sake I mean come on.*

He ran his hands along the package. Why would someone send him a bomb from North Dakota. Middle America bore him no grudge; he was an alum of one of its finest educational institutions. People out there didn't mail explosives to random strangers, unless you counted the Unabomber, and he was off fermenting in prison. It was probably a, he had no idea.

The paper concealed a plain white box, sealed at both ends with industrial-sized staples. He pried them free with his housekey, loosing a flock of foam 8's.

He said, 'Son of a bitch.'

It was a monster of a trophy, four feet high, acromegalic cousin to the Stanley Cup, with 'gold' grapevine handles and a 'marble' base. Jonah spot-appraised it at ninety thousand cereal-box UPCs plus $13.95 for engraving.

MAJESTIC JONAH STEM
SAVIOR OF WOMENFOLKS
PAYER OF THE ELECTRIC BILL
YOU RULE THE EVERLOVING COSMOS
WITH A GOLDEN SCEPTER OF WONDER

When he got done laughing, he brushed it free of packing material and lugged it upstairs, double-stepping over muddy puddles that had gathered on the uneven linoleum. His front door was ajar and he walked right in.

'You're insane,' he called. 'Where'm I supposed to put this?'

'He's not here. He said I could wait until you came home.'

Jonah turned around. There, on the sofa, sat Eve Jones.

CHAPTER 6

The place she suggested was a dingy basement bar six blocks away. 'It's the first place that came to mind,' she said, biting her lip as she looked around at the rotting plaster walls. 'I used to live near here, but it's been a while.'

He reassured her that it was fine. 'My standards are low. I don't get out much.'

They took a booth; she got them drinks. He asked how she was.

She displayed her bandaged palm. 'Plus my shoulder. All told, sixty-two stitches.'

'Jesus.'

'You're the reason it's not worse,' she said. 'And poor you. Look at that.'

He realized she was referring to his injured elbow. 'Won't even scar. And if it does, I have a good story.'

She smiled. 'Thank you,' she said. 'So much.' Up close, her features were even more delicate than in the newspaper photo: scimitar-chinned; mouth in permanent half-pucker. Beneath a close-fitting turtleneck, her breasts sat small and high. Her eyes were cups of smoke. Her ears, china

73

saucers, were multiply pierced: her left tragus bore a diamond stud, and a garnet swung on a gold chain threaded through her right earlobe. When she moved, everything glittered, as though she was crying out of the sides of her head.

'I hope they gave you adequate time to recuperate,' she said.

'I was back at work on Friday.'

'That's shameful. You deserve . . . I don't know. Bravery leave.'

He laughed. 'Tell it to my chief.'

'And the article, you saw that, I presume.'

He groaned.

'What?'

'That photo,' he said.

'What about it.'

'It made me look like a tool.'

'Oh stop,' she said. 'I thought it was lovely.'

'Plus he fabricated everything,' he said. 'I'm not a resident, I'm not a surgeon, I'm definitely not Superman.'

'At least he got your name right.'

He raised his eyebrows. 'Your name's not Eve?'

'It is. But he misspelled it.'

'How else do you spell Eve?' he asked.

'Not that: Jones.'

'How else do you spell *Jones*?'

'With a gee.'

'G-O-N-E-S?'

She nodded.

He smiled. 'Like, gones fishing?'

74

'It's pronounced Jones, jay. But it's spelled Gones, gee. They mean the same thing, but somewhere along the line, it went kablooey. G and J are close on a keyboard, and if your penmanship isn't too meticulous they look similar in lowercase. Your name is interesting, too. Stem, like a plant, the root of all goodness, the benevolent earth god.'

'That's me,' he said. 'Heed my power.'

'Where does it come from?'

He swallowed an ice cube. 'Also a mistake. It used to be Stein, someone at Ellis Island screwed up.'

'How blunderful,' she said, 'we're partners in error.'

He smiled and drank.

'At least it's a real name,' she said. 'Unlike Gones.'

'It's uncommon,' he said. 'But fair enough.'

'It *means* something. I have to call credit-card companies five and six times. My driver's license picture is dreadful, but the hassle of a new application is unthinkable. Passports, bank accounts, diplomas, standardized tests. You name it. I've never had a single piece of correctly addressed junk mail. Another?'

He looked down at his glass and was surprised to find it dry. How long had it been since he'd had alcohol on a school night? Never, he never had, not since starting at HUM. He had classmates who showed up to work hungover; that was not him. He had Responsibilities.

On the other hand. A little enforced relaxation couldn't hurt. Not after the day he'd had. He was human. And they had been working him into the ground. And Hannah, and George . . . the worst that could happen was that he'd sleep solidly, and what a relief that would provide, after so many bouts of nightmares.

He nodded, and she went back to the bar.

While she waited, he examined her shape. She was slender and her hair draped around her shoulders. He could make out the bulge of the bandage on her back. He felt a strong urge to touch her.

She returned with a fresh drink and a bowl of peanuts.

'Thanks,' he said.

'You saved my life. I think that's worth at least a couple of gin-and-tonics.'

'Fair enough.' He took a sip. 'They're watered down, anyway.'

'I know, I'm sorry.' She sighed. 'This place used to be *the* place. Everyone came here. My mother kissed Ray Davies while leaning against that wall.'

'*The* Ray Davies?'

She nodded. 'The one and only.'

'For real?'

'When I was growing up, the East Village was still the East Village, not the theme park it's become today.' She bit her lip. 'I didn't mean that the way it came out. No offense.'

'None taken. I live here cause it's close to free.'

'Rent-control aunt?'

'Trust-fund roommate.'

'Oo*ooh*,' she said. 'The rarer subspecies.'

'Was he high? When you met him.'

'I'm awaiting the results of my urinalysis.'

He laughed, losing a cheekful of drink across his chin and the table. Embarrassed, he reached for a napkin that wasn't there – because she had picked it up and folded it into his other hand. He wiped himself off. 'Suave.'

'Fret not. Everybody snarfs. Isn't that a song?'

He laughed again. 'He – Lance, he goes out five nights a week to the movies with this girl, not his girlfriend but another filmmaker he met at a festival. They get stoned and go to BAM or Film Forum, or Angel – I don't remember what it's called.'

'Angelika.'

'That's the one.' Regretting his impromptu caricature, he added: 'He's a good guy. He lets me stay as long as I pay the utilities. He's smart. A little lost.'

'I know the type.'

Still feeling bad, he changed the subject. 'This place is one of your haunts.'

'Was. It used to be crowded.' She glanced around to confirm that they were the sole customers. 'Now . . . It's rather bereft, don't you think. Although I guess it's early.'

Her diction made him smile. *Rather bereft*. Like a Brontë transplant, her sentences draped in lace; stick-on savoir faire. Or the other way round: she was trying, and failing, to hide impeccable breeding.

Does the zebra have white stripes on a black body or black stripes on a white body.

'Although,' she added, 'I haven't been here in over twenty-five years.'

'You're – thirty?'

'Thirty-one.'

'Twenty-five years ago, that would make you six.'

'I said *over* twenty-five years,' she said. 'I was younger. Three or four.'

'Your parents took you to bars when you were three?'

'They didn't believe in babysitters.'

'That's . . .' Every normative objection he could come up with sounded hopelessly bourgeois, so he went with a factual one: 'How could you remember?'

'How could I forget?'

'But that's too young to, to remember—'

'I remember things from when I was one and a half.'

He put his glass down. 'Okay. Not possible.'

'It most certainly *is*,' she said. 'I remember being on a swing set at my grandparents' house. I remember wearing pink overalls, and my father amusing me with a plastic duck. When I was eight I asked what had happened to that duck. He said, "What duck?" "The plastic one from grand-mama's house.' He said, "That?," that we threw it away the day we got it. It smelled bad.

'One day,' she said. 'I played with it once. But I could draw it for you.'

'You're reconstructing,' he said. 'From a picture, or from what he told you.'

'There are no pictures from that day. And he never mentioned it before I brought it up. It took *him* a long time to remember what I was talking about.'

'Then your mother mentioned it.'

'By that time she had been gone for three years. Her kiss with Ray Davies ended in San Francisco.'

'Your mother ran off with Ray Davies.'

'Briefly. I presume it didn't last terribly long.'

'And then?'

'And then she never came back.' She sat back, smiled, crossed her arms triumphantly. 'Crazy but true.'

'That's – wow.' He took a handful of peanuts. 'I feel pretty boring.'

'Nonsense. I want to know all about you. That's why I came to see you. Frankly, Jonah Stem, I'm having a hard time understanding if you're real or not.'

'I'm real.'

'What you did was exceptional. Are you aware of that?'

'Whatever.'

'Don't minimize. I'm alive because of you.'

He looked up. 'All right.'

'Thank you,' she said.

'You're welcome.' He almost added *I'd do it for anyone* out of modesty's sake, but seeing her – her perfect neck, her china ears – he wondered if that

79

was true. If she had been hideous; if it had been Raymond Iniguez getting stabbed?

He said, 'Tell me about you first.'

'Well, on last week's episode, my nuclear family fell prey to the British Invasion. Sadly the plot weakens considerably from there on. My father was a car salesman, which he continued to be after he and my mother divorced. I went to high school. I went to college. I received my master's. I lived in Brooklyn until it became *Brooklyn*. Presently, I'm ensconced in the great quasi-urban eczema known as Hoboken.'

'You came all the way over for me,' he said. 'Back to the old theme park.'

She smiled. 'The least I could do.'

'Where'd you go to college?'

'Yale.'

'No shit.'

'Lux et veritas.'

'My sister went there,' he said. 'Class of . . . '94? Her name is Catherine. Or Kate. Kate Hausmann. That's her married name. Back then she was—'

'Catherine, or Kate, Stem?' Eve said.

'Uh.' He laughed at himself. 'Yeah.'

'I knew I recognized that name. What a small, small world we live in. Have you noticed that overeducated white New Yorkers all seem to know each other?'

He snickered. 'Two degrees of separation.'

'I remember your sister, she was popular.'

'That'd be her.'

'Tell me she married someone from our class, that would be too rich.'

'Nope. A business-school guy. He's German.'

'As in from *das Vaterland*?'

'He was born in Berlin. He works for Deutsche Bank. They live in Greenwich and have a daughter. She's two and a half. Her name is Gretchen. She's pregnant again. Kate, not Gretchen.' He took a breath. 'That's pretty much the deal.'

'I never would have pegged your sister as a full-time mom.'

'She isn't. She works for a hedge fund in Connecticut. She also has an MBA, from Wharton.'

'Good Lord,' said Eve. 'What else can you tell me. Give me the facts, Jonah Stem, I'm finding this all very intoxicating.'

He talked about himself, about his family, about Scarsdale. He talked about being a child and playing with his father's stethoscope; being a teenager and overcoming the reluctance to follow in his father's footsteps. Not drinking for two years had turned him into a serious lightweight; Lance could down a fifth of gin and two dime bags, and drive nails without injury, whereas Jonah already felt loose-tongued. His limbs tingled pleasantly. He decided to go with the flow. She listened. She was funny, and also pretty, and also intelligent, and most of all interested: taking him in as though what he said mattered. He supposed he had to matter to her: he had saved her life. But he saw more: saw something gorgeous and honest; she cared; and he felt a swell of what did not register as attraction, not at first, as the machinery had been so long dormant. He talked and she talked and he learned about her and she about him, and, sensing heat, he observed out of the corner of his eye that their fingertips were nearly touching. He told her that his father went to Radcliffe and his mother went to Harvard, and she asked if they'd had sex-change surgery, and he laughed and said *No more drinks*.

'Well anyway that's some oligarchy,' she said. 'What Ivy grows on you?'

He shook his head. 'University of Michigan. Our mascot is the black sheep.'

She sighed. 'We can't all be so lucky.'

'Oh please shut up.'

'I take it your educational decision did not wow the electorate.'

'They didn't have a choice. I might have gotten into Brown or Columbia, but I didn't *want* to go to Brown or Columbia because I was an angry young man—'

She giggled.

'I was, I'm not anymore. Not angry, more like . . . stubborn.'

'Jonah Jonah quite contronah.'

'Yes, and I thought that a state school was the best way to irritate them.' He finished the last of the peanuts.

'And unfortunately for you, they were disgustingly supportive,' she said. '*Dans nos temps modernes, il n'existe pas de horreurs plus dignes que celle.*'

82

'*Yo hablo español*,' he said.

'I said, "Poor you."'

'Now you're showing off,' he said.

'My rap sheet includes several convictions for armed snobbery.'

He laughed.

'And let me guess,' she said. 'Your girlfriend went to Princeton.'

'. . . no.'

'I said something wrong.'

'No, no.' He could tell from the way she was frowning that he must look furious – which he wasn't; he was simply unused to answering the question. Eve began to apologize and he said, 'It's all right. You didn't do anything.'

A horrid silence ensued, in which he could see her weighing her options: make a joke, apologize again, find a new tack, need the bathroom, call it a night. Unhappily he considered the same list, and then one option came storming forward, violent and demanding: tell her. He had saved her life, the least she could do was help roll the elephant off his chest. He never talked about Hannah. His family had learned not to ask; and Lance – who'd known her since childhood, who had been the catalyst for crissake – got jumpy, refusing to say her name, as though she had ceased to exist, a superstition that indicated to Jonah a feeling of partial responsibility. Other than them, only Vik knew the whole story, and Vik was smart enough to know that Jonah didn't *want* to talk about it. Not usually. But on days like today he felt alone, and unable to keep his doctorly face up, and he wanted to talk about it, and now there was someone sitting across from him.

More than someone. He wanted to talk about Hannah, yes, but more important, he wanted to talk about Hannah *with Eve*. Unknown and intimate, the ideal listener, because as much as he liked her right now – liked her a lot, in fact, had a hell of an erection – liked her because after two hours of casual talk she seemed to anticipate him – he doubted that he'd see her again after tonight. And although he expected to hate himself, expected telling her to sound self-indulgent, a cheap ploy for sympathy, as he talked he felt the spring uncoiling, and the alcohol gave him an assist, and she did her part by listening, nodding, listening. She listened, and when he finished, she reached across the table and touched his hand.

He said, 'I'm sorry. For all that.'

She looked at him. 'Never, ever apologize for being in love.'

As they approached his apartment he again expressed his regret, this time for cutting the evening short. 'I have to be at work in five hours.'

'Stop apologizing, Jonah Stem, it's unbecoming for a superhero.'

They arrived at his building. He faced her. 'It was nice talking to you, Eve.'

She nodded and said *Yes*. Her body inclined toward

84

him, and he did what felt natural: he gave her a hug. Her arms around his neck felt strangely familiar. She was roughly Hannah's height, the top of her head brushing the soft underside of his jaw, now sandy with eleven-o'clock shadow, so that when she leaned back her hair stuck to him like Velcro. He laughed and moved to brush it away, but she raised up her face and brought his down to meet it, and her mouth was quite soft.

She stepped away, gave a short wave. He watched her disappear into the warm mist, then let himself into his building and headed upstairs, staggering a tiny bit, wondering why he hadn't had the presence of mind to ask for her phone number.

CHAPTER 7

From page seventeen of the *Guide to the Third-Year Clerkships*, the official literature distributed by the Office of Student Life, the Teaching College of the Hospital of Upper Manhattan:

> In particular, the clerkship in surgery can be a time of significant stress. Hours can be long, and the daily tempo is highly accelerated. Students who fail to take adequate care of themselves, either physically or psychologically, will find that they are less likely to perform at an optimum level. Remember: *A healthy student is a successful student.*

From page nine of the Book, a stapled packet of collective HUM student wisdom, first compiled in 1991 by third-years Gary S. Glaucher and Connie Teitelbaum, now blissfully wed and running a lucrative orthopedics practice in Tenafly, New Jersey:

HOW TO SURVIVE SURGERY,
or,

I'M PAYING TUITION FOR THIS?
The basic principles of surviving surgery
are as follows:
no food,
no sleep,
No problem!

By his third week on the colorectal service, Jonah
had begun to feel at home among piles of guts.
Once the custodial staff had removed the last copy
of the *Post*, the residents gave up their crusade to
put him in his place, and began to treat him like
any other medical student: *i.e.*, like a gimp.

His team consisted of Yokogawa, the chief; one
senior resident; two junior residents; two interns;
and two third-years in addition to him. Collectively,
they answered to an attending Jonah had yet to see,
a mysterious and legendary surgeon named Holtz.
On the ward, their team was known as Holtz Two.
There were also Holtzes One and Three, whom
Jonah imagined as clones of Holtz Two, so that he
had not one but two doppelgängers roving the ward.

His fellow HUMmers were Lisa Laroux, a
pimply redhead with modest pediatric aspirations,
and Patrick Nelgrave, a short, hirsute, belligerent
gunner who came in on weekends because he was
bored. Lisa was okay, but Nelgrave was a nightmare, nakedly desirous of making his peers look

as stupid as possible in front of their preceptors. He used his copy of *Surgical Recall* – a handbook of pre-prepped pimp sessions carried by all third-years – to look up obscure facts, later just happening to 'think them out loud' during rounds. *What's the difference again between Bochdalek's and Hesslebach's hernias? Oh right, one passes through the posterior diaphragm, frequently on the left, and the other is under inguinal ligaments* lateral *to the femoral vessels, riiight.* Jonah learned, when asked a direct question, to answer as fast as possible; any hesitation prompted Nelgrave to barge in, brandishing his vocabulary. He was a horse thief, a double-talking backstabbing toadying panjandrum, upstaging everyone, a tactic that Jonah considered transparently juvenile until he realized that many of the surgeons were the same but with bigger mortgages and less hair. Gunners were gunners at any age.

But this was surgery: you ate shit and declared it pâté.

He arrived at 5:25 A.M. to preround and do scut: standing at the nurses' station, he banged away at an ancient computer, copying vitals from the master spreadsheet and pasting them into another spreadsheet with his team's patients. This simple-enough task often required upward of a half-hour, because the consoles weren't networked, and without fail the overnight interns would update one console and not the others, with the result that every computer had different patient lists and different stats. It fell to the HUMmers to race around the floor, gathering the correct figures on floppy disks that they'd purchased out of pocket.

Then came rounds. Yokogawa's motto was *Colorectal hauls ass.* They didn't spend time assuaging patients' fears. Get the ins and outs: eat, piss, bleed, gas, shit, vomit. Heart. Respiration. Wound healing? Febrile? As soon as a patient could fend for himself, get him Off the List. OTL & OTD ASAP or SOL. The watchword was turnover. Anybody who didn't fall into line was a Pollyanna, a sapling, deserving of an AKA (Above Knee Amputation).

Invariably, the team had to contend with aches and pains that had bloomed, like crocuses, with the new day. *While I'm here for my hysterectomy* these patients seemed to say *why don't I develop a bad rash, as well? Or how about conjunctivitis? I could get pneumonia, if you'd like.* Patients praying and braying and clutching their liver-spotted hands to their sagging breasts. They had halitosis and flaky skin and creeping cancers that would kill them sooner or later. They went incontinent and shried about the blandness of their meals. They got annoyed when you couldn't bask in their reminiscences. Crotchety old-timers ripped straight from the pages of *The House of God*, they confirmed what his father had once told him: every branch of medicine was a subspecialty of geriatrics.

Jonah (or Lisa or Nelgrave, always frickin Nelgrave) would stand at the foot of the bed, discoursing animatedly on sphincter muscle tone and the state of the patient's rectal vault, which he imagined as bolted down with a mammoth brown padlock. *The documents are in the rectal vault, 007, set to self-destruct. Guaiac before it's too late.*

The medical student's real job during rounds, however, was to carry the Bucket, a turquoise emesis basin filled with gauze, dressing, scissors, syringes, gloves. Tegaderm patches in three sizes; if the resident called for a medium, and all you had was small and large, the world screeched to a halt as you sprinted to the supply closet. Lots and lots of Surgilube. Especially on colorectal. Yokogawa would stick out his glove. *Lube me, Superman.* Jonah felt like a hot dog salesman.

He felt lucky if he had time to wolf down a granola bar while jogging to the OR. Often not, which left him standing, unfed, through eight or ten hours' worth of colecystectomies, rectal polyp removals, appendectomies. He snipped and sutured and suctioned and retracted. Up to his elbows in ligature, he learned, first, the two-handed knot; then the one-handed knot; and then spent a whole surgery woozily considering the philosophical implications of a *no*-handed knot.

On colon resections he wielded the staple gun, a device that looked like an early-80s rendition of 'futuristic weapon.' *Preparing to fire* it would say in its creepy electronic voice. The attending would nod, and Jonah would pull the trigger.

Firing!

And lo, the Bowel was One.

He met a lot of surgeons. There was Kurt Bourbon, who came in twice a week to work in eighteen-hour blocks, a schedule that freed up Tuesday, Thursday, Friday, Saturday, and Sunday for the pursuit of extramarital affairs. There was 'Phat' Albert Zakarias, the Hip-hop Doctor, who liked to operate while hollering along to 'Real Niggaz Don't Die.' There was Elliot Steinberger, who – though lanky, balding, and potbellied – had clearly once strutted Lothario, his yearning for the bygone manifest in long rants about how unbearably hot he found his daughter's friends. They were thirteen. Was that wrong?

In the afternoon, the calendar gurus printed up the following day's OR schedule, which privacy laws forbade circulating. Anyone who wanted the information, attendings and residents included, had to come to the nurses' station to read the master. What actually happened was that Jonah's team sent him to make Xeroxes, a blah task made challenging by the fact that, most days, he had to do it while fending off a mob of neurotic HUMmers sent by *their* teams, all grabbing at the blue-vinyl binder, trying to locate the lists for *their* surgeons and get them into the copier that wouldn't start without a solid hipcheck. Ever fastidious, the HUMmers invariably made extras, which got left in the paper tray or tossed, unshredded, in the trash – thus annihilating any semblance of privacy and along with it the whole point of having a master copy.

Before evening rounds he redid the morning's charts, noting daytime vitals and whatever lab results had come in. Writing labs was like memorizing pi. It went–

Kim, Hyun Joo	Sodium 135 Potassium 3.9 Chloride 101
Blackwell, B.	Sodium 144 Potassium 4.2 Chloride 106

–for thirty values per patient.

The work got interesting when a patient registered numbers through the roof or the floor. Then at least he could marvel at the remarkable elasticity of the human body, and the fact that the poor jerk would be dead before prime time.

He swam in jargon: drowned in abbreviations. ABG, BIH, COPD, DDx, EGD, FAP, GERD, HCT, IBD, JVD, LLQ, NGT, ORIF, PICC, SBO, TURP, VAD, XRT, ZE. Words he thought he knew took on new meanings. 'Cabbage' wasn't a soup-or-salad vegetable; it was a Coronary Artery Bypass Graft. 'Fast' wasn't a rate of motion; it was a Focused Abdominal Sonogram for Trauma. PERRLs and SX and PEEPS and HOs; he was living in a rap video.

As in the argot of superstitious old women, cancer became CA. Centimeters were *saunt*imeters, like the hospital had imported a shipment of the word from France. A sucking vortex of MediCode, a pit of incomprehensibility separating the patients from the healers, the uninitiated from the elect, a burdensome and privileged vocabulary that, once accepted, rendered real-world conversation impossible. No wonder doctors married nurses or other doctors. After this there was no real world.

Here, you accepted the outlandish. Here, humanity distilled down to a dying child; a patriarch with grasping heirs. The staff, the patients, the families: everyone playing roles, having taken their cues from melodramatic films. To Jonah the suspense of watching someone's lungs work outdid any fiction. Such drama – real drama – made it all the more preposterous that the residents spent their free time in the lounge, watching TV shows about being a resident.

He got pimped senseless. He took abuse. He excused surgeons their gruffness and arrogance. They had to fend off malpractice and maintain their mortality ratings; they had to worry about hotshots with steadier hands. As an eyewitness, Jonah could appreciate their miracles in a way that patients – who went under feeling crappy and woke up feeling worse – could not. He wanted to be a part of this world, and yet did not. He hoped he appeared more confident, more competent, than he felt. He was tired. He was a furnace of guilt. He wondered how he would survive. All in a day's work.

WEDNESDAY, SEPTEMBER 1, 2004.
COLORECTAL SERVICE, WEEK THREE.

The final patient of that morning was a seventy-five-year-old Hungarian man whose wife hovered by his bedside, intimidating entrants with her considerable beehive. Mr Szathmáry was pre-op but had been hogging a bed for a day and a half, a curious luxury in the days of managed care. His prolapsed rectum and ill temper had rapidly earned him the designation 'the asshole whose asshole fell out of his asshole.'

They entered the room with one goal: to get him to sign his consent form. Instead they found themselves sparring with Mrs Szathmáry, who insisted they had no right to take away her husband's breakfast.

'I brang for him,' she said, waving a Tupperware tub of lekvar pierogies.

'That's very sweet of you,' Yokogawa said, 'but it's not good for him.'

'He has not eat,' she objected, reaching for the box as Jonah spirited it into the hallway and handed it off to a confused janitor.

Jonah returned to hear Gillers, the intern, explaining that, despite his crushing hunger, her husband had to fast this morning.

'He can have something to drink if he wants,' Gillers said, 'but no solids.'

'He can have water?'

'Water is fine, yes.'

'Tea?'

'Uh. Well, it's better, ma'am, if—'

'Juice?'

A purpling Lisa Laroux ate her fist. Nelgrave wiped his nose and took notes.

'He can have ice chips,' said Yokogawa.

Mrs Szathmáry said, 'Maybe leettle toast?'

'No, ma'am, no toast.'

'Why no.'

'Toast isn't a liquid.'

'*Hajna, Hajna,*' said Mr Szathmáry. '*Maradj cs . . . ndben . . .*'

'My husband say heess hungry.'

'Let's please run over the procedure,' said Yokogawa.

This, too, took longer than usual. Mrs Szathmáry, translating, kept leaping in to editorialize or to pelt the doctors with questions. Why did they have to put him under? Was it dangerous? Was the procedure necessary? Where did they get their degrees? Were they married? She had a bad headaches, they could prescribe her to help with?

Yokogawa said, 'And once we've reattached the rectum to the anus—'

'Ainus?'

'Uh – yes.'

'Whatsis ainus?' She sort of sounded like she was saying *hyenas*, and Jonah imagined the surgeon sewing a wild dog to Mr Szathmáry's butthole.

'His, uhum.' Yokogawa looked around helplessly.

'I don't know whatsis ainus.' She turned to her husband. 'Ainus?'

It was obvious to Jonah that he was the one best holding it together. Huberman was engrossed in his armpit. Gillers looked like he wanted to punch himself in the face. Stricken with a coughing fit, Lisa Laroux had left the room.

'The anus,' said Nelgrave, 'is the opening at the inferior end of the alimentary canal, open during defecation but closed at other times. Rectal prolapse, in contrast to mucosal prolapse, involves—'

Mrs Szathmáry's hearing aid shrieked, causing them all to jump. Her husband scratched at her shoulder and pointed to her ear. She turned it down, then addressed him with teary vehemence, until Yokogawa, having had enough, said, 'Mrs Szathmáry.'

'He need ainus?'

'Very much.'

She conveyed this information to her husband, who grunted assent and feebly shook Yokogawa's hand.

Gillers muttered, 'For God's sake.' Nelgrave wrote that down.

Vik said, 'I'm calling on behalf of my girlfriend.'

Native to Brookline, Massachusetts, Vikram Rakhe was laconic, dry, rational – all qualities desirable in a future trauma surgeon. A two-time winner of the New England Teen Tennis Invitational, he'd first walked into anatomy lab wearing a warm-up jacket embroidered with his club seal and, below it, his nickname: *The Boston Brahmin*.

I think we're sharing a cadaver. Holding up a sheet.

Over the last two years Jonah had come to appreciate his paternal mien. He was a good lab partner, reliable and knowledgeable, always letting others take their share of credit even when he was the only one who'd done the reading. He nicely countervailed Lance; around Vik, Jonah got to enjoy being the loose cannon.

The girlfriend in question was a management consultant who traveled five days a week. Jonah, copying *Pontebasso, Salvatore*'s T-cell count, couldn't remember where she was at the moment.

'Omaha.'

'What's in Omaha.'

'Nothing,' Vik said. 'That's why they need a consultant.'

The plan was to go skiing. Deanna had found a prime rate on a Vermont cabin for the first week of break. Vik intended to call some of their other classmates, Olivia and Jeremy and Harold and Anita. It would be fun.

Jonah thanked him but declined. 'I'm busy.'

'You're going away?'

'I'm staying with Hannah.'

'Mm.' To an untrained ear he might have sounded indifferent, but Jonah got his sympathy. As usual, Vik gracefully changed the subject. 'Did you get my flowers?'

'Thanks.'

'You're welcome. Take a lesson. How's surgery?'

Jonah gave him the five-minute summary, sharing tips for when Vik came through St Aggie's in the spring.

'Always carry a chart. That way, someone tells

you to go do something, you can say, "Sure thing, as soon as I'm done with this chart . . ."'

'Clever.'

'Do the busywalk. You know the drill, I'm sure it's the same on medicine.'

'Pretty much.'

Jonah briefly considered mentioning Eve Gones. So far he'd told no one, and that she had not returned in the last four days seemed to confirm his earlier suspicions: what happened happened: a one-off. Even now, as his jaw sawed indecisively, he felt the heat she'd conjured up – in one stroke, like a match igniting – burning down, intensifying as it reached the end of its pathetically short life.

He said, 'Tell Deanna thanks for thinking of me.'

'I will.'

Ten minutes later a nurse poked him in the arm. 'Some guy here for you.'

She nodded toward the elevator bank, where a stocky man in shorts and a purple messenger bag stood cracking his knuckles. Jonah went over. 'Can I help you?'

'Jonah Stem?' The guy fiddled inside his bag and withdrew a sheaf of papers, which he thrust into Jonah's hands.

'Consider yourself served,' he said. Then he smiled and walked away.

Jonah said, 'What?' but the guy was gone.

He felt as though someone had tossed him a dirty diaper that he idiotically continued to hold. Several nurses – along with an attending who was grading him – were staring at him. *Served* was a word he associated with restaurants and hotels, people working to make your life easier. Although he was pretty sure that his had just gotten harder.

CHAPTER 8

'Well,' said Belzer, 'no good deed.'

'This is not – not – *not right.*'

'Stop pacing, kiddo, you're going to give yourself a stroke.'

'*They're* suing *me?*'

'Hang on a minute. Don't let's get carried away. Nobody's sued you yet.'

'What do you think *that* is.'

'As far as I'm concerned, a lawsuit's not a lawsuit till the other guy's won. Until that it's wishful thinking.'

'I didn't do anything *wrong.*'

'Of course you didn't, b—'

'Did I?'

'No. You didn't. Will you siddown? Siddown. *Thank* you.' Belzer touched his phone. 'Mandy, can we hydrate my client here? Perfect. Now. Let's focus on the positives. First of all, you got your health, don't undervalue that. And you're in the clear, criminally speaking. Downtown called this morning. The cops talked to the hospital. Everyone gives you a thumbs-up. The DA's never going to gimme a guarantee, but I'd put the odds of them charging you at about two hundred to one.'

The relief Jonah felt startled him. Fear of incarceration had gotten lost in a thicket of more dominant anxieties. 'Thank you.'

'My pleasure. Now let's talk about the Iniguez family. The brother, what's his – can I have th— thank you.' Belzer put on his reading glasses. 'Simon Iniguez. See-moan. He has a thingy over the O. Isn't that a girl's name?'

The door to the office opened, and a willowy blonde entered with a tray of Fiji water, which she set on a wooden folding table. She smiled at Jonah and slipped out. Belzer held out a bottle.

'From now on, nobody hands me anything.'

Belzer chuckled. 'You're learning. Okay. Simon – I'm going to call him Simon for now, because Simón is too hard for me to remember. Let's imagine what's happening here. Iniguez is bereaved. He gets a call from this guy who tells him that he's got rights, he can win money, he can take revenge. This shyster, Roberto Medina, I know this guy. I bet you've seen him, he's got ads on every bus in the Bronx. Angry bastard. He does commercials on late-night TV. Screams a lot. I'll say one thing for him, he's fast. What's it been, two weeks?'

'Not even.'

'Good turnaround. They must really want your dough. First thing, I'm going to talk to him. I'll tell him what the DA told me, what the cops said, what this Eve Jones lady said.' He paged his secretary again. 'Call this putz. Medina. Me-*di*-na. Roberto. Tell him I'm representing Mr Stem and I want to schedule a time to speak with him ASAP. How about next week. Okay? Thanks.'

Next week sounded nothing like ASAP, but Jonah kept his mouth shut.

'As far as I'm concerned,' Belzer said, 'they're dick-waving. Any reasonable court will throw this case out in a second. To win money for wrongful death they have to show negligence on your part, and economic loss on theirs. Let's remember the facts, shall we? The guy was unemployed, unstable, and wielding a knife. He was about to commit a murder. Everybody read about it. No judge, no jury in the world is going to punish Superdoc.' Belzer cracked open his water. 'Now that doesn't mean that they won't try and squeeze you anyway. If they think you're a pushover, why *not*? That's what they're hoping for, a quick settlement. If they're made to see that we know the case is unwinnable, and that we'll countersue their nuts off, I can all but promise you they'll crawl back into their hole.'

'What do I do.'

'Nothing.'

'I want something to happen,' Jonah said.

'It'll happen, all right? That's what I'm telling you. Let me handle it. The first thing we're doing is filing a motion to dismiss.'

'What if that doesn't work?'

'It will.'

'But what if it doesn't?'

'It *will*. There's no case here, kiddo.'

'What if there is?'

Belzer sighed. 'Like what.'

'I don't know, *anything*.'

'You saw her crawling up the street.'

Jonah nodded.

'She had stab wounds.'

'Yes.'

'He tried to stab you.'

'Ye – I—'

'Okay, forget that. Lemme put it this way: you felt *gravely threatened*.'

'. . . yes.'

'Of course you did,' Belzer said. 'Anybody would, and you know why? Cause it's *reasonable* to feel gravely threatened when it's late at night, and there's a screaming woman, and the guy's talking to himself, and he comes at you with a knife. We've gone over this. By definition you're not negligent. Negligent is if he spits on your shoes and you smush him with a cement mixer. You acted to save your life and hers.'

'I know.'

'Then what are you worried about?'

'I don't like being sued.'

'Nobody does,' Belzer said. 'But it's a part of life.'

'Not mine.'

'Welcome to the big leagues. You're gonna be a doctor, you're gonna get sued. Think of this as a crash course. Don't worry about a thing. You look worried.'

'I *am*.'

'Don't be. We're going to nail em to the floor and varnish em. Get it?'

'Yeah.' He got it; but that didn't mean he had to like it. He felt bad enough as it was without having to let off salvos at Raymond Iniguez's grieving family.

He supposed this was the way it went: they pushed; you kicked. They cocked a gun; you shouldered a bazooka. American tort law didn't leave much room for turning the other cheek.

'Good,' Belzer said. 'How's life otherwise? School?'

'It's fine.' He'd skipped out early to come here. Tomorrow would bring a beatdown. 'Stressful.'

'Cheer up. Life ain't so bad.' Belzer stood up. 'My regards to your folks.'

Too restless to go home, he got off at Union Square, wending through a loose crowd of demonstrators concerned about the upcoming election. Mixed in were several other causes, people objecting to everything from the administration to globalization, meat to SUVs, each cadre occupying its own fifty square feet. A pair of dreadlocked men ambled through the fray, hawking essential oils and hemp bracelets that smelled of patchouli. Jonah watched the skateboarders, watched a group of emaciated breakdancers in matching orange T-shirts that said BOMB SQUAD. He counted the people going in and out of Starbucks. He wandered south on Broadway and ducked into the Strand.

He hadn't been in in a while; he liked its tottering, womblike stacks. During his junior summer he'd done research at Rockefeller, and would come down to the store after work to stand at the back, plucking titles at random and reading until he got bored. One time he read all of *The Bridge of San Luis Rey*, three hours rooted in place. Afterward he felt bad and paid for it.

Books – non-med books – reminded him of home. The living room of his parents' house had floor-to-ceiling units packed with acidulated New Directions paperbacks, anthologies of Russian plays, presidential biographies, out-of-print treatises on secular humanism. His mother had a large poetry collection; at one point she had aspired to write. (Asked why she gave up, she said *Because I gave up*.)

His parents had already read and reread it all. They kept the shelves stocked, Jonah knew, to inspire their children to a life of the mind – their own intellectualism having dwindled to support for public television and an epidemic explosion of magazine subscriptions. They got the *Atlantic, The New Yorker, Smithsonian,* and *The Economist.* They got *Cook's, Harper's, Granta,* and *American Art Review.* They got *National Geographic, Scientific American,* and *The New Republic.* Plus his mother's guilty pleasures (*Us Weekly*) and the annals of whatever hobby his father had taken up most recently (the *Astronomer*, lepidopterists' quarterlies). Accumulating in heaps atop the japanned coffee table. Sometimes Jonah thought of his home as a clearinghouse for waiting rooms everywhere.

To his chagrin, over the last two years, he'd come to fear and hate reading. One day, he'd return from the trenches and go back to books for pleasure. Assuming he wasn't blind by then.

'Jonah Stem. Shall I call a doctor?'

He turned from a row of weathered military histories.

Eve touched the small of his back. 'Are you having a hypnagogic episode?'

'I didn't see you,' he said. 'What are you doing here?'

'This is the one place I miss most in the City; I stop in after work sometimes. Are you feeling all right?'

'. . . yeah,' he said. 'Yeah.'

'You look decidedly hang-dog.'

'I'm . . .' He shook off the cloud, smiled. 'I'm better now.'

'Are you?'

'Much.'

'Good.' She squeezed his hand, then turned to the books. 'Is this your secret hideaway?' She poked at the spines. 'Which one opens the Batcave?'

They left the bookstore and went east as though they had laid prior plans.

The apartment was empty. Lance had left the remains of his dinner – a pizza, glazed over like a waxwork – along with a Post-it that read *Eat me*. Jonah checked the fridge and found nothing. He suggested the Yaffa Cafe. Or Café Gigi, or—

She said, 'Do you have a blanket?'

They climbed the fire escape to the roof and spread Lance's flannel throw across the tar paper. The sky was full of stars screaming to make themselves heard over the light pollution.

She said, 'I've been thinking about you.'

'Me too.'

'I don't know quite how to explain it,' she said.

'Me neither.'

'Then let's not try.'

He nodded.

She said, 'Come here.'

The blanket smelled like Pabst Blue Ribbon and designer weed. Jonah sensed the presence of people watching from adjacent windows as Eve knelt on his arms, unbuttoned his shirt, opened his fly.

He closed and opened his eyes at four-second intervals, finding her reborn with each shutterclick. First the gloss of distraction as she found her rhythm. Then trancelike, swiveling, reading his naked torso. Then rapturous, her face waxing and waning: full and heart-shaped; gibbous in semi-profile; an ecstatic sliver. He reached for her breasts but she grabbed his hands, brought them beneath her skirt, slapped them against her. She seemed to like that, and he did it again. Salsa music and honking from the street below. Gravel in his hair. Far-off watertowers applauding. They were not alone. Eight million pairs of eyes watching them. The aurora of the Empire State Building, streaking jetliners, her finger between his lips.

She said, 'You see that?'

'What.'

'How many people live in that building, do you think?'

'It's . . . what. Seven stories? And let's say five apartments on each floor. That's thirty-five. And probably two to four people in each. Call it a hundred.'

'A nice round number,' she said. 'Good for percentages.'

He nodded.

She said, 'Out of a hundred people in that building, think how many are going to the bathroom.'

He laughed, stroked her nape. 'I don't want to think about it.'

'Do, for a second. How many people are having intercourse. At least eight.'

'Is that what you think when you walk down the street?'

She nodded against his chest.

'The world must look surreal to you,' he said.

'Everywhere I go,' she said, 'I wonder how many people are doing what at this very instant. In a hundred people, at least eight are having sex, and another eight are masturbating. A handful are eating, and an equal number are watching television. There's overlap between those two groups. We could make a Venn diagram. Some are reading, some are ironing, some are taking a shower, and some are removing their contact lenses. Or swallowing an aspirin, or smoking. Some are dying and some are contemplating divorce. One is contemplating suicide. He might be committing suicide as I say this; he might have a razor against his wrist. And if a great hand came along and ripped off the exterior wall, exposing each little hole that people crawl into to do their dirty deeds, you and I could watch them like exhibits in the Museum of Human Frailties.

'That's what I think about when I see that building.'

A silence. Jonah shivered.

'It's hot out,' she said. 'Are you cold?'

'No,' he said.

'I'm always cold.' She plucked at her woolly sweater. 'I have poor circulation.'

'I'd tell you to get it checked out by a doctor,' he said, 'but we don't do shit. Go to an acupuncturist.'

Much later, when they came down the fire escape and climbed back into his apartment, they became aware of noise coming from the third bedroom, Lance's studio: a seven-second snippet of shower-singing, played over and over. Jonah raised his eyebrows at Eve. She giggled. 'I think we should leave the maestro to his work.'

'I'll walk you to the subway.'

At the Ⓛ, he said, 'This time I'm not going to forget: your number.'

'Would you believe I'm the last person in the Western world to go without a cell phone?'

'That's admirable.'

'Cheap, Jonah Stem. Cheap.'

She gave him her e-mail address. 'Honestly, that's the best way to reach me. I can call you when I get a moment from work.'

He gave her his cell, his pager, his home phone, and his e-mail. 'And you know where I live.'

She kissed him on the chin. 'I know where you live.'

The same snippet was still going when he got back. He decided to give Lance five more minutes before telling him knock it off, bedtime. As it turned out, an unnecessary deadline: a loud crash, followed by silence, solved the problem.

Jonah sighed and dutifully headed down the hall.

In the studio Lance kept a hoard of top-of-the-line AV equipment, much of which currently resided on the floor in an incredible, disastrous heap. Lance, in full combat fatigues, smoked a Gauloise and scratched his chin. 'You try and find one lens.'

Jonah looked him up and down. 'I thought you were antiwar.'

'Ruby and I are playing laser tag,' he said. 'You in?'

Jonah thanked him, declined, and went back to the living room.

'I need the break,' Lance said. 'I've been busting my tail. The Internet is a thing of beauty, dude. My subscriber base is expanding by the minute.'

'You have subscribers.'

'Sixteen. Most are my friends, and one is my mom, but a couple are from Canada, and one guy's in Kuala Lumpur.'

'Get out.'

'At a dollar ninety-nine apiece,' Lance said, 'that's thirty bucks a month for letting people watch me crap.'

'Please tell me you don't take the webcam in there.'

'It's part of my image. Honesty. That's what keeps them tuning in.'

'I guess so.'

'I keep the view partially obscured. You can't see my unit. You have to leave the viewer wanting more, it's an elementary principle of the tease. A pinch of mystery engenders like nine hundred Troy ounces of fixation. It's like my stepmom.' Edward DePauw's current wife was a plastinated real-estate broker half his age, the very one who'd found him a penthouse after things went awry with Original Recipe Mrs DePauw.

'She knew where it was at,' Lance said. 'Major

cocktease, dude. She made sure she had the rock firmly in hand before she put out.'

Jonah had his doubts about this theory, but nodded.

'Which reminds me: my Mom's got a new boyfriend, too.'

'Oh yeah?'

'He's a count.'

Jonah found this hilarious. 'Does he wear a cape?'

'For real, dude.'

'Four, four husbands, mwa-ha-ha-ha.'

'As far as I can tell he's less of a spaz than the last guy. He offered to take us to see his castle. We're going for Thanksgiving. Do you think he has a moat?'

'Where is this castle again.'

'Venice, I think.'

Jonah pointed out that all of Venice had a moat.

Lance beamed. 'You're so fucking wise, my friend. That's why I love you.' He sat down on the floor and whipped out the raw materials for a joint. 'You're up late.'

'I ran into a friend.'

'Yeah, who.'

'Eve Gones.'

Lance nodded in a way that suggested no recognition.

'You remember her,' Jonah said. 'The woman from the newspaper.'

'Oh. Sweet. She's like a friend of yours, now?'

'She came by to thank me,' Jonah said. 'You let

her in the apartment a few days ago, don't you remember?'

'I did?'

'That's what she said.'

Lance put down his rolling papers, scrunched up his face. 'What day are we talking about?'

'Saturday. She said you gave her permission to wait here.'

'I . . . I might have.'

'Were you high?'

'Was I high. Saturday, was I high. Was I – wa-*hoa*. Yes. Yes, I believe I was.'

'How high were you?'

'Fubar.'

'You can't remember if you met her or not,' Jonah said.

'It wouldn't be the first time.'

'Doesn't this cause you problems at family reunions?'

'We don't have family reunions, dude. My parents don't speak to each other.' Lance licked and rolled his joint. 'So she thanked you, that's cool. A little bit of manners in our boorish age. Whad she do, fuck you?'

'*What?*'

'No need to yell.'

'Why did you say that?'

'Because you deserve it.' Lance scrutinized him. Then he leapt up, sowing marijuana seeds into the rug. 'She *did*. She *did*, didn't she.'

In that instant Jonah understood what it was like

to be clinically paranoid, to see conspiracy every-where. Lance had been watching them, he was sure of it, through a satellite-spyware-privacy-wrecking technology heretofore restricted to the U.S. military, illegal in forty-seven states and Puerto Rico.

Then he thought: it's *Lance*.

As if in confirmation, Lance said, 'Duuude . . . ,' said it in a googly-eyed way that made the whole thing ridiculous. Jonah expelled his held breath in a laugh, picked up his books, and headed for his room. As he closed the door he heard *You fuckin wildebeest, I'm getting you another trophy.*

CHAPTER 9

Over the next week he saw Eve every night. He wandered, dazed, through his work-day, obsessively checking his watch until they turned him loose. Crowding onto the subway; rushing down 14th; turning the corner to discover her on the front stoop or beneath the stunted elm. Up the stairs, grabbing at each other, five flights in ninety seconds, no prelude, no seduction. He never managed to get her fully undressed; she insisted on keeping her top on, which spiked each encounter with a dash of the illicit, like they were sneaking into an airplane lavatory.

With Lance out, they exploited the apartment in full. The kitchen, the sofa, the hallway, the bath-room, the bathtub, the toilet, the coat closet, the editing studio: every square foot revealed its potential. Their couplings were architectural, fleeting feats of biomechanical grace that collapsed as they took a mutual breath and reached for another crooked knee, another arched neck, another greedy handful. There is no limit to the number of contortions available to two bodies with young joints and loose imaginations.

They invented records and strove to shatter them: How Many Times in an Hour, How Far Will a Leg Go in That Direction, How Hard Can You Do That Before It Hurts, and then How Hard When It Hurts. At one A.M. she would kiss him and leave him to drift off for three and a half hours.

At moments he regretted his inability to deny her – Monday morning, while sleepwalking through his presentation, drawing puzzled stares from Yokogawa, schadenfreude glowing behind Nelgrave's eyes; or on Tuesday night, when she made him come five times in the space of an evening, and it hurt to walk to the bathroom.

But how could he say no? She provided exactly what he needed: release. Release from the pressures of being good all the time. Being smart all the time. Being watched. Being sued. In the brief time since they had met, summer had banged closed, a mousetrap, and he could sense the days shortening. Three weeks of coming and going to work in the dark had begun to take its toll on him; he had entered a world with no sun.

In the midst of this whirlwind, his time with Eve acted as a tether to reality, a reminder that the insanity of the surgical floor was not how most people lived, a fact so easy to forget when you spent all day under the thumb of your superiors.

Sex helped, but mostly he relied on her as a confidante. The intensity with which she drew him out made him feel as though she'd plugged one end of a cable into his brain and the other into hers, direct downloading. He had never been the one in the room to attract attention by running off his mouth, but around her he burst with words, and the more he spoke the more he needed to speak, confessions snowballing. He felt like a teenager, storing up all his witty thoughts and observations over the course of a day in order to share them with her in the evenings, as they lay spent and laced up in sheets.

He admitted that he didn't know what kind of medicine he intended to practice. He had always been sure he wanted to cure cancer. Then, after Hannah got sick, psychiatry had appeared a natural fit – a Duty, the hand of God reaching down to orient him in the correct direction (not that he believed in God, he told her, and she said she didn't either, so there was yet another thing they had in common). Was he being ridiculous? Was it possible to choose what you wanted to do with the rest of your working life based on a few weeks of desultory apprenticeship? Really, he complained, medical education had some screwy ideas about how people made decisions.

Eve did not judge him, did not press her opinion on him, did not tell him he was being petty. She listened and said *You're very hard on yourself.* And he said *I guess.* And she said *You are.* And he said *Okay.*

He admitted that he often felt so angry at Hannah that it terrified him. He sometimes wanted to hit her, as though that would show her that he meant business: no more fooling around now. Get with the fucking program. The nicer he had to act, the harder it was to control his temper; and the angrier he got, the guiltier he felt. The whole cycle had gone bad. *Of course* she said; one can only repeat one's lines so many times before they ring hollow. *You're not an angel, Jonah Stem. You weren't sent here on a Heavenly Charge. Unless it was to save me.* He laughed. He said *I'm not an angel*. She said *I know, I know you're not.*

He did not stop to question whether it was Eve in particular he wanted to talk to, or simply another human being. To him the question was academic; it was enough to know that he felt better. For once he decided not to torture himself with excessive self-awareness.

She acted like white noise, masking the more disturbing frequencies in his head: the first time he saw a patient die, for instance, which had happened on Friday and left him with a weekend of bad dreams, in which the corpse rose up from the table – lines trailing, monitors going berserk – and crashed back down – up down up down up down – on some ascents with Raymond Iniguez's face, and on others his own. *Poor Jonah Stem.* That was what she said: *my poor poor Jonah Stem.* She knew when to speak and when to be quiet. He reminded himself that she was in real life a therapist (although not a dance therapist; Christopher Yip had gotten that wrong; she was a drama therapist, whatever that meant; and he didn't want to betray his ignorance – or to condescend – by asking what the hell she did all day), so it made sense for her to understand how to comfort him.

One week of honesty. He wasn't eighteen anymore; he no longer took honesty for granted, and could appreciate its rarity and value.

'I'm starting a new service next week.'

It was Friday, September 10. They were on the roof again, slumped against a tar-paper pyramid that rose near the east edge of the building, his head in her lap, his fingertips lightly tattooing his bare stomach.

'Jolly,' she said.

He smiled. He had decided that her quirks of speech were genuine, rather than an affectation. 'I have to see what my schedule's like. We'll have to play it by ear.'

'Jonah Stem, I know you can fit me in somewhere.'

'I don't know how much longer I can last with three hours of sleep.'

'Well,' she said, 'one day at a time.'

He nodded.

'Speaking of which: tomorrow. I had a splendid idea.' When she said the word she revealed her teeth, her tongue. 'What say you to this: we can – uh-oh. Already methinks you're not so keen.'

He said, 'I have to go visit Hannah.'

A silence.

'I'm sorry,' he said.

'It's perfectly all right.'

'I'd much rather spend the day with you, believe me.' She said nothing, so he added, 'I would.'

'. . . all right.'

'Listen—'

'Jonah Stem. I find that statement somewhat disingenuous.'

'What, I would.'

She looked down at him. 'Then you should.'

'Eve . . .'

'I am merely pointing out that you're not under threat of *imprisonment* if you don't go out there.'

'I know that.'

'You're a free man.'

'I know.'

'With free will.'

'I know, Eve.'

'All right. Then as long as you know. You're free to make your own decisions.' And she sat back against the tar paper, tilting her head up at the stars.

Another, longer silence passed.

He said, 'I can't back out on them.'

She nodded faintly.

'I told George I'd be there.'

'Of course,' she said. 'Duty calls.'

'Knock it off.'

'I'm serious, Jonah Stem. One of the many things I admire about you is the way in which you follow orders.'

'I am not following—'

'Even if you're the one who's issued the orders,' she said.

'Eve.' With difficulty, he sat up, got on his knees facing her. 'Stop that.'

'Stop what.'

'I promised them I would go out there.'

'Then you promised. You can't have it both ways, Jonah Stem. Either you promised, in which case you don't have to make excuses to me, or you have misgivings, in which case you don't have to make excuses to yourself. Either way, stop waffling, it's very unbecoming.'

He stared at her, waiting for her to make eye contact. She did not. He got up and walked around in circles. 'It's September eleventh tomorrow,' he said.

'I'm aware.'

'What'd you want to do? You can't have a party on September eleventh.'

'Not a party.'

'I wouldn't feel right.'

'Jonah Stem. Are you telling me that September eleventh will be a black day for you for the rest of your life?'

'Yes,' he said, disliking the defiance in his own voice.

'Even the Greatest Generation got over Pearl Harbor. You don't imagine, do you, that they continue to spend that day draped in mourning? Limits, Jonah Stem. Limits.'

'For crissake, I just asked what you had planned.'

Now Eve looked at him. 'So you're interested.'

'Of course I'm *interested*—'

'Excellent.'

'No, Listen. I can't do it. I'm interested in knowing what you had planned, but I can't do it.'

'Then I don't see why I should tell you.'

'It's a secret?'

'Yes. Yes, Jonah Stem, it is.'

'Why?'

'Because I share myself with you on the understanding that you have a certain level of commitment to me, and if you—'

'Eve—'

'—if you can't be bothered to break your date – a date which we both know is not good for you, except insofar as it reconfirms to you your extravagant sense of rectitude – then I'll wait until you can.'

'It's one afternoon. It doesn't mean anything.'

She said, 'My point exactly.'

All throughout the following day she kept asking *Isn't this fun?* as though worried he would change his mind and go to Great Neck after all. He reassured her, smiled and put his arm around her, giving onlookers, he imagined, the convincing impression that they were *an item*.

Truthfully, he was more worried than she. (Surgery had taught him well how to feign coolheadedness.) In the end he had chickened out, not calling George to cancel. While he and Eve ate a leisurely breakfast at The Mudspor, he kept reaching for his inside pocket, touching his cell phone as if to assuage it: *don't ring*.

By noon he began to relax. Maybe George was more reasonable than he'd thought. Surely he understood that Jonah would not visit every weekend for the rest of his life. Surely he understood that Jonah had to develop normal relationships with normal girls. He and Hannah had talked about getting married; but that wasn't the same as being married. Until now, admitting that had seemed like an acceptance of failure, not to mention a pretext for his mother's carping. But at some point, expedience trumped pride. Besides, where was the pride in denying himself? He wasn't a monk.

Not to mention that by keeping up the charade, he had fostered in Hannah a terrifically unhealthy dependence. With him around all the time, babying her, serving her memories, how could she achieve even a moderate level of independence? This wasn't Hollywood. He couldn't love her back to health. She was sick, and getting worse, and probably never going to get better. She might have brief peaks, but the troughs that followed would always be deeper, and by presenting himself to her – *reparting his hair* – he gave not love but a facsimile of love, a wobbly bubble of misleading romantic postures, and one that would pop if she ever found the wherewithal to reach for it. He could not fool himself, and he wasn't a good enough actor to fool her – if she was fooled. Real courage, he told himself as he paid the check, was the ability to say *no*.

So he wasn't caving in to his mother; he was

growing into himself. The harder she had pushed him to reintegrate, the more recalcitrant he'd become. He was in this way a typical youngest child, politely obstinate, less outwardly aggressive than his sister but the only one who dared resist a parental command. His mother had never experienced what he went through; he had over her a certain kind of wisdom, which he had used to justify his refusal to leave.

As Eve led him to the uptown ©, though, the real reason dawned on him. He was afraid. He needed Hannah as much as or more than she needed him; clung to her because, without her, his future was a complete blank. He needed a cause.

But now there was an alternative.

The alternative had lips and hips and breasts and a smile like sunlight on water.

The alternative was holding him around the waist and making jokes about the number of bacteria residing in one square inch of subway-car pole.

The alternative was kissing his Adam's apple and leading him above-ground at 168th Street.

The alternative was describing what she knew about the neighborhood. *You see these row houses? They're built to look old. They're in fact a recent project, an enclave of white yuppies in what is otherwise East Harlem. The same thing has happened all up the West Side, and in parts of Washington Heights. The same thing happened in Brooklyn while I was living there. You could accuse me of being part of the problem and you'd be correct. How do I know so much about this? It's our City, Jonah Stem. Don't you take an interest in civic affairs? The Museum of Human Frailties, writ large. Get in line, marvel, throw a coin into the fountain.*

Not far from the station, they came upon a quaint, tree-lined square that Jonah at first took to be a park. Then he saw the towering outline of a white colonial house, situated on the diagonal to the wrought-iron gates demarcating several acres of untended lawn. He was agog. 'What is this place?'

'The Morris-Jumel Mansion,' she said. 'The oldest standing house in Manhattan.'

The brick path to the entrance was in bad shape, missing pieces and covered in foliage. An obese man with a ponytail and a devilish goatee, his Parks and Recreation Department shirt dark with sweat, scraped a rake across the front steps. He looked at Jonah and Eve as if they had landed in a giant flying toaster.

'Good afternoon,' Eve said. 'May we?'

He let them in and sold them tickets. They were the first visitors in weeks, he said. 'Nobody cares about history.'

'Jonah does,' Eve said. 'He well-nigh lives in the past.'

They read the placards. Built in 1765, the house was more accurately described as Palladian in style. Its original estate had stretched clear across the island, from the East River to the Hudson, the hilltop location affording a cool summer retreat for the builder, a British colonel named Morris. With the Revolution, Morris decamped for the Motherland, and the house briefly quartered General Washington (*although* Eve said *isn't that what they say about all these old houses, George Washington slept here*) before being converted to an inn. In 1801 a wealthy Frenchman and former Caribbean plantation owner named Stephen Jumel bought it, leaving the property to his American wife, Madame Eliza, upon his death in 1832. Herself possessed of a suspect past – in her youth she had been a prostitute – Eliza had a knack for picking notable, if not wholly well-disposed, husbands, choosing a second partner in aging former vice president and duelist Aaron Burr. Their union lasted less than a year, ending formally with the serving of divorce papers on Burr's deathbed.

Eve said, 'Rather an obstreperous lot.'

The house changed hands once more before the City of New York decided to put an end to its tumultuous history by turning the place into a museum. Someone in the bureaucracy had had the good sense to leave the interior intact, and much of Eliza Jumel's attention to interior design remained in evidence: antique glass, pristine French Empire furniture, grandfather clocks, and a small but lavishly adorned bed.

'Purported to have belonged to Napoleon,' Eve read.

'Oh come on.'

'That's what it says. Museum placards are *never* wrong, Jonah Stem. They have the brilliance of gospel. The Jumels lived in France for a time, where they insinuated themselves into the Emperor's circle.'

'So he gave them a bed?'

'*Étrange, mais vrai*, Jonah Stem. Are you aware of what that means? It's very likely the oldest bed in New York. It has experienced more than you and I ever will.'

Jonah spun on his heel, causing the floorboards to creak. 'What do you think this place is worth?'

'Oodles.'

He rubbed at the molding near the door. They were on the second floor. The house was otherwise empty, and he imagined for a moment what it would be like to have so much money and idle time. What would he have done? Been a doctor, probably. Or perhaps a Man of Discovery, a Benjamin Franklin type. He wistfully imagined a time when a single person could shove all of science forward with one moment of experimental serendipity – unlike today, the age of specialization, when researchers' primary efforts went into writing grant proposals.

He turned around to share some of these thoughts with Eve, but his mind went instantly blank. 'What are you doing.'

She had her skirt up around her waist. 'Let us join the ranks of history.'

'Get off the bed.' The window behind her showed a landscape warped by the old, uneven glass: rippling lawn; rippling wrought-iron gate; rippling sidewalk, buckled further by surfacing roots. The Parks Department guy was out of sight. He might be around the other side of the house; or letting in more visitors; or coming to check on them.

'Get up. Get up.' Jonah stepped over the velvet rope, and she responded by reaching for the back of his head and pulling him face-first into her woolly sweater. In the ensuing struggle he knocked what he believed were several three-hundred-year-old embroidered pillows to the ground. Hell she was *strong*. And laughing, too, laughing hysterically, like a loon, whispering in his ear to stop being such a mop. He tried to look over his shoulder, at the doorway, where he expected to see a big fat Parks Department employee coming at them with a rake and handcuffs – did they carry handcuffs? – *sitting* on them until the police arrived to bust them for defilement of a historic artifact, and Eve wrenched his face toward her, kissed him as though she wanted to suck up his stomach. Her hands inside his pants, her tongue between her teeth, so pretty and wicked and laughing and he grabbed between her legs, he was possessed. The bed croaked awfully, as though it was going to collapse in a pile of chiffon and velveteen and lace edging and oak and goosedown. He went as fast as he could – which was very fast, given that he had both fear and Eve's thumb encroaching on his hyenas – and as he neared the end she curled his fingers around her ponytail and showed him how to give her hair a good hard yank, and when he did she made an unearthly noise, like a whale song. Then he fell against her, both of them panting and sweating, Eve giggling, her face eraser-pink. In his ear she said *Vive le roi, Jonah Stem*.

CHAPTER 10

That Monday he started a new service, euphemistically known as Blue Team but more cruelly (and accurately) referred to on the floor as The Fatties. The St Agatha's Bariatrics Clinic provided one of the department's main sources of lucre, and its doctors were renowned for their ability to get patients OTL. In Jonah's opinion, a tad more post-op TLC would have been nice, or at least helpful in preventing the kind of complications he'd witnessed on the Night of the Exploding Formerly Fat Lady.

That was the least of his concerns, though.

The shock of recognition must have been evident on his face when he showed up to meet his new chief, because Devon Benderking PGY-2 – he of the harelip – said, 'What's wrong, shitmouth? You aren't happy to see me again?'

Jonah spent the next five days getting spit-roasted. When Benderking wasn't in scrubs, he wore a bilious print tie that looked like it had been knotted once and left over a bedpost, nooselike, every night thereafter, as though to remind his students that their grades were swinging from the gibbet. Abusive to everyone, he appeared to take particular relish in referring to Jonah as 'Scut Bag' or 'Scut Slut' or simply 'idiot.' Vociferously he opined that, in a contest of wits between his pet cat and Jonah, Jonah would come in second. (Jonah felt it unwise to point out the supreme lameness of a single man lauding his cat.) He would send him to the library to retrieve articles that didn't exist, to fetch Egg McMuffins that he took one bite out of then trashed, to change his scrubs because he didn't like the colors.

While Jonah wanted to attribute an educational purpose to this tyranny – or a reason, *any* reason; maybe Benderking had gotten recently dumped; maybe his brother had been murdered by someone who looked like Jonah – in its frequency he perceived the truth, shining in big white letters like the exit ramp for hell: Benderking was a sadist.

You're going to kill people, Slut, you know that? You're sloppy. Where'd you go to college?

Michigan.

I have an uncle who went there.

Cool.

Cool? It's not cool. I am disgusted to be related by marriage to someone who went to the same school as you, you inept little beetle turd.

Adding to his stress, all the surgeries were laparoscopic. The medical student's role during laparoscopy was to drive the camera, a job specifically designed to be botched. Surgeons refused to believe Jonah's brain wasn't hardwired to their hands. If he performed well, nobody noticed; but if he missed one movement, once, one single—

'Back,' said Benderking. 'BACK.'

'Sorry.'

Plus, the image on the screen showed up inverted. Right was left, and left right; up down, and down up. Or – he forgot – down down, up up, right left, left right, or—

'IDIOT. LEFT.'

'Sorry.'

When it wasn't getting him chewed out – CENTER – Jonah admired the technique's elegance. Leave it to the Nintendo generation to invent video-game surgery. Working through a five-cm. incision, the surgeon guided long, slender tools with the grace of a painter . . .

'Move that camera any closer to his bowel, idiot, and you're gonna burn a hole right through the tissue.'

. . . and the temperament of a chef.

'Sorry.'

It's about the person; think about the patient. Not any patient, but this patient, an individual human, a white man in his mid-forties with an unquenchable priapism: an erection undaunted by full anesthesia.

'Another member of the teenie-weenie club. UP.'

Jonah barely heard him; he'd gotten used to continuous streams of barbs about weight, pimples, exceptional genitals, arboreous back hair. Everything became fair game when the patient couldn't hear.

'Thank God it's not bigger, it'd get in the way.'

Although Benderking's crassness repelled him, Jonah had begun to understand the urge to dehumanize. All surgeons did it to some degree, even the good guys; they had to. The less respect you had for someone, the less petrified you'd be of killing him. And the act of surgery itself made it easy to forget that the log of flesh under your knife had desires, thoughts, relatives, dreams. The only other way to conceive of the process was as an extreme intimacy, a lovemaking that – given the presence of a crowd, and the unconsciousness of one of the parties – felt more like a gang rape.

'If I were his wife, I'd invest in a banana plant. Right. RIGHT.'

'Sorry.' The screen appeared in triplicate; Jonah grayed out; his hand swerved. Then something hard and sharp cracked him on the shin, bringing the world back in full color. Benderking had kicked him.

'Morning, idiot. Want to do your job?'

'Sorry.' But he wasn't sorry. He was angry. As he returned to looking at the screen, he fantasized about all the things he could do to hurt the bastard. Krazy Glue his locker shut. Ex-Lax in his coffee. Cut the brakes on his bike. His imagination for revenge wasn't very powerful; he did not indulge that kind of thinking. Still, it'd be nice. He wasn't that type of guy, it would be so nice.

* * *

133

He said to Eve, 'Fucking motherfucker.'

They sprawled in the living room. It was Friday night. The coffee table had been pushed aside, stacks of PlayStation games knocked humble. In the building across the street – the one Eve called the Museum of Human Frailties – select windows shone. A woman doing yoga. A toddler hurtling past, victimized by the heaviness of its own head. A shirtless man tapping ash into a window-ledge flower bed.

She said, 'What now?'

'He made me stay late.' Jonah tried to scratch his back, could not reach the spot. Eve wordlessly did it for him. 'He has this *mug*. It's his special coffee mug, and the handle got smashed. He made me glue it back together. That's why I was late. It took two hours. It was in tiny pieces. He probably broke it on purpose.' He punched the air.

A silence.

'I don't understand why you put up with it,' she said.

'He's fifteen percent of my grade.'

'You're not a urinal, m'lad. Fight back.'

'Sure.'

'Feller needs to be learned manners sumpin good.'

'I wish he'd just disappear.'

'Consider it done.' She waved her hands like a conjurer.

He snickered. 'Sleep with da fishes. Makehiman-offah. Fuggeddaboutit.'

'I think I owe you one, Jonah Stem, do I not? Simply say the word.'

'Go for it.'

'I will.' She got up, went to the kitchenette, took down the speed-kettle. 'Tea?'

'Nnn.' He got up and began buttoning his shirt. He checked his watch: eleven thirty. He needed to get some studying done. He had to get up early. Eve sopped and discarded a teabag, talking about weekend plans. She had an idea for another outing, not dissimiliar to last week's but different in that—

'I can't.'

'What?'

'George called. He was pissed that I skipped out.'

'Who cares what he thinks? The man is a leech.'

'It's not him.'

'Who, then, Jonah Stem? Did the Ghost of Duty appear to you?'

Jonah said, 'He said Hannah was crying.'

Eve took one sip of her tea, made a disgusted face, poured the rest into the sink. She faced away from him, her hands on the countertop, her shoulders bunched. He did not know what to do. He came up behind her, put his arms around her waist, but she wriggled away and went to stand by the window.

'I'm sorry,' he said.

She said nothing.

'I can't stop cold turkey,' he said. 'It's not right.'

'It's not right to treat me like a second-class citizen.'

'This is a complicated thing.'

'Is that so, because it seems straightforward to me.' Her voice shook.

'If it were up to me, I'd—' He was about to say *never go again* but changed his mind. 'I'd add five hours to the day.'

'Thanks.'

'I go to work,' he said. 'That's an obligation, you understand that. You don't expect me to skip that.'

'Your analogy stinks, Jonah Stem.'

'Why?'

'Because she is *not* an obligation.'

'Yes she is.'

After a long silence, she said, 'I love you.'

His heart hiccupped unpleasantly. He said, in his most measured voice, 'It hasn't been – I mean – it's been less than a month.'

'There isn't a minimum requirement.'

He rubbed his temples. 'I—'

'You love me, too.'

'Eve—'

'You put your life in danger to save me. You knew when you saw me that you loved me, and that I would love you in return, and that was why you did what you did. You could have called the police. You could have stood at a safe distance.' She turned to face him. 'You put out your hand to me.'

He felt short of breath.

She said, 'Every moment I continue to live on this Earth is because of you. The consequences are self-evident: I love you. Even if I didn't want to, I'd have to. I'm constantly building up debt to you.'

'I forgive it,' he said.

'You can't. The moment you do, the debt starts to build once again. As long as I continue to breathe, I belong to you.'

He wanted to say *Come on, be serious* but he could not. He could not; because as half-baked as all this sounded to him, to her it was quite obviously real. This had to be a record.

Although – when he and Hannah – but that was different. They'd gotten carried away. And now it was happening again.

Wrong to lie, worse to do nothing. He came toward her; hugged her; kissed the part in her hair.

'Seeing her doesn't say anything about how I feel about you.' He stroked her back. 'We'll have the evening.'

She said nothing. He was about to make a joke, restore the mood. Then he felt her stomach convulsing, tears running down his arm and beneath the loose gauze on his elbow. Despite the scab, it stung. The human lachrymal glands exude at a salinity of approximately nine parts per thousand.

As if to punish him for last week's absence, Hannah refused to come out of her room. She ignored the food, rolling over and going back to sleep. Plate on his lap, Jonah sat in her pink wicker chair and watched her weather a bad dream. He had managed to please nobody.

Eventually he went back to the living room.

'Eight letters, "one member of a needy pair." S blank blank B I.'

'Symbiont.' Jonah ate half a slice of American cheese and slipped the rest to Lazy Susan. His cell phone was flashing.

Two new messages

George said, 'You know what I could really go for?'

Jonah held up a finger.

received today at one thirty-seven P.M.

Hey it's me. [Vik.] *My roommates are throwing together a hold-em tournament, twenty bucks buy-in. It's going to be up at the dorm at six. Call me if you want in.*

It was three. By the time he got home it'd be seven, and anyway he was wiped, and anyway he had to see Eve. He glanced at George – curving the newspaper to make it rigid, chewing on the butt end of a mechanical pencil – and deleted the message.

The second message had come while he was upstairs with Hannah.

Hello Jonah Stem.

He sat up sharply.

I bet you're ensorcelled to be hearing from me in the middle of the day.

As though ejected by the couch, he sprung up and into the kitchen.

'Jonah?'

—wanted to apologize for that shamefully petty display of jealousy—

He crossed to the laundry alcove and crouched beside an industrial-size bottle of bleach and a wire basket heaped with crusty towels.

—hope you're in a private place. Relax. Lower the lights. Perhaps you want to light a few candles—

'Jonah?'

'One minute.'

—ose your eyes, go on, Jonah Stem. Close them and listen.

Ridiculously, he obeyed.

I know you've got them closed. Now picture this:

She began to describe obscenities.

He admired her vocabulary.

'Jonah?'

He closed the phone and stood up with an enormous erection. Quickly, he bent over, pretending to thumb the dials on the washing machine.

'What're you doing? Are you doing laundry?'

'One second.'

'If you're doing laundry already, there's some—'

'Just – gimme *one*, I'll be with you in *one second*.'

Blood-faced, he waited, squeezing the phone, until he heard George mutter *Sure thing* and pad out of the kitchen.

He counted to two hundred, wet a paper towel, passed it over his forehead. Adjusting himself inside his boxerbriefs, so that his penis lay flat against his left leg, he forced himself to walk back into the living room. George, writing, noticed nothing as he took a seat and drew his bag over his lap.

'Six letters, "eager creature," question mark.'

'I – I don't know.'

'You okay?'

'I got some . . . surprising news.' He noticed George looking at him expectantly. 'My – mom. She's publishing a poem. In a magazine.'

'That's nice.'

'. . . yup.'

'Tell her congratulations for me.'

'I will.'

'Suggestions?'

'What's it again.'

'Six letters, "eager creature," second letter E. Wait, I got it. It's beaver.'

'Sounds good to me.'

'Jonah, are you sick?'

'. . . no.'

George sucked down an ice cube. 'You want a drink?'

'No thanks.'

A few minutes later, George said, 'We're flying to Florida. That's where the ship departs from. Or you don't say depart, you say "sets sail." Or "embarks."'

Jonah wondered who this *We* was. Unless George had adopted the royal We as justification for taking autocratic liberties with the vacations of others.

Psychological eminent domain: your free time shall be confiscated for the public good.

'Anyhow,' George said, 'I arranged for Bernadette to be here during the day. We'll discuss it further when the time comes, but how much cash you think you'll need?'

'Can we discuss it when the time comes?'

'Sure, yes, yeah. I'm, y'know, leaping out of my skin.'

'I bet.'

'I appreciate it. Don't think I don't. One thing's come up.'

Jonah gritted his teeth. 'What's that.'

'Bernadette. You know what she's like.'

'No, what.'

'Stubbon.' George chewed his pencil. 'Tough as nails, which is why I trust her. She's giving me sort of a hard time about being here on Christmas.'

'. . . uh-huh.'

'She's Catholic. Devout. Incense and holy water. I said I'd pay extra, but I don't think that's the sticking point.'

'Offer her more.'

'No but that's what I'm telling you. The money doesn't matter to her. She wants to go to church, spend time with her family.'

'That's understandable.'

'Certainly,' George said. 'I mean, who wouldn't.'

'Yup.'

'So it comes out that I'm going to need someone for that night and the day of.'

Jonah let the sentence float off into the stale air.

'You might be able to help me out?' George said.

'I'd like to spend time with my family.'

'You don't celebrate Christmas.'

'Not as a religious holiday, but we celebrate having vacation.'

'Had you gone skiing with your friends, you wouldn't have seen them at all.'

'Fine, but—'

'Never mind, never mind. That's not the point. I'm not asking you to come on Christmas. That's not what I'm talking about.' George folded down the paper. 'Is that what you thought I was asking?'

'That's sure what it sounded like.'

'What do you take me for?'

Jonah made a conciliatory gesture.

'What I meant was I'm looking for another nurse. You might know someone from the . . . you honestly – come on, Jonah, a little credit, please.'

'I'm sorry. I don't know what I thought.'

'Well, whatever the case may be. Hannah doesn't take easily to new people, as you're aware, but if we introduce whoever it is a few months in advance there won't be any surprises come December. I'm letting you know, put it on your radar.' George got up. 'You sure you don't want a drink? Some lox?'

'I'm all set.'

The fridge gasped open, and the cat mewled as George slipped it fish.

Aggravated, Jonah got up and went to the back room. The treadmill did not respond to his touch;

he found the plug and the outlet, and set the belt to two mph, clenching the bars of the machine until his hands began to turn cold.

For some reason, the baseline chutzpah they'd gotten along with now grated on him something awful: the feigned offense; the liquor; the ratty boxer shorts, as though George couldn't be bothered to put on pants. *It's Jonah, not the Queen of England.*

He stopped the machine and crossed to the mantel, where hung a series of mustard-toned prints of Hannah's mother. Always serious – freckle-faced with ironed hair; grim in bell-bottoms and a suede jacket – Wendy Richter had been fair and fleshy, making it hard to see her daughter in her until the late 70s, when a strange convergence began: the more pregnant Wendy got, the stronger her resemblance to Hannah grew, mother and child meeting at a common physiognomy.

Did George think of his wife as a mistake? If so, did that make his daughter a mistake? At what point did bad decisions cease to be an interruption of life and become life itself?

He went back to the living room. 'George.'

'Mm.'

'Are you going on this trip alone?'

A brief silence, then pencil on newspaper. 'Why do you ask.'

'I'm curious.'

'It's—' George erased, blew. 'It's really not your business.'

Jonah said nothing.

'But as a matter of fact, no.'

'Does Hannah know about her?'

'This is private,' George said.

'Fine.'

'And no, she doesn't.'

'Are you sure?'

'I don't know why she would.'

'She's not stupid. She can figure things out.'

'I don't think she's stupid, I think that there's no reason for her to know.' Proudly, defensively: 'Her name is Louise.'

'You don't have to tell me.'

'I'm not ashamed. Am I' – George's voice dropped – 'am I not supposed to be *alive*?'

'You are.'

'It's bad enough having to sneak around my own house.'

'Then don't.'

'You say that like I can do whatever I want, when you know full well that—'

'Because of Hannah?'

'No because of *Lee Harvey Oswald*.'

Jonah swallowed a retort. 'She might like having a woman around.'

'She can't handle that. *Either* of them.'

'How do you know?'

'Because she's my daughter and I can gauge what she can and can't handle.'

'I don't think you're giving her enough—'

'Don't start this, don't, don't, *don't*.'

'What about Louise? If you need a reason to

introduce them, that's a good one. She can help you out.'

'Her life's been hard enough, I think I can spare her.'

'So what, you're going to lie to Hannah indefinitely?'

George crushed the newpaper into a ball. 'What the hell do you think you know about it. You're here twice a *month*. What about the other twenty-nine days a month. Monday through Friday. Where're you *then*?'

Stunned, but recovering fast, he said, 'I don't have to be here at all.'

'Then don't do me any favors, if you're going to make my life harder. I don't care what you do. You can come if you want or stay home if you want. But you think you can start lecturing me about how I spend my private time, you can go to hell.'

A silence.

Jonah went to the sofa and began jamming books into his bag.

'Where are you going?'

The zipper stuck and he yanked, breaking it entirely and leaving the bag uncloseable. He threw it gaping over his shoulder. 'Find someone else for Christmas.'

At that, George – who had been sulking placidly – leapt up. 'We had a deal.'

'Not anymore.'

He made it halfway down the block before George pulled up alongside him in his Acura. 'You promised me.'

145

He wanted to break into a run, but it wasn't as though George couldn't keep up. Not to mention the shedding of dignity that running entailed. He kept walking, looking straight ahead.

'It's not me you're hurting. You know that. It's her. She asked for you to stay.'

'You can tell her it's your fault that I'm not.'

'Jonah. Get in the car.'

'Fuck you.'

'I'm going to ignore that.'

'Then I'll say it again. Fuck y—'

George zoomed ahead, pulled over, and got out, leaving the motor running. Jonah clenched the strap of his bag. He was bigger than George, and presently he felt three times normal size.

'Why are you doing this to me?'

'What am I doing to you, George.'

'I'm a human being. You understand that? I need to get away. I need help. What I *don't* need is you prying.'

'You won't have it,' Jonah said. 'You won't have me doing anything. You won't have me to worry about, or to pick up from the train station – not that you ever remember, every fucking time – and you won't have me to babysit. You can *pay* someone. You want someone, you can fend for yourself. Hire a service. Hire a Jewish nurse. Who do you think works on Christmas Eve?'

For the first time, George looked genuinely frightened. 'I didn't mean t—'

As Jonah brushed past he felt a hand on his arm, and his immediate instinct was to lash out. But he shook himself free, reshouldered his bag, and headed up the block alone.

CHAPTER 11

That night Eve did not come over. Jonah, hepped up on adrenaline, was exasperated; he wanted to tell her what had happened and to share with her the decision he'd made on the train home.

As angry as he was, he admitted that Hannah, not her father, stood to suffer most from an abrupt end. But done gradually, like tapering a medication:

Through Christmas he would come regularly; it was three and a half months away, and already he had tolerated twenty months of nonsense. Three and a half months was fourteen weeks, which at his current rate amounted to five or six visits. That much he could stomach; he would do it for Hannah; in her honor; in memoriam.

And he owed her the first week of vacation. Reneging didn't bother him, but he got sick thinking about what George would tell her if he didn't show. *He doesn't want to see you anymore.* Even if Jonah let him dangle for a bit, even if he wrung an apology out of him, in the end, he had to go.

The threat to duck out had been ninety percent bluff, anyway, designed to elicit a reaction both from George and from himself. He needed to see how it felt to say *no*. And now he knew: it felt okay. Not good, but he would adjust. He'd adjusted to the opposite extreme.

After Christmas all bets were off. Starting in January he would scale back to – say, once a month. Then every two months, every three. Her birthday was in April; he would make an exception. Beyond that he made no promises.

He wanted to tell Eve, because although she couldn't claim credit for putting these ideas in his head – they had been gestating longer than he cared to admit – he did owe her a debt of gratitude for jump-starting him. And telling her would go a long way toward demonstrating that she *was* important to him, even if he wasn't exactly – or at all – ready to say that he loved her. *You showed me the light* he would say. A good way to satisfy everybody, at least in the short run.

He waited up. At midnight Lance came home and went straight to the PlayStation.

'You're still awake?'

Jonah, grateful for the distraction, put his books aside. 'Insomnia.'

'Bummer.'

For a half-hour he watched Lance fend off zombies.

'What's this game called again?'

'Dude, I'm glad you have me to fill in the steel-meltingly huge blanks in your map of contemporary cultural literacy. This is a classic: *Resident Evil.*'

'Is there a character named Benderking?'

'What what?'

'Never mind.'

After biting the dust several times, Lance switched off the TV, and stood solemnly looking at the dark screen. 'I don't know if I've accomplished anything today.'

'You honed your hand-eye co-ordination.'

'*The* definitive parental rationalization of the late eighties and early nineties,' Lance said. 'Is there any medical evidence for that?'

'Not as far as I know.'

'I take it back, I did achieve a lot today. Footage galore. My *Citizen Kane*.'

'You'll have to show it to me sometime.'

'You got it, kemosabe.' He rushed from the room.

'No, not n – I have – Lance. Not—'

'It's a digest of the most recent work.' Lance returned, waving a DVD. 'Groundbreaking shit.'

Jonah endured four minutes of Lance reading a German film magazine, using a pocket dictionary while his lips moved; two minutes of Lance doing sit-ups; six minutes of Lance styling his hair; nine minutes of Lance smoking and watching the ceiling.

'I feel like it really gives a sense of who I am.'

After thirty seconds of Lance brushing his teeth, Jonah had had it. He was about to say as much when the screen went to a low-lit shot of the living room.

Jonah Stem.

'This is one of my all-time personal favorites,' Lance said.

On the screen, Eve walked across the living room. Barefoot, a gray pencil skirt, her usual woolly sweater. Jonah recognized the outfit as one she'd worn a week prior.

He said, 'Oh God.'

'It's hard to make out what you're saying unless you turn it way up. During the talking part I mean. Once the action starts it's plenty loud.'

Jonah didn't reply; he was absorbed by the arm at the bottom left of the screen. His own arm. That put the camera – where? He tried to extrapolate, but it was like reading the laparoscopy monitor.

'I'm shocked, shocked, that you haven't had the cops called on you. You guys are feral; it sounds like someone's dying.'

Jonah watched Eve climb on top of him. They fell halfway out of the shot as she pulled him to the floor. He tried to remember if this was the night she'd thrown his tie out the window. Oh yes, there it went.

He'd liked that tie.

'You never told me about your exhibitionist tendencies, dude. That's the beauty of good friends: you're always learning something new.'

Eve exuded patience: a ballerina partnered with a hippopotamus. He, on the other hand . . . that's what he looked like? Strained, pixelated, clownish;

like the portraits theme parks offer after you toddle, addled, off a rollercoaster. He decided that if more people could see themselves in the throes of lust, they'd enter the priesthood. In her limpness as he struggled to get her sideways he inferred a certain . . . *passivity*? She spun into the frame, on top of him, and the camera's vantage showed him something new: although Eve was grunting, and bucking her hips, and thrashing around, her expression was flat. *Passive*, he saw, wasn't the right word. The right word was *bored*.

He grabbed for the remote and Lance danced back. 'Wait, this is the good part.'

'Turn it off.'

'Are you kidding?'

'I don't need to see this.'

'Why?'

'*I was there.*' Jonah tried to get at him, and Lance took up a defensive position behind the easy chair.

'Whoa,' he said. He held up Buddha palms. 'Chill.'

'I can't fucking believe you.'

'You guys did all the work, you get all the credit.'

'I told you not to put a camera in here. Where is it.'

'Dude—'

'Where.'

Lance pointed: atop the fridge, nestled between two half-empty boxes of Frosted Flakes. Right where he'd been forbidden to put it in the first place. He rushed to whisk it away. 'I moved it a couple of weeks ago to film myself, and I forgot to take it down. Then it happened to snag nuggets of your amorous dalliance. You were so in the moment, dude, I couldn't stop once you got rolling.'

'Yes you fucking could.'

'You've quadrupled my audience. You're one of the more popular segments—'

'I am not a segment, you shitty shithead.'

'Look, I can't help it if you want to do it all over the apar— *hey*.' Lance ducked a flying mandarin orange that left a Rorschach on the wall. 'You're gonna injure me. Please listen to reason, dude, I – put that down.'

Dangling the PlayStation out the window, Jonah said, 'Gimme the camera.'

'The camera is a vessel, man, you the artist fill it with – please put the gaming console down.'

'I'm on the Internet.'

'No, no, no, I deleted you off the server. This is the only copy.'

'Somebody might have saved it.'

'No, dude, no w – uh.' Lance pursed his lips. 'Correct.'

'Yeah, *correct*.'

'Web video has a short shelf life, dude. You'll be forgotten in a week, I promise. It's not like you're a celebrity or anything.'

'No more broadcasting.'

'At all? Come on—'

'Not in here. No more cameras in here.'

'Fine. Fine. You got it. Set her down gently.'

'The *camera*.'

With a sigh, Lance handed it over, and Jonah repatriated the PlayStation to its dust-free rectangular patch atop the television. Then he ejected the DVD and snapped it.

'Dude, that wasn't necess – whoooaaaokay chill, chill. I just think it's tragic that you can't appreciate your own work. When can I get my camera back?'

Jonah threw the disc in the trash.

'My mom e-mailed me,' Lance said. 'She thinks your chick is faking it. She said it doesn't sound real. The guy from Kuala Lumpur wants to see a money shot.'

Jonah wound up and pitched the webcam into the street five stories below. It shattered on the opposite sidewalk, causing a pair of girls sipping from a brown paper bag to shriek. Lance joined him at the window and slipped a fraternal arm across Jonah's shoulders. 'I'm sorry I upset you, dude. Really. I love you.'

'I love you too, Lance.'

'Listen, I have a great idea. You and me should take a trip to Atlantic City. Or maybe we could drive to Graceland. We'll shoot the whole thing. Think about it: you're stressed, I could use a vacation – aww don't walk out while I'm talking, it's uncivil.'

CHAPTER 12

Any resemblance Simón Iniguez bore to his brother had been effaced by good grooming. Thickset, with a black moustache and a cleft chin, he wore a leather jacket and sunglasses.

'Scarface wannabe. Meet his attack dog.' Belzer opened another file, full of Xeroxed letters, motions, decisions, a bar certification. He liked to have photos of everyone he was dealing with; it helped him keep people straight and – he claimed – identify their weaknesses. Roberto Medina wore a trim gray three-piece suit and a gold watch chain. With the exception of titanic eyebrows, he had dainty features: a smug pretty-boy smile and cheek-bones like a Latin pop star.

'Class-A prick,' said Belzer. 'He comes in here, makes a point of walking around the room, checking everything out. 'Wonderful view,' he tells me. 'Must be nice to have a nice big office. My office is real small, you know, up in *Da Bronx*.' Like that's supposed to impress me, or else gimme a guilt trip,

I don't *know* what. He starts telling me about putting himself through law school at night. "I was a busboy." Then he looks at that' – Belzer indicated a lithograph on the far wall – 'and he goes, 'What's that, how nice.' He reads the fucking placard. You believe that? 'Ellsworth Kelly, is he famous?' I'm sitting here, waiting for this guy, he's reading the placards on my art. 'Just like in a museum,' he goes. 'I didn't have much art education. *Public school.*' Prick. I swear, kiddo, canning this guy's going to be more fun for me than it is for you.'

Jonah wasn't listening. He was thinking about what Benderking had said to his request for two hours off.

I'm not your mommy. If you don't want to make the commitment to being here, that's up to you. Your actions have consequences, and you'll have to deal with them.

The last thing he needed was to flunk surgery. It was far from impossible: two or three HUMmers who'd been forced to repeat during fourth year could be seen skulking around the floor, cadaverous and daunted, like Sisyphus at breakfast. His grade took into account other evaluations, not to mention the upcoming Shelf exam; but if Benderking made it his sole mission to destroy Jonah, he had the power to do so.

Belzer took his time explaining the nature of the Iniguez family's claim, enumerating technicalities that, he promised, hamstrung the case.

Jonah said, '*Racism?*'

'That's what he's saying. He says that the guy was acting in self-defense.'

'She was crawling. And – and – how do they know? They weren't there; I was.'

'Hey, kiddo, don't need to convince me. I'm telling you what Medina said. His claim is, you arrive on the scene and assume that when a man of color – that's what he called him, a "man of color" – and a white woman are having a fight, the man of color is automatically the attacker. Don't look at me like that, kiddo, *I'm* not saying it. *He* is. Listen to what he wrote: "Mr Iniguez matched your client's bigoted stereotype, and your client took it upon himself to use excessive force. He should pay for that mistake."' Belzer looked up. '"Bigoted stereotype." How's that for concision. Look, these guys, they're all talk. Medina's not dumb. He'll lose; he knows it. They just wanna give the white man a good scare.'

'What did you tell him?'

Belzer said, 'I said, "Fine, Bob. We can call Ms Jones to the stand and ask whether she felt her life was in danger, given the three stab wounds in her back and the one in her hand. I think people will see it our way when I tell them about Raymond's extensive history of violence, including the charges filed in 1992 when he assaulted a co-worker with a baseball bat. Or the fact that he was almost expelled from his halfway house for brawling with staff. Or, if you want to go a different route, we can hear from the ADA who spoke to my client, who's gone on record calling him, quote, one of the bravest people she's ever encountered, unquote. I bet they'll find it interesting that Raymond – whose death you claim has caused your client, quote, significant financial hardship, unquote – has not paid any income tax in over a decade, not cause he was avoiding it but because he had no income to *report*. I bet people will find it interesting that, according to his bank, your client was sending his brother five hundred dollars a month in spending money. I'm scratching my head at that one, Bob, cause it takes some pretty advanced math to make the *loss* of a six-thousand-dollar-a-year liability into a significant financial hardship. I bet people will find it interesting that you sent a process server to harass my client at the hospital, distracting him from work on critically ill patients, recklessly interrupting vital medical procedures, and damaging his reputation. And I'll bet that they'll find it interesting that my client has experienced extreme mental anguish warranting its own suit for punitive damages. I bet they'll find it interesting enough that any jury – white or black or whatever color you please – will give my client a truckload of money on behalf of the estate of Raymond Iniguez, which is the responsibility of your client."' Belzer paused for breath. 'Something like that. Maybe not verbatim, but close enough.'

Jonah said, 'And what did he say?'

Belzer shrugged. 'He said, "We'll see you in court."'

★　★　★

By Tuesday night Eve had not shown up for four days, and Jonah began to worry. He kept getting up from his studying to look out the window for her. He sent her e-mails. He wished she would get a goddamned cell phone; he'd pay for it.

Without her around he felt his resolve weakening. On Wednesday he called George and mumblingly agreed to a truce. Nobody apologized but both of them seemed to imply that they would act differently, given the chance to redo the afternoon. Jonah said he would still come for the week, adding that he was doing it for Hannah's sake. To which George replied *I'm having you for her sake.* There was a pause. They hung up, and that was the end of that. Not the definitive result he'd hoped for.

He opened his wallet and took out a corner torn from one of Belzer's folders; on it, Jonah had copied Iniguez's home number while the lawyer used the bathroom.

The phone rang three times and was answered by a woman with a DJ's voice. Jonah asked for Simón.

'Who is this?'

'A friend of his brother's.'

Kiddo what the hell do you think you're doing we're not trying to make friends

A second extension clicked on; saxophone and drums softly in the background.

'Yes?'

'Mr Iniguez?'

'Yeah, who's this.'

'My name is Jonah Stem.' He paused. 'I'm the—'

'I know who you are.'

'I'm sorry to, to disturb you, I – Chip – my lawyer, he wouldn't want me to say this, but I wanted to, to apologize for what happened to your brother. You may not believe me but I didn't mean for him to get hurt. I swear. This is the worst thing that's ever happened to me, and I feel like shit for it. It probably won't mean much to you, but, but I wanted you to know.'

Iniguez hung up.

Unable to concentrate, Jonah spent the evening in front of his laptop. He had Googled Eve a zillion times before, always turning up the same paltry results. Find-a-person sites couldn't locate Gones, Eve; Gones, E.; last name Gones, instead offering to put him in touch with old classmates, a proposition he found pathetic to the point of heartbreak. His attempt to close the browser met with a barrage of popups (*Spycams, You are the 1,000,000th visitor!!, Vaporize the bunny and win a FREE MP3 PLAYER*) that multiplied faster than he could pick them off. He was glad when Windows crashed.

He didn't have a phone book. Nobody under thirty-five did.

Verizon had no listing under the name Eve Gones or Eve Jones. Not in Hoboken, not in New York, not in the entire metro area.

He called his sister.

'Jonah-face, it's good to hear your voice.'

'You, too.'

'Can you get me some drugs? I want to sell them at work. Everyone I work with takes sedatives. Except me.'

'You sleep?'

'No. But sometimes I black out for hours at a time, regaining consciousness in a motel room off I-95, with my purse and underwear gone. What's shaking?'

'I wondered if you could look someone up for me in the Yale alum database.'

He heard the meaty slam of her Sub-Zero, followed the snap of a can and a lusty slurp. 'The best part of pregnancy is that I'm not allowed to drink diet,' she said. 'You forget how good real corn syrup tastes.'

'You're not supposed to drink caffeine, either.'

'It's Sprite,' she said. 'Mind your own beeswax. Who went to Yale?'

'I met someone in your class and wanted to do some research on her.'

'Ooooh, Jonah-face has a girlfriend.'

'She's a friend.' He sounded about six. Leave it to a sibling.

'Jonah and *some* girl, sitting in a tree, she wants him for his M.D.'

He waited.

'All right, Jeeeez. Let's go check it out . . . Oh boy. My office is such a mess. Can you come clean it up for me, please?'

'No.'

'Thanks, my darling brother, I love you, too.' Channeling Mom again. He pictured Kate in the stately downstairs library she'd converted for personal use: bookshelves soaring up to kiss crown moldings at an altitude of eighteen feet. When she and Erich first bought the house – with equity coming out of their ears, they'd snatched it up during a lull – she told Jonah that they planned to call one of those dealers that sold archaic, unreadable hardcovers by the yard.

Jonah had never confessed how much he disliked the place. It was drafty, with big Camelot stones and stained glass that tried much too hard. The decorator, a schoolmate of Erich's from Berlin, had gone ornate retro-neo-bobo. Divans, settees, ottomans. Lots of spots to sit with nary a backside to fill them: their owners worked too much. Spending the night there, drowning in pillows and down, made Jonah feel like a monarch, one due for a beheading come morning.

'What's her name?'

'Eve Gones.'

'I don't remember anybody like that.'

'Think about how many people you had in your class.'

'A lot, but I'm surprised I don't have any . . . What college?'

'I don't know.'

'Huh. Well, let's look.' He heard her clicking

keys. 'Eve Jones . . . Oh you know what? Gretchen drew you a picture.'

He smiled. 'Yeah?'

'I told her you were a doctor. So she drew a picture of a doctor. It's a masterpiece. Pollockesque. She employed a lot of white crayon. I never understood why they made white crayons, paper is white, how pointless is that. Okay, Eve Jones. Nope. Sorry. Nothing.'

'She said she knew you. She remembered you.'

'She *knew* me?'

'Not that she was a friend,' he said. 'But she definitely implied familiarity.'

'That's weird.'

'Yeah,' he said. 'It is.'

Then he thought *Of course*.

'Katie? I made a mistake. Can you look up a different name?'

'You don't know the name of your own girlfriend?'

'She's not my girlfriend. Her name is spelled with a G.'

'Huh?'

'It's Jones but with a G.'

Kate snickered. 'Like G-J-O-N-E-S?'

'There's no J.'

'Gones?'

'It's pronounced Jones,' he said, which made her laugh harder.

'Jonah-face, that's not a name.'

'That's how she spells it.'

'They don't let illiterate people into Yale.'

'I'm not kidding.'

'— not many.'

'Would you please look in the database please.'

'Guh-Jones . . . From now on can I call you Guh-Jonah?'

'Kate.'

'Calm down, I'm looking . . .' She paused. 'Nope. Maybe she's not registered. Did she change her name? Get married?'

'I don't think so. Can you – do you have a year-book around or something?'

Kate sighed. Then he heard her drag something across the parquet.

'What are you doing?'

'I need the stepladder, it's all the way on the top shelf.'

'Why don't you have Erich get it?'

'He's at the office.'

'It's nine o'clock.'

'The life of a moneymaker.' She grunted. 'Crap. It's about two inches . . . let me get the ladder from the kitchen.'

'Kate—'

'Keep your frickin shirt on.'

'You don't have to get it right this second. I don't want you to hurt yourself.'

'Jonah-face,' she drawled, 'I'm pregnant, not a cripple.'

He timed her. Three minutes, during which he pictured her on tip-toes, her taut belly brushing up against *The Natural History of Nova Scotia Vol. VII.*

Once he'd thought of pregnancy as a delicate, motionless phase of life. His sister had disabused him.

'Whoo.' Kate belched. 'Excuse me. Okay. Got it. This'll be fun, I haven't looked at this in a while . . . Okay. Jones or Guh-Jones, is that right, Gonah-face?'

'That's right.'

'Wow, look at that.'

He stopped pacing. 'You found her.'

'No, I found a picture of my friend Robbie building the Beer Can Eiffel Tower. He worked on it for six months before his roommate came home wasted and—'

'*Kate.*'

'Jeeeeez. Yessir. I am on the job. I am at your service. Um . . . Goldstein. Gomez. Graves. There's no Gones, here, Gonah-face.'

'Are you sure?'

'I know how to use an index. There's an Elizabeth Marion Jones, a Jennifer Jones, and a Samantha Erin Jones. No Eve Jay-jones or Eve Gay-gones. Sorry.'

'Can you flip through it?'

'There's thirteen hundred people in my class.'

He sat down on his bed, flicking his big toe and breathing heavily. He zoned out long enough that when he came back he thought they'd been disconnected. 'Hello?'

'I'm here. I'm looking at – oh, gosh, there's me. That's so sad, I was so skinny.'

He said, 'What the hell.'

'Maybe she made it up to impress you. It happens all the time. My junior year there was a woman who got into the graduate program in microbiology by faking her entire application. It turned out she was a total psycho. They arrested her. True story.'

'I don't understand,' Jonah said.

'What's not to understand? People lie, they do it all the time. They lie on their job applications. When I recruited for Lehman, I couldn't believe what people would put on their CVs. Where does she work? Call them, they'll have her info.'

He slapped himself in the forehead. 'That's a good idea.'

'Glad to help. Should I tell Mom you have a new girlfriend?'

'No, please, no—'

'I'm kidding. Love you.'

The man who answered at the Beacon Transitional Housing Facility didn't sound altogether official; he seemed confused when Jonah said he was looking for a way to get in contact with Eve Gones.

'This is a men's-only residence.'

'She works there once a week,' Jonah said.

'Nobody by that name works here.'

'Are you sure?'

'Yeah.'

Jonah pursed his lips. 'Can I ask who *I'm* speaking to?'

'I'm the head night-shift nurse.'

'You've never heard of Eve Gones?'

'I don't know.'

'You don't know if you've heard of her, or—'

'Can I ask who *I'm* speaking to? Are you press?'

'I'm a friend of hers,' Jonah said. 'I'm trying to track her down.'

'Look, I can't help you. I can't speak to you. I have to go.'

The man hung up. Annoyed, Jonah dialed again. It rang eighteen times.

CHAPTER 13

Lately he'd grown accustomed to spending his days in a funk, but the following morning he was so nonplussed by his conversations with his sister and the man at the Beacon that he failed to notice that the usual cause of said funk wasn't around. At lunchtime he asked one of the interns what had happened to Benderking, and received a noncommittal shrug.

He wasn't about to question this gift. Not until afternoon rounds, when Benderking showed up in a beastly mood – sans tie, wearing an illfitting shirt and a large gauze eyepatch – did Jonah care to ask a notoriously gossipy nurse.

'Somebody threw a cup of coffee in his face.'

'What happened?'

'She comes in, yelling at him, "You piece of this, you piece of that," Whhooosh.' The nurse made a flinging motion. 'Right in his eye.'

'It was a *she*?'

'You know what I think, he was playing around on her.'

Disturbed, Jonah asked what had happened to the attacker.

'Ran off. You undercover? What you want to know for?'

He said, 'I wanted to know.'

He expected her that night, and sure enough, she was under her elm, its foliage slaughtered by the oncoming fall.

'Hello my love,' she said.

They went upstairs. He dropped his bag and stood with his arms crossed while she made herself a cup of tea.

'I need to apologize,' she said, reaching for the box of chamomile. 'I've been frightfully out of touch.'

He said nothing.

'Oh my, don't we look rather vexed.'

'Why did you do that.'

'Do what.'

'You can't do that,' he said. 'You *can't.* That's not – I mean, I can't believe you *did* that. And please don't try and tell me that you didn't, because—'

'Jonah Stem.' She set her tea down. 'Kindly allow me to get a word in.' She cracked her knuckles, cleared her throat. 'First I must explain where I've been. I've had a number of things on my mind, and a number of obligations to attend to. First and foremost, you must be aware that the difference between success and failure is most often a matter of planning. With likely only one chance to have my say with this fiend who's been venting his wrath upon you, I took it upon myself to—'

'You did do it,' he said.

'You're interrupting me.'

'You're not going to, I don't know, *pretend*?'

'Why should I pretend? I was going to tell you, I wanted it to be a surprise.'

'Oh it was.'

'Then good. Don't act so oddly. I was explaining to you that doing the job properly entailed a fair amount of thought on my part, not to mention effort, in determining when and where the best time to strike would be, the most appropriate means of reprisal. I thought coffee worked well—'

'Oh my God.'

'—symbolically.'

'Jesus. Eve.' He walked around the room, beating his fists together.

'You don't agree?'

'Agree with *what*.'

'The symbolic value of—'

'What are you *talking* about.'

'Coffee,' she said patiently.

'What about it.'

'After what he did to you? Making you glue his mug together? I suppose I could have hit him with a mug itself, but this was so much more – well, *cinematic*. I wish you'd been there to witness it first-hand . . .' She traced the path of the imaginary coffee through the air. 'A direct hit.'

He stared at her until she frowned.

'I'm getting a bad feeling from you, Jonah Stem.'

'No shit.'

'Is something wrong?'

'Of *course* there is, you assaulted my resident.'

She shook her head as if to say *And so . . . ?*

'Why did you *do* that.'

'He deserved it.' She looked surprised. 'Are you going to tell me he didn't?'

'I—'

'All you've been saying for a month is how much you'd like to sauté his innards.'

'That was—'

'Frankly,' she said, 'I was expecting a little more gratitude.'

'*Gratitude?*'

'Why yes.' She was wide-eyed. 'I did it for *you*, you know.'

'Don't even say that.'

'I did.'

'Don't even try and say that.'

'Well I did, you can't get around it. Just because the results aren't what I anticipated – and I'll be frank again, I think you're getting a tad histrionic here, Jonah Stem – doesn't mean my heart wasn't in the right place. You said—'

'I said I didn't like the man, I didn't—'

'You said—'

'I didn't say I wanted him *injured.*'

'You told me to,' she said.

'I never said *any* such thing.'

'You most certainly did.'

'When.'

'You said, "Go for it."'

'When did I say that.'

'We talked about it. You told me you wished he'd learned some manners, and—'

Now he remembered. 'I never said that, *you* said that.'

'And you acceded to the point.'

'I—'

'And I offered to teach him some manners, and you told me to go for it.'

'Figuratively.'

'Well,' she said, 'that wasn't very clear.'

'It should be.' He leaned against the wall. 'I mean for God's sake if I'd said to kill him would you've done *that*?'

She didn't answer.

He turned around to look at her.

She said, 'You did it for me.'

A silence.

He said, 'I need to – excuse me.'

He locked himself in the bathroom and sat on the edge of the tub. Benderking had suffered a corneal burn. He'd recover, but it would be painful and could take weeks.

He replayed that conversation, trying to remember if there had been anything in his tone, his phrasing, his facial expression – anything at all . . . *Go for it*. That wasn't a command. Was it? Could he be held accountable? What it would look like, having this woman who he had ostensibly saved testifying that he'd put her up to an act of violence.

Nobody died he thought. That was the main thing.
But somebody could have.
But nobody did.
From down the hall he heard something break.
He went back to the kitchenette and found Eve at the counter, her hands in the sink. Her face was pale.

'Eve?'

'I – I dropped it.'

The teacup lay in fragments near the drain. Blood ran from Eve's palm, spotting the watery stainless steel, mixing and swirling with dishwater and dishsoap.

'Let me see,' he said.

'It's nothing, it's – I'm sorry about the cup.'

The cut was shallow but long. He didn't think it would require anything more than a tight bandage and some antiseptic. He tore a length of paper towel off, bunched it together, and told her to apply pressure.

'Jonah—'

He went to the bathroom and scrounged stuff to patch her up. When he returned with a handful of Band-Aids and a tube of Neosporin, she had begun to lay the shards on the counter.

'I can fix it,' she said. 'I'm so sorry.'

'Give me your – op – hold it open.'

'Please don't be mad.'

'I'm not mad.'

'I'm sorry I – I'm sorry.'

'Hold still, Eve.'

'I love you.'

'Hold your hand open.'

'I do, I love you.'

'Eve—' He looked at her, and what he saw startled him: an immense chasm of despair, dividing her top to bottom, a book with its pages torn out.

'I love you,' she said. 'I'm sorry, I made a mistake. Please don't be mad.'

He had put on too much Neosporin; her skin gleamed; it was hard to get the Band-Aids to stick. 'Hold still.'

'Are you mad?'

'I'm not m— *Stop moving around.*'

'You're mad, I can hear it.'

He took a breath. 'You need to let me do this.'

'I'm sorry.'

He wiped the area around the wound clean.

'I'm sorry,' she said. 'I did the wrong thing. I'm sorry. I'm so sorry, please, I can't stand it when you're mad. Please don't be mad. I'm so sorry, Jonah, please, I love you. I won't do anything like that again. I made a mistake. I did it because I thought you would be happy but I was wrong. Tell me you're not angry.'

'I'm not angry.'

'*Good,*' she said. 'Good, good – I promise – I'll make it up to you, what I did, I'm sorry.'

'You hurt *him*,' he said. 'Not me.'

'I know, I'm sorry, I'm sorry . . .' She leaned her head against him.

He finished with the dressing. It wouldn't hold

for long but it'd do for the time being. He tried to step away from her but she put her arms around his neck. Crying. Yes. She was crying. As angry as he was, she was once again small, and despite his best efforts he felt bad for her. His hands went around her. He pulled her close and she moaned gratefully.

'You need to promise never to do anything like that again.'

'I understand.'

'I mean it, I need to—'

'I'm not a child,' she said in a remarkably child-like way. 'I understand. I won't do it again. I made a mistake.'

'All right.'

'Haven't you ever made a mistake?'

Yes he wanted to say *but it never involved physical harm.*

Then he remembered that that wasn't true.

'I'm trying to be explicit,' he said, 'because when I wasn't you took my words out of context.'

She said, 'It won't happen again.'

'Fine. Then. Then I don't think we need to – I want to forget about it.'

'Forget what.'

'I'm being serious. I don't want to – I could get nailed at school, or—'

'Why would you?'

'If he found out—'

'Jonah Stem, nobody knows that I know you. Do you think I gave him my card?'

'They called the police.'

She shrugged. 'So?'

'So they could be looking for you.'

'With all due respect, I think the NYPD has greater priorities.'

'You're not worried at all.'

'No.'

'Fine,' he said. 'Then let's forget about it.'

'Consider it forgotten.' She smiled. 'All better?'

He paced around. 'I called my sister yesterday.'

'Really. And how are things on the money farm?'

'I called her because I was trying to find you. You didn't show up for five days.'

'I'm sorry. As I explained earlier, I had things to attend to.'

'I asked her to look you up in the Yale alum database.'

'I'm not in there,' she said. 'I find it a bore.'

'I called the Beacon and asked for your phone number, and they didn't recognize your name.'

'Ah,' she said. 'That's because the director sent a memo to all staff instructing them not to answer questions about me. After my little run-in with Raymond they were getting bombarded by media. Bad PR, you know, to have one of their patients – or *citizens*, as they call them – stabbing staff members. It wasn't the first time Raymond had done that. He got into a fight last spring and they wanted to kick him out. I interceded on his behalf.'

He recalled his conversation with the night nurse. *Are you press?* Eve dug in her purse and

176

found a wrinkled business card with her name and the Beacon logo.

'Is this your number?'

'It's a direct line for the center.'

'I've been trying to reach you,' he said. 'I wrote you e-mails.'

'I know, and I'm sorry.'

'Don't you think it's a little strange that I don't have your phone number?'

'No.'

'It's been a month and half, Eve, that doesn't strike you as weird?'

'You've never expressed this displeasure before.'

'I haven't needed to call you,' he said. 'You've always been around.'

'And here I am, *c'est moi.*'

'But you weren't,' he said. 'I needed to speak to you. You have my number.'

'You have testicles, and I don't. Call it even.'

He stared at her. 'What's going on here?'

'. . . nothing.'

'Then why are you acting this way. What is this. Is it a – a security issue?'

She bit her lip.

'Eve. What's wrong.'

She went to the window and looked out. All stations in the Museum of Human Frailties were offline, as though they had darkened the displays to install new ones. 'I don't think it's fair that I should have to give myself to you if you won't do it in return.'

He said nothing.

She said, 'I love you. I don't have any problem saying it.'

'You'll give me your phone number if I tell you I love you?'

'Yes.'

'That sounds backwards to me.'

She returned to looking out the window.

He had wanted to tell her about his blowout with George, about his plan to scale back. If she had been around a few days earlier . . . and if she hadn't done what she did. He saw now that this was going to be impossible. He wasn't prepared to say that, though, not with her hand cut up and his head hurting from all the activity. He would formulate a strategy. He would worry about it later. He couldn't think about anything except what was right in front of him, and at that moment she turned and said, 'Let's go to bed.'

CHAPTER 14

For the next two weeks they reverted to their previous schedule, he going to work and she greeting him upon his return home. She would ask him how Benderking was behaving these days, and though Jonah was loathe to admit it, he had noticed a change: although still outwardly gruff, Benderking took care not to cross the line between *jerk* and *psychopath*. Jonah didn't tell her, of course. First of all, who knew what had caused the shift. Benderking might be scared; but he might also be quietly plotting his revenge. Maybe she'd given him a stroke that had burned out the cruelty center in his brain.

Plus Jonah didn't want to encourage her. Overnight he saw Eve differently. They continued to sleep together, but he no longer felt compelled to tell her everything that had passed through his mind; and he tried hard to look at her *objectively*.

Two memories dogged him. One was her face on Lance's video. He tried hard to put the image out of his head but it nagged him, cropping up while they rolled around on his bedroom floor. He found himself sneaking peeks at her, wanting to catch her in the act. Not that he would know what to do if he *did* catch her. Jump up with trembling finger: *faker*. Why did he need to have his suspicions confirmed? If he knew she was doing it – and he knew she was – he could either accept it or not. But torturing himself by looking, and looking, and looking . . .

The other memory, the worse one, the one that kept him awake after she'd left, and frightened him when he admitted it to his consciousness; *you did it for me*. He could not abide that analogy, and if she saw what he'd done in that way, then, well, then he didn't know what to do.

He felt the tiniest bit scared.

He had never been good at breakups, but if his experience with Hannah had taught him one lesson, it was that you saved everyone a good deal of grief by heading things off at the pass. Not yet but soon. He had a month of surgery left, plus the Shelf, and he didn't want to get tangled up in nightly heart-to-hearts, face-to-faces. He would miss the regular release, but there was always the Internet.

WEDNESDAY, OCTOBER 6, 2004.
BLUE TEAM, WEEK FOUR.

He exited the OR around one, and with ten minutes before his next Fatty, ran for the bathroom. On the way back he came across Nelgrave puddled in a chair.

'Patrick.'

Nelgrave's head lolled and swiveled. He had a sharp widow's peak that Jonah could swear had gotten more severe over the weekend. 'Huh?'

'Are you okay?'

'I passed out during surgery.'

'Shit. Did you hit your head?'

'I fell forward. On the patient.'

'. . . whoops.'

'His chest was open,' Nelgrave said, his voice cracking. 'I landed on his lung. I contaminated the entire sterile field. Then I vomited.'

'On the patient?'

'No. By that time, they'd thrown me off. That's when I hit my head.'

'Man,' Jonah said. 'That sucks.'

'I wanted to do plastics. Do you have any idea how competitive that is?'

'They won't flunk you for one bad day.'

Nelgrave shifted around in his chair. His scrubs were a mess. His neck looked like it hadn't been washed in a month. 'They might.'

'Look,' Jonah said, 'you know way more than I do.'

This seemed to cheer him. 'That's true.' He got up, smiled, patted Jonah on the shoulder. 'You always know the right thing to say, Stem.' Then he walked away.

Although bariatrics was a nonemergency service, he took call like everybody else. He reported at eight for what turned into one of the busiest nights of the year. Three ped-strucks (a couple in a crosswalk mowed down by a taxi; a tourist dashing through Times Square); a man beaten up in a bar fight, both collarbones and his jaw broken; a recent patient whose wound, improperly tended, had turned gangrenous. They removed the arm at the elbow, slicing through the joint.

After one A.M. things slowed down, and Jonah snuck off for a nap. He managed thirty minutes before his cell phone buzzed.

'Get down here.'

As he sleepily tied his shoes, the phone rang again.

'Don't bother. He died.'

He went back to bed.

Waking shortly thereafter to extremely proximate yelling.

'MEDICAL STUDENT.'

Jonah rolled over. 'Yuh?'

'I paged you *an hour ago*.'

'Y . . . you said he died.'

'Died?' The resident shook the lounge's bunk bed. 'Are you nuts? You must've dreamed it. Hey – you're the guy from the paper.'

Jonah nodded.

'Let's make use of your talents. I have a new job for you. You won't pass out on me again, will you? Good. The copy machine's broken, go fix it.'

Jonah didn't know how to fix a copy machine. They had copy-machine repairmen whose job it was to fix copy machines.

'Okay,' he said.

182

It was The Paper Jam That Ate Milwaukee. He sat down crosslegged with a pair of dissecting forceps and picked out toner-besmirched confetti. The tedium caused him to repeatedly pitch forward, snoring. At one point he grazed one of the machine's hot internal organs, raising welts on his hand. An hour later, a test copy – of his extended, injured middle finger – came out clear. He went to tell the resident, who gave him a hearty clap on the back.

'Good job, Supercock.'

By three thirty A.M. Jonah had been in the hospital for twenty-three hours, on his feet and active for the vast majority of those. He felt like a bald tire. He was heading to clean up for rounds when a wad of paper beaned him on the back of the head.

'Hello, Jonah Stem.'

He hurried over. 'What are you doing here?'

She giggled. 'You look adorable in your coat.'

'You can't be *here*. You could be arrested. Where are you going.'

She descended to the basement. The few people they passed nodded at her as though she had every right to be around; her bearing conveyed a sense of divinely mandated authority, the cushion of air found beneath the heels of movie stars, royalty, maître d's. Jonah tailed her at a distance, voicing dissent.

'Geeeez,' she said. 'Cease and de*sist*. If I didn't love you so much, Jonah Stem, I might find you a real downer.'

'You can't go in there. It's locked.'

'Rubbish, I've done my research.'

'This is illeg—'

'*Shhhh*,' she said in a stage whisper. '*Someone . . . might . . . HEAR . . . us.*'

And like that she was inside.

'Eve,' he said to the wall. 'Eve.' He had a feeling that, were he to try and wait her out, she would win. He didn't want to be caught standing here, doing nothing; that could lead to much worse. He'd have to go in and get her out as quick as he could. He turned the knob and stepped into MRI room 4.

She was staring at the machine. 'I have always fantasized about being able to see through things. You know what this reminds me of, those early computers, behemoths that ran three city blocks.' She laid a hand on its smooth tan shell. 'One day we'll shrink these down to a size convenient enough to carry in your handbag. Everyone will own one, they'll be like telephones or credit cards. We'll all walk around with MRI glasses, seeing people without their skin on.'

'We can't be here.'

'I thought our romantic life could use a pick-me-up,' she said, prancing around the far side of the machine. 'Something's been feeling off to me.'

He glanced at his watch, at the door.

'You could scan us while we did it. You could see our insides as it happened.' She poked her head into the tunnel. 'You could watch your glands in mid-contraction.'

He made a show of refusing – if they got caught, oh holy fuck – but when she climbed into the MRI machine he was right behind.

Miraculously, they fit. The mechanical bed was in the out position, giving them an extra six inches, not that that helped him: he could barely move in any direction, squirming against a rubberized cable, depilating the nape of his neck. He corkscrewed his body and his back sang *nooo*. He felt like a dolphin lodged in a waterslide.

Whereas she was positively acrobatic. She came to rest atop him, her woolly sweater bunched against his nostrils; he sneezed into her throat. *You're a master of your trade, Jonah Stem. I knew the minute we met. You're a prodigy.* She grated long itchy sleeves down his flanks and undulated and emitted what he could tell were fake moans. He felt angry at her for lying to him and he said *Stop it.* He tried to push her off. She arched against the top of the tunnel, exerting tremendous downward pressure.

Be good she said.

I don't want to do this.

You do, you do.

He tried to will himself soft but he could not. She was in his face. *Do something for me.* She grabbed his arm and brought it to her cheek. *Here.*

He stroked her face lightly.

Harder.

He didn't understand, and then he understood. She wanted him to hit her. This was new. They

185

had done what normal lovers do. But this was different, and no way was he going to comply. He jerked his hand away; she grabbed his other arm and he retracted that, too, so that he seemed to have flippers, Thalidomide Baby Versus the Humpamatic 3000. He refused. He told her *No*.

Hearing this, she said *Fine*.

Swiftly winding up, she bashed her head against the tunnel wall.

The noise was ferocious, as though he was sitting inside a church bell; as though he'd been the one brained. She bent to do it again, and *did* do it again, *WHAM*, the whole room rocked. His mind filled with wild pictures: Eve killing herself, her stiffening corpse trapping him, her skull opening like a soft-boiled egg, brains and cerebrospinal fluid and blood across his face. She wound up to do it again. He reached out to restrain her, and she seized his hand. *Good boy*. What could he do to stop her, *hit her*? And he felt her growing excited. This was why she liked it when he grabbed her buttocks; this was why she had him pull her hair. This was what she wanted, and although he felt sick to his stomach and there was no way he would allow it to happen, he allowed it to happen: he wanted to be surprised, but wasn't, not really; he had earned this. He offered his arm and let her flog herself. She made her whale songs; every sinew tight; pummeling herself in the face one two three times, kept on until her nose bled and splattered his forehead like bird droppings, and just as he could bear it no longer she shook and said *Oh oh oh* and her insides contracted on him and he could not help it, he came.

The machine hummed. He had never had an MRI before. Hannah had had one on her shoulder. He felt a curious mixture of dead peace and electrical agitation. Eve's weight atop him was a blanket, a burden. A vein in her neck drummed against his cheek. She whispered to him. Blood, her blood, sledded through the bristles of his two-day beard, tracking a route to the corner of his mouth. He was freezing. His hand throbbed; later he would see that he'd opened a huge gash along his knuckles. They'd contaminated the inside of the MRI. He would have to sterilize it. Red smudges along the walls like bad cave art. She sat up, her tongue bulging out her lower lip, rooting as after a persnickety piece of spinach. She drooled a bloody chunk into her hand. Her eyed widened, and she displayed the bounty: a tooth.

Her smile disclosed a newly formed gap. She collapsed against him again.

'There, my love,' she murmured. 'Was that so bad?'

CHAPTER 15

His last month of surgery consisted of two two-week subspecialties. Ophtho wasn't bad. The attendings all had beards, like it was a board requirement.

'You're shivering.' The surgeon, Dr Eisen, was pointing a gloved finger at him.

'It's cold in here,' Jonah said.

'You're not used to it by now?'

'Some things you never get used to.'

He'd never replied in any way more profound than *yes* and *no* and *sorry*. Now everyone in the room stared at him.

'True,' said Eisen. 'And that's why I left my wife.'

The patient on the table was a twenty-nine-year-old M with sympathetic ophthalmia. He'd lost one eye when a moving van plowed into his gypsy cab. In one of the body's great tragicomedies, the other eye, though unscathed, had started to die – an auto-immune response that, if left unchecked, would leave him blind. To save the good eye, they

188

enucleated the injured one. The patient would have to settle for blurry, nonstereoscopic vision. On the plus side, he'd have a prosthetic eyeball that would make for a good party trick (*watch this*).

Eisen had a basset-hound face and a dreamy voice. He pimped Jonah languidly about the Rube Goldberg apparatus of sight: the optic nerve, the ciliary ganglion, the straps of controlling recti muscles.

'Here's a toughie. If you can answer this, the team will remark on the high quality of med student we're getting. What writer's blindness was the result of sympathetic ophthalmia?'

Jonah couldn't remember too many blind writers. James Joyce. Wasn't Homer blind? He gave up.

'James Thurber. A surgeon told me that when I was a third-year. And now I'm passing it on to you. Don't say you didn't learn anything practical. Have you ever read *The Secret Life of Walter Mitty*?'

'In high school.'

'You should reread it,' sighed Eisen. 'It means a lot more once you get older.'

At seven thirty he left work. On the way to the train, he checked his voicemail.

Kiddo, how ya doing. Do me a favor and give me a buzz. I'm at the office until seven, after that you can get me at home, 212—

He stood near the entrance to the 50th Street

subway station and called. A puberty-ravaged squawk answered.

'Hi, Jonah Stem for Mr Belzer.'

'Daaad.'

Another extension clicked on. Jonah heard canned laughter from what he imagined to be a superb 7.1 surround-sound audio system channeling a plasma-screen TV opposite a leather recliner and an end table with a tumbler of Macallan, neat.

'Evan? Hang up.' The first receiver tumbled back into place. 'Yallo.'

'Chip, it's Jonah.'

'Oh hey kiddo. Lemme' – the TV piped down – 'thanks for getting back to me. Everything all right? How's school?'

'It's fine.'

'You got tests coming up?'

'Soon.'

'Must be rough. You work too hard, kiddo.'

The earnestness of small talk jangled his nerves. 'Is something up?'

'Up?, no. It's more a question of what *hasn't* happened.'

'. . . okay.'

'You remember we talked about the weakness of their case.'

Jonah sensed that he was supposed to answer in the affirmative.

'Good,' said Belzer. 'I told you at that time that I was going to file a motion to dismiss. Now, before I say anything, you need to understand something about the nature of that kind of motion, what it is *not*. What it's *not* is a motion to have the case thrown out on the basis of a lack of substantive merit. That is to say, what I mean is, there's no law says you can't file a case full of holes. With me so far?'

'Uh-huh.'

'Now that you understand what it's *not*. I can explain to you what a thirty-two-eleven motion *is*. What it is, it deals with whether an argument has any legal merit. Not factual merit. You see the difference. Meaning, if and only if there is a *technical* objection to it. Despite the fact that it's a shitty case, which our friend Roberto Medina knows it is. So a thirty-two-eleven will sometimes get denied if the judge feels that the plaintiff has any legal legs, no matter how bad, to stand on. It depends on how their case is worded, and what kind of judge we're talking about. And in our case, the two of those happened to coincide in a particular way, and the motion was denied.'

Belzer sipped. 'I can't emphasize enough that this is a minor setback. It's not a setback. For all we know they may give up the ghost once they figure out that they're actually gonna have to go to trial rather than get a quick settlement.'

Somebody shouldered past him to get into the subway. Distantly, Jonah heard her say *people need to get by here.*

'Trials like these – assuming there ends up being one – don't happen for months. Medina ain't the type to bill by the hour, he takes fifty percent of

191

the client's award. Since I know, and he knows, that that number's going to be zero, or close to it, he'd be shooting himself in the foot by pressing further. My prediction, we'll hear from them within a couple of weeks, whaddaya know, they want to negotiate—'

'Chip?'

'Yeah?'

'Zero, or close to it. Which one.'

'Whassat?'

'If we lost,' Jonah said, 'then it wouldn't be zero.'

'I can't make pre*dictions*,' Belzer said. 'I'm not *God*.'

'Then why did you say "close to it"?'

'It's a figure of speech. Look, I can't deliver it to you sealed in *wax*. But based on my extensive experience with the justice system, I see no reason to worry. Zero is an extremely educated guess. Would I bet my mother's life on it? No. But I'd bet mine.'

Jonah wondered how many civil suits Belzer had tried. He thought back to the glam trials of the last ten years: O.J., Michael Jackson, Scott Peterson. Not a group he wanted to have dinner with. They all had separate criminal teams and civil teams. Why hadn't Belzer passed the baton? Immediately, Jonah inferred the answer: because he thought the whole thing was a big joke.

'They could be trying to bully you, get you scared about damage to your reputation, so forth.'

'I *am* scared of that.'

192

'There's no reason to be. You got to trust me.'

'You said before it was going to be dismissed.'

'I never said that. I *never* said that, outright. I said that the case is weak, and that it *should be* dismissed. But if the judge looks at what's being presented and believes that there's enough ground to stand on – *statutorily* – then he has no choice but to let it through. That's the law. The ruling says absolutely nothing about the specifics of our case. Now we lean on them that much harder to get them to stop messing around.'

As Belzer continued to talk, Jonah's throat constricted to the diameter of a pencil, a swizzle stick, a needle, a thread. '. . . yeah,' he managed when Belzer asked *You okay?*

'Don't sound so depressed, kiddo. This too shall pass. You have more important things to deal with. The world needs more people like you. Good Samaritans.'

The Brooklyn-bound Ⓛ was a colloid of hipsters suspended in minorities. The girl on his left, her heavy houndstooth jacket no longer, he realized, unseasonable, used a pen cap to pry a scab from her thumb. One out of every three passengers wore white earphones, an army of drones remotely controlled by Steve Jobs. People got off, got on, trod patterns in the floor grime. A pair of teenagers in knee-length T-shirts entered the car via the end door, carrying boxes of candy bundled with duct tape.

Ladies and gentlemen we are selling candy today not for any basketball team or any charity but for ourselves to keep out of trouble off the streets and to put some money in our pockets today we are selling M&M's M&M peanuts Snickers for one dollar

Whatever debt Jonah had felt toward Simón Iniguez and his dead brother was rapidly fermenting into a sour hatred. Who did they think they were? He kneaded the fabric of his backpack, unsticking the Band-Aids covering his wounded knuckles.

Shucking, jiving Second Avenue carried him past a loud Mideastern takeaway where he stopped to order falafel. While waiting for his food he wandered out onto the sidewalk. Astor Place and its turning cube; two Starbucks, one block apart. He imagined himself on trial. His only point of reference was *Law & Order*; he kept hearing that *duh duh* noise, seeing white titles and an establishing shot of his neighborhood.

APARTMENT OF JONAH STEM
AVENUE A AND 11TH ST.

Duh duh.
Alone, he sat on the sofa, studying to no avail. He noodled on his computer, discarded his sodden pita, got up for a soda. He hooked his fingers round the fridge handle, did not pull it open.
My love was that so bad

194

Actually, it was. Actually, he did not like it, at all. The need to *head things off at the pass* seemed far more pressing than it had before.

He stood there dreaming up worst-case scenarios, failing to notice how much time had passed until the downstairs buzzer shrieked. He glanced at the microwave's LED display; he had been standing in place for nearly thirty minutes.

He went to the intercom. 'Hello?'

In singsong: 'Jonah Steeeem.'

He let her up.

While she climbed the stairs he formulated his plan: tell her. Honesty the best policy. Whole truth and nothing but. No time like the present. He hoped she appreciated his candor.

As her tea steeped she smiled to show him the new tooth she'd gotten to replace the missing one. 'They did a smashing job, didn't they?'

He walked to the window, preparing his opening.

'Jonah Stem, are we moody?'

He said nothing. She came up behind him and hugged his chest, her thin arms tightening like an écraseur. He pried free and stood facing her.

'We need to talk.'

She appeared paralyzed. Then she reached for his crotch.

He arrested her. 'Wait.'

Behind her eyes flared something greenish, chemical, rotten. She reached for him again; he grabbed her other hand. His fingers hurt, and he wanted to let go, but as soon as he loosened his grip, she made another go for him. She smiled, and he smiled, too: a contrived exchange signaling either the onset of détente or the circling of beasts.

He could throw her out. He didn't want to because – because he wasn't like that, a guy who threw women around, and also because he was worried that she might enjoy it.

'No,' he said.

'Why not.'

'I don't want to.'

'Then why,' she said, grinding her knee into his groin, 'are you hard.' Backed against the kitchen counter, their arms cruciform, he shying away and she curving in conformity, like a bimetallic strip, compressing his erection with her pelvis and saying *Jonah Stem   You can't say no   I can feel it I can feel that   Are you going to tell me that I'm imagining   I can feel it in my hands   I can taste it*

She dropped to her knees, gnawed him through two layers of fabric. Still he had her by the wrists; she couldn't open his pants; then she opened his pants using her teeth and found her way inside, why hadn't he worn a button fly.

Stop

He grasped at world health statistics and open chest wounds and any other repellent image capable of leaching his desire: thought of his mother, of his mother having sex with Lance, thought of Hannah, of the black crud he washed from her armpits, thought of the time she threw her shit at him, he thought of the time

196

please stop

Raymond Ramon Iniguez, the dying sough, he thought of cancer and AIDS

st sto s

To the couch, straddling her chest, in her mouth; she began bobbing back and forth, doing crunches attached to his penis. He closed his eyes. One last time and then no more. Get it over. Fast as possible. Enjoy it, not too much, but enjoy it. It is happening. He wanted it to be over. *Out. Out. Out. Out. Out*

At that moment he heard several loud thumps. He opened his eyes: Eve, bobbing, with each descent banging the base of her skull against the armrest.

He reached out to cup her head, but she batted him away *bang bang* and kept *bang bang* going. Although initially worried about her *bang bang bang* head he fast began to fear for the *bang* sofa, and the floor, and the building, as though she could *bang* bring the whole City *bang* down, crack its foundations, *bang bang bang bang* drop it *bang* into the sea, replace it *bang* with a smoking crater of *bang bang* rage and lust *bang bang bang BANG BANG BANG BANG* he couldn't help it couldn't help himself.

Sweat from his forehead dripped on her nose. She blinked rapidly, as though seeing double; wiped her mouth with her hand; smiled dreamily. 'You never fail me.'

While he stepped into his pants, she crossed to the kitchen sink and drank two glasses of water,

197

returning to the sofa with excessive poise, as though demonstrating sobriety for a highway patrolman. She sat and tugged her skirt down over her knees.

'What do you see,' he said. 'While it's happening.'

She looked out the window. 'Stars.'

He rinsed his face, then re-emerged, twisting the washcloth.

'I don't think we should see each other anymore.' He waited. 'Eve?'

'We can see the people across the street. That means that they can see us in here. We're in our own Museum. Have you ever considered that, Jonah Stem?'

'I've been thinking about it and I'm sorry it has to end like this, we can talk about it if you'd like, but that's what I feel and I hope you can respect that. It's only been a couple of months, we can pretend like it never happened.'

She looked at him. 'But it did.'

He said, 'Do you want to talk about this?'

'There's nothing to talk about,' she said.

'All right, then.' He crossed to the front door and held it open. 'Good-bye.'

She smiled. 'No. Not good-bye.'

On the way out she pressed something soft and square into his palm. It was a jewelry box. He waited till she was gone, then opened it. Set in silver, on a silver chain, was a human tooth.

CHAPTER 16

His mistake, he decided, had been one of tone.

Several shades of meaning lurked inside the phrase *I don't think we should see each other anymore*. It might embody a backhanded attempt at self-analysis, a reaction provoked in order to see how that reaction provoked you. Or some sort of perverse romantic refresher: *let's fight and then do it on the bathroom floor. I'll get the chardonnay*. Or else a dignified camouflage for solicitation: *you have done wrong, crawl back with apologies and all will be okay*.

Or: *Go away*.

He could not shake the sound of her calling *Not good-bye*. As though she could speak and have it be, a God-of-Genesis mastery, commands lobbed from the heavens to resurface the world on her whim. Her confidence awed him. No way could he compete with that voice, in which every word carried the sweet pompous vinegary sting of inevitable victory. By comparison he stood not a chance, especially when the animal part of his brain still desired her, still wanted to submit, no matter how much he instructed it otherwise.

Really, though – who was submitting to whom? He thought about the broken teacup; about the MRI tunnel wall, the armrest; and he saw a pattern that he did not like. She'd looked bored on the video because she *was* bored. And while he had encountered plenty of people, plenty of girls, who liked being controlled, even pushed around – Hannah came to mind – there was a big difference between faux rough stuff and what Eve wanted. He perceived a clear escalation, headed toward . . . where. He did not care to find out. She needed what he could not provide, and in her demands he felt strong-armed, both top and bottom, master and servant.

He looked at his own injured hand, palpated the scab on his elbow. Take the bandage off in one quick rip. Tugging gently helped nobody.

Still, he worried about how she would react when she really *did* get the message. Then what? Was he obligated to prevent her from harming herself? Killing herself? She had already demonstrated a willingness to act where most would stop at threats. He did not want the responsibility but, as usual, fate had failed to seek his permission.

All next day he tweaked his speech. A train-stopper, Churchillian in its grandeur, mercifully swift and thorough, leaving no room for misinterpretation. Women were the most captious creatures in the universe, Eve a credit to her gender.

That was the idea, anyhow. What little he'd readied glided out of his consciousness, dissolving in the wake of an arm, as he came up the block.

'Jonah Stem. *Yooooo-hooooo*.' She was on his front step.

Be a good Scout. Earn your courage badge.

'I'm glad you're here,' he said, stopping on the second step, cocking his elbow jauntily. He hoped he looked cool. He felt not cool. He felt like a poseur extraordinaire.

'Right-o.' She smiled expectantly. 'Upstairs?'

He said, 'I understand how you've been feeling.'

Her face changed. 'Not this again.'

'Hear me out—'

'Jonah Stem, you are not going to regargletate that tired hash. Please, spare me the trouble of having to correct you in public.'

'I understand that you're put off—'

'What puts me off is having to have a fatuous conversation twice.' She leapt at him, began kissing his neck. 'This is lovelier. My my. Hello down there, Jonah Stem.'

He backed out of her arms, bag swung round to conceal the front of his slacks. Eve covered her mouth and laughed. 'Oh my.'

'Don't say anything. I want to say something. And don't touch me.'

'But I like to.'

'I *don't*.'

'You never seemed to complain before,' she said. 'You seemed quite content to stick your ding-dong into my hoo-hah, and never a peep out of you. This attack of qualms I find extremely suspect, and rather upsetting.'

'Can I talk, please.'

'Go right on.'

'Without you interrupting me.'

Eve made a lotus flower, bent her head. 'As you wish.'

He took a moment to marshal his thoughts. Part one, concession and acknowledgment of fun had. Part two, semicolon HOWEVER comma. Part three, amplify rationale, drawing attention to unfeasibility of long-term involvement, scheduling conflicts, lifestyle incompatibilities, etc. Part four, anticipate rebuttals; dispatch. Four-A, in response to hurt, console and support. Part five, conclusions.

'You look pained, Jonah Stem.'

'I'm choosing my words carefully.'

'I expect nothing less.'

'Now,' he said, 'while it's true we've had a very compelling, uh—' He tried to locate himself on the page. 'I was – okay. Now. While it's true, it's *been* true, that we've had a good time together, I'm sorry to tell you, sorry to say it but I'm no longer okay with the way you and I get along. I admit that the past two months have been great. But to my mind that's outweighed by the fact that I can't see it going anywhere, and that I'm a little uncomfortable, actually *very* uncomfortable with the way you've been behaving recently. I don't like the, the – I don't think I can provide what you need.'

'You can.'

'Can I—'

'Sorry.'

'Please.'

'I'm sorry.'

'I – shit. Okay, look. Now I know *you* think I can, but the last few – times, have shown me that – I'm not . . .' He stepped closer to her. 'I'm not going to hit you.'

'You don't have to.'

'Or allow you to hit yourself, or get involved with, with that.'

'Jonah Stem. May I interject? I'm not sure you understand what I'm all about.'

'That's probably true, it's certainly true, but all I can tell you is how I feel about what happened last time, and I – I don't want to do that. I don't want to be with someone who needs that. It sucks for me to have to say that, and I'm sorry to be so blunt. But I want you to understand exactly where I'm coming from, it has nothing to do with what kind of person you are. You're a terrific woman, and you deserve someone who can give himself to you one hundred percent, who won't feel conflicted. It's not right for me to get any more, uh, involved. So this is it. I'm sorry. It's been crazy, the way we've – and the – but now it's over. No more. Am I making myself clear?' He wiped his forehead with his sleeve.

'Well said,' she said. 'Shall we to the boudoir?'

'Are you – did you hear me?'

'I did, Jonah Stem. Hand me your keys, you're not well to drive.' She reached for his coat pocket, which he stapled shut with a slap.

'Very well.' She began to sing 'Why Don't We Do It in the Road.'

'Eve.'

She sang *You drive me crazy, Jonah Stem.*

'Eve.'

You're such a cutup, Jonah Stem.

'Talk to me like a normal human being.'

'Think of all the ways in which you've tooouuuuched me,' she sang. The original melody had been lost.

His hands sweaty and her staring at him, he dropped his keys, and as he bent to get them she dove forward; they knocked heads and she went tumbling down the front steps, rolled around on the sidewalk, holding her head and laughing. He snatched up the fallen keys and went quickly to let himself in. Not fast enough; she slipped in behind him and began following him up the stairs, talking as she went.

'Let's explore your feelings,' she said. 'How long have you hated your mother?'

Five fucking flights. He ached from standing all day; his bag dragged like granite.

'You're certainly in a hurry.'

'I know what you're doing,' he said. 'You're trying to provoke me. I won't do it, so forget it.'

'Don't you think you're being a tad hasty?'

'No.'

'I love you.'

'You do *not* I—'

She screamed. The noise pinned him to the wall.

'Now that I have your attention,' she said.

'Jesus Christ . . .'

'The problem is you're not aware,' she said. 'You've never seen my work, you can't apprehend the perfection of our fit.'

His ears were ringing. 'Jesus fucking *Christ.*'

'Love is powerful and blinding. But get to your feet, lad.'

She opened her arms.

He bolted, taking the steps three at a time.

'Jonah Stem, don't run.'

His legs were much longer than hers, and he outpaced her; but the ground he gained disappeared in the time it took him to turn the lock. He tried to slam the door but didn't quite succeed; a hollow crack rang out as Eve blocked it with her head. She stumbled into the apartment, crashing into his arms. For twenty or thirty seconds they staggered around.

'What the fuck are you *doing.*'

'I hurt myself,' she said.

'What was *that.*' He dragged her to the sofa. 'What the, what the *fuck.*'

'May I have a glass of water?'

'You may get out of here is what you may do.'

'Look.' She touched her head; her palm came away bloody.

'*Shit.*'

'I'm going to stain the upholstery, call for a transfusion. Medic. Medic.'

He laid her on the living-room floor. Like most scalp wounds, hers was superficial but profuse. He cleaned it roughly, making it bleed worse.

'You're so good,' she slurred. 'I love it when you heal me.'

He said nothing.

'I would die for you.'

'I'm not asking you to.'

'I'd do it anyway,' she said. 'I'll send you some of my portfolio. We can do a new project together, I have ideas . . .'

He applied Neosporin. Much more of this and he'd have to start ordering by the case. All the while she mumbled.

Jonah Stem shall we have children? Jonah Stem do you want to kiss me? Jonah Stem I think we ought to find a studio in the countryside so we can work undisturbed.

When he finished he pulled her up. She was too unsteady to put up serious resistance. He wrestled her out onto the landing, and forced her to sit on the top step.

'I'm coming out here in ten minutes,' he said. 'And if you're not gone, I'm calling the police.'

She fingered the ugly sharp line of bruise on her temple; the messily dressed wound. She held up her bloody hand. 'What will you tell them?'

He stared at her. *Believe me, officer—*

206

He walked back into his apartment.

A few minutes later he heard her leave.

He kicked his backpack across the room. He should've slammed the door on her a second time, a third, kept at it until her skull bulged. This was not him; he did not have these terrible thoughts. Throw her against the wall and pound her body until her womb fell out like an overripe peach. Push her out the window and watch her scatter into a billion irreconcilable fragments, like the camera. This was not him. He ran to the fridge and took a beer in one long draught, not for thirst but so he could crush the can and whang it against the far wall. *Primum nocere*. He wanted to throw the easy chair against the TV; wanted to hear the vacuum tube crack; wanted to tear the stuffing from the sofa with his hands until springs poked up like little frozen upside-down lightnings. This was not him, this was her effect on him; this was what she wanted, to turn him into a thing of violence. He opened a kitchen drawer and grabbed the largest deadliest object, a chef's knife with a stained blade, he hammered it into the counter, left it there, grabbed the crisper drawer from the fridge, and dumped out its contents. The knife left a black line in the Formica as he yanked it out and went to work: scallions bent and bleeding; her kidneys, mushrooms hacked apart. Her heart a tomato puking seeds and slime; her lungs two long hothouse peppers crushed flat. Juice slashed the cabinetry; tendonous stems and wrinkled vegetal skin matted his forearms, landed in his hair. He beat maimed killed. Not him. He took out five eggs and broke them one by one in his hands; he squeezed a stick of butter and it squirted from the ends of his fist like a deep-sea fish reeled in too fast, coughing up its own swim bladder.

From across the room he watched himself, his black-hearted double, sinking knees-first into a mess of his own creation.

She did not come for a week and a half. Every so often, once a day at first but then more frequently – every two hours or so – she would call; he could identify her by the words that displayed on his phone in block letters.

ID UNAVAILABLE

He deleted her voicemails without listening to them. He didn't care what she had to say, as long as she continued to steer clear. Eventually she would see it his way.

FRIDAY, NOVEMBER 5, 2004.
SHELF EXAMINATION.

The written half of the exam consisted of a hundred questions ranging from boring to extremely boring. Passing was a shade over fifty percent, and he finished with time to spare. Then came the oral, a ninety-minute one-on-one pimp-a-thon. The attending asked 'thought questions,' open-ended cases for which Jonah had to present an appropriate plan of surgical treatment. As a test of his knowledge such questions were wholly inappropriate: for twelve weeks he had ceased to think, functioning as an android, executing tasks – and menial ones, at that. It wasn't as though he could cure anyone. When asked, 'How would you begin to deal with a patient whose neglect of a peptic ulcer has resulted in hemorrhagic shock,' he had to bite his tongue in order not to respond, 'By paging the resident.'

He began by inquiring after dietary habits, allergies, socioeconomic status—

'The patient is bleeding to death,' said the examiner. 'Life moves at a speed that's not always convenient for us.'

Jonah didn't know whether to be flattered or repulsed. *Us.* What earned him admission to that club? The American Association of Obnoxious Doctors. The League of Being a Smarmy Jerk. The Society for Intimate Knowledge of What It's Like to Watch Other People Writhe Within Your Grasp.

But he faked his way through that question and the questions that followed. As he talked, the noise of St Aggie's leaked through the vents: carts and beds and humans in transit. Rattling chests. Feet in paper slippers. Beeps and blurps and *whoopsy-daisy*. Halfway through Jonah's sermon on nuclear scintigraphy, the examiner said, 'Don't mind me,' and, in flagrant violation of hospital policy, produced a pack of Marlboros and an ashtray carved from a hockey puck. Smoke filled the room, invading his clothes, tickling Jonah's sinuses. Sweet and cheap, an offering to a low-rent god, the God of Surgery. Bowels and blood, the insides of the insides, Holy of Holies, places no man is meant to look at, private lives torn open.

Not bad.

'Not bad.' The attending squinted at him. 'Aren't you Superdoc?'

Jonah said, 'That'd be me.'

'Huh. Who knew. Well, congratulations. Fly on home.'

He rather staggered out. He had a dehydration headache and he would need to dry-clean his blazer. But he was done cutting people up.

He stepped inside his apartment and let out a victory yawp that drew Lance out of the editing room.

Jonah said, 'You are going to buy me a slice of pizza.'

'Roger that.'

On their way out Lance pointed to a pile of mail that Jonah had been neglecting for two weeks. 'Your public awaits.'

Jonah flicked an envelope. 'The electric bill's probably due.'

'It came on Saturday.'

'Sorry, I'll get to it tonight.'

'Done and done.'

Jonah was touched. He said thanks.

'You looked busy. But, look, can you stop being a depresso-stressball now? Cause I'm sick of you sounding like Eeyore with a fuckin head injury.'

Lance deemed pizza an inadequate reward. They needed to live it up, and that meant knishes from Yonah Schimmel's. The bakery itself was closed, but he knew a pastry-pushing restaurant where they resold after-hours at a slight markup. Belching, potato-breathed, they then wandered to a Lower East Side dive favored for its spectacularly coherent design scheme: a top-to-bottom reproduction of a New York City sewer. The walls glistened with runoff and multicolored 'moss.' The bar, a slab of concrete, leaked steam at strategically random points and was slathered in unidentifiable sludge (as were the bartenders themselves). After blowing seventy-five dollars on four drinks, they moved to another bar, this one made up like a Vietnamese village and called Napalm. Its delicate, obsequious waitstaff dove for cover when customers made sudden movements. Lance's tips induced kisses on the cheek. *Have another.* A Jersey girl bachelorette party asked Jonah to sign the bride's left bra cup. He obliged and they graced him with a necklace made of plastic penises. *Have another.* A band called Liquified Chicken played a noisy thirty-minute set that concluded with a radically deconstructed cover of 'I Have a Little Dreidl.' Lance bought the bassist an absinthe. *Another*. A flashbulb popped *another*. By this time Jonah was as wasted as the entire U of M rugby team, and Lance acutely desirous of going home to get stoned.

Somehow they got upstairs. Lance ducked into the bathroom with his stash and a roll of duct tape. Jonah sorted mail. He flipped through a Victoria's Secret catalogue. How'd they get his name? He didn't mind, he found catalogues an affirmation that he filled a desirable marketing demographic. A tuition bill from HUM. A thank-you card from a wedding he'd attended a year ago. A postcard from a local theater company. A package addressed in his mother's hand; for some reason, his parents insisted on *mailing* him the mail he got in Scarsdale. He had tried to get them to stop wasting postage. He didn't need his high-school alumni newsletter. But his father said *Tampering is a federal offense*. From Kate he received a malapropian headline snipped from a financial newspaper: PROFESSOR ASPIRES TO BE FED CHAIR.

Chortling, he went to use the bathroom.

'. . . hang on.' Lance sounded strangled.

'Are you gonna be long?'

Smoke snaked through the doorframe.

Jonah rattled the knob. 'Lance?'

'I am on Venus.'

The door popped with the sound of ripping tape, and smoke poured out, making Jonah's eyes water. Lance, lying in the bathtub, floundered like an overturned crab. The sink was full of ashes, formerly eight hundred dollars' worth of mari-juana. 'Close the door, you're letting it out.'

It was too late to contain the gray cloud spreading into the hallway. Thankfully, the smoke detector was dead. As Jonah prized open windows, he noticed that his room looked funny, everything looked funny, the world fishbowled and dripped. He was well on the road to being extremely high.

Groaning, he opened the front door to wave smoke out.

There was something on the threshold.

It appeared very far away. He squinted, swayed, knelt, picked it up. A manila envelope, addressed to him in tight cursive. He tore it open and shook out a sheet of single-spaced type and a jewel box.

My Dearest—

Doubtless you wonder where I've been.

Having confined myself to thoughts of our most recent exchange, I find myself culpable. It is my unpardonable coyness that has caused you to act this way. It's not easy to find people who sympathize at all with my passions, much less complement them as sublimely as you. Perfection is a rare and precious bird, thought by many extinct. Surprising, then, when it alights on our sill and pecks for entrance. We may pardon the skeptic.

It is important that you watch the enclosed portfolio carefully and to the end. You must understand the project as a complete Body of Work / Work of Body if you intend to contribute to its future. Remember,

nemo enim ipsam voluptatem, quia voluptas sit, aspernatur aut odit aut fugit, sed quia consequuntur magni dolores eos, qui ratione voluptatem sequi nesciunt,

neque porro quisquam est, qui dolorem ipsum, quia dolor sit, amet, consectetur, adipisci velit, sed quia non numquam eius modi tempora incidunt, ut labore et dolore magnam aliquam quaerat voluptatem.

This, I believe, is what has been missing. Our Love, already resplendent, will achieve wholeness. You will like what you see, and you'll understand what a mistake you're making in being so recalcitrant.

You are a great artist. Now we can create together.

Yours sincerely,
in Love and War,

Eve Gones

CHAPTER 17

The DVD was unmarked, its readable surface red and shining like wet meat.

After checking on Lance – he'd passed out in the tub – Jonah locked himself in the editing room and pulled a chair up to the elaborate AV rack, which housed four DVD players, two VHS decks, a cable box, and various devices to accommodate Super-8, 16mm, and various unfamiliar media, all wired to a fifty-five-inch flat-screen TV. He wondered if this was the best time to start watching whatever it was she thought he'd find so compelling. He felt faintly sick, and could sense a massive hangover kicking up dust in the distance.

He looked at the disc. He could throw it away.

Getting the screen on took a fair bit of fiddling. The sound ran through an old Pioneer tuner; hearing nothing, Jonah twisted the knob up, curdling the background hiss to a growl. He tripped across the room and eased into Lance's rolling desk chair with the bent leg, the one that would slip out from under you if you weren't careful, which Jonah was not; he pitched sideways, his stomach burbling. He righted himself, waited.

PURE BEAUTY

fade

A PORTFOLIO
PREPARED BY EVE

fade

FOR HER ONE AND ONLY LOVE
JONAH STEM

fade

PART THE FIRST: JUVENILIA
(THE EXPLORATION OF SENSATION)

Then nothing.

Wondering if the disc had jammed, he stood up to check, getting midway across the room before a mindsplitting screech sent him reeling, his chest a popping grape. He fell on the chair for support, causing it to roll out from under him, dumping him to the floor, hands clamped over his ears, the AV system's towering wood-paneled speaker stacks vibrating like lawnmowers, the detritus atop them – pencils, quarters, cigarettes – skittering like spooked rats. He thought that he'd died, that what he was listening to was his soul being torn from his body. Where was Lance, how could he sleep through this. He tried to get to the tuner but standing – while he was this drunk, without unclamping his ears – proved impossible; and he was crawling for the door when without warning the sound broke off, leaving a vacuum that seemed somehow louder, filled as it was with the roar of his own blood.

The screen burst alive with what could have been a direct shot of the sun, or a close-up of a lightbulb. No sense of space: it could have been a racquetball court or a decompression chamber or the inside of a septic tank, a place blank and depthless. The shifting contours, rolling across the gigantic screen, made it seem as though the room itself was moving, inverting itself, the corners moving away as the center drew close, a swelling belly of emptiness pressing against him and mashing his bowels, Jonah getting seasick. He should turn it off, he could not turn it off. Unsteadily he sat, falling back on his elbows. Now he discerned a horizontal. The camera pulled back and there appeared a person – a woman – lying facedown on a table. She was naked. She did not look real; she was liquid. The image was grainy and scarred, a copy of a copy of a copy. The camera repeatedly softened and sharpened, his head hurt. The woman was Eve. He could tell. Not exactly naked: a jungle of loose ropes, hung from above, effleuraged her back. Ropes?, ropes. They began to go taut.

The ropes were attached to her back with hooks, glinting like mouthless teeth, two dozen stingers left by bees the size of babies. Her back spiked; grew stalagmites of skin. She extended her arms and began to fly. Legs aligned and stiff; head up; beatific. Rising from the table, attached to the ropes attached to her skin. She bled. It coursed down her ribs. The camera tracked upward until she stopped rising, and hung in space, sculptural, swinging in and out of shadow, like a cast-off angel plummeting through the clouds. Repulsive, beautiful; and his whole head was wet but before he could get up

blackout

And at once the screen again flashed bright: Eve, naked from the waist up, handcuffed to a post, being flogged with what appeared to be a belt, although the whipper stood off-screen, and all Jonah could make out was a flicker of motion and a popcorn *crack*. Red stripes appeared across her back. *crack* As her skin showed no marks, he intuited that what he was watching had occurred much earlier or much later. *crack* Her back bled; she cried out. Shifting in one direction earned her lashes from the opposite side. When one well-placed hit sliced open her shoulder, she fell to her knees, screaming in a way he found familiar, almost lovingly known, an idiosyncrasy like *that's all folks* or *finger-lickin good*. The disembodied hand dropped the belt and began to beat her viciously about the neck and head; she slumped like cloth;

and as the hand stopped clubbing her he heard
an electronic buzz, whimpering

blackout

JONAH STEM, I REGRET THE POOR QUALITY OF
THESE IMAGES.

fade

AT THE TIME, YOU SEE, I COULDN'T
AFFORD A DECENT CAMERA.

fade

I AM THEREFORE INCLUDING ONLY TWO OF THE
EARLIEST CLIPS.

fade

SHORTLY THEREAFTER, MY LUCK IMPROVED,
I CHANCED INTO SOME DECENT EQUIPMENT.

fade

HENCE THE GREATER VARIETY AND SUPERIOR
QUALITY OF THE FOLLOWING:

fade

PART THE SECOND: LATER WORKS
(THEORY/PRAXIS)

The remote control. He could turn this off. He did nothing. He was sewn to the ground.

Eve, again: older, a clear, close shot of her bare back. He had never seen her fully naked in real life and now he understood why. Between the previous movie and this one, she had changed, horribly: her upper body not that of a young woman but a twisted mass of scar tissue, pink and white swellings like melted Styrofoam; injuries healed and reopened so many times that her torso was gone, smothered, a slum atop the ruins of a palace.

Gloved hands, holding a screwdriver and a barbeque lighter, appeared on-screen and then retreated. *Click*. The screwdriver reappeared, its tip smoking. Eve raised her arms above her head and the screwdriver moved to her left flank.

He covered his face until the sizzling, the screaming, stopped. He would get up and leave. He would do that. Open his eyes and get up. He heard nothing. There was no screaming, probably the tape was over. He would get up without looking at the screen. He put his hands flat against the unwashed floor and started to push himself to his knees. But drunk and sightless he lost his balance, slipped, and as his eyes opened reflexively he caught a glimpse of the screen, a fifth of a second but it was long enough, more than long enough, a pair of scissors clipped off the tip of a nipple.

He scrambled across the room, slamming the door behind him, which failed to drown out another bout of digital-quality screaming dressed atop reports of (no; but yes) snapping bone. Like a dog he flopped in front of the toilet, losing undigested hunks of dough and tropical liqueurs and then nothing, nothing but retching still, drooling crystal and viscous. He cleared his burning sinuses into the toilet; took off his shirt and wrapped himself in a towel. He instructed himself to *think clinically*, recast her as a series of component layers: skin and fat and muscle and bone and vessels and nerves. Not a person but a model. You trained to see the human body as an object. Like a car, like a coloring book. You kept your distance. And in his mind's eye he saw scissors and a ragged bloody hole where there should have been supple pink and, to his amazement, he vomited again.

Lance rolled over in the bathtub, murmuring about Nam.

The bathroom tiles smelled of Gold Bond; the grout was black. Jonah shook. Invisible bugs crawled all over him, down his pants and across the soles of his feet and into his armpits. Furiously he sawed the towel against his skin. Something was wrong with him. He was seeing things. There was no letter, no DVD. He was asleep or blacked out in his bedroom. Pot always put him over the top, especially in quantity and quality and after a long hiatus. The sight of the toilet made him want to throw up again. His stomach cried out for something to sop up the sloshing acid. He grabbed the towel rack to hoist himself up but the screws pulled out of the wall, sending plaster raining down on him. Cursing, he got to hands and knees, got up, gargled sinkwater, washed his forehead. He put down the toilet seat and sat, scraped out and sweating.

A few minutes later he felt well enough to stand.

Inside the editing studio, the DVD was still going. He waited outside, listening to what sounded like a normal conversation; a girlish laugh he recognized as Eve's. He entered expecting to make a dash for the screen, but stopped instead in the middle of the room to watch something new.

The man on-screen had an uneven moustache. Soft-shouldered but muscular, his shapelessness seemed the result of poor maintenance rather than genetic disadvantage. He wore a Yankees cap and looked at the camera with longing.

Are you ready? Eve's voice, behind the camera, swallowing the microphone.

The man said *Yeah.*

Excited?

Yeah.

As am I. As am I. Her laugh. *You want me to touch you now?*

Yeah.

I will shortly. Would you care to say anything first?

No the man said. He was sitting on the floor, his back against a squat cherrywood nightstand. Behind him, a window whited out with mid-morning glare.

Who are you? Show me who you are.

He held up an old photo of a black man – not him.

And who am I?

He held up another old photo, this one of a white woman – not Eve.

Do you love me? How much do you love me. How much.

The man smiled.

Say good-bye.

The man continued to smile.

Say good-bye.

Good-bye.

The image jerked, then jumpcut to a dark exterior. Close rustling, as though someone was swaddling the camera in rags.

Twenty feet away, across a street, the same man stood in front of a Dumpster. He swam inside a threadbare coat whose sleeves dangled past his wrists. With pendular regularity he glanced up the block, down it. Once he paused to wave at the camera.

The rustling stopped and Eve walked into the frame, crossing the street to join him. They talked inaudibly. She demonstrated a downward motion which he copied until, satisified, she pecked him on the cheek and pointed off-screen.

They turned toward the sound of an oncoming car.

A taxi passed through the frame.

They watched it go. Eve said something. The man went in the direction of the taxi, returning thirty seconds later, shaking his head. She shrugged, kissed him again, this time on the lips, and jogged back toward the camera, disappearing behind it. The focus went in, out; fixed. *Okay*.

She crossed the street and stood with her back to the man. He took something out of his pocket and positioned himself ten or fifteen feet behind her.

Eve called *Go* and began to walk away from him.

He ran up behind her and stabbed her three quick times in the back. She turned to fend him off and a fourth stab caught her across the palm. Screaming, she fell to her knees. He hung back as she began to crawl away from him. He followed her at a distance of several feet.

oh my God he stabbed me

The man took a step forward, and then – seeing something off-screen – retracted his hands into his sleeves. Eve was screaming, screaming, screaming like a song.

please help me

Then came a new voice.

hey

Jonah watched himself step into the frame.

The man glanced at the camera. He looked lost.

please look at me

The man looked at him.

nobody's going to hurt you

I'm dying

you're going to be okay can you do something for me mister please take a step back

The man tried to come forward but Jonah blocked him.

okay hang on I don't want to

Eve scampered away from them, across the street. The man made to follow her but Jonah grabbed his arm.

listen I don't

Eve slipped from the frame.

nobody wants

On film it looked awkward, anticlimactic, incongruent with his memories. The Raymond he remembered had pressed forward, but the Raymond on the screen was pulling away, losing ground to a Jonah that the real Jonah did not recognize. Yet this was how it had happened. He watched and relearned, his preconceptions shriveling and blowing away. At that moment – as if to emphasize the new truth – something incredible happened, something that allowed Jonah to see firsthand the confusion and terror and dumb trust in Raymond Iniguez's face.

The camera zoomed in.

The fall that he remembered as direct was in fact staggered: Raymond reared back, lifting him off the ground. He convulsed, causing Raymond to tilt and fall to the side. As they went down, Jonah's head banged against the lip of the Dumpster. His legs folded and he pulled Raymond down on top of him, landing hard and hitting his head a second time against the sidewalk. Raymond fell chinfirst atop the knife. He turned over, grabbing at the ground and at his throat. Then he seized up and was still.

That was how it happened.

On-screen, Jonah fumbled out his cell phone and dropped it. He felt around, found it, dialed, dropped it again, reached

blackout

PART II

PSYCHIATRY

CHAPTER 18

'They're growing people for food.'

'Who is?'

'The Polish government. They have them in pods. They incubate them for a hunnert twenty-eight days, number of days you need to become fertile, and then the flesh has properties, the hunnert and twenty-eight languages of the world match, language is fire, they use the bodies for fuel, they have a chamber, the walls are nine thousand cubic meters deep, and a hunnert, a hun – they, all, they they pump the electricity running through the brains, the juice, they feed them juice from Florida, where they built the American Polish consulate.'

So many places to begin. 'You have electricity running through your brain?'

'No. The Polish. Yes. I have electricity in my brain, they put it there.'

'Who did?'

'You're not telling me the truth.'

'Who put the electricity in your brain?'

'Eastern European Jews of Ashkenazi descent. You're a liar.'

'Mr Hooley—'

'They'll grow them and eat them, burn the bodies for fuel, to heat the secret chambers of the Polish information. They breed embryos. You can eat them if you're hungry but then they get angry because they want them for fuel to make orange juice.'

'I see.'

From page twenty of the *Guide to the Third-year Clerkships*:

> The clerkship in psychiatry will be an opportunity for you to learn about many of the most important issues facing medicine today. Treatment of psychiatric disorders constitutes one of the nation's single largest health expenditures. In the course of her or his career every physician will encounter patients requiring mental health care in addition to the primary care being sought.
>
> The clerkship is often less physically demanding than others due to its regular hours and relatively relaxed pace. However, it can be equally – if not more – emotionally demanding. Mild depression is common, as are conflicting feelings about the appropriateness of treatment. These emotions should not be considered unusual or a sign of weakness. Nor should they be ignored; students are encouraged to speak

with their supervisors or call Student Health (× 5–3109) to discuss and resolve issues as they arise.

From page fourteen of the Book:

I AM LOSING MY MIND

or

PSYCHIATRY FOR NONPSYCHIATRISTS

All those of you who aspire to be headshrinkers may flip past this section and go find something useful to read, like a comic book.

Psychiatry is best summed up in one simple phrase: **SPARE TIME**. Now would be a good time to catch up on your sleep or your studying. One of us completed an entire research project while doing psych. It got published, too (*Missour. Jour. of Med.* Vol. 13 N. 2, check it out!), so you could say that we got something out of the experience.

Along with its attendant teaching college, the hospital of Upper Manhattan occupied a demilitarized zone between the Upper East Side and Spanish Harlem. As such, it served two radically different patient populations; helmet-haired Park

Avenue matrons attended by harems of sweaterset-clad daughters roamed the hallways alongside *abuelitas* leaning on Medicare-issued walkers. The neighborhood wasn't truly upper Manhattan, unless you ignored everything north of 96th Street, which plenty of people did: taxicab mapmakers, for instance, who sold tourists on the quaint notion that the Apollo Theater was the farthest tip of the known universe.

The central building of the hospital was similarly split: a decrepit old tower that faced north, overlooking the projects, and a shiny new wing, designed by a Pritzker Prize–winning architect, who had sought and achieved a strict obedience to feng shui. The skylit central atrium that allowed natural light into every patient room also turned the lobby into a massive greenhouse. Shirts adhered to backs; terrazzo planters in full thriving bloom.

The department of psychiatry occupied two non–feng shui'd, non-naturally lit, nonplantered floors of the old wing. Big Green, as the ward was known, had cheery yellow walls. Its nickname had nothing to do with Dartmouth or Fenway Park or jolly canned vegetables, deriving instead from the ostentatious plaque that announced that this portion of the hospital had been funded by a generous grant from the James B. Green Foundation. Other plaques dedicated the nurses' station, the dayroom, the Quiet Room, and the Larson Center for Electroconvulsive Therapy. The looped central hallway was a gift of Frederick and Betty Hall. Nobody called it the Hall Hall.

Compared to surgery, the hours were a joke. He came at eight and left at five; earlier, if there wasn't much to do. Morning conference – table-talks held without the patient present – bled into hour-and-a-half lunches. In the afternoons they paid visits, tweaked meds, offered solace, and called it a day. During stretches of downtime, residents would slip out to jog around the north end of Central Park, returning damp and flush-cheeked.

Along with two other HUMmers, a social worker, and two residents, Jonah belonged to Dr Hugo Rolstein, a spacey, longhaired Freudian relic. Flouting current fashion, Dr Hugo didn't care much for dosing. Nor did he bother to meet with patients, relying on secondhand reports to craft baroque etiological analyses that made reference to his own specially designed psychometric, the Rolstein Curve of Ano-Oral Growth. Chess problems absorbed much of his day, as did a plodding quest to complete the novels of Anthony Trollope.

The real work fell to the senior resident. Four-foot-ten, freshly pressed, flawlessly complected, Bonita Kwan boasted an M.D.-Ph.D. from Johns Hopkins. In childhood she had toured the world as a violin prodigy; one of the HUMmers brought in a CD for her to sign. At the team's introductory meeting, she announced that her interests included the translation of Appalachian folk ballads into Mandarin, Gustav Klimt, and computational neuronal modeling of anxiety across Class Mammalia.

Bonita took everything extremely seriously, providing a necessary foil to Dr Hugo's unstructured disquisitions. Rolly Rounds – conducted from the refuge of his office – could linger on one case for an hour or more, moving on only when Bonita insinuated that perhaps they'd exhausted the implications of whether the man who believed he was de Gaulle had ever witnessed the glory of springtime in the Loire Valley.

There were enough beds to accommodate fifty-five people, mostly in-house referrals or rollovers from the psych ER. The bulk of the patients were either psychotic or depressed, although this was a distinction far from sharp. One woman had tried to hang herself because her husband and all four of her children had died in a housefire. She had no high-school degree, no living relatives in the United States; she hovered over a financial abyss, and her HMO had recently begun to deny her claims, asserting (falsely, she swore) the presence of another provider to cover the cost of her diabetes medication. If her misery didn't justify suicide, Jonah didn't know what did.

Nothing did. Recurrent suicidal ideation was a symptom of mental illness, *Diagnostic and Statistical Manual of the American Psychiatric Association*, Fourth Edition, p. 327.

He said, 'I'm so sorry.'

'You sorry you have to listen to me. You'd rather be playing golf.'

In general, such acid logic – the honesty of pure melancholia – was a rarity on the ward. More typically, patients spent the day doped up, in front of the TV: gowns littered with crumbs; running their hands over oily, discontiguous hair. They talked to themselves or with each other, conversations that never went anywhere, each participant a prisoner of his own quiddities.

Schizophrenia destroyed people in two ways: first, by coring them of speech and affect, and then by slapping over the husk a wild mask of paranoia and delusion. Meds took reasonable care of the latter problems but had little impact on the former, with the result that patients often appeared not docile but crushed and impotent. Their language was alien, a mosaic of non sequiturs that could melt from innocuous to bizarre to sinister in seconds. Taking a history was like being stuck on an exquisitely difficult blind date.

Have you been employed recently?

Oh sure. Got to try. Got to keep going. Pratice makes perfect.

What do you mean by that?

I once thought about trying to see, but how many years did it take the prophets? Plenty. My father went for a lesson on the road. They went fishing.

Fishing?

What I said, practice makes perfect.

They called it 'flight of ideas' but the term didn't fit. There was nothing elevated or soaring about these semantic wrecks, these verbal crash-and-burns. And if it was confusing, frustrating, or frightening to listen to, it was a thousand times worse for the speaker: living with a mind that gagged itself, wrestled itself, cut out its own tongue.

Aside from the man afraid of the Polish conspiracy – whose membership rapidly expanded to include Bulgarians, Romanians, Russians, and the hapless citizenry of Djibouti – there was a woman who believed herself invincible and liked to drink, would drink anything, would chug a gallon of contrast dye; a man who talked to stave off the voice of his dead uncle, a priest, whom he described as 'a little faggot living in my ear'; a bus driver who'd gotten into a scuffle with a cop over a purported threat of impalement (not *necessarily* false, said Dr Hugo, citing Abner Louima); and a one-legged crack addict who insisted he was John Lennon. To prove his point, he would launch into 'Sweet Home Alabama.'

Jonah suggested that they try sending him to music therapy.

'He gets too upset. He thinks he wrote all the songs.'

You had to laugh. If you didn't, you'd drown. All pain, from adolescent heartbreak to the throb of a burst appendix, originated in the brain. Mental illness, then, was a distillate of pain, pain without physical pretense. Just as heroin produced

236

a euphoria unconnected to – and therefore better than – reality, psychiatric disorders created agony without referent or peer. The hallways of Big Green fairly swam with suffering. You saw it in the unwilled movements and bodily agitation; in the eyes that never settled; fearfully, constantly, seeking the next distraction, a new suspicion. You saw it manifest in a hundred piddling regulations: no pens, no safety razors; no nail clippers, CDs, cameras, cellular phones, or iPods.

'iPods?'

'They use the hard drives to cut themselves.' Bonita pointed to four screwholes in the Quiet Room ceiling. 'We had to remove the smoke detector. Someone broke it open and tried to slash her wrists.'

The suffering surged, foamed, receded, returned. Supplied by the patients, it was refracted in their families and friends: torn up yet bored; embarrassed at what had become of their loved ones; further embarrassed at being embarrassed; then angry for being made to feel embarrassed; then ashamed at having insufficient grace and patience. An awful negative feedback loop that Jonah knew like catechism.

What got him worst was seeing his first Code. On a medical floor, Codes meant cardiac arrest. All available doctors would come running, swinging their credentials like tomahawks, ready to deliver badass emergency resuscitation; and – upon discovering, inevitably, that the situation had been stabilized – would commence to mill around, restless and disappointed, like the crowd at a political concession speech.

Psych Codes, on the other hand, meant that a patient had gone violent, pitching furniture around the room; threatening to injure or attempting to do so. Jonah's second day on the job, while conducting an intake interview, he heard the page, the shouting, and leaned his head out to see if he could help. A young woman, frothing at the mouth, delivered imprecations and sobbed as several brawny nurses and one cop fitted her into four-point restraints and dropped a syringe into her thigh. She fought and fought and then she was still, dead still, flash-frozen, spittle trickling down her slack cheek. Though he knew they were acting in her best interest, Jonah could not bear to look, because the girl had black hair and he attributed features to her face that he knew weren't there.

Over the last five years of his life he'd mastered the art of splitting himself in two, the better to cope with divided loyalties and morals. That week, however, he achieved a new level of dissociation.

Professional at work, he soothed his patients and participated in the ward's gallows humor. His superiors praised his knowledge and remarked on his maturity. He had a knack for keeping people calm, they said. He said he'd done some charity work.

The moment he left the hospital, though, his heart began to pound, and he found himself plagued by the same sorts of ideas he heard all day long from people he knew to be severely – clinically – paranoid.

You are a great artist.

Now we can create together.

He saw her ogling him as he hurried to the subway. Heard her snicker when he slipped going up his front steps. Streetsigns and shop signs, festooned with her visage, sprouted and then receded as he turned to look. Crossing 12th Street, nearing the elm – her elm, the spot where she had greeted him every day for two months, thrown her arms around him like he was a war hero – knotted his throat, brightened the low-grade nausea that nagged him all day long.

On Thursday night, he took out his *DSM-IV* and flipped to the section on anxiety. His own behaviors fell across an alarmingly wide range of disorders, so that he could not simply shoehorn himself into GAD or PTSD. This in turn worried him further: worse than cracking up was doing it without a validating nomenclatural imprimatur.

The key difference between him and his patients was that they feared the impossible; whereas the movie of him was *him*. The other stuff might be fake (he prayed it was; that angry *snip* kept tunneling up through his consciousness), but *he* was real. The fight was real. A genuine tape of a fake stabbing that had led to a mistaken but actual death.

If the lawsuit accused him of misreading the situation, leaping to attack the Dangerous Ethnic Man

239

– that was true, wasn't it? Why *had* he assumed that the man was the attacker? That Raymond had been carrying a knife and mumbling to himself; that Eve had been crawling and screaming – none of that seemed as salient now as the clues and traces of clues that *something had not been right.* He should have asked why a woman would be walking alone in a lousy neighborhood at that hour. He should have noticed how slowly she'd been moving; should have noted the choreographed quality, the mise-en-scène of it all. He should have seen the reluctance in Iniguez's face, obvious when watched from a different angle and without the lens of adrenaline. He should have spotted the camera; should've called the cops instead of rushing in to play savior.

And why hadn't she said anything? Too busy zooming in. *Oh that's great, so spontaneous, I'm loving it, LOVING IT, brilliant, give in to the moment and run with it baby run run run run run.*

He had made the worst mistake possible. And she had managed her angles.

Certainly she was taking her time, allowing him to digest this new information; though he believed she might appear at any time: as she had that first night on his sofa, as she had in the bookstore. Had she been following him then? Why not. Maybe she had been following him before that. Maybe she had set the accident up. How far back could he spool out this insanity? The answer, if he wound himself up sufficiently, was forever.

In the meantime he would take no chances.

On the second Monday of his new rotation, before leaving for work, he peered out the window and saw a woman in a puffy coat waiting up the block, a size and shape close enough to hers that he took his bag and went creeping idiotically down the fire escape. As he reached the ground he discerned that it was not Eve but an old man smoking a cigar.

He thought *No chances.*

For days he had trouble sleeping. The DVD sat buried in his desk, its presence pushing up through the wood. He kept waiting for the room to burst into flames.

He told no one. Who would it help. Not him. Not Raymond Iniguez or Simón Iniguez or Roberto Medina. These people already wanted to string him up, and admitting that he'd made a mistake – however well intentioned – was not likely to earn him Most Favored Nation status. Moreover, he had no one to tell. His parents? Vik? Lance? All they could do was freak out. Belzer?

Wear a sign says Please Sue Me, why doncha. Cmon, kiddo, what's done is done.

He had no crime to report – except his own. Eve hadn't done anything besides talk oddly and get him off in public places. She'd never threatened him, never made a suggestion of harming him. She would never. Because, of course, she loved him.

That was what was so disarming about his anxiety: transformed into a basketcase at the flip of a switch, he knew he had flipped the switch himself. Having made the slightest gesture, she stood back to let him stew in silence, knowing that his dark imagination, his overcooking guilt engine, would provide the rest. A sickening litany of *maybes*. Maybe he was a murderer. Maybe she intended to do to him what she'd done to Raymond. Maybe she would do nothing.

Silence; *maybe*; terror. Three synonyms in the modern lexicon: one way to win and an infinity of losses.

He was eating himself from the inside out.

You are a great artist.

And she believed he liked it.

Without a clear sense of the tape's legal ramifications, he balked at calling the police or the DA. He didn't consider himself a criminal. He had acted decisively at a moment of crisis. Human error. People nevertheless liked to assign blame; they sought moral deep pockets. Spreading the tape around was the surest way to bring the consensus to bear on him and, maddeningly, him alone. As far as he knew, it wasn't illegal for Eve to stand by and say nothing.

Or maybe it was. He had no clue. Either way, she didn't seem overly concerned about sending him a copy, knowing, perhaps, that he'd be too scared to show it to anyone else. She was right. Glued together in a private truth; a universe of two, exactly as she wanted.

CHAPTER 19

FRIDAY, NOVEMBER 19, 2004.
INPATIENT PSYCHIATRIC SERVICE, WEEK TWO.

Bonita said, 'You're buzzing again.'

ID UNAVAILABLE

He switched off his phone and resumed eating his burrito. 'It's my mom.'

'She must really like you, that's the sixth time in the last ten minutes.'

'Is it?' He fanned himself with his oily paper plate. 'I hadn't noticed.'

That afternoon he came up from the subway at first Avenue, and there she was, umbrella-less in the rain, outstretched arms forking the pedestrian traffic, and grinning, grinning.

'My love.'

He pivoted like a wooden soldier retreating into the body of a clock and turned onto 14th, ducking into a Subway sandwich shop and running to the counter, coming face-to-sneeze-shield-to-face with a pimply kid who said *Can I help you.*

A stack of cheese with hard edges; a bucket of gloppy tuna fish; gray cold cuts.

Behind him, two men in painter's jeans and construction-company sweatshirts devoured meatball subs. They were built like armadillos, all neck and shoulders. One of them wore a Giants cap with a long, flat, stickered brim; the other a blue bandanna, tied sweatband-style, that moved as he chewed and studiously pored over the nutritional information printed on his napkin. Cap said, 'Yo man, you *learnin* some shit?'

Hoping to wait her out, Jonah bought a large drink, his grip on the proffered cup shooting fault lines across its waxy surface. He stood at the soda dispenser, back to the storefront, adding one half-inch spurt at a time, letting that fizz out completely before adding another. The meatball eaters got up and left. When the cup was full, Jonah poured three inches out and started again.

'No refills.'

Jonah said, 'Is there a woman outside, brown hair, about five-three, wearing a purple skirt and a down jacket?'

'I don't see nobody.'

Leaving the soda on the counter, he exited and went east, hurrying past delis and Immaculate Conception and the post office. He began to feel safe, he'd gotten away from her, *good job, Superman* and then a hand fell on his shoulder.

He flew one hundred eighty degrees, bumping into a white girl with cornrows who yelled *Asshole* and speed-sashayed away, her negligible frame lost beneath gigantic jeans with dirty, curling cuffs.

Eve laughed. 'You're agitating the natives.'

A neon sign outlining MILLER TIME coppered her hair. He had never seen her in braids before; they took five years off her already young face. She was beautiful, no way around that, and he unexpectedly began to get hard, and had to shove his hands into his pockets, tamping down desire by picturing the bombed-out body beneath her coat.

'No,' he said.

'No what? I haven't said anything worthy of reply. Unless you mean to dispute my statement about the natives and agitation and so forth, in which case, I concede. It was a throwaway comment anyhoo.'

'I'm not talking to you.'

'This is public space, Jonah Stem. We're standing in the middle of the street. And why shouldn't I come here?' She gestured to the towers of Stuy Town. 'Fond reminiscences. Childhood. A stroll down the lily-lined lanes of youth. Why have you been avoiding me.'

He turned to go and she came in front of him.

'Get out of the way.'

'You're being very rude,' she said. He started around her and she danced back. 'I take it you received my gift?'

He removed her hand from his arm and walked on.

'Is that a yes?'

'You're sick,' he said.

'*Tsk*.'

'I called the police.'

'No you didn't,' she said.

He said nothing.

'You're being rather cold, don't you think?'

'You want to do fucked-up stuff like that, find someone else.'

'But you're so good at it.'

He said nothing.

'I've waited for you to no avail. I tried waiting for you in the morning but you never seem to come out, either. What gives? I call and you don't answer. Do you get my messages? I love you. Then I said to myself, said I, Eve, you should go straight to the source. I went back to the hospital but you weren't there. Hence today's plan. Well, it worked. Why are you walking away.'

'Don't touch me.'

'It's been three weeks, you must be exploding.'

Again he tried to go around her, but she got in his way and puckered up and threw her arms around his neck. Startled, he jerked back, pulling their bodies flush.

'Let go.'

'Is this about another woman?' she asked. 'Is this about Hannah?'

'Let go of me, Eve.'

'Don't you see that I love you?'

'For the last time: *let go.*'

She kissed his chin, his neck. 'I'm better than her.' He was pushing her away, twisting his face away from hers, keeping her at bay but barely. Then the strain on his back octupled: she had lifted her feet up and was dangling from his neck, so that he wore her like a living necklace, a rapper's berserk accessory. His spine torqued and pain shot through his trunk and he emitted humiliatingly feminine grunts. She sucked at his face. *Think of her as a child, you can't hit a child whenever it makes you angry.* He would not hit her. Anything but that, because he knew she wanted him to. He ground his fingers into her solar plexus; she responded by using both legs to tourniquet him at the waist, trapping one of his hands. He would not hit her. He pressed a thumb into her throat, pushed it harder, it could not have been less natural for him to do this but he had to. He pretended that he was strangling an inflatable doll. His thumb disappeared in her neck up to the first knuckle; he felt her windpipe giving in. And she hung on, gagging, her saliva running down his neck. He could not bear her weight. He fell to his knees. Immediately she capitalized on his lack of balance by springing on top of him, her belly to his back, her head near his tailbone, flattening him facedown on the wet sidewalk. She clamped her thighs around his head: his neck was a champagne bottle and his skull a stubborn cork.

Her pantyhose sandpapered his cheeks. She sunk her fingernails in his hamstrings, her nose in his ass, as though she intended to munch through the seat of his pants. He had never seen the ground in the City this close-up before. Filth gummed up the cracks in the sidewalk, got under his fingernails as he tried to do a push-up and his wrist slid through an oatmealy glop of cigarette butts and newspaper.

He got partway up when a suckerpunch of light caused him to slip and fall. A skinny kid in an NYU hoodie stood focusing a 35mm. Jonah cursed at him through a blinking field of red dots and green pennants and he sauntered away. Two women passed; one of them muttered *Filming*. What the hell was wrong with New Yorkers that they could watch people wrestling in the middle of the sidewalk in the rain and comment solely on the situation's aesthetics? He needed a superhero wannabe, someone like him, who'd read about his deed in the paper and spent nights prowling Manhattan, awaiting his chance. Although for all he knew it looked like *he* was the bad guy.

With a heave he straightened up, dumping her on her back. On her way down she grabbed his shirt, causing his top button to pop off. She latched onto his leg like a fungus round the base of a tree.

'Let go of my fucking— *let go*.' He yanked at her ears, pressed her throat again. 'I'm going to break your fucking neck.'

'You're losing your property,' she said with a nod. He turned to see a guy picking up his backpack.

'Hey,' Jonah yelled. 'That's mine.'

The guy looked at him, at Eve, and walked on, dropping the backpack in the gutter.

'Always looking out for you,' she said.

He spoke into her ear. 'Enjoy this,' he said, 'because it's going to be the last time.' Then he slammed his elbow into her temple. She went loose, and he shook free, grabbed his backpack, and stumbled down the block.

He'd covered no more than five yards when she let out a bloodcurdling howl.

Stop him he stole my bag

Instinct instructed him to stop and defend himself. *What do you mean* your—

Not the time. He ran.

Stop him stop somebody stop him

He barreled down Avenue A, his bag jiggling against his body like a potbelly; fishing out his keys, slotting the correct one between his fingers, glancing back—

Stop him

He didn't see it coming; all he felt was a gritty jawbone crunch, like he'd bitten down on a marble, followed by the miserable sensation of involuntarily changing vectors, a kite nosediving in a murderous crosscurrent.

When he opened his eyes he was on his back, surrounded by four columns of white, paint-stained denim. Two broad, wary, disgusted black faces peered down at him, as though from a great height. Jonah wondered for a moment if he was in his own grave, waiting for dirt to fall. He hurt too much to move.

Cap was holding the backpack.

'Is he okay? Jonah?'

'I got your bag,' said Cap. 'He'll wait here with you, I'ma call the cops.'

Eve brushed her fingernails across Jonah's forehead. 'My love . . . It's all right,' she said to the men. 'He's my husband. We had a fight. We'll be fine.'

The men exchanged a look.

'My love, are you okay?'

Jonah moaned.

'Thank you.'

'You sure you don't want us to call the cops?'

'Thank you. Yes. That was brave of you.'

Cap shook his head, prompted Bandanna with a shrug, and they ambled away.

'Wait,' Jonah croaked.

'Shh . . .' Eve restrained him. 'Rest, my love. Convalesce. Recuperate. These heavenly tears shall cleanse you. They have healing properties. Shhh . . .'

Rain came down in waves, forming pools in the crenellated asphalt. His hair sopped up City juices; his shirtfront grew heavy. Eve's face floated over his, the dripping ends of her braids echoing the soggy denuded canopy of the elm, her elm. Rain stung his eyes, went up his nose. Cornices wept. He smelled sewage and cat hair. He was going to drown in the middle of the East Village.

'It's Fate,' she said. 'I'm your mission, Jonah Stem. And you mine. When you walk, I am the stones beneath your feet. When you come home at night, I am your bed. During the day I'm your air and when you die I will be the earth that enfolds you. I am everywhere. So it's not worth mucking about.' She smiled. 'Now. Shall I take you up and make you some tea?'

He forced himself up. His head fucking killed.

'Lucky you,' Eve said, 'I was there to tell them to let you go. Chivalry lives.'

He grabbed his backpack, staggered up, staggered across the street.

'A little gratitude,' she called.

He mounted the steps to his building.

'Can't we be courteous about this? Must I resort to extremes?'

He reached into his jacket pocket for his keys.

'Are you going to answer me?'

His jacket pocket was empty.

'Looking for these?'

As she hurried away he slipped on the wet concrete steps, reaching out to grab the stone bannister, missing, grating the back of his hand.

'Are you sure this is necessary, dude?'

'I told you, I'll pay for it.'

'That's not what I mean, I mean are you like

having a, like a . . .' For want of a conclusion, Lance wiggled his fingers in the air.

'They got my ID and my keys,' Jonah said.

The locksmith said, 'Better safe than sorry.'

'This is the strongest one you make?'

'Medeco. Only Superman could break it.'

'Dude, that's you.'

Including the fee for evening service, it came to three hundred nineteen dollars. Jonah had never been happier to write a check.

'I'm putting the chain on when you go out,' he told Lance.

'I won't be able to get back in.'

'I'll take it off before I go to sleep. Or I'll wait up until you come home.'

'Aren't you being—'

'Better safe than sorry.'

'They say that so you'll buy more product, dude. It's a cliché.'

'If someone follows you, don't come into the building. Walk around the block. In general, try and keep a lookout.'

Lance gawked. 'Are you sure – okay, dude, don't tweak, I'll keep a lookout . . . You know, your face looks pretty fucked up.'

'I told you, the guy hit me. I need some ice, it'll be fine.'

'You don't want to get out for a—'

'I'm sure, Lance, I'm sure what I need is to *relax*, okay?' He went to his room and dialed his parents. As the phone rang the front door creaked open and closed, making his heart gulp. He peeked out. The living room was empty. *Lance leaving, that's all. You have a new lock, use it.* He turned the bolt as the machine picked up.

You have reached the home of Paula and Steven Stem . . .

'Mommommommom—'

'Golly, golly, here I am. Hold your horses, lemme—' Feedback squalled and died. 'Hello, my dear son. Calling me on Friday night, how thoughtful.'

'Mom, listen. I had my keys and my wallet stolen.'

'Oh no, where?'

'I d – at the gym.'

'Did you have a lock?'

'Yes, but—'

'Sometimes they look closed,' his mother said, 'and then they fall open. You should make sure it's locked.'

'I will, next time, I promise. Listen, you need to change the locks at home.'

'Here?'

'My driver's license has that address on it.'

'We have a good security system,' his mother said.

'Mom, please. It'd make me feel better if—'

'Cripes, we're going to have to cancel the credit card.'

'What?'

'My card that you have. The Mastercard.'

'No, no – you don't need to cancel that.'

'Why not?'

'That card in particular wasn't lost. I have it, uh, I keep it separate.' He felt in no state to be ad-libbing.

'You're going to need a new driver's license.'

'I'll handle it, okay? Just please change the locks.'

His mother sighed. 'Jonah . . .'

'Please.'

'All right, all right. I'll get somebody out here on Monday.'

'Can't you do it now?'

'It's ten o'clock, Jonah.'

'They come twenty-four hours. We had someone here tonight.'

'If your license has our address, why did you change *your* locks?'

'Just – I – I have another ID. With this address on it.'

'You have *two* driver's licenses?'

To get her to comply, he had to resort to yelling, which he hated to do, and he hung up feeling like a jerk. He insisted on getting his way, though, because doing so gave him a sense of achievement when in fact he felt oarless.

Tackling him counted as an assault, he supposed; although who was to say that he hadn't gone after her first? He had hit her in the head, after all. She was probably just as banged up, probably worse, and she was a woman. A small woman, a helpless woman. Everybody wanting to save her, little girl lost, her heroes.

Besides, it would take more than an upper-middle-class twit med student whinging about a playground scuffle to get the NYPD in gear. They had better things to do than run cover for him. *Don't you read the news? This isn't storytime, it's Jihad Vigilance Fucking Central.*

He changed the icepack on his chin and lay down, his chest backfiring with each of those cause-less cracks people call *the house settling.* The ice passed from cold to painful to warm. He'd been bleeding from the head when he came in. Scalp lacerations looked worse than they were. He'd seen them before. He could handle it on his own.

CHAPTER 20

He spent the weekend holed up, ordering Chinese, leaving money in an envelope taped to the door, with written instructions to put the food on the ground. The delivery men nevertheless rang until he acknowledged them.

You wan receipt.

Leave it in the bag.

Okay mistah.

He waited by the door, waited for a silence unattainable in the City. He waited, knowing that his food was getting cold, the syrup collecting at the bottom of his General Gao's chicken, the breading peeling like a popped blister. He didn't care. He waited until hunger and shame got the better of him, then unlocked and unchained the door.

Each time his cell phone rang – and it did so with increasing frequency – dread punched through his neck.

ID UNAVAILABLE

He called his provider to ask about blocking her number. Someone in Bangalore politely informed him that without the actual number they could do nothing.

He took the battery out of the phone.

On Saturday morning he called the super – a cantankerous Slav with watery eyes and torrential postnasal drip – and confessed that he'd lost his keys along with his wallet. Yes, they should probably put a new lock on the building. Yes, he'd pay. Yes, he was sorry. Gesundheit, Mr Randjeiovic. No, it wouldn't happen again. Yes, goddamn Steinbrenner, maybe next year.

Mr Randjeiovic's locksmith charged thirty percent more than the other guy. Cutting keys for all the residents added up, too. Jonah didn't care. He'd barely spent a dime over the last six months; the constraints of third-year inflicted an involuntary frugality. He briefly considered installing an alarm.

He told himself that all these precautions were just that: precautions. Rations of time and peace of mind. Besides, living in Manhattan made hermitage seem not only reasonable but ideal; people paid heavy premiums for privacy. What could be more exclusive, more private, than never ever leaving your apartment?

Lance, mystified by his roommate's sudden agoraphobia – and characteristically willing to accept new weirdnesses without question – stayed in as a show of solidarity. They sat in the living room, playing a video game in which shirtless homies vied to be the most ruthless gangsta in da hood. It was Sunday evening.

'This game encourages moral values.'

'Yeah.'

'If you could pick any criminal in history to be, who would it be?'

'Al Capone.'

'I *knew* you'd—' Lance jerked the controller. 'No. *No.* NOOOOO.'

They watched his character eat a hand grenade.

'What about you?'

'Me, I'd totally be the Riddler. The greatest criminal mind of our century.' Lance revived his character. 'Crap, I have to get the bazooka all over again.'

Forty-eight hours of this had driven Jonah to the brink. He saw himself as the character in the game: vaporized by stasis, returned to the beginning of the conversation to make the same stupid jokes. The apartment had begun to smell like the psych ER, its atmosphere congealing, as though they were breathing broth.

'We're living in a submarine,' Jonah said.

'A yellow submarine?'

'More like a depressing shit-brown submarine.'

Lance said, 'You're going to need groceries.'

Jonah made him promise to check for strangers before entering the building.

'Whatever you say, dude.'

'It's important.'

'Ten-four. I'll stock you up so you'll be okay while I'm away.'

Jonah blinked. 'Away?'

'I'm going to see the Count. Uh-membuh?'

He hadn't.

'It's been on the books since the summer. Dude, you sound *baked*. You're going to miss me, huh? Don't worry, I'll write.'

Lance came back from the bodega with peanut butter, bread, some apples.

'Did you see anyone out there?'

'All clear.'

Jonah nodded. While Lance had been gone, he'd put the battery back in his phone and discovered 47 MISSED CALLS.

'Do you think I should bring a bathing suit? The guy definitely has an indoor pool. Check out what he sent me.' Lance stopped his packing, pawed through his bag until he found a jewelry box, in which sat a pair of matte gold cufflinks inset with rubies. 'If I play my cards right this could be serious Paycheck. My mom wants me to like this guy. She told me she thinks he might be The One. Believe you me, I'm as skeptical as you. It's mathematically impossible for him to be The One. At best he can be, like, The Seven. I don't think my mom's ever had a first boyfriend. She started dating in the womb. She dated sperm.'

'Thanks for sharing.'

'It's either embrace the concept of my mom being a total fuckin slutbag, or resent her and further denormalize our relationship.' Lance rolled up a pair of wrinkled cargo pants. 'I hear the Count has fabulous taste in hydroponics.'

'It's nice that you have common interests,' Jonah said.

'We're botanically inclined. The family that smokes together, stays together.'

'That doesn't rhyme.'

'The truth doesn't fuckin rhyme, dude. It doesn't need to.' Lance strapped his video camera into its padded case and absentmindedly wound the power cable around his hand. 'Someday they'll discover the chemical that causes infatuation. Vitamin L. The world as we know it will come to an end. Have they found that already?'

'It's called alcohol.'

Lance laughed. He hefted his luggage and found it acceptably light. 'You sure you're going to be okay without me?'

Jonah nodded.

'Cause I don't want to hear about you having a spaz attack in my absence. In case of loneliness, I keep a limited but high-quality selection of adult entertainment under my bed. You know where the real movies are. Feel free to get cultured.'

Lance's flight left Kennedy at nine, and for the first time in their roommateship he went to bed first. Unable to sleep, Jonah sat watching the Museum of Human Frailties. It was raining again, the asphalt a mirror.

MONDAY, NOVEMBER 22, 2004.
INPATIENT PSYCHIATRIC SERVICE, WEEK THREE.

In the morning he left in a hurry. He took a circuitous route to the subway, stopping to buy snacks he did not want and crossing 14th.

When you walk, I am the stones beneath your feet.

He jogged through Stuy Town, then doubled back and descended into the station, bypassing an old Russian woman hobbling along with a laminated picture of a bearded man in a cassock.

When you come home at night, I am your bed.

Instead of pushing through a turnstile, he crossed in front of the token booth and ran up the other stairs. Above ground, he dashed for the uptown bus.

During the day I'm your air

There he changed to a crosstown, catching the ⑥ at Grand Central.

and when you die I will be the earth that enfolds you.

Nobody on his team seemed to care that he was fifteen minutes late. Rolstein greeted him with a wave. Stifling a yawn, Jonah donned his game face and took out his notes. He had patients to present. He was a professional. Wake up.

Bonita passed him some files, along with a Post-it on which she'd scribbled *OK?*

I am everywhere. So it's not worth mucking about.

He wrote *water pipe emergency sorry* and pushed the note back to her.

★   ★   ★

At the hospital he was required to leave his phone on, should a patient or resident call, and was thus unable to do anything except play calm when he got a call from ID UNAVAILABLE, which by two P.M. had happened fifty-nine times.

He could get a beeper and leave the cell at home. Or get a new cell, with a delisted number. It wasn't a big deal to change your number. People did it all the time.

Are you going to get a new identity, too?

Going home he got off three stops early and flagged a cab, instructing the driver to overshoot his street and drop him at Avenue C and Seventh, enabling him to approach his building from the opposite direction. He skirted Tompkins Square Park, passing supafly whiteboys in rastafarian hats and a swish middle-aged man walking a Yorkie in a green Burberry vest.

As he crossed near the 7A diner, the oily scent of french fries hit him hard. He had eaten nothing today, not for lack of time but because his gut was a trampoline, waiting to deflect whatever he consumed in the form of heartburn. He reshouldered his backpack and fell in line behind a bookcase of a man lumbering up Avenue A. Between Ninth and Tenth the man stepped into a doorway, killing Jonah's screen and affording an unobstructed view of the intersection at Eleventh.

Eve was nowhere.

He took the stairs in long, dorky leaps, rushing into his apartment and throwing all the locks.

Panic lubricated irrationalities: had she been on the train. Had she paid off all the cabbies in lower Manhattan to be on the lookout for him. Could she have been watching from a window. Was there any other way in. Could she squeeze through the vents like human toothpaste, scale the exterior wall, slip through the crack beneath the door, will you think normally, you're inside, you're here, she's not. Calm down, calm down, *calm the fuck down*.

The radiator hammered to life; he jumped.

Several hours later, he felt calm enough to try for sleep, so he put his books aside and fell into nightmares. The first found him in a deserted urban war zone, the sky apocalpytic orange, burnt husks of cars and ravaged bodies of dogs and faceless children. He was running with someone piggybacked, his legs wearing out, he could not carry her (it was a her, he knew, and she was alive, although he could not see her face), he would have to dump her to save himself. He heard an air-raid siren. Then he woke up but the air-raid siren continued.

He rolled over. It was three in the morning.

The downstairs buzzer brayed again, fell silent.

He put on his robe, went to the living room, checked the locks. Again the buzzer went on-on-off-on-on-off. *I'm here* it said. I'm here I'm here I'm here. A brief silence; then the pattern changed to an impatient cha-cha: on, on, on-on-on. *Bz bz bz-bz-bzzzzz.*

He closed the door to his bedroom and wrapped

his pillow around his head. Soon the buzzing stopped, displaced by the ringing of the phone. He disconnected it and unplugged the answering machine. He switched off his cell phone and laid in bed, working over his knuckles like a junkie.

She's half your size. (She shakes you like a doll.) Leave her out there. (Ignoring her baits her.) You don't have to leave the apartment, you can stay up here. (You have to leave sometime.) She's not going to put up a tent outside the building. (Why not?) She can't get inside. (She can follow someone else in.) She's persistent but harmless. (They're not mutually exclusive.) You can call the cops. (And tell them what.) She'll go away. (She won't.) She'll go away. His breathing slowed. *She'll go away.* There was silence. *She went away.*

She went away.

He went to the bathroom and swallowed an Advil. He could do this. He had no reason to wig out. First he would allow a margin of, say, a half-hour. Then he would get up, collect his belongings, proceed down the fire escape – with dignity – and get a cab. He would find a cheap hotel for a few days. It would be like a vacation, a characterless room and white walls, he could get some sleep. He was not sweating. He blotted his forehead on his pillowcase. There, he wasn't sweating at all. On Thursday he would go home for Thanksgiving, and there he could relax and make a plan. Once he wasn't feeling so run-down. He would go to work and help people with problems much more serious

264

than his. He felt fine. He wasn't run-down, he was fine. He felt serene, unprecedentedly serene, gulls adrift over the Pacific serene, Carnival Cruises serene. He blotted his forehead again. It would all be taken care of as soon as he had some space, not a problem, there was a knock at the front door.

CHAPTER 21

Jonah Stem.

Jonah Stem, why won't you answer the door? You're not going to make me wait here. Are you?

So cold.

Perchance the changing seasons have cooled your blood.

Where has my fondle-happy lad gone, that lad I know and love so well? That lad knows my crevices. That lad seeks my darknesses.

He's there, I'm sure of it. He yearns for me.

I can feel you behind these walls. These walls are nothing. They are thin and I can tear them down to reach you. At some point, my desire shall overcome my respect for private property. And then I'm coming in.

Let's not let it get to that point.

You have no reason to act like this. We've been heading in one direction the entire time. You can't claim to be *that* surprised. You're a bright young man.

Oh dear. I feel so alone.

I've been nurturing an idea. Do you want to

know what it is? A new project for you and me to execute together. Her most ambitious work yet, sayeth the critics. A rocket of incendiary imagination, a soul-shaking geyser. *The New York Times. The New Yorker. The New York Review of Books.* All waving accolades, paging through thesauri for a particularly pretentious panegyrical pablum to best encapsulate our idiom. You and I, Jonah Stem, we knock em dead.

I thought we could—

Well.

I'm not going to tell you while I'm standing here.

You have to let me in. Then I'll tell you.

You're going to love it.

You're hurting my feelings.

At any rate I thought it would be preferable to have this conversation in person.

Did you enjoy work today?

You looked tired. My poor poor love. Let me give you succor. Don't shun the one who would bind you in her arms. You are a gift and I the bow.

Open up.

This hallway smells. Think of me out here. Your neighbors are probably phoning the authorities as I speak.

Dear officer, there's a poetess on my landing.

But I wager that, if I smiled, Mr Policeman would let me go, and possibly try to buy me a beverage.

Men do that all the time, Jonah Stem. Give me things. One time in the middle of Herald Square a man came up to me out of the blue. He was quite handsome, though not so handsome as you. He put a hand on my neck and whispered in my ear *I bet you taste like maple syrup*.

Do you believe that? What a silly twit. I wonder what his success rate is. It must have worked at least once or twice. This is a big city.

We went to his studio. He had Ansel Adams posters. He had a CD tower in the shape of a large S. His bathroom was tiled in black and white, and the handtowels stank of Calvin Klein. He put on some truly abysmal jazz. There must be a special store that sells music that wretched. Really, though, the sound of mediocrity.

I sat on his papasan. Although I can't be certain, I think he was salivating.

His tongue was like corned beef. He spent a great deal of time kissing the area behind my knee. Some former girlfriend must have told him that that is an erogenous zone. It's possible he read it in a men's magazine.

Before he could do what he intended to do, I said: By the way, Roger – I don't think his name was Roger – Roger, by the way, I want you to know that I have syphilis.

Isn't that funny?

He almost went through with it anyway.

As a present, I left my panties in his kitchen sink. One point for feminism.

Jonah Stem, my back is starting to hurt.

I'm afraid I've offended you.

Have I offended you?

If so, it's only fair to allow me to speak with you face-to-face, so that we may clear the air. I love you to death. Frankly, I find this little display of obduracy disgustingly smug. It's presumptuous of you to believe that I don't know you're there.

I see you from across the City. All I have to do is follow your glow. I could track you across the globe. If you dove into the ocean I would follow in your steamy wake.

We should take a trip together. There are so many places I want to go, so many experiences waiting to be had. I want you to flay me on the silty banks of the Amazon. I want you to lick my wounds like fresh snow atop the high misty peaks of Mount Fuji. I want you to distort me in the halls of Versailles.

Open the door, Jonah Stem.

It doesn't bother me to throw myself against it. I have a thick skull. Did I ever tell you that? When I was but a wee lass I toppled headfirst off a jungle gym. These were the days before playgrounds came with rubber padding standard. But I was fine.

I'm getting bored out here.

To pass the time, and to help you see it my way, I'll tell you a story about a man named Raymond Iniguez. Raymond wasn't much of a collaborator. He was more like a tape recorder.

Now, far be it from me to imply that he was

stupid. To be honest I have no idea how intelligent he was. I never much listened to what he said, and even had I, I would've been in no position to judge.

My understanding is that he was at one time quite vital. Rumor had it he'd once been a contender to play professional baseball. Regardless, I'm sure that the old Raymond could scramble eggs, drive a car, or tell a decent joke.

Not the Raymond I met. By the time I met him, he had the vocabulary of a child. This should help you understand why my work with him was so primitive.

Why it remains unfinished is obvious. For that I have you to thank.

My concern was not his intelligence or lack thereof. My concern was that ethereal quality, that unpinnable *je ne sais quoi* that separates the men from the angels: *talent*. I have a nose for people, Jonah Stem, which is how I knew about you. Raymond gave off a similar scent of promise, although not as subtle and complex as yours.

His was thick and sugary, cloying, at times. You might even say like maple syrup.

We met in one of those classes I used to give to him and his compatriots. Once a week I went to that horrid place they have the gall to call housing. I don't want to begin to discuss my personal feeling; they coop them up like steers. Nothing could be less conducive to the repair of the psyche. Men need to release, Jonah Stem. You

270

can identify with that, I'm sure. But that's neither here nor there.

Raymond fascinated me, because despite what I knew about him, he seemed satisfied and earnest. It was an act, natch, but I could not help admiring him: what a feat of trickery. To look so placid and yet be the epicenter of such rumblings.

Do you know that he almost killed a man? Another teacher at the school where he used to work. He coached high-school baseball. Then he lost his mind and attacked another teacher at the school, breaking his arm with a bat.

Think about that.

People didn't understand; they sought to ameliorate him with drugs and creature comforts. Fill him up, give him ballast, and he'll stay plumb.

They misjudged him. Raymond's turmoil didn't stem from a void, it stemmed from a surplus. He had too much life force; it burst from his eyesockets and tried the tensile strength of his skin. He was gravid, eructing; he was the Übermensch.

The Superman.

Like you.

What misfortune for him, then, to be born into our normative culture.

Raymond was profoundly unhappy, Jonah Stem, and this was why I found his cheery countenance so fascinating.

Both of you have that same determination to be good, although yours is more willing and less knee-jerk. You are both lost. Your goodness springs from

271

hatred, like grass from burnt soil. You don't belong in this world. It would almost be merciful to kill you, Jonah Stem, and spare you the disappointment.

In the difference column, let us note that he often had problems maintaining an erection, a misfortune that has never darkened your doorstep.

Raymond and I didn't communicate well at first. I found him uncouth and – well, I shall come right out and speak it aloud: he *was* stupid, Jonah Stem, stupid as soap.

Now, that isn't always a liability. True, Raymond never appreciated the totality of my work, thinking it all a game. But stupidity is also an emollient. He never argued, the way you do. He did whatever I commanded.

And he was strong. He had arms like most men's legs.

I brought him into the modern world. No mean feat, mind you. Teaching him to type was one of the greater accomplishments of my adult life.

Oh, we had some good times, Raymond and I. Not on the order of the times had by you and me; they lacked the intellectual verve. But enough to whet a lady's appetite.

He helped drag my ideas out of the laboratory and into the big bad streets. As you saw on the tape, he was hardly my first collaborator. Those others, the disembodied hands you saw – niggly prigs, to a man. Too *cerebral*. Always wanting to talk.

Raymond was ready for action.

Parenthetically, love, I add that you are the

perfect blend of bookish and brutish. I feel a fool never having sought out a doctor before; you lot are familiar with the body, and educated as to its limits. What luck: of all doctors, I found *you*.

Your arrival confused him. While I'd warned of the possibility that we could be misunderstood, when it came down to it, he couldn't break character.

I didn't know what to make of you, either. At first I thought to call the whole thing off. I didn't want *you* to be hurt. So messy. But you got going, I couldn't stop you. It was gorgeosity. One of art's glories is that no amount of meticulousness can best the impulsive gesture. You are a creator of the highest order; your instincts, unerring.

Pain is spectacular, Jonah Stem, in the sense of *spectacle*, drawing the eye. Properly done, it's as transformative and cathartic for the performer as for the audience. Think of all our world religions.

The only thing worth watching is the suffering of others. Depending on how close the observer is, the result is either comedy or tragedy.

Watching you and Raymond was a bit of both.

I'm getting tired.

I think I'm going to leave now, Jonah Stem.

I'll see you very soon.

I love you.

CHAPTER 22

'Oy, kiddo. *Oy*.'

'That's what I'm telling you.' He was supposed to be in a seminar on tardive dyskinesia; instead, he was in a room cluttered with Nerfs and paperbacks, standing by the window, gazing out over the Metro North rails where they came aboveground. In two days, he planned to be on one of those trains.

He said, 'She's written me two dozen letters in the last week. And that's not even close to the . . . the number of phone calls.'

'Has she otherwise threatened you? Bodily harm, et cetera.'

'As in, "I'm going to blow up your building"?'

'Anything at all.'

'Not – not exactly in so many words.'

'Did she hurt you?' Belzer asked. 'When she tackled you?'

'. . . no. It wasn't her who—' Jonah shifted the phone to his other ear. 'She didn't exactly *tackle* me.'

274

'Did she *exactly* do anything?'

'She – there were these guys—'

'She has guys with her.'

'They were more like – no.' Raking a hand through his hair. 'I'm not hurt.'

'Okay,' Belzer said. 'Lemme get this straight. She calls. She writes. She follows you around.'

'And breaks into my building.'

'Now wait a second.'

'She was there, she stood there for an hour.'

'All right, but we've got no way of demonstrating that.'

'If they came and, and, took fingerprints—'

'Kiddo, you ask the cops that and they're going to laugh at you.'

'That's a serious crime. Breaking and entering?'

'If if if. Your real problem'll be convincing them to come over in the first place.'

Although he had had much the same thought, hearing it confirmed was like a hammer to the kneecap. 'Isn't there a law against—'

'Against being annoying? There's harassment statutes, and stalking statutes, but they're broad and mostly for when there's more serious stuff going on.'

'This *is* serious stuff.'

'Kiddo—'

'Can't we get a restraining order?'

'That's not what they're used for. They're for people on notice, under arrest, a summons. The cops don't go around making people be nice. Tell her to get lost.'

'I did.' Jonah breathed through his teeth. 'Why are you so averse to me calling the police.'

'You called to ask my advice – I'm glad you did – and I'm giving it to you. I'm not averse to calling them, per se, but I want you to remember that we're still in the process of dealing with a lawsuit to which this woman is not irrelevant. She's not a dealbreaker, but if we can keep her on our good side—'

'You're shitting me,' Jonah said.

'I'm imagining a cataclysm. Not that you should be concerned, but we have to be prepared. What could happen, let's think: Medina gets her to retract. He could have her say something like, "I was scared, I didn't want to implicate him, I wasn't thinking, but *ya know what*? Now that I think about it, prolly he *wasn't* in danger. My imagination ran wild.' They could make anything up. The guy is a liar. He could promise her a cut of the winnings. Who the hell knows. Not that it should make a difference, let me stress, because I don't believe anyone would buy it. But it would make me happier if she wasn't out to get you. Golly, kiddo, what've you gotten yourself *into*?'

Jonah started to object to that phrasing but faltered. He had called Belzer intending to tell him about the DVD; but he no longer knew what that would achieve. 'Last night I barricaded myself in my apartment.'

'Jesus. Jonah, are you nuts?'

'She's scaring the shit out of me.'

There was a silence.

'Is there something you're not telling me?' Belzer asked.

Down the hall a door opened, and two residents emerged, laughing. One of them said *New meaning to the phrase double-blind* . . . Jonah waited until the squeak of their soles faded, then said:

'I slept with her.'

'You what? Why did you do *that*?'

'She started – showing up. We – it happened. I know it was a bad idea—'

'No kidding it was a bad idea.'

'I know, but it's already happened.'

'This is . . .' Belzer paused. 'I don't know *what* this is.'

'All the other stuff happened after I'd told her I didn't want to see her anymore. I'm sorry I didn't tell you earlier, it was personal.'

'Oy.'

'I'm sorry.'

'*Oy* . . . Well, what can I say. It's a free country.'

'If I thought it would help to call her, I'd do it in a second. It won't. First of all, I tried telling her, in person. And second, I don't have her phone number—'

'Look it up.'

'She's unlisted. I don't have her address. I don't have anything.'

'There I may be able to help you,' said Belzer. 'She gave a statement to the police. Lemme see what I can dig up. Meantime steer clear of her.

Next time she shows or does anything bizarre, call nine-one-one. If you get lucky and they do decide to bust her on harassment, they'll put out a TOP. Temporary Order of Protection. Then if she violates that, that's criminal contempt, which is a felony.' He sneezed. 'Although – look. It's still only a piece of paper.'

Jonah said nothing.

'Have we told Mom and Dad?'

'Of course not.'

'You're my client. I'd never disclose anything. But I think they should know.'

'With all due respect, Chip, that's the worst idea in the world.'

'As a father, I can tell you that any initial worry is nothing compared to what you feel when you find out your kid's been keeping something from you. You start wondering about all the *other* things they haven't told you.'

'I'm twenty-six.'

'I'm saying, is all.'

'Help get her off my back and they never have to know about it.' Having unburdened himself, he was starting to relax; and now he wondered if he'd blown the problem out of proportion. He said, 'It's not a big deal.'

'Don't tell the police that,' Belzer said. 'Not if you want to get any help.'

'If there's a way to fix this without getting them—'

'Kiddo. Where you coming from? First you call

me up like a madman, now you tell me it's not a big deal. Either it is or it isn't.'

Jonah was silent.

'I understand that you don't want to run yourself into the ground. But you gotta tell me: you want to take steps to stop this or not?'

'Yes.'

'Then fine. I'll give her a call, make lawyerly noises. That'll send her packing.'

Jonah shook his head. 'Sure.'

'If it's a big deal, we'll take care of it. If it's not a big deal, it's not a big deal. Either way you're gonna be fine. I'll call you in a few days. Have a good Thanksgiving, my love to everyone.'

'Okay.' Jonah hung up. The ward flooded back into his consciousness: agony, futility, fury. He straightened his tie and went back to work.

WEDNESDAY, NOVEMBER 24, 2004.
INPATIENT PSYCHIATRIC SERVICE, WEEK THREE.

His mother pretended not to care that he couldn't come home early.

'We're happy to have you at all,' she told him. 'Although you did promise.'

'I said *might*. I have to work.'

'What time is your train?'

'I'm taking the ten twenty-three.'

'Tonight?'

'A.M. Ten twenty-three A.M.'

'Oh.' His mother sighed volubly.

'Cut that out.'

'I'm allowed to sigh,' she said. 'Someday soon you'll sigh, when your children would rather work than spend time with you.'

'Mom—'

'Sometimes I cry at night, thinking about how empty my nest has grown. I weep and weep . . . there's water damage in the master bedroom.'

'Maybe if you made Peking duck I'd come home more often.'

'*Touché*, my lovely son.'

He smiled nervously. His heart was beating too fast. He glanced at the window near the fire escape, where stood the upended sofa, filmy bottom facing him, the whole shebang buttressed with chairs and his nightstand. As a finishing touch he'd pushed the dining-nook table over and weighed it down with all his books. If nothing else, he'd created a psychological deterrent. 'I get in at eleven. Are you going to pick me up?'

'Someone will,' she said. 'I'm not going to promise it'll be me. I don't make promises that I can't keep.'

CHAPTER 23

Thursday, November 25, 2004.
Thanksgiving.

He almost missed the ten twenty-three. Nightmares kept him up until three, and when he finally sank under, he slept deeply, knowing he did not have to get up for work. He hit the snooze button four and five and six times. When the radio announced it was 1010 WINS News time nine thirty-six, he grabbed his backpack and a bottle of wine and flew down the steps, and hailed a cab trundling sadly up 14th Street.

'Grand Central, please.'

'Tucky day,' said the cabbie.

'Excuse me?'

'You gwan to eat tucky today.'

'Uh – sure. You?'

'*Yyyuh.*' The cabbie winked at him in the rearview mirror, put in an earpiece, and began a rapid creole patter.

The train car he picked had a smattering of people spaced two and three rows apart: a ruddy girl in a Barnard sweatshirt; a lady in stretch pants clutching a snakeskin bag as though it had previously attempted to escape; a youngish guy in a trenchcoat and Timberlands, thumbing a portable video-game console. Apparently, most good children had kept their promises to their mothers and gone home yesterday.

The ticket taker wished everyone a happy holiday. When he came to Jonah, he motioned to the wine and said, 'Personally, I prefer Chianti, but you shouldn't have.'

Manhattan devolved into the Bronx's moonscape. Somewhere out there – beyond donut shops, concrete crapstacks, discount-furniture warehouses, incomplete urban renewal, unrestored parks – lived the Iniguez family. Were they celebrating? Did they have a turkey? Did they plaster paper pilgrims to the insides of their windows? Did they say grace and go around the table praising God for another twelve months of His Mercies, all the while cursing Him silently for taking their Ramón? Did they pray that Jonah Stem, medical student, superhero murderer, a grainy newsprint face, would die violently? Did they know he was on a train? Did they chant *let it crash let it crash*? Did they cry into their stuffing and accept one more beer than usual?

Overtired from excessive sleep, and generally morose, he got out his headphones and MP3 player, and spun the dial to a Tom Petty album.

From the adjacent car came a tall, well-groomed

man wearing a fitted gray suit, a dark coat slung over his shoulder. A pink necktie poked from his briefcase like an earthworm. It was his brother-in-law. He collapsed into the empty four-seater across the aisle and instantly fell asleep.

'Hey.'

Erich opened an eye. 'Oh. Hello.' He appeared to be calculating the necessity of cordiality. He scooted over one seat. 'I didn't see you.'

'You can sleep if you want.'

'No, I shouldn't. I will when we get home.' As usual, Erich gave the impression that he considered chitchat a waste of oxygen. He gestured around as though pointing out the majesty of their surroundings. 'We're on the same train.'

'We sure are.'

Jonah couldn't remember the last time they'd been alone together. He guessed it was his sophomore year, shortly after the engagement, when – acting on Kate's orders – they went out for a drink. He recalled the conversation as one of his Top-Five Most Strained, a real achievement considering that he had almost two years of George Richter's Awkward-palooza under his belt.

They had jointly improvised a comparison of American and German soccer culture. Erich asked twice whether Jonah owned a tuxedo or would have to rent. Jonah squelched his need to wipe away a fleck of foam caught in Erich's goatee.

As they neared the bottoms of their mugs Erich said in an offhand way *There's an opening in my department. A beginner's position but with the potential for upward mobility.* His pinched mouth became a manhole when he smiled. *You could work near me. It would be fun.*

That's an idea Jonah said.

Clearly, this was Kate's doing. Jonah didn't want a finance job; Erich didn't want to give him one; and yet, out of respect for her, they sat there taking the idea seriously, giving each other nods of encouragement, two atheists planning Mass.

Actually he told Erich *I'm going to medical school.*

Oh? I didn't know you had done the preparatory work for that.

I'm taking the classes.

Erich said *In Europe people commit to their future careers at a much earlier age.*

Then I'm glad I was born here.

Since siring Gretchen, Erich had made scant effort to get simpatico. He didn't have to: his place in the family had been fixed. Dropping a kid was dropping anchor.

He unwound his scarf and waved at the window. 'In Germany, I enjoyed rail travel. The trains there are clean and convenient. When I was a teenager we used to tour the countryside or go to see the castles in Bavaria. Once I left my radio on the train. Two days later, on our way back to Berlin, I returned to the station. They had my radio waiting at the front desk.'

'Wow.'

'American trains, however, are another breed. My commute has erased all the joy. Every morning I go from car to car, looking for one that doesn't smell like someone pissed on the seats.' He folded the scarf and laid it across his lap. 'Your mother told me you were coming home yesterday.'

Your mother and *your father*; never Mom and Dad. Erich thought it silly to pretend to be their son when he wasn't. It drove Kate bonkers. While initially Jonah had taken offense, too, he'd begun to see things Erich's way. A little distance seemed fitting.

'I had to work,' Jonah said.

'Ah.' That appeared to close the subject. Jonah moved to replace his headphones when Erich pointed and said, 'May I?'

Jonah handed him the wine.

'It says here,' Erich said, 'that this vintage has affinities with poultry and fruit.' At some point during the last five years he'd rid himself of the goatee, with the effect of widening his wide smile. 'Well chosen.'

'I try.'

'I will never get used to the idea of American Thanksgiving. In Germany we have a similar holiday, but it's not the elaborate production that your mother makes.'

'Few Thanksgivings are.'

'My grandparents took me to church on *Erntedankfest*. I haven't been for years.'

'To church?'

'Kate and I are raising Gretchen to find her own beliefs.'

'I'm sure she'll appreciate that later in life.'

'How's school?'

Jonah was glad to have a conversation this boring; it restored his sense of order. 'Fine, thanks.'

'Have you been in the papers recently?'

Jonah smiled. 'Not recently. Work?'

Erich shrugged. 'Oh, you know. Busy. I slept at the office. I haven't had a bath in two days. We have showers there but I can't stand them. It's a brutal life, be grateful you're going into something calm.'

Jonah wondered if his brother-in-law grasped what he did all day. He said, 'The night before Thanksgiving? Aren't most things closed?'

'Not the European markets. Not the Nikkei. You think too provincially, Jonah. That's not how business is conducted these days. These days, the whole world is trading, night and day, nonstop. If I wanted to live in the office I could. As it is, I've slept there several times in the last few months.'

'That must be rough.'

'Quite. You're listening to music.'

Jonah handed over his headphones.

'I like it,' Erich said. 'Is this new?'

'Not so much.'

Woodlawn the conductor called out. *Woodlawn Station next stop.*

'All right, Jonah. If you'll excuse me I'm going

286

to rest my eyes. Shake me when we get there, please.'

As he began to snore, it occurred to Jonah that their talk had been unusually jocular. Evidently, the holiday spirit had gotten into him.

Like a blimp he thought. like a blimp, or a watermelon, or a woman pregnant with triplets. Huge; much bigger at six months than she'd been with Gretchen. She met them on the platform with two bouquets of flowers, waving as she shouted their names.

'I wondered if you'd run into each other,' Kate said, grabbing Jonah. 'Poor Erich's been away forever.' She turned her attention to her husband. 'Are you okay? You must be so tired. I missed you. I love you. My back hurts.'

They climbed into her blue Mercedes. Kate explained that she'd been contemplating getting a more practical car – a tanklike mommy-van – but was reluctant to abandon the sedan, 'the last vestige of my independence,' she explained gloomily. Its cream leather interior presented well, though Jonah could detect traces of chemically removed baby food. He sat in back, his arm nestled inside a carseat redolent of animal crackers and apple juice. 'You look great, Katie.'

'Why thank you. I have the glow of motherhood. Isn't that right, honey?'

'Absolutely.'

'Erich thinks I should be a maternity model. One

of those women who does ads for big clothing. I wouldn't mind having my picture taken, but I wouldn't want to have to stay skinny while pregnant. It's bad for the baby. Movie stars, starving themselves. Have you seen some of these women having babies? Honey?'

'It's not healthy.'

'Celebrities shouldn't have children, it's not their job.'

When Kate made a pronouncement, Jonah tended to believe it. He'd always thought of her as impenetrable, and found it a discomfiting inversion of his worldview that he'd ended up as Superman instead of her.

'Mom said that you – aharggh.' Kate rooted in her bag for her ringing phone. 'Honey, can you please – thank you. Catherine Stem-Hausmann. What's up. I thought I told them not to p— He said *what.*'

With one hand she held the phone; the other hand alternately tended the steering wheel and punished it for the sins of other drivers. From Kate's remonstrations Jonah gathered that someone had bought something long after the correct time to buy had passed. She demanded to know why Jonathan and Stuart hadn't asked David F. and David M. about scraping together cash from . . . His sister appeared to be the sole female involved in these transactions, and Jonah had to admire the way she roared *It's your job, not mine!* before hurling the phone down and reaching to stroke Erich's sandy cheek. 'You look so tired.'

'I could do with a nap.'

'Did you sleep on the train? Jonah, you have to tell Erich to sleep more.'

'Sleep more,' Jonah said.

'There, hear that? The doctor has spoken.' Kate glanced over her shoulder. 'People in the office asked me if I was related to you. You're famous.'

'Hardly. Thanks for the flowers.'

'Yes, they're delightful,' said Erich.

'Really? Not too girlie? I wanted to get you each a present, but I couldn't think of anything. Next time I'll buy you weights or single-malt scotch. For now you'll have to make do with flowers. You're sure they're not too girlie?'

'Not at all,' Jonah said. 'Uh – Kate.'

'What. Oh.' She swerved to avoid a cat. 'That's okay,' she said. 'I'm allergic to them anyway.'

Jonah's mother, aproned, met them in the driveway.

'Did you kill anything?' she asked Kate.

They exchanged kisses as though they didn't see each other twice a week. His mother drove to Greenwich to babysit so Kate could get to the office. If he knew his sister, she'd work until her water broke. Jonah wondered if she'd bothered to lie down while giving birth to Gretchen. Like a peasantwoman squatting in the field.

'How thoughtful,' his mother said, taking the wine. 'Thank you. To the manor?' She clasped Kate by the arm and escorted her up the gravel walk.

Erich looked at Jonah as if to say *Women*.

And Jonah thought *Women I love*.

Photo collages lined the entry hall: Kate and Jonah sledding, Kate's high-school graduation, Jonah in lacrosse uniforms. The entire family in Paris, posing by the base of the Arc de Triomphe. Gretchen had a collage to herself, hung near the painted folk-art umbrella stand that stood sentry over a line of galoshes and duckboots.

The last one in, Jonah lingered to watch their three forms, bejeweled by light percolating through the transom: his mother, waiflike, her pinned hair puffing flour as she shook her head in response to a question; his sister, waddling mightily in defiance of gravity; and Erich, broad, Teutonic, handsome.

Jonah longed to be part of this wholesome scene, but he felt too sullied: by sex, by sickness, by death. He bore the mark of trampled innocence.

He closed the door quietly and left his backpack in the hall.

He wandered into the living room, picking up and discarding myriad magazines before finding one he'd never seen before: *American Photographer*. He deduced that his father had gone on an enthusiast's kick.

Muffled motherese squeaking through the heating vents; the satisfying slap of a butcher knife crushing garlic; the drone of the den television left viewerless. He put his feet up on the coffee table, clicked on the brass reading lamp, and paged through the camera magazine, enjoying pictures and ignoring captions.

His father appeared on the second-floor landing. 'Welcome home.'

They met on the stairs and had an off-balance hug before proceeding to the kitchen, where his father took a bottle of Pellegrino from the overfull fridge and dipped his finger in a bowl of cranberry sauce.

'Steve.'

'I'm tasting it.'

'You can taste it during dinner.'

'Needs sugar.'

'Thank you, Interfering Man. Leave the kitchen.'

Jonah followed his father back upstairs, fielding rapid-fire inquiries about life in the clinics. Steve Stem asked questions efficiently and in sequence, as though he'd written them out in advance.

'Nothing's changed,' he said as Jonah described vending-machine lunches. 'Although we didn't have a Student Wellness Committee.'

His father's cardiology practice belonged to a private doctor-run collective, a no-insurance-taken attempt to cut out the middle man. A hundred physicians and an equal number of nurses worked out of a sleek building forty minutes north of Scarsdale, catering to upper-income families, including that of a former President of the United States. He missed the bustle of the down-and-dirty, though, and since Jonah had started medical school, an element of professional camaraderie had colored their talk.

'Did I ever tell you about the time I was working for this fellow, Brooks.' They followed the well-worn Persian runner that stretched the length of the second-floor hallway. 'I was an intern. We were called on a woman whose EKG had started to act up. He takes one look at her and says, "Digitalis, immediate delivery." Then he gets paged and leaves, and I do as I'm told. Five minutes later another cardiologist, Ragolonsky, a South African – good doctor – shows up. "Everything's under control," I tell him, very proud of myself. "Digitalis IM." Well, he goes ballistic. As it turns out, she's seriously dij toxic. The shot I gave her is basically going to kill her.'

Though Jonah had heard this story at least five times, it still made him smile. He said, 'It's crazy out there.'

His father grunted, as if to say *You understand*.

They mounted three steps to his office, a hexagonal addendum at the back end of the house. Normally impeccable, the room had grown a second skin of newspaper, pimpled by bottles of wood glue and thimblesize pots of paint. Pages torn from an instruction manual blanketed the desk. In the center of this mess stood a glistening blue dollhouse, three feet high and wet to the touch.

'I planned on giving it to Gretchen before dinner,' he said. 'But it might have to wait until

Christmas. Still missing windows, and' – he pried up a section of cork shingles – 'I can't get these to stick, for some reason. Any ideas?'

Jonah had no clue. 'It's stupendous, Dad.'

'We've gone back in time. A hundred and fifty years ago you had to make everything by hand, or buy from someone who did. Then the world went industrial, and you got all your goods mass-produced. Now we're back to DIY. Your sister quilts, did you know that?'

'You're kidding.'

'She's making a blanket for the new baby. That's why I'm doing this for Gretchen, so she won't feel jealous when he's born and everyone stops paying her exclusive attention. Parents have to be careful. Your mother and I were.'

'It's a he?' Jonah said.

His father's mouth hung open. Then he said, 'Pretend to be surprised.'

During the day he helped his mother mash pota-toes, helped his father experiment with a variety of adhesives, helped his sister and brother-in-law take care of their child. In the end they'd given their au pair the day off, which did not prevent Gretchen from asking for her every five minutes.

'You want a story?' Jonah asked.

'Dah-lene.'

'Uncle Jonah will read you *Sadie's Great Big Competition*.'

'Dah-lene.'

Jonah put his niece on his lap, opened the book. Like the seats of Kate's car, it was enlivened by bold-colored stains, emitting the sweetish odor of a diabetic's breath.

'There's a whole series,' Kate said. 'Sadie and her friends go on great big adventures.'

'Ah-veh-chuh,' confirmed Gretchen.

Sadie turned out to be a sunflower. Along with companions Desdemona the Daffodil, Gertrude the Geranium, and Carlotta the Chrysanthemum, she engaged in loony and outrageously motile activities. The *Great Big Competition*, volume three in a series of forty-odd, pitted the characters against one another as they strove to be the prettiest. Bedlam ensued; nobody won; the moral of the story emerged as *It's more important to be nice to your friends than to win.*

Jonah would have enjoyed reading aloud, but Gretchen beat him to it.

'Isn't she kind of young to be literate?' he asked Kate.

'She's not. She's memorized it. Darlene reads it to her a hundred times a day.'

'Dah-lene,' said Gretchen.

'She *is* reading,' Jonah's mother called from the kitchen. 'She's a genius.'

'Ah-gay.'

Kate said, 'Erich and I call it *Sadie's Great Big Repetition.*'

'Dah-lene.'

'Not today, honey. She's home on vacation.'

'Vaca-shuh.'

'That's right. And so are you. And so is Mommy, and Daddy, and Grammy, and Grandpa, and Uncle Jonah. We're all here! Here! Where are we?'

'Gammy.'

'That's right, Grammy's house. And where do *we* live?'

'Conneck-uh.'

'That's right! So smart. And who's that?'

Gretchen craned around and peered at Jonah. He opened his eyes as big as he could. 'Hello, Gretchen. Do you know my name?'

'Dah-lene.'

'Darlene?'

'Dah-lene.'

'Darlene? I'm not *Darleeeene* . . .' He swept her up, tickling her until she turned plum and kicked with delight. She rolled free and ran to shelter behind her mother's legs.

'She must love you. Normally she doesn't let people tickle her. She scratches. Believe me.' Kate showed tiny white marks near her hairline. 'No, sweetie, Mommy can't pick you up, Mommy's going to slip a disc.'

'Dah-lene.'

'That's Uncle Jonah. Can you say Uncle Jonah?'

'Sadie Gay Big Com*pi*-shuh.'

'Uncle Jonah will read you the book if you say his name. Can you say Uncle Jonah?'

Gretchen squirmed.

'Say Uncle Jonah.'

'Hey Gretchen,' Jonah said, 'my name is . . . *Uncle Jonah*!' He chased her around the living room. She spun in a circle, yelping *Unka Jonah*, stamping her feet and flapping her stumpy arms like an overwrought penguin.

'Very good,' Kate said. 'Unka Jonah.'

'Unka Jonah! Raaahr. Raaaahr.'

'I'm not sure she understands that it's my name,' Jonah said. 'She might think it means "Back off, bitch."'

'Baga, bish.'

Kate moaned. 'You can't swear in front of her.'

'Don't be a tightass,' Jonah said. 'Can you say "Mommy's a tightass?"'

'Ty-tah! Ty-tah!'

'Oh brother.'

'Bruh! Ty-tah! Raaahr.'

They read the story three more times before dinner. Gretchen nodded off on the couch and Kate followed suit. At quarter to six his mother came downstairs, having washed up and donned a silk blouse and pearls. She lit candles on the sideboard and asked Jonah to fetch everyone.

He put a hand on Kate's forehead. She stirred, yawned, kissed his wrist.

'I don't think we can leave her there,' she said, referring to Gretchen, limp in a pile of pillows.

'You want me to put her to bed?'

'I'll do it. Come with me.'

As they went upstairs, Kate put her arm around

Jonah. 'This is the way it ought to be,' she said. 'Just the family.'

Eat eat eat eat eat eat eat.
  'Who wants pie?'
  'I am going to *die*.'
  'You're eating for two.'
  'I ate for nine.'
  'Everything is exquisite.'
  'Thank you, Erich. Steve? Pumpkin or cherry?'
  'Both, please.'
  'And of course Jonah wants both.'
  'Just pumpkin is fine.'
  'Erich, what kind.'
  'Cherry, please.'
  'Okay. Pass to Jonah, please.'
  'Mom. I said just pumpkin.'
  'I couldn't hear you, I must be going deaf.'
  'Here, Erich, take mine.'
  'No no no. I've already cut him a piece.'
  'He can have two.'
  'What are you, on a diet? Steve, Jonah's on a diet.'
  'I'm not on a diet.'
  'You're on a diet?'
  'I'm not on a—'
  'Maybe he has a special friend.'
  '*Kate.*'
  'Do you?'
  'No.'
  'Why not?'
  'This pie is exquisite.'

'Thank you, Erich. Why don't you have a girl-friend, Jonah?'

'I don't have time.'

'Steve.'

'Mm.'

'When you met me, did you have time for a girl-friend?'

'I made time.'

'Maybe his special friend is a nurse. Do you like nurses?'

'Hey Kate?'

'Yeah? – achhh, you shtunk.'

'Don't throw whipped cream, Jonah, it's not polite.'

'Hey Mom?'

'Dooon't.'

'Jonah-face, tell us about this nurse of yours . . . Wave that around all you want, I don't care, you already ruined my pants.'

'She's not a nurse.'

'Aha! Steve, you heard that? Our son's marrying a nurse.'

'She's not a nurse.'

'Then what does she do?'

'She does nothing.'

'Well she must do something. Are you in love with an unemployed woman?'

'She does nothing, because there *is* no – fine. She's a mechanic.'

'Perfect, a doctor and a mechanic. America's two most secretive professions.'

'Erich, more pie?'

'No, thank you. It's exquisite.'

'Thank you. Well, Jonah?'

'There's no one. Really.'

'Did you hear that?'

'What.'

His mother got up. 'Someone's at the door.'

'Jonah-face,' Kate said. 'My friends from college have sisters who live in the City. They're all editorial assistants and weigh ninety-five pounds. Interested? Where you going?'

He did not answer her. He'd gotten up to follow his mother but stopped midway across the kitchen.

I can't believe he didn't say anything.

I'm so sorry, Mrs Stem. I apologize. I thought he'd mentioned – dessert. I brought this for you. If it's inconvenient—

Not at all, not at all. Although I wish he'd said something about it. Oh how thoughtful. It's nice to meet you. We're in the middle of dessert right now. Come on in.

His chest bottomed out like a flushed commode.

'Jonah,' his mother called, 'you didn't tell me you were inviting a friend.'

CHAPTER 24

'You look so familiar,' said Kate. 'Have we met?'

'At Yale.'

'Ohhhhh. *You're* the friend who went to Yale.'

'You didn't tell me you had a new friend,' said his mother. 'Jonah?'

'What year were you?'

'Same as you,' Eve said. 'But I wasn't terribly memorable in college.'

'Everyone knows Kate,' Erich said.

'Not everyone. But thank you, honey. What college were you?'

'Calhoun.'

'No kidding. Did you know Jenny Ballentine?'

'She was Council Chair.'

'And Robbie Sevenza?'

'The Beer Can Eiffel Tower,' Eve said.

Kate laughed. 'Wow. How funny we never met.'

'I graduated early. And senior year I lived off-campus, in the Grad Ghetto.'

'Well it's nice to meet you now. Jonah, you never told me she lived in Calhoun.'

'You never told me she existed at all,' said his mother, smiling at Eve.

Eve squeezed Jonah's shoulder. 'He's bashful.'

'Where did you meet?' his mother asked.

'In a bar,' Jonah blurted.

Kate snickered. 'That's so sleazy, I love it.'

'Behave,' his mother said. 'I met your father in a bar.'

'No you didn't.'

'Your mother and I—' began his father, stopping when Kate wrung her hands. 'What.'

'Every time you start a sappy story that begins "Your mother and I," it goes on for an hour and ends up making me cry.'

'I was simply going to remind the table that love can evolve from humble beginnings.' His father gestured around the room. 'Our family.'

'Fuck, I'm going to cry,' Kate said.

'I didn't know you had time for bars,' his mother said.

'I – don't, normally.' Under the table, Eve was raking her nails toward his crotch.

'The hand of fate,' his mother said.

'. . . I . . . I don't . . .' Sharply, he bent one of Eve's fingers back. She made a series of near-silent chuffing noises and withdrew. She'd taken out most of her piercings. To cover the holes she'd worn her hair loose around her turtleneck. A pleated skirt, ladylike navy stockings, burgundy penny loafers: she could've stepped out of *Preppy Quarterly*.

'So Eve,' said Kate, 'since my brother is in *suuuuch* a friendly mood, I'll talk to you directly. What do you do? Are you a mechanic?'

'I work with the mentally ill.'

'How appropriate,' said his mother.

Eve laughed. 'Jonah and I have a lot in common.'

'I always knew you'd find a Yale girl,' Kate said. 'Didn't I say that, honey?'

'We all know Yale women are exceptionally beautiful,' Erich said.

'That is the overstatement of the century,' Jonah said.

'*Jonah*,' his mother said.

'How do you put up with him?' Kate asked.

'I like him just the way he is,' Eve said, mussing his hair as she began another round of Exfoliate Jonah's Pants.

'I ate too much,' Jonah said. 'I'm feeling groggy.'

'That's the tryptophan,' said his father.

'The turkey was exquisite,' Erich said.

'Thank you. More pie, Eve?'

'No, thank you. Everything's delicious. I'll have to get your recipes.'

'Oh?' His mother sounded inordinately pleased. 'Do you cook?'

'Recreationally. But I'm a dilettante, compared to Jonah.'

'Jonah cooks?' his mother said.

'Mm. Very well.' Eve's laugh exposed her neck.

'When did you learn to cook?' his mother asked him.

He had pried three fingers away. Her shoeless toes rubbed his foot. 'I don't.'

'What else haven't you told us?' Kate said.

'He's too modest,' Eve said.

'Are you hiding other skills from us?'

'He's quite an artist,' Eve said. 'Did you know that?'

'I most certainly did not,' his mother said. To him: 'You should *share* these things . . .'

'How bout embarrassing Jonah stories?' Kate asked. 'I'll trade you one for one.'

'Nothing would make me happier,' Eve said.

'I think it's time to clear the table,' Jonah said.

'Oh sit down,' said his mother. 'One meal a year, we get to linger.'

'Which ones should we tell,' Kate said. 'Why don't we let him pick.'

'How bout the time I embarrassed myself by leaving the table in the middle of Thanksgiving dinner,' he said, reaching for Eve's plate.

'My golly,' his mother said, 'let her eat.'

'If you're not going to pick a story,' Kate said, 'I'll pick one anyway, and then you won't have any choice in the matter.'

'I have a request,' Eve said. 'Tell me about his childhood fears.'

'Where to begin,' his mother said, and laughed. 'Steve? Wine?'

'No thank you.'

His mother poured herself a half-glass, smiling as she geared up her story. 'To see him now you'd never know, but he was a *very* skittish boy, a regular nervous Nelly.'

Eve demurred.

'It's true,' Kate said. 'Everything set him off. Movies, loud noises, rollercoasters. He was such a fraidy-cat that he wouldn't go to the bathroom alone.'

Eve laughed and brushed Jonah's temple. He stared at his plate.

'Mom took us to see this traveling group do *The Pirates of Penzance* – you remember that? Jonah?'

'I remember,' he mumbled.

'I assumed it was a production suitable for children,' his mother said.

'It *was*,' said Kate. 'Just not for Jonah.'

'They did a sort of gothic staging, ghoulish and spooky, cobwebs in the seats.'

'And the pirates were dressed up as skeletons,' said Kate. 'How old was I?'

'You were . . . well, Jonah was two and a half, so you were about eight.'

'After that he started seeing ghosts everywhere. There's a big black birch outside the upstairs bathroom, and he would see things in the branches. He would sit down to make a number two, and next thing you know we'd hear him crying *Help! The Pirate King! Except . . .*' Kate laughed, coughed, beat her chest. 'Wooo, *ahem. Except*, that at that age he had a *wuh*. So it sounded like *He-wup! The Pie-wat King!*'

Everyone laughed. Eve pinched his cheek.

'He was *darling*,' said his mother. 'To protect himself, he would ask Katie to come with him into the bathroom and wait while he did his business.'

'No!'

'Yyy*yes*,' Kate said. '*But*. He was too embarrassed to go with me watching him, so I had to stand in the shower and face the other way.'

'So together,' his mother said, 'yet so alone.'

He could not think of a way to communicate the urgency of ending this conversation without sparking a riot. He was skittish, all right, but the Stem women were human landmines. They found him funny because they were worse.

Part of him wanted to slug Eve right there, right at the table. He doubted she would fight back, not in front of everybody else. Though he had underestimated her before, and she had the cutlery at her disposal.

He bent back another intrusive finger.

'And as a baby – *oh* . . .' his mother sighed. 'Too much. Too *much*.'

'I bet,' said Eve.

'Are you done,' Jonah said, seizing her plate and striding into the kitchen, ignoring the swell of protest.

I don't know what's gotten into him.

He's stressed Eve was saying. *He works so hard.*

He scraped piecrusts into the trash compactor. In the dining room they were entertaining themselves at his expense.

He would announce that he had work in the morning, studying to do. If he left, Eve would have to leave.

Unless his mother asked her to stay. She reveled in her role as hostess, and it was conceivable that she would try to carry on without him. She might invite Eve to stay the night. *We won't allow him to be a party-pooper.*

His mother called, 'Eve would like some seltzer, Jonah.'

He went to the laundry alcove. On the floor was a half-empty case of Pellegrino; beside it, bottles of bleach, Windex, Liquid-Plumr.

He could put something in her drink.

Keeling over, clutching her chest as her esophagus dissolved, spitting bloody tissue out on the ironed linen tablecloth, his sister screaming and his mother screaming and his father baffled and Erich stuttering in his hyperrational way, all of them recoiling, pushing back in their chairs, knocking over the candlesticks, flinging aside water goblets and silverware with musical—

'Jonah?'

His mother watched him from the doorway. 'Did you hear me?'

He nodded, did not move.

'Would you like to rejoin us?'

He nodded again.

'What's the—'

He made a shushing motion. She frowned,

mouthed *What*. He sequestered her in a hug. She said, 'Honey?'

'She's not supposed to be here,' he whispered. 'I never invited her.'

His mother's arms tightened around him. 'Oh my God.'

'Act normal. If I leave the house she'll follow.'

'Is she—'

'Do you understand me? Act normal. Promise me you can do that.'

She nodded.

'If you don't know,' he said, 'she won't know.'

They went back to the dining room.

'Mission accomplished,' his mother said. She opened the seltzer and poured two glasses, the first for Eve and a second for herself. A seamless performance.

'I'm telling Eve about the time you threw up onstage,' Kate said.

'I think that's enough hazing for one night,' his mother said cheerily.

'Poor Jonah-face,' Kate said. 'You know it's only cause I love you so much.'

'Why don't we adjourn?' his mother asked. 'Steve, you look sleepy.'

'Don't mind me,' said his father.

'I'm feeling sluggish myself.' His mother smiled. 'Tryptophan.'

'If you'll excuse me,' Erich said, 'I'm going to check on Gretchen.'

'Is that your daughter?' Eve said to Kate.

'Yes.'

'She must be scrumptious,' Eve said. 'Who does she look like?'

'You know what I think?' Kate said. 'I think babies never really look like anyone. What happens is, people identify the older relative who looks the most babylike, and then say, "The baby looks like *them*." Gretchen, she's a new era of cute, she makes the Gerber baby look like a gnome.'

'May I come see her? I *love* children.'

'We should be getting back,' Jonah said. 'We should get on the eight oh six.'

'It's five to, you'll never make it,' Kate said. 'Take the next one.'

'I have work tomorr—'

'Puh-lease. Even I can turn it off for one day.' Kate stood. 'We're going to gaze at my beautiful daughter.' She took Eve's arm and led her out.

There was a brief silence as Jonah looked at the space in front of him: a clean circle of tablecloth, bounded by the indentation from his dinner plate, rice and gravy dotting its perimeter. His father leaned over, kissed his mother, thanked her again, folded his soiled napkin, and took the dessert plates to the kitchen, where he could be heard rinsing them and slotting them into the dishwasher. Erich excused himself to read.

Jonah said, 'Shit.'

'Why didn't you say something earlier?' his mother whispered.

'I didn't have the chance.'

'What is she *doing* here, if you didn't invite her?'

'Put us on a train and I'll call you later.'

His mother checked her watch. 'You're not going to make it.'

'We will if we hurry.'

'Can we wait an hour?'

'No,' he said, getting up. 'We can't.'

'Shhhhh.' Kate steeped into the hall. 'Don't run, you'll wake her up.'

'Tell Eve we're leaving.'

'She's looking at Gretchen.'

He stepped past his sister and into the darkened room. Gretchen was asleep on the bed, a drooly thumb loosely between her lips. Eve knelt beside the bed, stroking her; the sight of them touching made his mouth run dry. He wanted to kick her away.

'We have to go.'

Kate shushed him.

'Right now,' he whispered. 'Come on. We're leaving.'

'The embodiment of happiness,' Eve said.

'We're going to miss the train.'

'So you'll take the next one,' Kate said. 'Chill out.'

'It's *important*,' he said. He hoped she could intuit him, see through what he knew sounded like a tantrum.

Kate said, 'Jeez. Somebody needs medication.'

309

Eve raised the hem of Gretchen's shirt and touched her tummy. Smooth, perfect baby's skin, untainted and unblemished. Remembering, he imagined, what it was like to have such a body. Her fingers would leave scars.

'We need to *leave.*'

He grabbed her by the biceps and pulled her up. She jerked back, bumping into the painted chest of drawers that had been Kate's, then his, and was now the baby's; slunk into the corner, behind the rocking horse near the changing table. Kate said *Stop it you'll wake* and then he lashed out and struck Eve in the face.

A tap; less than nothing. But she collapsed, whimpering and shrinking further when he stepped toward her.

Kate grabbed him. 'What is *wrong* with you.'

His brain went off like firecrackers: his sister was going to stab him.

'What are you *doing.*'

'I'm sorry.'

'Get out of here.'

He held his hands up to show defeat. 'Kate—'

'*Get out.*'

He hesitated, then said, 'I'll wait downstairs.'

My God. What has gotten *into* him.

It's not . . . not his fault.

I don't care if he's my brother, it's disgusting.

It's my fault.

Don't blame yourself, that's sick.

He didn't mean to . . .

It looked to me like he did.

He was trying to hurry me up. I . . . sometimes I need to . . . I space out. He'd never hurt me. He wouldn't, he loves me, I love him. It's not what you think, I promise. I – I overreact, sometimes.

That didn't seem like an overreaction to me. He *hit* you for God's sake.

No, I – it wasn't – it was a minor, he barely – I over-reacted. I made it seem like it was a bigger deal than it was. Please – can we, can we not talk about this.

You can't be with him if he treats you like that. Does he treat you like that?

I don't want to talk about it. I swear that you have nothing to worry about.

How d'you expect me to believe—

Let's talk about something else. Let's talk about Gretchen.

Eve—

Please. Look at her. She's so beautiful. She's gorgeous, Kate. She reminds me of a Botticelli cherub. Jonah wants to have kids, he wants to have lots of kids. We're – well, we haven't picked, it's not official yet. But . . . Don't tell your parents yet, please? We're keeping it under wraps. But – I feel like I can tell you. What. Why are you – please don't look upset, it's cause for happiness.

A silence.

I shouldn't have said anything. Kate.

Nothing—

You're missing the big picture.

311

Nothing justifies —

Please. Be happy. I'm happy. I want to be happy with him. He's happy. You want that. He's . . . suffered so much.

Jonah?

Yes. With that girl.

What g – you mean Hannah?

Yes, her. He's suffered. He sometimes has trouble expressing his emotions in front of other people. He's under so much stress. You don't know what it's like to be a doctor, I see him every day, people die in his hands. It's torture for him, and he has no way of letting it out. It's something we've worked on. And he's been working on it with his therapist. I sent him to a friend of mine. He and I have something special, you have to believe that. He takes care of me in the way that I need. Believe me. He's a wonderful man, and I love him.

He *hit* you.

He gets angry sometimes and he doesn't realize his own strength. It's me who —

Don't indict yourself, it makes me want to vomit.

I know it sounds that way, I know. You have to take my word for it. I could never love somebody cruel. He isn't. You've known him your whole life, has he ever been?

No.

So there you are.

. . . I don't know.

I can only give you my word. You do love him, don't you?

. . . yes.

He loves you, too. You're lucky to have each other. I don't have any brothers or sisters. My parents died when I was three. I didn't know them at all. It wasn't a car accident, if that's what you're thinking. They got cancer. It's all right. I barely knew them. It didn't register until I got much older. I've been alone for so long. I was raised by my aunt, who was sort of a spinster. She was strict. I didn't have a boyfriend until college. It wasn't someone from Yale, I can see you were about to ask that. He was a friend from high school who later became a boyfriend. I've never been in love until now.

With my brother?

Yes.

A silence.

. . . God, look at me.

You're allowed to cry.

I'm so emotional all the time. Hormones – sometimes when too many things happen . . . I'm sorry, Eve.

Katie. Here.

. . . thank you.

Be happy for us if you can. You have to remember, the accident. People who go through trauma of that magnitude sometimes act out. That's why I'm not scared: because I know he would never do anything to hurt me. He's venting the pressure, he's learning to express it in a more normal manner, but he's been damaged. He wakes up in cold sweats every night.

. . . I didn't know.

So please don't look at him like that. I love him. You love him, too.

I . . . of course I do.

He's aching inside. He's like a wounded animal. He needs everything we've got. I promise you that's all that you saw. It's nothing worse than that.

. . . okay. Okay.

It's funny. You know? I think about all the people I could have met, but didn't . . . You and I were in the same place for years. But I suppose it's better late than never? For us to be friends. And now we have a common passion.

Choking, clotted with rage, he stopped halfway down the stairs, pressing his forehead to the banister.

His mother was waiting for him in the kitchen. 'We missed the train.'

'We'll take the next one,' he said, heading for the back porch.

'Jonah? What's going on here?'

'It's fine, Mom. I need some air.'

'Jonah—'

The evening had turned cold. Across the leaf-strewn backyard, his father stood mounting a bulky camera on a tripod. Jonah approached, rubbing his hands together.

'I'm thinking of getting a telescope,' his father said. 'For virtually nothing you can get a setup with GPS. Joe Schmoe's doing university-quality work. Truly an age of exploration. I got this last month and already it's obsolete. Have a look.'

Jonah twisted the lens, focusing on a window upstairs. Eve was holding Gretchen up while Kate opened a package of baby wipes. All three laughing.

'Give it a try,' his father said.

Jonah swung the camera away and shot a picture of the weathervane.

'Look at that sharpness,' his father said.

'. . . great.'

'Eve seems nice.'

Jonah nodded.

'In a bar, huh?'

'Yup.'

'Because, to my eye, she looks a lot like the woman from the paper.'

Jonah said nothing.

'I wasn't going to mention it,' his father said, 'but Erich noticed, also.'

Jonah shrugged.

'Should I not ask?'

'Please don't.'

His father nodded, glanced at the window. 'She and Kate seem to get along.'

Jonah said, 'Don't tell Mom, okay? That you recognized her.'

'I'm sure she'll figure it out on her own.'

'She hasn't yet,' Jonah said.

'Discretion is the better part of valor.'

'Thanks.' Jonah toed the earth. 'I have to go to the train station.'

'Am I driving you?'

'Mom said she would.'

'All right. You know you can talk to me, if something's wrong.'

'It was good to see you, Dad.'

His father said, 'I love you.'

Looking at the window, Jonah reached for and found his father's hand. 'You too.'

CHAPTER 25

They looked like any normal couple waiting for the nine oh six, pacing the platform with their arms entwined – or perhaps not any couple, but like newlyweds, unwilling to break touch. Jonah struggled to remain stiff-backed, the stake around which she grew like a hothouse creeper.

A whistle sounded.

'Homeward bound,' she said.

Most of the empty seats were singletons. With Eve attached to his sleeve, Jonah passed from one car into the next: butt-brushing, ruder than excusable, raising consternation and causing tongues to cluck. At the end of the car he pulled free of her and stepped up his pace.

'Honey,' she said. 'Where are you going?'

'To find a seat.'

'There's no seats together,' she said.

As he walked on she called *wait please darling wait*. He was aware of people giving him dirty looks like he was some sort of abusive asshole.

Honey please I love you can we talk this over?

When he reached the last car, he about-faced. He tried to slip past her but she clung to him.

'Your family is so charming,' Eve said. 'I think we got on famously.'

'Yeah, you're one of the gang.'

She bit her lip. 'Don't be upset.' Cringing, teary, childish, their height differential monstrously exaggerated. 'Please don't. They love me, why can't you.'

They might've stayed there for the duration of the trip had not a man on his way to the bathroom said *Excuse me.*

As they shifted to accommodate him, Eve recovered her composure. In a loud voice she said *I never expected it to be this crowded, did you, honey?* She turned to a boy marking up a physics textbook and asked if he wouldn't mind moving over to the opposite side of the aisle so she could sit with her husband?

'Sure,' the boy said and began piling his stuff up.

Jonah wanted to make another break for it, but it wasn't as though she wouldn't be able to find him. They were going to arrive in Manhattan at the same time, get off the train at the same time, make it back to his apartment at the same time. Accepting that constraint he began to wonder if there were not a way to take advantage of the situation.

The physics boy relocated, and Jonah sidled in, resting his bag in his lap. Eve snuggled up next to him.

'My love,' she murmured.

He said nothing.

'My love, my love. Well I for one was happy to meet your family.'

He was elsewhere.

'It's not very festive of you, my love, to ignore me.

'Well, suit yourself.

'It makes me very sad.

'Our seatmates must think I'm pathetic.

'You think I'm pathetic, don't you?

'I love you. How can you treat me this way? Your own sister said it.

'Please look at me. I love you so much it comes out of my eyes.'

Between each sentence passed a considerable silence.

'I had a friend who owned a dog so intoxicated by her, every time she petted it, it lost its bladder.

'Please look at me. Please won't you. Please.

'You are killing me.'

For a long time it went on like this. He let her nuzzle him, lick him, let her tongue play the ridge of his ear. He pretended she was Lazy Susan harassing him during a nap. He wiped her kisses from his face. She reached around, put her hand on his fly. He wanted to throw her into the aisle. But that wasn't the way to win.

'Please, my love, let me love you.' She stroked inside his pants. 'Let me.'

The way to win was not to give anything. In the window reflection he saw her making a scene of herself, attracting attention. The physics kid across the aisle had definitely abandoned his homework.

'Jonah Stem. Jonah Stem, what's wrong with you. Pay attention. Do I need to take more drastic steps.

I will, right here on the train. I'm going to, Jonah Stem. I'm going to do it if you don't give me what I want. I want a sign of life. I'm going to. Are you listening? I will. I'm doing it right now.'

A woman from across the aisle to Eve said *Ex-kuh-yuuse me, miss, this is a publ—*

'Shut your fat fucking face.'

The woman made a gargling noise and hoisted herself out of her seat.

Hunched over, Eve made a garish display of sexual elan. But he was winning. When after several minutes she sat up, panting savagely, her face purple, her hair erratic. 'Too much wine, Jonah Stem. That's *your* problem. We'll resume our normal course. I know. I know you, Jonah Stem. Pay attention now. *Pay attention.*'

She climbed atop him, and he felt her fingers guiding him. No use; he was winning. He moved her away in his mind. He was winning. She couldn't get him inside. Beneath her skirt her hands typed hectically. He was winning, and she knew.

'Everything all right here?'

A conductor; behind him, the fat lady glowered and wheezed.

'Miss . . .' the conductor said, and reached for Eve. She snapped at him, literally, and, with a sob, dashed down the aisle toward the vestibule. Jonah hurriedly zipped up his pants, sank back, and closed his eyes, ignoring the conductor until he heard him leave and heard the fat woman tramp away. He was fine. He had won.

320

Several minutes later: '*Mister.*'

He opened his eyes and found three conductors staring at him. White, black, and Filipino, uniformed like some sort of comedy troupe.

'Your friend won't calm down.'

'She's not my friend.'

'We're going to have to do something about it.'

'Be my guest.'

'You want to come talk to her?'

'No.'

'Sir—'

'I' – Jonah turned to face them – 'I don't have anything to do with her.'

The white conductor said, 'She's humping you in the middle of the train, you think I'm gonna believe that?'

'I've never met her before.'

'If you don't go take care of her I'm going to call ahead the station and have them hold the *both* of you.'

He followed them to the cold, clanging vestibule, where Eve had curled up on the floor, her face pressed against the filthy metal wall, weeping like an orchestra.

'I want to die,' she said. 'I want to tear myself apart. You make me feel like a maggot. Every moment I'm alive I'm rotting.' A gag, a laugh. 'Heal me. Don't let me bleed to death. Without you I am ragged, I love you, please love me please please please please please—'

The conductors looked at Jonah sorrowfully,

although it was unclear whether their sympathies lay with him or her. He started back to his seat, and one of them caught him by the arm.

'Man, look at her.'

Snot embroidered the front of her shirt. She'd torn a hole in the sleeve of her turtleneck, and was in the process of tearing another in her stockings so that she could slice open her shin with a broken bobby pin. Jonah reached down to take it from her and she grabbed his neck.

'Don't ever let me go. Don't ever let me go.'

He gave in, sank to his knees and let her cry into his collar. At first he wouldn't put his arms around her, but keeping his body away got to be too much of a strain. She cried. *I love you don't ever let me go.* He wanted to help, he wanted to hurt; every cell of his body moving in two opposite directions, rending down the middle, disgorging its watery contents, leaving him divided, ruined, a mush of ambivalence. The train rocketed southward and she gripped him tighter, tighter, soaking him with her misery. They stayed like that until the conductors announced Grand Central, and people poured into the vestibule, crushing their bodies flat like palms met in prayer.

He took her home.

He paid for the cab, pulled her upstairs. She looked ready to disintegrate.

'I'm so unhappy,' she said.

He grimaced and shifted her weight to one hip, angling in his pocket for the keys to his front door.

'I've never been happy, not once in my life.'

He took her to his bedroom, put her on her stomach.

'Every minute I want to die.'

He tucked a pillow beneath her head. Crowned with splinters of streetlight; a triangle on her forearm; dappled toes; a malformed ring between her shoulder blades, like her halo had slipped off. She tried to sit up and he forced her prone.

'Go to sleep.'

'I can't unless you're with me.'

He slipped off his shoes and got in beside her. The average person took seven minutes to fall asleep, but nothing about Eve suggested that she was in any way average, so he decided to give her double that. Counting in ten second segments, he got distracted, thinking about his sister, who probably thought he was a demon, along with the people in the train and Belzer and Lance's Internet audience. Quite a reputation he'd built himself. He lost count and had to start over. At a hair over five minutes, she kissed his shoulder absently. *My love.* It was dark and warm and a body beside him. He fought to keep his eyes open; dug his wrist against the sharp steel corner of his bedframe. He was winning, he would win. *My love.* He heard her as though through a bad connection. Falling asleep, he bit down on the inside of his cheek, tasted blood. He would win.

Her body shuddered and then set.

He got up as slowly as possible. She scratched at his shirt. He said, 'I have to go to the bathroom,' and replaced her hand atop her hip. She shivered and was still.

He sat on the edge of the tub and dialed Belzer's home number. It rang three times and then he hung up without leaving a message.

Soon she would come looking for him. What if she hadn't been asleep?

On his second try, he spoke rapidly into the machine.

'Chip, it's Jonah. She's here at my place. She came to Thanksgiving. She showed up at my house. I don't know if I should call the police – if you're there pick up. I don't know what to tell them. Shit. Please pick up.'

He would've gone on babbling indefinitely had it not been for the slam of the front door. He almost juggled the phone into the toilet before swatting it down.

He reached the first floor landing in time to see her disappearing in a flash of tartan. He called her name but she did not look back.

Upstairs, his bare feet red and wet, he turned all the locks, put on the chain.

His phone had come apart when he dropped it, the battery skittering under the bathmat. Upon reassembly it leapt to life.

ID UNAVAILABLE

He pressed TALK.

Silence. Breathing.

He tried to locate her by the background noises: honking, loud music, and shouts. She was probably on St Marks or Second Avenue. He could put on his shoes and run; he could be there in five minutes. 'Eve?'

She said, 'You should not have done that.'

CHAPTER 26

FRIDAY, NOVEMBER 26, 2004.

Belzer called at lunchtime, and Jonah – who, on his day off, had not left the apartment – recapped the previous evening, at every point attempting to explain his rationale: why he hadn't said anything to his parents when she'd showed up at the house; why he hadn't called the cops *then*; why he'd brought her to his place.

'I didn't know what else to do,' he said. 'She was holding my *niece*.'

'I wish she'd been more explicit.'

'I don't.'

'The clearer the threat is, the better off we are if we talk to the cops.'

'It's clear. Believe me.'

'She's a *woman*. You're a *man*. That's the world, kiddo, take it or leave it. And while we're cutting to the chase, let's note that she's never done anything illegal except tackle you, and that's pretty weak. You didn't call them then.'

'She broke into my apartment.'

'Write that off,' said Belzer. 'No proof.'

'She came to my *house.*'

'And your mother let her in of her own free will. Let's look at the here and now, okay? What she said connotes a threat to you.'

'Of course it does.'

'I agree. I agree. However. We gotta problem: not much the cops can do without knowing where she lives.'

Jonah was confused. 'I thought you were going to get that from them.'

'I did. None of the information she supplied is real. Address, phone. Tell you the truth I got my doubts about her name, too. Gones with a G? Whoever heard of that?'

Jonah said nothing.

'Any other way we could track her down?'

Jonah said, 'Not that I can think of.'

SUNDAY, NOVEMBER 28, 2004.

The trip out to the Bronx took about an hour on the ⑥, during which he had plenty of time to script and revise his opening lines.

I'm sorry to bother you like this.

I'm sorry to bother you on a Sunday.

I'm sorry if you don't want to see me.

I'm sorry—

He'd considered cooking up a story; he could pretend to be from the Beacon. But he was too nervous to keep up a front, and if it collapsed he'd be in no position to start making demands.

I'm sorry to show up unannounced.

I'm sorry I ruined your year. Your decade. Your life.

I'm sorry.

He stretched in his seat and picked up a discarded copy of *Hoy*. When that proved tedious, he read the subway ads. A new thriller out by someone he'd never heard of; he didn't read thrillers. New malt beverages promising an exciting nightlife populated by people with great hair. You could get free information about *la prevención del VIH* by calling the number indicated by the cheerily infected woman. The MTA map had been red-rafted to include stops such as *Bitch* St and Ave. *Pussy*.

George had been suspiciously generous that morning when Jonah called to beg off. *Everybody needs time away. If anybody gets that, Jonah, it's me.*

Thanks.

I know how hard it can be for you. You know that, right? That I know.

Yes, George.

I can always count on you. One week missed is not a big deal.

(So generous that Jonah had begun bracing for a bombshell.)

As long as we're still on for Christmas.

Christmas break.

What?

Break. You told me you'd find someone for Christmas itself.

Right. I know. Bernadette can't come, you know.

You told me that. You said you would find someone else.

Mm . . . I haven't found anyone yet.

Is that right.

Not yet. I'm still looking.

I can get you a recommendation.

No. I've got it all taken care of.

Are you sure?

What?

Are you sure you're going to be able to find someone. Because I don't want—

I'm sure, sure I'm sure. Listen, do you think you can come out next weekend? Instead of this one.

I – I don't know, George.

If you didn't . . . we wouldn't see you until I was ready to leave for my trip. But. Whatever's most convenient for you.

He got off at Parkchester and clomped down from the elevated platform to the center of Hugh J. Grant circle. Above, tracks shuddered and wheels ground, showering him with rustflakes as the train pressed on. Next semester he had OB/GYN around here. He'd considered subletting a studio near the hospital so he wouldn't have to get up at three in the morning every day. So his presence here wasn't entirely indefensible; he could pretend he was apartment-hunting.

From the street he saw the Cross-Bronx, which resolved, miles down the line, into various destinations: New England, La Guardia, Nassau County. It was ten forty A.M., the sky pigeon-gray and flat.

329

Following his printed map, he walked beneath the train tracks for several blocks. A tattoo parlor, a beauty parlor, two check-cashing places, a brown building with an ambiguous logo and sans-serif lettering: PARKCHESTER ELECTRICAL SUPPLY. The supremely unappetizing Papa Mell's Old-Style Sizzlin Hizzlin Cajun Chicken Fry marked his turnoff, where the main commercial drag grew semiresidential tentacles. He came to an intersection where a boy in a baggy parka and dark jeans was pulling figure-8's on a tricked-out BMX. The seat was so low that the tail of his jacket scraped the ground. He saw Jonah, stood up on the pedals, and raced away.

A church.

Another church.

The neighborhood seemed to have been hit by a neutron bomb. A flier taped to a telephone pole asked if Jonah felt like he was starting a new diet *every Monday???* The wind rattled street signs and wove a plastic bag (THANK YOU ☺ PLEASE COME AGAIN) through the fractured lattice of a midsized crabapple.

On a short street crowded with compacts and a handful of glittering SUVs, four identical brownstones – 'weathered' for 'character' – opposed a towering apartment complex that ran the length of the block. After the brownstones came a series of mottled brick houses sharing common walls and sitting atop sunken garages. In one driveway sat a large truck belonging to a produce company;

the adjacent home had been converted into a dentist's office for Dr L. Sruthi, who accepted Medicaid and union insurances in both English and Spanish.

Dominican flags, American flags, Puerto Rican flags: three permutations of red-white-and-blue. Hanging from fences and staked in yards; flapping in the breeze; the motion effacing their individual features so that, in times of turbulence, the neighborhood seemed united in patriotism.

Near the end of the block he found the one he was looking for. At the side of the front steps lived a planter in the shape of the swan. Colorful pennants inexplicably gathered in a flowerpot; an uncoiled garden hose. From an open window across the street drifted a melody familiar to him from the wards: the querulous soprano of Old Woman, currently giving holy hell to a telemarketer. Jonah jammed the map in his back pocket and mounted the six steps to Simón Iniguez's house.

The doorbell summoned slow, heavy steps.

'Yes?' The screen door stippled Iniguez's face. He was wearing those same mafioso sunglasses. In an instant Jonah forgot his prepared speech.

Iniguez frowned. 'Hello?' He pushed through the screen door and stepped onto the threshold, forcing Jonah to back up.

'Who's there,' said Iniguez. Leaving one hand on the doorknob, as if to moor himself, he reached out, his free hand swimming through the space between them. Jonah hopped down the stairs.

'Mister, sorry, Mr Iniguez.'

'Who's that.'

'I'm very sorry to, to bother you, like this. Like – I'm, I hope it's not an inconvenience to come here without ca – I wanted to say—'

Iniguez frowned again.

'My name is—'

'I know who you are.'

A silence.

'What do you want.'

'I need your help.' Jonah saw himself reflected in Iniguez's dark lenses: bulbous, pleading, absurd. The old woman across the street continued to pour forth invective.

Iniguez scratched at his smooth, cologned cheek. His arm bulged inside his sleeve. Slippered, in wool drawstring pants, he managed to make Jonah feel both overdressed and slovenly. His resemblance to his brother was stronger in person: identically beefy necks, identically incipient jowls. And somewhere in his genome lurked some of the ore that, fired in the crucible of experience, had become madness.

The wind stirred a neighbor's leaf pile into a swarm.

Iniguez said, 'You can come in.'

The house was solidly middle-class in its accoutrements: a wire umbrella stand; a hallway credenza that smelled of Pledge; a coat closet, ajar, stacked with bulk-bought cleaning supplies and shrink-wrapped packages of lunchbags. The foyer opened onto a living room, a gallery of family photos: Simón, an extremely blond and handsome woman who could have been a Swede, and two puckish-looking boys.

Notably, the room lacked a television. A mammoth stereo – on but at zero – predominated, surrounded by tall shelving units built to accommodate LPs and CDs, filled with hundreds of the former and thousands of the latter. A forest-green loveseat bore the bactrian imprint of a man's behind; on the floor was a stack of Braille newspapers and a half-full mug with a TASCAM logo. The hearth rug was askew.

'Drink?' Iniguez asked.

'No thanks.'

'I have coffee on.'

'All – all right—'

Iniguez walked past him into the kitchen. Jonah stood reading the CDs, which appeared in no particular order. Janis Joplin rubbed elbows with Dr Dre and Celia Cruz. The Beatles occupied one full shelf, as did Tchaikovsky and David Grisman. At the right end of every shelf was a small Braille label.

'Sugar? Milk?'

'Milk's fine, thanks.'

Iniguez reappeared, holding a mug steadily at chest level. 'Take it from me.'

The coffee was mild and good, a welcome change from the razorblade brew he usually took. Jonah found a spot on the sofa amidst piles of toys and stray CDs.

'You're lucky it was me who answered the door,' said Iniguez, reseating himself. 'My wife wants your head.' He reached down, seemingly to plunge his hand into his mug. Then his fingers curled to receive the handle. 'She took the kids to church.' He paused. 'We have some left-over pie.'

'No thanks.' Jonah glanced at the front hallway, half-expecting the Wife and Kids to walk in and chew his ears off for molesting their patriarch.

Iniguez picked up the papers and folded them in his lap. 'So. What.'

Jonah said, 'I – first I want to tell you that I meant what I said. When I called you. I still mean it, I'm sor—'

Iniguez raised a hand. 'Why's it matter to me whether you're sorry or not? Those are words. What good does that do?'

'. . . nothing.'

'Correct. Nothing. So don't tell me you're sorry anymore.'

'I' – intending to apologize, he finished with – 'won't.'

'Your shrink send you here?'

'No.'

'I didn't see a shrink,' Iniguez said.

' . . . it's not for everyone.'

'I think it's for people who can't deal with problems on their own.'

'That . . . may be true.'

'Your lawyer sent you.'

'If he knew I was here he'd kill me.'

'What, then. It's like a pilgrimage?' Iniguez's mouth twisted up. 'Cause I don't know. I let you in here, give you a drink, offer you some pie. I'm hoping you'll entertain me a little. Give me a reason why I shouldn't beat the shit out of you.'

Jonah said nothing.

'I'm a strong guy,' said Iniguez. 'I guess you're about five eleven. Am I close?'

'And a half.'

'One eighty-five?'

'About.'

'Okay. Then tell me why I shouldn't break your arm.' Iniguez drank, stretched his fingers around the mug as though it were a neck. 'You have thirty seconds.'

Jonah said, 'During the accident—'

'Don't call it that.'

Jonah said nothing.

Iniguez said, 'You must feel like a real asshole.'

'I do.'

'That's too bad.'

'I don't expect this to mean anything to you—'

'I told you not to apologize.'

'I'm not going to,' Jonah said. 'I'm not trying to get you to feel bad for me.'

'I don't.'

'All right,' Jonah said. 'But what happened that night was a mistake.'

Iniguez nodded. 'Know what? I haven't given you one second of thought.'

'You're suing me.'

'Yeah.'

Jonah said nothing.

'Does that sound fair to you?' Iniguez asked.

'. . . not really.'

'Yeah. Me neither. Too fucking bad.'

Jonah set his mug down. 'You're right,' he said. 'It wasn't an accident.'

'No, huh?'

'No.'

'You want me to call Roberto up? You can tell that directly to him.'

'Your brother is dead because of Eve Gones.' Jonah paused, licked his lips. 'And you know that, but you're suing me instead.'

'I see. You're the Truth and Justice Committee.' Iniguez smiled. 'Let me tell you something. You and me? We're not partners.'

Jonah said, 'I don't expect anything.'

'You don't have the right to.'

'I don't.'

For twenty ticks of the grandfather clock, Iniguez drummed his fingers on his knees. Then he got up and went to the shelves, finding a CD without use of the labels. He raised the volume knob to eight o'clock and dropped in the disc.

A solo guitar drew a faint, sultry line between jazz and Latin, backed by an upright bass that pulsed on offbeats, like the music's own heart.

The melody took three steps in one direction and one in reverse, unfolding the minor scale.

Iniguez said, 'That's Raymond on the bass.'

'I didn't know he played.'

'Of course you fucking don't,' said Iniguez. 'That's why I'm showing you. So you know something about him.'

The guitar relaxed into a secondary role. Jonah thought of bass solos as lugubrious, but Raymond's was clear and spare, notes hanging like ornaments, peaking needily in the upper register; then – as though ashamed to have sought attention – slinking, chastened, down the fret-board to resume the original pulse. The guitar regrasped the wheel, and Raymond Iniguez became background.

Iniguez pressed STOP.

'Our mother,' he said, after a while, 'would leave us alone together when I was seven and he was four. That's how I learned to cook without cutting off my thumbs, by making him dinner. I taught him to play the bass. He was my baby brother. He was my only brother. Now you know something.'

Jonah said, 'That song is beautiful.'

'I used to play it for him. It calmed him down.' Iniguez lifted his glasses and rubbed his dead eyes.

A long silence passed.

'That lady is bad news.'

Jonah said nothing.

'Is she calling you up?'

'Yes.'

'That's how it started with us.'

'She broke into my apartment. She crashed my family's Thanksgiving dinner.'

Iniguez nodded. He turned and walked into the hall. 'Bring my mug?'

In the the kitchen he took down a box of Equal packets, took the carton of milk, lifted the coffee pot. The tiniest pause preceded each decision, a microprayer before his fingers closed around an object. He would've appeared fluent, had Jonah not been watching closely.

'She was taping it. The night he was killed.' Jonah felt nervous using the passive voice, but Iniguez either didn't notice or decided to let it slide. 'She knew what was going on but she didn't say anything.'

'She told my brother that it was an art project.'

Silence.

'She used to call up here. She said she was his girlfriend.' Iniguez smiled sourly. 'I was like, news to me. Raymond has a girlfriend, that's fantastic. He hasn't had a girlfriend since the eighties. I told my wife, she started to cry she was so happy. She's more protective of him than me, even after he – This lady, she did classes at the Beacon about a year ago. She starts flirting with him. You imagine what that's like for a guy like him. She got him to break curfew. He stopped taking his medication cause of her, stopped going to sessions, he was almost on the street again. With meds he had no problems, not for years, and then, *pshp*, everything up in smoke. They wanted to throw him out. He got into a fight with one of the staff members. That wasn't him. He fought when he got scared. They told me at the Beacon that he was getting aggressive for no reason. That never happened before.'

Jonah, remembering the baseball bat, said nothing.

'I know what you're thinking, he should've been living with us.'

'I wasn't thinking that.'

'It doesn't work. We've tried. The kids . . . But I wasn't gonna let him be homeless. Do you know what I had to do to get him into that place? They require more paperwork than the IRS. I had to sign waivers' – a hand at chin level. 'He was doing better. A *lot* better. They got him a job, he made friends. Then he met her, and things changed.' He paused. 'One time he called me up real late. He couldn've been calling me from the Beacon, they lock down the phones at midnight. I didn't ask where he was. With her, probably. He's going crazy. Calling me names. *I* don't deserve that. Ungrateful shithead. My wife is asking, 'Who is it, who's calling at three in the morning.' And I don't want to hang up on him, because he could be standing on the top of the GWB. So I listen, and finally he starts to talk instead of shout. He tells me he's angry, nobody ever lets him be angry. I say, 'Yeah, Ramón, cause you have to *behave* yourself.' Iniguez was ashen. 'He hung up on me.'

'Was this before he got in the fight at the Beacon?'

'That was February. The fight was in April, right around my son's birthday. I remember, cause I'm on the phone with the balloon-animal guy, who's saying under no circumstances can he stay an extra half-hour, dealing with that, and then the other line rings and it's the Beacon people. You need to come pick him up, he's being evicted.'

'What happened?'

'He trashed the TV room. I had to pay to have the wall replastered. He hit some guy, who was fine, but Raymond broke a bone in his hand.' Iniguez faced Jonah. 'It was like she pulled a cork out in him.'

'Did you talk to her?'

'Not then. I made Raymond promise he would stop seeing her. He didn't get in any trouble during the summer. It was behind us. He came over for the Fourth of July, we had a barbeque. But I guess he didn't stop. He just got better at sneaking out.'

Jonah understood Simón Iniguez's purpose in hitting back: to hit. Eve hadn't pulled a trigger; her crime wasn't on any book. Who else but him to blame. He said, 'Do you think you're going to win the lawsuit?'

'I don't know.' Iniguez smiled faintly. 'What do you think?'

'Our lawyers seem to get a kick out of shooting at each other.'

'That's cause they're lawyers.' He walked to the fridge. 'Sure you don't want some pumpkin pie.'

'I'll have a piece. Thanks.'

As he cut them: 'How old are you?'

'Twenty-six.'

'Raymond got sick when he was twenty-seven.'

'He was a teacher.'

'He coached at PS One Seventy-five and ran Little League. There was nobody like my brother. Huge Yankees fan. You should've seen his room at the Beacon, posters everywhere. The worst thing about him getting sick was it happened right when my first son was born. My kids never got to meet the real him. His friends forgot him, our parents are dead. The only people who know the truth are me and my wife.'

'I'm sorry,' Jonah said. He remembered he wasn't supposed to apologize.

Iniguez said, 'Me too.'

They ate in silence. The crust was soggy.

'I'd say get her out of your life, but I know it's easier said than done.'

'I'm trying to get a restraining order.'

'You think that'll work?'

'Probably not.'

Iniguez nodded, rinsed his plate in the sink.

'The thing is,' Jonah said, 'I don't have her address or her phone number, which they need.' He cleared his throat. 'Did Raymond have them?'

Iniguez stood the plate on the drainer board. 'He might've.'

★   ★   ★

The garage had been converted into a recording studio. Foam-covered walls made the place feel more cramped than it was – which was very cramped, a paella of instruments, speakers, cables, microphone stands, computers; milk crates of analog tape; wavy, silvery columns of CDs. A single forty-five-watt bulb burned. Iniguez stepped past a nylon-string guitar on a stand, stopping to pluck the low E.

'My wife brought this back from the Beacon,' he said, hefting a cardboard box.

While Jonah sorted through its contents, Iniguez picked up the guitar and sat in the chair by his workstation, playing a tune recognizable as a slower, more elemental version of the song they'd listened to upstairs. Jonah took out a few shirts, refolded them, set them aside on the steps. Some bed linens. A handful of fliers; the *Beacon House News*; a *Post* sports section talking about the pennant race.

'When we were kids, me and Raymond made money playing in a Mexican restaurant in Brooklyn. This was our, you know. Signature song.'

Jonah didn't know what to say. 'What's it called?'

'It doesn't have a name. Raymond called it "The Song." "Let's play 'The Song.'" Playing live we made it last a quarter of an hour. When I set up my first studio – I used to live near the zoo, before I got married – and we did that version I played you upstairs as an audition piece. It was mostly to test the equipment.'

342

Jonah wanted to know how Simón had met his wife, how he had come to his profession, how he managed to navigate this morass without sight. But too many questions were too many questions.

'Not much here except clothes.'

'I bought him a computer,' Simón said. 'That's not there?'

'I don't see it.'

'Then it's back in the corner. Have a look.'

Jonah parted a picket fence of boom stands and knocked into a low metal table covered with a checked tablecloth and a half-dozen green-blinking devices, all plugged into the same overloaded surge protector. Lifting that, he found a slim, dusty ThinkPad.

He brought it back to Iniguez, who said, 'I got him this so he could look for jobs or, you know, write a résumé. I don't know what's on here, but it's private.'

'I'll look for the number,' Jonah said.

'I don't want my wife coming and find you here. Take it home.'

Jonah hesitated. 'Are y—'

'Don't tell me what you find, I don't want to know. Call before you bring it back. It's listed under Cross-Bronx Studios. Call first.'

'I will.'

Iniguez started back up the stairs. 'You can let yourself out.'

Jonah said, 'The rest of the stuff—'

'I'll take care of it. Unless you want something. You want a shirt?'

343

'No. Thanks.'

Iniguez stopped at the top of the steps, his big body outlined in yellow light. 'You can take it all,' he said. 'I don't want it around the house.'

CHAPTER 27

Adults got diseases; children got sick. A thirty-year-old had epilepsy; a nine-year-old had Seizure Disorder NOS (Not Otherwise Specified) – as though by avoiding a label you could delay a lifetime of grief.

The practical reason for NOSing kids was that they frequently failed to fit familiar diagnostic patterns. Nowhere was this truer than on ped psych, where the first order of business was to identify where normal childhood flightiness ended and illness began. All five-year-olds are a little bit psychotic.

Matched one-on-one with a softhearted shrink named Shervan Soleimani, Jonah walked the floor on consults. The patients they saw that morning were inadvertently hilarious, popping with off-the-wall ideas, mimicking the doctor's soft Persian lilt. Most were Wacky Kid Not Otherwise Specified. Others suffered from externals – violent homes, severe neglect – such that their imaginations seemed to have been pulverized; they looked at Jonah with cold pity, as though he still had a lot of growing up to do.

One such girl, a sickly six-year-old from Spanish Harlem, had been at the hospital for two days because Social Services couldn't decide where to send her. Her mother had brought her in to shelter her from an abusive father, then had an MI in the middle of the peds ward and died. Dad had drifted into the ether, although general consensus held that to be for the best.

The girl had been crying so hard that she'd given herself a nosebleed, which Jonah attempted to stanch. She gnawed at her uneven braids, hiccupping sorrow and swinging her feet.

'DeShonna?' Soleimani said.

The girl sniffled and squirmed away. 'Stop touching me.'

Soleimani indicated for Jonah not to be offended. Jonah nodded, dropped the bloody cotton balls in the trash.

'We talked to your aunt today,' said Soleimani. 'She is going to come take care of you for a while.'

This piece of news caused DeShonna to cry even harder.

'I don't want her, I want my *mama*.'

'I know you do,' said Soleimani. 'It must hurt a lot. Sometimes talking about it can make you feel better. If she was here right now, what would you say to her?'

She dropped the pigtail and gave him a businesslike stare.

'I'd say, Fuck you, bitch.'

That night Lance returned home bearing boxed panettone and an improbably intense tan.

'UV beds, dude. A European favorite. The Count keeps one in his basement. I was on it like an hour a day. Do you think I damaged my reproductive capabilities?'

'One can only hope.'

Lance handed him the panettone. 'It's traditionally a Christmas delicacy, but in the age of mass tourism, you can get it all year round. The EU legislates production.'

Starved, grateful, Jonah put out paper plates. 'How was the trip?'

'Fuckin waste of time. All I did was smoke and tan.'

'How about the Count?'

Lance picked a raisin out of the cake and balanced it on his thumb before darting his tongue out, toad-like, to eat it. 'Bad teeth, good clothes. He owns a gondola. His house is attached to the hotel, right on the Grand Canal, with its own slip in back. It's pretty cool. In the morning you go out there and it's all foggy. Molto mysterioso.'

'The craziest part of that story is that you were up in the morning.'

'They're six hours ahead, so when you think about my schedule here, it's like I'm living their time zone, dude. Like, their nine A. M. is our three A.M. So that means I'm getting up when they're going to – Uh. That doesn't make any fucking sense. Whatever, dude, I was *jet. Lagged.* The three of us went out in his gondola. You remember Zeke from Alpha Sig? With the Steven Tyler lips? Dead ringer for the gondolier. Scary.' Lance grimaced and pushed his cake away. 'I have to say, though, it was an unfortunately *overt* vacation.'

Jonah raised his eyebrows.

'The place is old, dude. The walls . . . I could hear them going at it. All fucking night. My footage is *tainted.* I'm going to have to redub everything.'

'It's your Oedipus Rex.'

'My mom and I are close, but this was *evil.* Plus I think they were having a threesome. One morning I went for a walk at like six A.M. Our noon. Or – whatever, point is, when I come back there's this *chick* coming downstairs with her hair all *whhhraang,* wearing a mink stole and I'm pretty sure nothing else.'

'That's messed up.'

'Whatever.' Lance shrugged. 'He's coming for Christmas.'

Jonah sensed hurt – and a kind of puritanical contempt – behind this show of indifference, but he did not want to probe uninvitedly. He nodded.

They ate in silence. Finally, as though noticing it for the first time, Lance waved at the huge pile of furniture blocking their fire escape. 'It looks like Les Mis in here, what the shit is going on?'

Jonah sighed. 'Don't unpack just yet.'

He told Lance everything, concluding, 'It's not safe to stay here. I called Vik, I'm staying with him.'

'This is beyond wack.'

'Tell me about it.'

'Are you going to turn yourself in?'

'What for?'

Lance pondered this. 'True dat. Do you still have the DVD?'

Jonah got it from his desk. 'Turn the volume down,' he warned.

The screen filled with snow. The DVD player made unhealthy shifting noises and regurgitated the disc upon its tongue.

ERROR MEDIA NOT READABLE
IT MAY BE DIRTY OR DAMAGED (MESSAGE – 7.9)

Jonah turned the disc over to blow on its underside, and saw that its surface had gone cloudy gray. He rubbed at it with the corner of his shirt to no effect. 'When I first got it, the bottom was red.'

He handed it to Lance, who looked at it and said, 'It's a self-destructing disc. They go bad after they're exposed to oxygen.'

Jonah felt the blood drain from his face. 'Is there any way to recover it?'

'Not that I know of.'

They stood looking at the now useless piece of plastic.

Jonah said, 'Get your bag.'

Before clearing out of the apartment, he left a note for Eve taped to the door, in which he informed her that he was leaving town for a few days, apologized for betraying her trust, and again expressed a desire to end their relationship peaceably. This bunch of platitudes he didn't expect to achieve much, save to prevent her from breaking in.

Lance was gracefully accommodating. 'As long as we're taking proactive steps, dude. Don't let the cops search our pad. It's like a class-C felony in there.'

They parted ways at Union Square, where Lance headed to Ruby's in Park Slope, and Jonah – hoisting a large duffel containing books, clothes, and both his and Raymond Iniguez's laptops– went uptown. He changed trains and buses at random, ending up in Columbus Circle, where he sank into the posh bowels of the Time Warner Center. Whole Foods bubbled with neo-yuppies ogling lustrous produce. The odor of ripe cheese set off notes of damp cashmere and shoe rubber. He spent time examining Fontinas and Parmesans and sheep's-milk blues (*I got the sheep's-milk blues* he sang in his head) before selecting a pomelo and stepping into a line fifty strong. The first snow of the year had come down that morning, and although it hadn't stuck, folks looked despondent.

He took his fruit to the second floor, prying the rind free with cold, red fingers as he alternately checked his watch and over his shoulder. Through the picture window, taxis swirled like bees, hungrily swallowing pedestrians. Wind whipped streetlight banners, stripped newspapers from commuters running for the subway.

He braced himself and headed out into the storm, walking north on Central Park West until he spotted a cab, which he directed to the HUM dorm via the longest route imaginable.

By the time he got upstairs, it was nine thirty, bringing his travel time to two hours and forty-six minutes. He dropped his stuff near the futon. The apartment was quiet; Vik and Mike were out, and Cutler's door was closed, the light off.

Raymond's laptop had refused to start when he'd tried it at home the previous night. Having left it charging all day, Jonah now slid it from his bag and fired it up. It took forever to boot, getting snarled in a virus scanner that hadn't run for months. Up popped a wallpaper of Derek Jeter, his pinstripes straining as he swung at a ball stretched oblong by speed. Other than this one gesture toward customization, Raymond seemed not to have used the machine a whole lot. For that matter, Jonah doubted that it'd been Raymond who'd put the photo there.

Who was Simón Iniguez kidding? His brother couldn't sustain a job coaching high-school sports. Picturing him as connectophile, as data processor, as dot-com entrepreneur . . . It was too pathetic to think about, running shoes for a paraplegic. Jonah felt a dull wet pop; he'd destroyed more than a person: a talisman against hopelessness.

And when people looked at him: what did he represent? Did his friends draw strength from him; did his parents, or George? He didn't think so. They pitied him, like the little girl with the pigtails, DeShonna, did. In twenty-six years in the world he had failed to learn hardness, like a real person should.

The computer's beep poked him in the eye. The virus scanner needed to be updated. Would he like to do it now or to be reminded in fourteen days?

CANCEL
       CANCEL
              CANCEL
                     CANCEL

He spent an hour or so digging. The last websites Raymond had visited were exactly what Jonah would have expected: *Sports Illustrated*, MLB.com, the Weather Channel, pornography. The browser's cache held a worthless mess.

Upon opening, the mail client prompted him for a password. He tried *yankees* and *jeter* and combinations thereof, adding numerals and punctuation and misspellings. He tried *newyork*, *bombers, steinbrenner*; tried *bostonsucks* and *fucksox* and, feeling that he was reaching here, *mickey-mantle* and *lougehrig*. Then he typed *simon* and the program popped alive with an error message: the network could not be found.

The archived mail sat in the inbox. Jonah scrolled to the first e-mail, dated July 2003. Raymond's ISP welcomed him to the service, confirmed his username, and reiterated their Terms of Service in case he hadn't read them the first time.

For the first few months the mailbox served as a repository for rubbish-hucksters with spam-filter-evading names like Unforeseeable H. Mackenzie and Propeller E. Decipherable. They advertised cheap Viagra and the chance for him to *break down walls with your HUGE SHAFT!!* Every so often, Simón sent a note: circumspect encouragement couched in small talk. Weather and sports. Jonah recognized the authorial tone as the same one he used with Hannah, a frivolous, chary optimism that painted all successes as unarousing and all setbacks as minor.

Raymond never replied.

In October 2003, a new correspondent appeared. At first, Jonah bypassed the name, thinking the letters junk. But around January, they spiked in frequency. Someone named First Lady had taken a shine to Raymond. Jonah scrolled to the first one.

Dear Raymond Iniguez—
It was a pleasure to make your acquaintance.
You have nice hands.
Fondly,
Eve Gones

Jonah read it several times in search of some hint of what was to come.

It was a pleasure to make your acquaintance.

Its simplicity disarmed and depressed him.

You have nice hands.

She knew. She could divine latent rage.

It all started by complimenting a man's hands.

Three weeks later she wrote again, a longer letter referring to events that Jonah didn't understand. This time around, Raymond wrote back.

thak you i like yuo to

What started out as sporadic swiftly assumed an epic pace, not a correspondence so much as a monologue, as the ratio of her text to his got more and more exaggerated: fifteenfold, one hundred fiftyfold; one thousand polysyllables for every chickenpecked word; burning supernovae of language. It was unthinkable that Raymond understood her. Jonah – who considered his reading comprehension skills pretty sharp – could barely follow as she scampered through an impassable underbrush of adjectives and allusions. Ten densely written pages would elicit a single *yes* or a single *no*, leaving him to wonder what question Raymond was answering. Was it

Some would argue – and on this matter I avow agnosticism – that the duality (interior inaccessabil- ity/known universality cf Scarry) of corporeal sensations is precisely what make them objects of a sort of ekphrastic fixation, in that the primeval need to be confronted with an omnipresent always-applicable yet unknowable entity (formerly expressed as God-head reverence etc) has never truly disappeared, even in our deicidal age, becoming rather sublimated (and in many cases psychically dissolute to the point of pathologization), the impulse possibly assuming form as the Intellectual Quandary (eg quantum physics, Shakespeare's True Identity) or the Unworkable Ideo- logical Quest (eg Global Warming), although in my eyes for your money you're better off sticking with what you can grab in two hands that Raymond intended to affirm with his *yes*? Or was he trying to tell her that, yes, he did *like it when I touched you there?*

For several months she wrote him a half-dozen theses a day. Then, in late February – right before Raymond's fight at the Beacon – she took a turn for the terse, her e-mails shrinking to no more than a few lines, in which she exhorted him to carry out some small task. As before, it began benignly enough.

The next time you get on the subway, hold the doors till someone gets angry.

Or

Drop trash in the Turtle Pond.

Or

355

It would enthrall me, make me so happy, if you brought me a dead pigeon.

Soon she grew blunt, and alarmingly more specific.

If you love me, Raymond, you will put ink in Jerry's shampoo bottle.

I want you to go to Port Authority, walk downstairs to the bus depot where all the people are waiting, enter the women's restroom, and smash the mirror with a ball-peen hammer. Take a piece home in your pocket for me.

How many of these requests had he carried out? A few of her e-mails expressed gratitude for an unnamed act and promised a vaguely sexual reward: these were outnumbered by e-mails venting displeasure that he had disappointed her yet again, his noncompliance evidence of a feeble superego grappling with itself. The script for these scenes sat on the tip of Jonah's tongue. He had been a much better player, but the part was essentially the same, and he could not help but feel a sad kinship.

Oh, we had some good times, Raymond and I. Not on the order of the times had by you and me; they lacked the intellectual verve. But enough to whet a lady's appetite.

He read on with an unwillingly prophetic eye.

All her nonsense about keying cars and shoplifting Zippos and scaring tourists by spitting on their shirt-fronts: it was her way of testing mettle, figuring out if he was ready to do what she really wanted. *Where's the beef* he wondered.

Then, in May, she sent him an e-mail headed *Doggerel for Raymond.*
You make
me ache
Well done
my son
Jonah set the computer down, stood up, stuck his head out the window, and breathed the cold ninth-floor air.

By that time he had been reading for two hours; the machine computer whistled with overexertion, its internal fan whirring. He was debating whether to return to it when he heard a key in the lock. He rushed to close the computer and opened the door.

Snow had collected in Vik's erect, unkempt hair, making him look like a human shaving brush. His clothes were wrinkled and his face bloated. Under one arm he'd tucked a bag of groceries. Jonah went to help him unload the stuff.

'I left you towels,' Vik said.

'Thanks. How's OB?'

'It's a sorority. What're you on now? Psych?'

Jonah nodded.

'You must like that,' Vik said.

'It's interesting. I'm supposed to be following up one case for the next three weeks. This girl from the projects.'

Vik nodded. He looked spaced-out, and Jonah apologized for keeping him up. 'I'll put the rest of this away,' he said.

'All right.' Vik yawned. 'I round at five.'

'Shit. Well, go to bed.'

'You're okay out here?'

'All set.' He had said that he needed a place to crash for a few weeks, Vik's unflappability enabling him to ignore the inconvenience caused by such a request. 'Whatever you guys need while I'm here, I'm buying.'

'Not necessary.'

To press the issue would have been insulting, so Jonah thanked him and said goodnight.

As the crack beneath Vik's bedroom door went dark, Jonah returned to the computer to read the rest of First Lady's correspondence. It yielded nothing of further significance, and he was about to give up when he had an idea.

For this, Raymond's computer, lacking Web access, was useless. Jonah took out his own laptop, joined the apartment's wireless network (*Club Valsalva*), and searched for First Lady's e-mail address, striking gold among the newsgroups. Scores of threads filled up the monitor, all posted to a group called alt.rec.pain.

While First Lady had authored the bulk of the content, there were a few oddballs mixed in, posting anonymously or behind fake addresses. That people avoided using their real names didn't surprise Jonah at all, seeing as how the posts were invariably obscene, asking Mistress First Lady to punish them or spank them or whatnot. To one such suitor Eve replied:

You are mistaken. My interest is aesthetic. There are plenty of websites where you can indulge your asinine coprophilic fantasies without disrupting my train of thought. Go there.

And please stop posting here without proper grammar, spelling, and punctuation. Your ignorance turns a chapel into a corral.

In another post, overrun with quotes from Artaud and the Bhagavad Gita, she decried the 'petty anodynes' of 'standard bondage,' deriding the activities of 'mainstreamers' as 'jejune.' *Like Coke* she wrote *only the Real Thing will do.*

The real thing being – pain? Death? He could not make head or tails. Flung into cyberspace, the same heady rambling that had clogged Raymond's inbox read as animalistic, a maniac shouting into a wind tunnel. One item, however, caught his eye.

Req: vid will pay top $$$

He clicked on her reply.

E-mail me your phone number and we can discuss this in private.

He hoped he sounded like someone else.

Dear First Lady,
Your project excites me. What have you been creating recently? I would like to obtain footage of your work. I am unable to give you my phone number as I do not want my wife to answer. I can send you a money order. What are your

359

rates? Please send me your phone number or
address.
Sincerely,
Sam H.

CHAPTER 28

From page three of the *Guide*:

Your responsibility to a patient does not end when he or she is discharged from your service. **Continuity of care**, as affirmed by the bylaws of the American Medical Association (H–140.975, 5), remains a priority for physicians, especially those treating underserved populations, for whom a healthy lifestyle and continued access to medication may not be readily available.

Traditionally, because of the nature of the third-year clerkships, students do not often see the same patient for more than the duration of the hospital stay. This creates difficulties in developing ongoing relationships. To combat this problem, HUM has introduced the Home Helpers initiative, which allows the student doctor to follow a patient beyond immediate treatment. You are encouraged to look at the programs as an opportunity to forge a stronger connection to both the individual as well as the community in which you work.

FRIDAY, DECEMBER 3, 2004.
CHILD AND ADOLESCENT PSYCHIATRY,
WEEK ONE.

The Home Helpers program was the brainchild of the medicine department. Third-years would accompany attending physicians on housecalls, a way of ensuring that the most infirm and the most isolated, forgotten by the world, did not forget themselves, their pills, their diet regimens. Soleimani had been the one to integrate the program into the psych department, and it was with him that Jonah set out on foot that morning, accompanied by the social worker handling DeShonna Barnsworth's case. Yvette Wiltern's radiant smile underscored the fatigue etched in her fine brown face.

'I've been trying to get in touch with the aunt for three days. DeShonna should be getting out of school about now. Although I don't think she's been enrolled in years.'

'As in how long?' Jonah asked.

'As in ever.'

They walked north. Block by block the neighborhood degraded, chichi delis mutating into high-fat chain restaurants; dry cleaners becoming pawnshops. Clogged gutters created swamps of melting snow, rafted by six-pack rings. A van coasted by, woofers thumping, fanning water onto the sidewalk. They passed a block lined with nothing but funeral parlors and, turning east toward the river, met a vicious wind. Up rose the dead canvas of the projects.

Yvette said, 'I have another client here I was visiting last June – that heat? – when the trash didn't get collected for two weeks.' They crossed a court-yard and she pulled open the broken lobby door.

After colorectal surgery, Jonah figured that no smell would get to him ever again. He was wrong. Urine, bolstered by snack cheez and decaying phonebook. He felt as though he'd been jammed into the tank of a portajohn, and thought of Erich inspecting wine. *This vintage has affinities with poultry and fruit.* The smell of DeShonna's home had affinities with despair and poverty.

A dripping crack in the ceiling nailed him; he gave his head a canine shake.

Soleimani, commenting on the elevator, said, 'Slow.'

'It doesn't ding,' said Yvette. 'You have to watch close or else you can be waiting here for a half an hour.'

'We can walk.'

'They're on the seventeenth floor.'

Ever the optimist, Soleimani said, 'I need the workout.'

Jonah wondered aloud about DeShonna's mother's funeral.

'I'll ask the aunt.'

'What's her name?' Soleimani asked.

'Veronica Hutchins.' Yvette read from a spiral notebook. 'DeShonna's mother's sister. Three kids of her own, works at a perfume wholesaler on Lex. I leave messages with her boss, but she never calls back.'

'Are we sure someone's home?'

'We'll find out soon.'

The elevator came, and they crowded inside a scarred faux-wood box with an even chewier odor.

The hallway to Unit 20N-I was warped and grungy. Welcome mats had seen better decades. Cans of paint were stacked near the electrical closet.

'Home improvement,' Soleimani remarked.

Jonah decided that that could mean anything, including closing one's eyes.

The theme song of a daytime talk show blared, obscuring the doorbell. 'One thing you get on the job is tough knuckles,' Yvette said, pounding.

A doe-eyed girl of about sixteen answered. Leggy, in form-fitting jeans, she wore hairy yellow socks that undulated as she compulsively flexed her toes. Against her hip she held a scrawny, wrinkled five-month-old. Behind her the apartment was dark.

'Yeah?' she said.

'Is Veronica Hutchins home?' Yvette asked.

'No.' She shifted the baby to her other side; a tiny hand clawed the air.

'We're from the Hospital of Upper Manhattan,' said Soleimani. 'We're here to see how DeShonna's doing.'

The girl pursed her lips. 'She ain't here.'

'May I ask who you are?'

'You may ask it, yeah.'

Yvette smiled. 'Are you Veronica's daughter?'

The baby chirped crankily, and the girl shushed it. 'Yeah, so?'

'Did DeShonna go to school today?' Soleimani asked.

The girl shrugged.

'Can you give this to your mom?' Yvette said.

The girl crushed the card into her pocket, where Jonah thought it likely to stay for a long, long time.

'You from Social Services?' said the girl. 'Cause we got a problem here.'

She turned and went inside, plainly expecting them to follow. 'Look,' she called.

A television provided most of the apartment's light, bluing the floor, upon which a handful of choking-hazard figurines lay scattered, as though swimming, round the legs of two plastic chairs. In the corner was a pile of disarticulated cushions. Movement flitted through Jonah's peripheral vision, the darkness itself crawling: roaches.

'Look.' Near the kitchen baseboards, a greenish substance oozed from the floor.

'What is that?' Soleimani said.

The girl looked at him like *How the fuck do I know*.

'How long has that been there?' Yvette said.

The girl chewed her tongue contemplatively. 'Every day some more comes out.'

'Did you talk to your super?'

The girl snorted.

Yvette said, 'I'll call someone from the Housing Authority.'

The girl said, 'It's like *alive*.' She turned to them. 'You think it's alive?' Then, loudly, she began to cry. Nobody seemed to know what to do; Jonah looked at Soleimani, who looked at Yvette, who took the girl gently by the arm and led her to a back room. A door closed.

Jonah remained standing awkwardly by the kitchen, counting fissures in the ceiling. Soleimani walked to the window, peered through the savaged blinds. He looked down at the pile of cushions and clucked his tongue. Using a handkerchief, he reached into the cushions and withdrew a small, cloudy glass pipe with burnt ends. He sighed, wrapped it up, and pocketed it.

The playground chainlink gave a noisy cross-hatched view of the FDR's junction with the Triborough. Most of the equipment had been busted up or stolen, leaving a swing set with a lone intact seat. On it they found DeShonna, chewing her hair and singing to herself, heedless of the cold in a denim jacket and jeans a slightly darker blue. She did not see them approaching until Soleimani whistled. Then she glanced up, and her expression shifted from self-involved to dull.

'Hi DeShonna,' said Yvette. 'You remember me?'

The girl nodded.

'Are you out here all by yourself?'

'Yeah.'

'Where'd your Aunt Veronica go?'

'I don't know.' She kicked the ground.

'Did she tell you you could come out here and play?'

She shrugged.

'Aren't you cold?' Jonah asked.

'Yeah.'

'I think you should go inside,' said Jonah. 'Your head might freeze and fall off.'

DeShonna half-smiled.

'Let's get you upstairs,' said Yvette.

The girl shook her head.

'Well *I'm* going upstairs,' Jonah said. 'I'm turning purple.'

That earned a giggle.

Yvette said, 'I'll take her inside. I'm going to have to talk to the mother at some point, you don't have to hang around.'

'We don't have anything else to do,' Soleimani said.

They cajoled DeShonna into joining them. As they rode up she shyly reached for Jonah's hand.

'It smells like *shit*,' she said.

'You said it,' said Yvette.

Their knocking took twice as long to revive the cousin, who had ditched her baby but continued to stand crooked, as though her spine had remolded itself to bear weight on one side. She

367

yelled at DeShonna for leaving the house. 'You always runnin off.'

Yvette stepped in and diverted the conversation to the pocket of slime. In the meantime, Soleimani and Jonah sat with DeShonna in the room she shared with both her cousins and the baby boy, whose name, she informed them, was Marquise. Soleimani asked how she was feeling about her mom; how she liked living with her aunt; if they had talked about starting school. She gripped a limp teddy and chewed her hair, refusing to make eye contact with the doctor. Occasionally she shot a look at Jonah, whose smiles elicited one-fifth reciprocation.

After a few minutes, Soleimani excused himself to go to the bathroom. Sensing that the questions were closing her up, Jonah said nothing. They sat listening to baby Marquise shift in his blankets. 'He's pretty,' she said. She touched his nose. 'I want a baby.' The idea of her breastless body swollen with child made Jonah want to throw up.

Soleimani came in and announced that they were leaving. DeShonna went back to staring at the ground, and did not reply when the psychiatrist told her that she could call him whenever she wanted.

Yvette stayed behind to talk to the cousin, whose name was Adia, and Jonah and Soleimani tramped south down Third Avenue. The doctor complimented Jonah's listening skills.

'It is a gift,' Soleimani said. 'Certain people, you know you can trust them.'

At 100th Street he shook Jonah's hand and headed back toward the HUM parking structure. Jonah continued south, passing the Islamic Cultural Center with its verdigris dome and looming minaret. Scarved women and a man in a dishdasha waited for the bus.

All week long he had been taking different routes home, stretching the two-block commute from HUM to the dorms into ludicrous hour-long excursions. He now walked to 86th Street, land of headless, tinsel-decked mannequins sporting fluorescent fleeces. Inside Strawberry, a clerk picked a zit. He went into Barnes & Noble and toyed with the magazines, which gave him a nice, homey feeling. Enough was enough, he decided. He went outside, walked one more block west, and doubled back.

She was across the street.

He saw mostly hair as she ducked behind a newsstand. But he knew it was her.

He ran into the subway and jumped on the uptown train. He went one stop, getting off with the intent to switch to a downtown train. Then he changed his mind: she might have seen him go into the subway; she might've followed on the next train. Or she might be waiting at 86th. He didn't know. He wouldn't put it past her to be anywhere.

★   ★   ★

Three hours later, he got home.

On Sunday he checked the e-mail account he'd used to contact First Lady, and found nine new messages, eight of which were garbage.

> *Dear Sam—*
> *I am flattered at your interest in my work and am happy to discuss it further with you. While I prefer not to give out my phone number, if you are located in the New York area, I would be willing to meet you somewhere public.*
> *As a word of warning, I must inform you that copies of my work are not cheap, as purchasing them requires a certain standard of commitment on the part of the buyer. For every price, however, there is a taker, and perhaps you are that person.*
> *FL*

He hit REPLY.

> *Dear First Lady:*
> *I live in Florida but good timing, I'm in New York for a business trip. I have conferences all day and can be available by seven in the evening on Tuesday.*
> *Name the place and I'll be there with bells on.*

He wondered if he'd been too quick on the draw; perhaps she wouldn't get the e-mail until

Wednesday, and would assume that he'd left town; then he'd have to find another excuse for being in New York . . .

But at six oh three P.M. she wrote back.

Meet me in front of the Metropolitan Museum of Art at quarter past seven. I'll be wearing a red jacket.

CHAPTER 29

The crowds that blanketed the steps of the Met during more clement months had long since dissipated, leaving no short-distance camouflage. He watched from afar as she approached, her jacket against the white-dusted steps like a wine stain on a hotel bedsheet. She didn't look surprised to have been stood up, leaving after five minutes.

He tailed her at a distance as she disappeared into the park at 85th, walking along the reservoir bridle path, pitch-black and too cold for all but the most intrepid joggers. His feet on gravel, louder than he liked.

On the west side of the park she picked up her pace, and he did, too, huffing to a building on the corner of 96th Street and Columbus whose signage advertised luxury rentals and whose doorman welcomed her with a tip of his hat.

It was possible, he supposed, that this wasn't her

building; maybe it was her boyfriend's place. He could easily imagine her stringing along lovers, the female equivalent of those sad-sack bigamists who end up on Springer, sparred over by four nebbishy deluded housewives. *He tol me* I *wud the only one he errer loved.*

He took out a five-dollar bill, crumpled it in his fist, and crossed the street.

'The woman who came in here?' he said to the doorman, holding up the money. 'She dropped this outside.'

'How's that?'

'She got off the bus and it fell out of her purse. She came in like a second ago.'

The door man smiled. 'Good man.' He picked up the house phone and pressed a button. 'Miss Cove? A gentleman here has some money you dropped outside? Okay.' He hung up. 'She'll be down in a minute.'

'You know what,' Jonah said, 'that's all right. Tell her it was a Good Samaritan.' He put the money down on the reception desk and walked out.

Kate said, 'I saw what I saw.'

'Do you understand what I'm saying?'

'I—'

'Do you understand what *you're* saying?'

'I *saw* what happened, Jonah.'

'That's what I'm trying to explain.' There was a long silence. 'Kate.'

'Yeah?'

'I'm your brother.'

'I know.'

'You really think that about me?'

'. . . no.'

'You think I'm some sort of monster.'

She said, 'I never thought that.'

'You did.'

'Well you *hit* her, what am I sup*posed* to think?'

'You're supposed to give me the benefit of the doubt.'

She said nothing.

He sighed. 'Listen.'

Fifteen minutes later, he stopped talking.

Kate said, 'Holy fucking shit.'

'Yeah,' he said. 'Holy fucking shit.'

'Why didn't you say something?'

'I didn't want to get you involved.'

'Jonah, this is, that's, lunacy.'

'I know.'

'You let her in the *house*?'

'I—'

'You let her near Gretchen?' Kate was yelling now. 'What are you *thinking*?'

'If you'd listened to me instead of running off to have ladies' night—'

'I can't believe you, Jonah.' She was doing her best Disappointment, which normally stopped him dead in his tracks. 'I can't be*lieve* you could be so irr—'

'Shut up. *Shut. Up.* You can scream at me as much as you want in five minutes, but for the *time being*, give me some *assistance* so I can get her out

374

of my hair before she does something *bad* to me, can you do that for *one second*?'

A silence.

Kate said, 'I'm sorry.'

He exhaled. 'I don't care.'

'I – I shouldn't have jumped to conclusions.'

'Forget it. You have to keep this to yourself.'

'I apologize.'

'Listen to me: I don't care what you thought about me,' he lied. 'Promise me you're not going to say anything to Mom and Dad.'

'They don't know? They should know.'

'They don't need to, they'll just freak out.'

'*I'm* freaking out.'

'Everything is under control. Promise me you're not going to tell them.'

'I think it's a better idea if—'

'I don't care if you think it's a better idea. All right? Now *promise me*.'

Kate said, 'I promise.'

'Good. Thank you. Now get your yearbook. Her last name is Cove.'

He listened to her dragging the footstool, breathing hard, turning pages.

'I'll be darned,' she said quietly.

'She's there?'

'She's there.'

'What's her first name.'

'Carmen.' The phone fell away from Kate's mouth, was shoved back. 'There she is. I remember her now. Oh my God. She looks completely different.'

'Different how.'

'Back then she had this . . . butch haircut. She used to wear overalls all the time. I thought she was a lesbian.'

'Can you send me a copy of the page?'

'Jonah.' A change crept into Kate's voice. 'Jonah, this can't be her.'

'What.' He waited. 'What's wrong.'

'This girl . . . she was – she moved out of the dorms after her roommate died. Jonah, her roommate was murdered.'

Although Kate had always been big woman on Campus – familiar with faces and good for a salient factoid – in this case all she could say was *It was in the papers.*

The online archives of the *Yale Daily News* yielded a series of articles, the first of which was dated November 20, 1992.

MISSING JUNIOR PROMPTS INQUIRY

NEW HAVEN – **Police said yesterday that they had no information about the disappearance of a Calhoun College junior.**

Marisa Ashbrook '94 was last seen leaving her room Monday night. She told roommates she was going to a party and has not been seen or heard from since.

'We're treating this as standard missing

persons,' said New Haven police Cmdr. Paul F. Reed. 'We will investigate with every resource we have at our disposal.'

Reed added that investigators had not ruled out the possibility that Ashbrook had left campus of her own volition. The police have been in contact with her family, he said.

The next article, a week later, reported that Marisa Ashbrook's friends and swim teammates planned a candlelight vigil.

In a third article, right before winter break, the reporter covering the story shifted to an elegiac tone. Marisa's athletic achievements were lauded by her peers, who also recalled her sunny smile and charming Southern accent. Her ex-boyfriend called her *the sweetest person you ever met.*

The editor must have ordered the staff to pursue more active items, because Marisa disappeared from the headlines until the first week of March, when a group of hikers spotted an arm obtruding from a melting snowbank.

POLICE ID MISSING JUNIOR
NEW HAVEN – Police today confirmed that a body discovered in rural New Hampshire is that of a Calhoun junior missing since November.

Twenty-year-old Marisa Ashbrook '94 was identified using dental records.

Ashbrook, a member of the swim team, was last seen three months ago leaving her dorm room for a party.

'This is a tragedy for the entire Yale community,' said university president Richard C. Levin. 'We extend our condolences to the Ashbrook family.'

Although the Grafton County (NH) Medical Examiner's Office has yet to certify Ashbrook's death as a homicide, police there have already begun to investigate in co-operation with the New Haven County Sheriff's Department, said a department spokesperson.

Because Ashbrook was discovered across state lines, the spokesperson added . . .

The archives of regional papers turned up the same photo: dirty blond hair; a rectangular face; expensive orthodonture, which had probably made identifying her a cinch. Jonah was sure her parents wept over that: her braces. And her prep-school clothes. Her allowance, her first car, her prom dress. Childhood illnesses; six A.M. practices. Her father was a Chattanooga tax attorney. Another article called her a promising young athlete, although nothing he'd read indicated that she'd been anything more than run-of-the-mill. A National Merit finalist. A perfectly pleasant, bright girl.

Then he found a blog called EVIL FORCES OF DOOM AND OTHER GORY STUFF. The author of

EFODAOGS, as described on the ABOUT ME page, was an economics Ph.D. candidate at MIT and an armchair criminologist who liked to chew on cold cases. His analysis of the Marisa Ashbrook murder was detailed and grisly. Because the body had been under icepack for most of four months, he wrote, it had hardly decomposed.

Then why were dental records necessary to make the ID? Because before dumping the body, the killer worked her over pretty good. She'd been skinned.

There were no suspects.

WEDNESDAY, DECEMBER 8, 2004.
ADOLESCENT AND CHILD PSYCHIATRY,
WEEK TWO.

He had been given by Belzer to understand that cops weren't interested in issuing harassment violations; unless there was a bookable crime, no dice. Thus Jonah did his best to impress upon the officer at the Twenty-third Precinct the totality of Eve's – Carmen's – behavior. As much as he wanted to tell them about Marisa Ashbrook, he realized that claiming to have solved a decade-old murder was a surefire sign of crackpottedness; so he did his best to radiate Rationality, every now and again squeezing out Reasonably-sized pellets of panic in the form of tense chuckles.

It must've worked, because within the hour he received a visit from two uniformed cops: a swarthy block of a man and a woman with pensile breasts and kindly cow's eyes. They introduced themselves as officers Degrassi and Villanueva.

'I know you,' said Degrassi. 'Superdoc.'

They interrupted Jonah's story with a promise to look into the matter.

'Call us back if she bothers you again,' said Villanueva, giving him her card.

'That's the smart thing,' said Belzer. 'Let them handle it.'

'I have to wait *until* she does something?'

'Welcome to New York.'

Needing clothes, he returned that night to the apartment. To his surprise Lance was already there – and had been for two days.

'You told me you were going to stay at Ruby's,' Jonah said.

'I lied, dude. I missed my stuff.'

'It's not safe here.'

'Then why'd you come back?'

'I'm just picking up some socks, and then I'm leaving, and you need to, too.'

'Dude, I agree completely.'

'You're full of shit,' Jonah said. 'You said that before.'

'That's cause I didn't believe you.'

'And you do now?'

Lance paused. 'I'm going to tell you something but you can't get mad.'

380

'What.'

'Say you won't get mad.'

'I don't *know* if I won't get mad,' Jonah said. 'I might.'

'Then I can't tell you. I need immunity.'

Jonah sighed. 'Yeah, fine.'

They went to the editing room, where Lance turned on his AV system. 'I found this today while reviewing footage for volume two of the selfumentary's greatest hits.' He opened his media editor, found a file, hit the spacebar. A shot of the living room came up, marked 11/29/04 7:13 P.M.

'This is the night we left.' He fast-forwarded, the clock on the screen advancing by leaps and bounds to nine P.M. He hit PLAY.

The shot continued, static as before.

Jonah said, 'I don't—'

'Watch.'

At nine oh one there was a muffled crash. Because of the camera angle, Jonah couldn't tell exactly where it had come from. The fire escape? They had put the furniture back before abandoning ship.

Eve walked into the frame.

Jonah said, 'Fuck.'

She strolled around the living room, not touching anything. For several minutes she stared out the window near the sofa.

'I don't know what she could be looking at that's so interesting,' Lance said.

'I do,' Jonah said. The Museum of Human Frailties.

At nine ten she left the shot.

'I don't get it,' Jonah said. 'The window—'

'Wasn't broken, right? Watch.' Lance picked up the remote control and set the fast-forward to jump one minute at a time. Eve's onscreen figure zipped and dashed, disappearing from the room at eleven forty-eight P.M.

'She went out the way she came.'

'No,' said Lance. 'She went *that* way. She's sleeping in your room, dude.'

The clock races forward, seven A.M. Eight A.M. A quarter after eight.

Eve re-emerges, talking on a cell phone. She says something that sounds like—

'Is she giving out our address?'

Fast-forward again to nine fifty-eight A.M. A knock. Eve – who has been lying on the floor for two hours – gets up to admit a man in a jump-suit. He and Eve move off-screen, toward the fire escape. At ten twenty-nine A.M. he leaves the apartment.

Jonah said, 'Who the hell was that.'

'You'll see in a second.'

At eleven twenty-two A.M. she lies down to take a nap. At two forty-seven P.M. she gets up.

The man in the jumpsuit is back – with a friend. They carry something poster-sized, wrapped in paper. They take it off-screen: the sound of a drill. Forty-five minutes later, they leave. Eve crosses the room, carrying a broom. At four oh six P.M., she lets herself out via the front door, and once again the shot is static.

'One take-home lesson,' Lance said, 'need be, you can get a window replaced same day.'

Jonah said, 'I thought there wasn't supposed to be a camera in the living room.'

'Uh.' Lance smiled sheepishly. 'Immunity?'

'Where is it.'

'Dude, I di—'

'*Where.*'

From atop the kitchen cabinets poked a barely visible camera eye. Jonah got it down: a square body with a flexible appendage, at the end of which was a lens.

He said, 'Gimme the fucking phone.' He dialed Officer Villanueva. 'Stay right there,' he said to Lance, who was slinking from the room.

Villanueva listened to the new information and promised to call the next day so she could have a look at the footage.

'I'm sorry, dude.'

'You're not coming back here,' Jonah said. 'Not until I say. Get it?'

Lance nodded.

'You have everything you need?' Jonah asked.

Lance nodded again.

'Good,' said Jonah. Then he belted Lance in the solar plexus, dropping him gasping to the floor.

'*Duuude.*'

'We gotta go,' Jonah said, poking him with his toe. 'It's not safe here.'

CHAPTER 30

A s they waited for Yvette's knock to be answered, Jonah felt mild déjà vu: the hallway, cold as before; the blasting talk show. Adia appeared in the same slinky jeans, over which she had added a ratty bathrobe. She shivered and sweated and clutched baby Marquise to her body, not noticing Soleimani or Jonah as she zeroed in angrily on Yvette.

'I called the man you told me to, he didn't do nothing.' She began berating Yvette while Soleimani and Jonah slipped past.

DeShonna was seated crosslegged on the floor, her hair pulled into tight, even pigtails. She acknowledged their entrance by facing the wall.

'Did you miss us?' Jonah said.

She shook her head.

'Yeah,' he said. 'If I were you I wouldn't miss me either.'

384

Getting her to look at them – let alone respond – took a while. Soleimani managed to extract the fact that DeShonna's aunt hadn't been home in a week, and Adia had declared herself in charge.

'Where did she go?' Soleimani asked.

'She left.'

'Did she say where she was going?'

DeShonna looked at him as though the question was woefully stupid.

In the other room, Adia raised her voice several notches. *Fuck that. Fuck that.*

'If you want to tell us anything,' said Soleimani, 'we are here to listen.'

DeShonna looked at Jonah. 'I don't want to.'

Soleimani said, 'Why don't I go see how Yvette's doing out there.' He winked at Jonah and shut the door behind him, muting what had by now become an honest-to-goodness verbal brawl.

'She's loud,' said DeShonna.

'How do you feel about her?' Jonah asked.

'I hate her.' She wiped her nose on her sleeve. 'I wish she died.'

'Sounds like you know a lot of people like that.'

DeShonna nodded.

'Does she smoke around you?'

'Yeah.'

'Is there someplace you can go when she's like that?' he asked. 'A friend's?'

DeShonna shrugged.

'I'm here because I care about you. We all do. We all came back just to see you. That's three people who think about you a lot. It might not feel that way sometimes, but I promise you, I've been thinking about you all week.'

'Yeah *right*.'

'You think I'd ride in that smelly elevator for fun?'

She smiled weakly. Giving him an A for effort.

'I'd rather stick my head up a monkey's butt.'

'Maybe you should.'

'Maybe I will.'

'Maybe you should go do it right now.'

'I will. And I'll stick your head up a monkey's butt, too.'

'*No*.'

'It might help you feel better. It's nice and warm inside a monkey's butt.'

'Ew, *no*.' She giggled. 'Fuck off.'

'You have some vocabulary,' he said. 'I bet I could learn a lot from you.'

'Yeah,' she said. 'You could.'

Evidently, Yvette had pushed a button, because after Jonah said good-bye for now to DeShonna, he found both the doctor and the social worker under siege, Adia alternately shrieking at the top of her lungs about Social Services and coughing phlegm into a paper towel. Yvette vainly explained that she didn't work for DSS; she worked for the hospital. Adia called her a dumb trick and Soleimani a terrorist and waved the baby around like he was a magic wand. She trailed them into the hall, still yelling.

Yall walk out, you go on.

She got in the elevator with them, followed them out of the building and across the courtyard, lobbing epithets as they walked away. Jonah worried about her standing out in the cold with the baby, a concern neither Yvette nor Soleimani seemed to share as they beat a hasty retreat.

It was eight o'clock before he trudged up to the dorm. The security guard was drunk as usual, his breath spicy as he asked Jonah what he wanted for Christmas.

'Ah . . . haven't . . . made up my mind.' He was having trouble finding his ID.

'Forget it, forget it,' said the guard, waving him through.

'Thanks,' Jonah said and started to step inside.

'Hey,' said the guard, snagging Jonah's sleeve. 'You dint answer my question.'

Jonah glanced up the block. Nobody: the sidewalk clear to the corner save for a heap of trash bags and a dilapidated nightstand blocking the building's service entrance. 'I really have to get upstairs.'

The guard frowned. 'Am I gonna have to twist your nuts.'

Evidently, it was his day to be molested by substance abusers. 'I'd like a periscope,' Jonah said.

'A wha?'

'Look it up,' he said.

Inside Vik's apartment he returned a voicemail from Officer Degrassi.

'We spoke with Ms Cove this afternoon. She said she doesn't know what we're talking about. We instructed her to leave you alone.'

'That's it?'

'I'm afraid there's not much else we can do at the present moment.'

'But the video—'

'Officer Villanueva and I, we don't feel it would be expedient to pursue that element of the situation any further. Ms Cove denied being in your apartment—'

'You can *see* it on the tape.'

'I get where you're coming from,' said Degrassi. 'But let's think here. Now I haven't seen the tape, but let's assume it shows what you're saying it shows. She broke your window and then had it fixed. She didn't rip you off, and she didn't harm you.'

'Not yet.'

'And at the present moment we don't have anything to suggest she would.'

'She came into my house when I wasn't *there*,' Jonah said.

'Exactly,' said Degrassi. 'So she couldn't've done anything to you anyhow. And – hang on a sec – she says you *were* there.'

'*I* was there?'

'She said you were waiting for her in the bedroom.'

'I *wasn't*.'

'Can you prove that?'

'Look,' Jonah said. 'Either I was or I wasn't, and

388

this isn't a court of – yes, as a matter of fact, I can. I'm staying with a friend, he'll—'

'I understand your frustration. But we're not going to pursue it. Okay? I'm tryin to be helpful here. She doesn't have a criminal record, she's employed, and she sounded in control of herself when we talked to her.'

'When she talks to *you*,' Jonah said, 'fine, but that's what you're missing here, how she acts when she's around *me* is—'

'I'm not *going* to arrest her,' said Degrassi, 'because if I do, they're gonna let her go. See what I'm saying? She's in and out of there next day. She's a pain in the ass, grant you that. But that's not a reason to bust her. Some people are by nature a pain in the ass, and there's not much you can do about it. If she continues to bother you, give us a call. If she does anything to threaten you—'

'She *has*.'

'—*physically*, to threaten you physically . . . or verbally – and it's *credible*, then you give me a call back.'

Jonah said nothing.

'Okay then?' said Degrassi. 'Take care.'

'Wait,' Jonah said. 'You said she's employed.'

'Yeah.'

'Can I ask where she works?'

The officer sighed.

'I won't go start with her,' Jonah said. 'I'm giving you my word.' He paused. 'I'm curious. I never knew she had a job.'

Degrassi chuckled. 'Well, you're gonna soil yourself when I tell you what it is.'

The tiny preparatory preschool where Carmen Cove taught kindergarten was on the Upper East Side, a quarter-mile from the HUM dorm. Degrassi said, 'It's one of those places they test the kids with blocks before lettin em in.'

That night Jonah had a hard time studying, his focus cracked by the knowledge that, whether at work or home, Eve was at most two miles away. He had no plan of action, no legal recourse; he was at her mercy.

To calm himself, he thought about DeShonna. Things could be worse.

SATURDAY, DECEMBER 11, 2004.

'I fly down on a week from today,' George said. 'They supply the transfer to the boat. My flight's at six. I leave for the airport at four thirtyish. If you're here by noon I'll give you the rundown. That's the – the eighteenth. You're all set to—'

'Yes.'

'Good. Good.' There was a click; Jonah wondered if George had hung up. 'Jonah? Quick question. What are you doing that night?'

'Which night?'

'The night before, Friday. The seventeenth.'

'I'm going to be in the City.'

'Doing what?'

running scared 'Doing whatever I feel like doing.'

390

'Okay. Cause I was wondering if you might come out here.'

Jonah said, 'You were wondering that.'

'Do you think you might be able to?'

'You haven't asked me—'

'No, I know,' George said. 'But look over your schedule for me, would you? If you could make it, I'd appreciate it.'

'You can't get on the ship early.'

'I thought it might help, to integrate you, so that if you have any last-minute questions I can be there to answer them.'

'Whatever you want to tell me, tell me now.'

'I'm saying if questions come up.'

'Then I'll ask you that morning,' Jonah said. 'I don't understand the need for me to come out early if—'

'Then never mind. If you're okay, I'm okay. If it's possible for you to come out, I'm asking you to consider it. Cause you may think you know your way around the house, but things come up, there's bound to be errands I need to do. You know? Or if I wanted to go out and grab myself a bite to eat.'

'When.'

'That night, Friday night. I wanted to get out of the house for a bite.'

Having sailed the Caribbean with his family, Jonah knew full well that luxury liners carried half their weight in comestibles: enough for theme dinners, flambé surprises, the midnite choco-buffet. You didn't need a last supper to survive the week.

'You want to go to dinner with Louise.'

'It's our anniversary,' George said.

It no longer amazed Jonah, this spiky mixture of sympathy and anger. This was the way the world worked. He said, 'I'll think about it.'

SUNDAY, DECEMBER 12, 2004.

He woke late. Vik had already left for his post-call day; also gone were Mike and Cutler, who jogged in the mornings. Jonah perused the kitchen, scrounging a half-eaten box of instant rice, some soy sauce, and a stockpot. He set about preparing himself an austere version of the Traditional Japanese Breakfast. As he checked beneath the sink for a colander, a toilet flushed down the hall.

'Hello?' he called.

A woman's voice answered. 'Mike?'

'It's Jonah.'

'Hey you.' Deanna, Vik's girlfriend, appeared. 'I didn't know you were here.'

'I'm crashing for a little while.' He expected to have to give a reason, but she didn't seem to care. She retied her kimono and pecked him on the cheek and said, 'Good to see you. What time's it. My word, I just woke up. You want some coffee?'

'I didn't know you were here, either,' he said.

Deanna pulled open a cabinet and made a face. 'Gross. I had a red-eye from Hong Kong. I got

392

in at seven. Vik doesn't know I'm here, I came straight from Kennedy. Is there *any* coffee in this apartment.'

'How was your flight?'

'Lousy. But I got eight thousand miles out of it, which puts me over the top. I can fly my nuclear family plus our dog to the moon and back. And Cathay Pacific business class gives you goodies.'

Deanna Girardeau had benefitted from the mid-90s revival of 1950s style: the belted dresses she chose complimented her pinched body, and drastic cosmetics gave her heart-shaped face a black-and-white glow, classily defiant of the modern world's three hundred million colors. Her hair was swept back with chopsticks; her pedicure a vampy violet. 'I think we're Starbucks-bound. Want to come?'

'Sounds good.'

Makeup ate up a half-hour, as she styled her bangs, widened her eyes with mascara and grease pencil, thickened her lips cherry red.

'Very Gwen Stefani,' he said.

'I was thinking more Jayne Mansfield,' she said, 'but so be it.'

They took umbrellas. The guard – still hammered – burped and saluted as they exited the building. Halfway down the block a long wolf-whistle made Deanna smile.

Over coffee she talked about work. She hated her job but was a good solider. 'I chose it,' she said. 'I am a free agent.'

As they left, the wind inverted her umbrella, snapping two of its ribs. Jonah sheltered her as she waited for a downtown cab to do her holiday shopping. They stood hip to hip, her hand clutching the back of his jacket: after all her effort, she was desperate not to screw up her hair.

A taxi slowed and Jonah opened the door for her. 'Here,' he said, handing her his umbrella.

'You sure?'

'Lady,' hollered the cabbie. 'You getting my seat wet.'

She said to Jonah, 'You're a doll,' and smooched him on the cheek, leaving a lurid smudge. He turned up his collar and hurried back to the dorm. He hadn't been outside in twenty-four hours, and now he was soaked. Upstairs he hung his wet clothes in the bathtub.

CHAPTER 31

MONDAY, DECEMBER 13, 2004.
CHILD AND ADOLESCENT PSYCHIATRY,
WEEK THREE.

He expected his last week on the job to bring mixed feelings: regret that he could not follow the cases of kids he'd grown attached to; relief that the semester was over; a measure of pride at being able to look back and see how much he'd learned.

He did not expect to be whisked off the floor at eleven in the morning by a man he'd never met in person. He did not expect to be brought to Dr Soleimani's office and invited to sit down. He did not expect to be fidgeting like he had a tarantula locked in his rectal vault. He did not expect to have to defend himself.

'You have to understand,' said the psychiatrist, 'the legal issues involved.'

The man sitting on his left nodded.

Soleimani said, 'I am responsible for you, Jonah, so I have to ask you straight out if there is any truth whatsoever to—'

'*No.*'

'All right . . .' Soleimani mopped his brow with his handkerchief. 'I am asking a question, that is all.'

'The fact that you have to ask – the *whole thing* is—'

'I believe you,' Soleimani said. 'We all do. There is a presumption of innocence.' He glanced at the other man. 'I understand how you feel.'

Jonah said, 'Do you?'

'Not – no, but I *sympathize*, you must feel a bit under the microscope—'

'Good guess.'

'And I understand that.'

'When did she call you?'

'This morning.'

'And what did she say?'

Soleimani looked for guidance. 'I . . . I am not sure we should discuss that.'

'Oh come *on*, you can't sit there accusing me of—'

The man on Soleimani's left, Dr Pierre, the dean of students, folded his veiny hands across his knee and said, 'Nobody's accusing you of anything. We're trying to determine the truth, if any, of Ms Hutchins's allegations.' The dean sat back. 'We're trying to get to the bottom of it. It's in your interest to be co-operative.'

Jonah said to Soleimani, 'You were with me the entire time.'

'That is almost true, but if we are completely honest we must remember that—'

'You've got to be kidding me.'

'—that it was not the *entire* time.'

'You're *kidding*.'

'Ten minutes,' Soleimani said. 'Unattended. The door was closed.'

'Jesus fucking *Christ*.'

The dean said, 'Calm down, please, Jonah.'

Overheating; mildew in the carpet; shelves crammed with books on child development; walls papered with spindly line graphs, bibliographies, fMRIs. Soleimani declined to look Jonah in the eye, preferring to flick at a green Slinky on his desk, or to mess with the paperweights holding down a looseleaf manuscript of *The Early Intervention Handbook*, ed. S. I. Soleimani, M.D., MPH.

Of all the things Jonah wanted to say, he could find none not easily corrupted by an unkind interpretation.

I want to work with kids

I have never been accused of this before

I want to speak to my lawyer

It almost seemed easier to wave a white flag: he understood; sure, liability, sure, of course, sure. For the first time in his life he had an inkling of why people confessed to crimes they hadn't committed. Living with certainty – regardless how bad – had serious advantages over squirming, and he had been squirming but ten minutes.

The dean said, 'I've asked Ms Hutchins to come down here so we can discuss this together.'

'What did DeShonna say?' Jonah asked. 'Ask her, she'll tell you the truth.'

'I will talk to her,' said Soleimani, 'as soon as—'

'Ask her,' Jonah said. 'Call right now, *ask* her.'

'I think everyone needs to take a nice deep breath,' said the dean.

'This could ruin my career,' Jonah said. 'I can't *breathe* it away.'

Soleimani said, 'A problem like this—'

'I am not a problem.'

'I'm sure not,' said the dean. 'And we'll have it all resolved immediately. In the meantime, however, please take the day off. Dr Soleimani will be in touch with you as soon as is expedient, and we can get back to work.'

'What about the Shelf?' Jonah demanded.

'Pardon?'

'I'm supposed to take the Shelf on Friday.'

'For now let's focus on resolving this issue in the immediate. You'll take the exam when it's appropriate.'

On his way out, Dr Pierre left the door ajar. Soleimani got up to close it.

'I am sorry this has to happen.'

Jonah said nothing.

'For what it is worth, I still think my original impression of you is the correct one.' Soleimani came around and sat on the edge of his desk.

'Whoop-de-doo.'

Soleimani frowned. 'I want to help you.'

'Then believe me.'

'I do—'

'You're going to take the word of an adolescent crackhead who DeShonna doesn't even *like*? Isn't this about the most transparent thing in the universe?'

'Do you hear me arguing with you?' Soleimani swatted the Slinky so it folded over. 'We, the hospital, the department, as an institution, need to be careful. Even a hint of impropriety. You have to understand, the press. To question the victim—'

'There's *no victim*.' Jonah felt his temper rising again. 'It's a *third party*.'

'Okay, but you must see that the bandwagon gets rolling, and it ceases to matter who is guilty – and I am not saying you are, okay? I am not saying that. People sling mud. They do not stop to think. They assume, and that is harmful for you and for us.'

'It *would* be,' Jonah said, 'if there were any chance that it was true. There isn't.'

'*Perception*, how people *see* the – and, and okay, I can see that you do not—'

'No. No. No. No.'

'—let me – let me ask you something: you agree that we do good work here. Yes? And you agree that it is important that we be allowed to keep working. No one else serves this community with the same professionalism and competence. You saw the way the girl lives. Our program is a haven. We cannot endanger ourselves, either by sullying our reputation or by . . . If the problem *were* real – I can see you becoming upset again . . .'

Jonah shook his head. 'This is bullshit.'

'Hypothetically,' Soleimani said, 'if the problem were real, then you would agree that the issue at stake is larger than you and your career. Are we in agreement.'

'Fine. Yeah. Whatever.'

'No. Not *whatever*. It is a serious – look,' Soleimani said, leaning in, 'it so happens that this would not be the first time our department has confronted this issue.'

Jonah said nothing.

'I will not discuss the details with you, because it is far, far under the rug. But I assure you that the *last* thing this hospital needs is another child molester on staff.'

Jonah said, 'I am not a *child molester*.'

'Of course not,' said Soleimani. 'Of course.'

As instructed, he left work, skipping his afternoon lecture.

Do not beat yourself up, Jonah. We will clear this up faster than you can say boo.

He was tempted to go over to the housing project, find Adia Hutchins, and drag her straight to HUM. Or – better yet – bring in DeShonna herself. She would vindicate him. If Dr Pierre wanted to accept a tall tale, go ahead. Jonah would sue. Defamation of character. Harassment. Malice aforethought. He could retain Roberto Medina.

His walk down Madison Avenue coincided with the final bells of neighborhood schools. He sorted the fleeing kids by dress and demeanor: coed and corduroy-pantsed from Hunter College HS; prep anorexics in dark tights and sky-blue blouses, plundering the corner markets for Diet Coke and wasabi peas. Chatting on phones and chomping on pizza; comparing SAT tutors and dissing their teachers.

the last thing this hospital needs

During his first year he, like all his classmates, had contracted Medical Student Syndrome. If his feet throbbed from a long day in the anatomy lab, he had gout. If his head and neck pounded from hours hunched over a textbook, he had meningitis. West Nile, a brain tumor.

Now he began to do the same thing, except that the faults he found were moral instead of physical. What if DeShonna really *did* think he'd molested her? He could not imagine why, but his brain was in overdrive. What if he'd inadvertently crossed some line? You never knew what a kid was thinking – especially not a thoughtful, reticent, damaged one like her. Abuse might have left her sensitive to being touched even in the most innocent way: his hand on her shoulder, causing her to regurgitate a trauma. What if – somehow – anyhow – he really *had* molested her, full-on sleaze-bag molested her – but now *he* couldn't remember? He tried to tell himself that that was impossible. He *knew* it was impossible. But had you told him five months ago that he would stab a man to death he would have called that impossible, too. Look at how he had changed. How she had changed him, brought ugliness to his surface, like pools of fat rising in soup.

Fuming, he marched to the crosstown stop on 97th Street. As he strode to the back of the bus, he gleaned from the startled reactions of other passengers that he had on a hostile expression. *Good* he thought. The better to play nice with.

The doorman at Eve's building was different, a young Hispanic man with close-cropped hair and glasses.

'Carmen Cove,' Jonah said.

'Your name, please?'

'Jonah.'

The doorman called up. 'Mr Jonah is here? Yes ma'am.' He set the phone down. 'Eighth floor, eight G.'

In the elevator he couldn't stop cracking his knuckles. Stepping out purposefully – ready to barrel through her door – he collided with her.

'How nice of you to drop by,' she said.

'Fifty bucks,' he said.

'Pardon me?'

'A hundred?' He ran his palms down his pant legs. 'You bought her a vial of crack, was that it?'

'I must confess I don't know what you're—'

He punched her. Her head snapped back against the wall, making a sound like two hardcovers slapped together; she stumbled sideways, forward, and fell, finally, in a heap.

'Jonah Stem,' she mumbled, 'how I've missed you.'

He knelt and forced her face into a pucker; blood oozed out.

'I vit my tfongue,' she said.

'I know you did it,' he said. 'I want to hear you say it.'

Her eyes, liquid and vibrating, honestly so confused, and he began to think he'd made a mistake, that she had nothing to do with Adia Hutchins. Eve could not be blamed every time his life malfunctioned. He had made a mistake; he had made a terrible mistake; and shame divided, redivided, metastasized. He owed her an apology. He was going to give it to her – and then, beneath his fingers, her cheeks bunched into what would've been – had he not been juicing her face – a smile. The transformation dropped a sinker of revulsion through him. He backed away.

'You sent those two uniformed beasts round here to harangue me,' she said. She sat up, wiped her lips. 'What was I supposed to do? You did a bad thing, Jonah Stem, and you deserved a warning. I regret any inconvenience that this recent turn of events may have caused you. But frankly, you should be thankful. I could have told Officer Krupke and Co. about how you beat me.'

'It's not going to work,' he said. 'You're going to lose.'

'I'm an Ivy Leaguer, we hate to lose.' She cleared her throat. 'Would you care to come in for a cup of tea? This is not a conversation I care to have in the hall.'

'Marisa Ashbrook,' he said. 'Did you lose to her?'

For the first time ever, she looked caught off guard. Then she shrugged. 'There' – she wiped her mouth again – 'you've got it wrong. She was nothing like Raymond, or you for that matter. We had a special relationship, and what happened to her, while tragic, was nonetheless purely accidental.' She rolled toward him to stroke his ankle. If he wanted to, he could kick her throat in. He forced himself to take another step back.

'Don't touch me, you cunt.'

'Jonah Stem. I know for a fact that you weren't raised to speak that way. Speaking of – how's your family? I didn't have that growing up, Mayberry. My parents fought like cats and dogs. Life was rough. It was either listen to Dad whaling on Mom all night long or step in to stop it – in which case *I* got the belt. Sometimes I tried to help her and *she* gave me the belt for interfering. They had strict rules, my parents, unwritten and subject to constant revis—'

'Which parents would those be?' he said. 'The ones who died of cancer, or the ones who split up when your mother ran off with Lou Reed?'

She laughed. 'Clever boy. All right, if you must

know. My father is an accountant. My mother is a teacher. They live in Bal-di-more. Could I concoct a more prosaic creation myth? And for the record, they never fought. Not once, never. *Très ennuyeux.* I don't think they've had sex in eons.'

He had to leave. Before he hit her again. His black double was whetting itself, and she seemed to have read his mind; she smiled a little and sat up a little and spread her legs a little and said, 'Come here.'

He summoned the elevator.

'You know I saw you kissing her.'

He did not turn around.

'That woman,' she said. 'With the *lips*. It made me very jealous. I've half a mind to let her know how I feel.'

The elevator came.

He did not get in.

The elevator closed.

He said, 'That's Vik's girlfriend.'

'Waaall, she looked mighty enamored of you.'

'Keep away from her.'

'Maybe I'll go over and mark my territory.' She stood up.

He called the elevator again.

'Think of history's great romances,' she said. 'Antony and Cleopatra. Romeo and Juliet. Humbert and Lolita. Tom and Jerry. All forged in agony. They may be fictional but they're our only consistent cultural truths. Fashions change, their stories remain.

You know, I was expecting you to show up sooner rather than later. It's nice to know you're still the reliable man I fell in love with.'

He stepped into the elevator. As the doors closed, she said *I love you.*

CHAPTER 32

He was not to take the Shelf; that would be made up at a time TBA. He sat in Dr Pierre's office with Soleimani, Yvette, Adia, and the dean himself, who conducted the proceedings with a sort of detached, neurotic precision: Perry Mason as scripted by Franz Kafka. Judging by her loose carriage, Adia was sober. On the particulars she did not fare well, venturing a number of competing, equally ambiguous accounts. When asked to clarify how the alleged abuse had come to her attention, she said *She told me.*

Then they brought DeShonna in and spoke to her alone. Adia and Jonah sat outside the dean's office, in the waiting area presided over by a HUM seal. Adia switched off between sneering at him and retreating to the privacy of her poofy green jacket – its seams smoking with wisps of synthetic down – in a way that made her look

407

very frightened and very young. Irate, Jonah got up and went to the men's room. When he returned to the waiting area, she was gone.

The dean opened the office door and hooked a finger at Jonah. 'Where's Adia?'

'I don't know. She left.'

The dean frowned. 'Come in.'

DeShonna was crying. Yvette stood behind her, stroking her hair. As soon as Jonah stepped into the room, DeShonna turned to him and said *I didn't say nothing to her, I swear.* Yvette said *Cmon honey let's take a walk.*

DeShonna rose to promises of an ice cream sandwich. On her way out she clamped her arms around Jonah's waist. Soleimani and the dean both stared at the carpet.

'It's okay,' he said. He knelt down. 'Go with Yvette.'

She nodded and let go. Yvette said *Chocolate or vanilla.*

Soleimani bought him lunch and they went to the MD lab, a humorless room on the twentieth floor, with northern and eastern panoramas of eddying snow, blight forests, two bridges, Randall's Island.

'Did you know that the East River flows in both directions?'

Unoccupied, the room had a slight echo.

'It is not a river but an estuary. It changes direction depending on the tide.' Soleimani chewed, swallowed. 'I think I intended that as the start of a metaphor. But now I cannot remember what I wanted to say.'

Jonah said nothing. Soleimani sipped his coffee and set it atop the lab station's hard, black, resin countertop. Like all the others, the station had two high-legged chairs, two microscopes, and two lockers, each labeled with the name of a second-year student. Jonah could see his desk from last year, where he'd spent so much time pretending he knew what medicine was.

'I want you to know that I think you are a gifted doctor. This week should not affect the way you think of yourself or your future. It is all politics. I never mistrusted you. A hospital is a bureaucracy. I hope one day you will understand my position.' Soleimani wiped his glasses on his coat, peered through the lenses: dirtier than before, now smeared with salt and lines of Funyun grease. 'How are you spending your break?'

'Going to visit a friend.'

'Enjoy yourself. You deserve it. Allow me to say one thing, though. My intention was to protect the department, not to defame you. You have performed admirably, and I will do everything I can to ensure that this will not affect your grade.'

That was sort of funny. For his trouble, he'd end up with honors. He'd have to send Eve a thank-you card. Jonah said, 'Good to hear.'

'I want you to know.' Soleimani wiped his glasses, held them up. Still dirty.

★   ★   ★

At Vik's he deflated the air mattress and bagged his clothes. Vik – after getting the full story – had gone to stay with Deanna in TriBeCa for the week. Jonah wanted them to leave town early for their ski trip, but Vik promised to keep an eye out.

You should call the police.

He explained that he'd tried, told him what the cops had said.

Vik said *You should get a gun.*

Which Jonah laughed at. Upon reflection, though, it seemed like a decent idea.

He had neither enough nor the right stuff, so he cabbed erratically back to the East Village to pack. The apartment felt foreign. They'd switched the heat off before leaving, and he left his jacket on as he rummaged through his dresser for sweat-shirts and jeans. Outside it had started to come down hard, the forecast calling for the season's first serious heavenly dump. He found the wool socks with holes in them, and the wool socks he'd mended himself. Once, on a lark, Hannah had shown him how to sew.

Status check: window intact; surfaces appropri-ately dusty. He could probably afford to spend one night here. He called George.

'I'm coming out tonight.'

George sneezed. 'What was that?'

'I'll see you soon,' Jonah said. 'I'm coming on the nine forty-nine.'

'It's Friday. I thought you weren't coming until tomorrow.'

'I wasn't. Change of plans.'

'I wish you'd told me earlier, I could've called Louise. Now it's too late.'

Jonah said, 'Meet me at the station.'

SATURDAY, DECEMBER 18, 2004.

The guest-room mattress was potholed and unsupportive, and when he awoke from a restless night, his back hurt. His sleeves bunched in his armpits; one pajama leg twisted around like a French pastry; the air stale with the effluvia of nightmares.

He came up from the basement and crossed the darkened living room, interrupting shafts of light busy with migrating cat hair. Outside, snow blew from the hedges. Aside from the imprint of *The New York Times*, the front yard was unbroken, bubble-bath white.

He washed his face and neck in the second-floor bathroom. He could hear Hannah talking in her sleep, something she'd always done, even in her well days. She would sleep on her stomach, her head wrenched sideways, laughing at untold jokes until he stroked her naked back to quiet her down.

Six months ago he might have gone in and done the same; but standing at the sink, he resisted the urge to perform an intimacy no longer called for.

At nine thirty-nine George galumphed downstairs, stopping at the liquor cabinet before running outside to snatch up the paper. He shook snow from his slippers and cleared a space at the kitchen table to scavenge the remains of Jonah's breakfast.

'How'd you sleep? Did you let the cat out?'

'Yeah.'

George bit down on a piece of bacon. 'I didn't know we had this in the fridge.'

'It was there.'

'I'll be darned . . . You want the sports?'

While glancing at the basketball scores, Jonah noticed that George hadn't shaved. Cultivating stubble for the Week of Romance?

Jonah made a list of provisions on a notepad with a floral pattern. He'd bought this notepad for them; now he couldn't remember why. He'd thought Hannah would like the flowers? Hoped that a designated 'to-do' list would increase overall household organization? 'I'm heading into town.'

George killed his drink and reached for his checkbook. 'You want a ride?'

'I'll walk.' Then, before he could stop himself: 'Need anything?'

George started to reply, shook his head.

'What,' Jonah said.

'I'll get it myself. Never mind.'

'I'm there already.' *Stem, you servile twat.* He needed to leave before he made some new unreasonable offer: to shave the lint from George's skivvies or scrub out the raingutters with a toothbrush and elderberry jam. He stood abruptly. 'I'll be back soon.'

412

As he went into the entry hall, George appeared behind him, waving a page torn from the notepad. 'Since you're there already.'

Jonah took the note.

3 pk Trojan reg lubricated

'Car's coming at four fifteen,' George said. 'Try'n be back before then.'

Plows had built up great glittering snowbanks; he walked in the middle of the street. Men clearing driveways stopped mid-heave, shielding their eyes from the glare to see who was coming. Sons unwillingly roused to help leaned sullenly on their shovels. A girl used two green bottlecaps to give sight to a snowman. Her mother, visible in the bay window, cupped a mug and cradled the cordless: a speech he could easily imagine.

Yes I can see her right now you won't believe how big she's gotten she'll be taller than Nate soon can I bring anything a salad well if you insist how about renting a movie we can all watch together that'd be so June Cleaver I suppose that's where we're at

At the supermarket he loaded up on nonperishables. The checker rolled her eyes when he asked for a delivery slip. 'Might take a while,' she said.

He said, 'I got nothing but time.'

Unready to face the music, he strolled around Great Neck Plaza, watching his breath rise and vanish. He got a haircut. He bought a collection of photos of 1920s dancers and had it wrapped for Hannah. He bought himself a new shirt and, on a whim, found the hunting counter at the sporting-goods store.

'Six months,' said the clerk when he asked about the waiting period on a handgun. 'State law. They need to check you out, make sure you're not prone to shoot, y'know, someone.'

As George flipped his suitcase into the trunk of the cab, the back of his parka rode up, disclosing a florid Hawaiian shirt. Jonah stood on the threshold, feeling the house's warm air rubbing at his nape and, on his face, the cold, setting sun.

'The emergency numbers,' George said, coming back up the front walk.

'Yes.'

'And the cash.'

'Yes.'

'I'll call from Miami. If there's a problem with the flight, I'll call from the airport.' George stared over Jonah's shoulder at the house. Hannah had refused to say good-bye. 'Tell her I love her.'

'I will.'

'Tell her I love her, though. Tell her I still think about her mother all the time.'

Jonah said, 'I'll tell her you love her.'

George leaned toward the porch, as though negotiating the bow of a tilting ship, as though he intended to go inside, go to his daughter and apologize for having his own life; for Wendy; for being short of patience; for drinking. Some of this history warranted an apology; some of it did not; and, unable to differentiate, he had left it all to rot.

He turned and went.

The tires spun in place until the tread caught and the car lurched into a U that expanded, by virtue of the Lincoln's long snout, into a three-point turn. The squeaks and crunches of vulcanized rubber on snow. Jonah watched them drive up the block, signal, and pull away. He lingered, listening to nothing. Then he went inside to deal with dinner.

The pizza place they normally ordered from wouldn't come out in the snow; he got the same answer from the Chinese place, the Mexican place, the Thai place. He scrambled eggs. It was going to be a cholesterol-heavy week.

The smell of frying onions brought Hannah downstairs. She sat on a kitchen chair, tucking her feet beneath her nightgown, her sleepgear of choice when she got around to taking off her jeans and bathrobe. In college she'd eschewed the standard baggy flannels and boxer shorts in favor of a frilly Victorian number that made her look like the ghost of Ophelia.

'Hey there,' he said, and smiled.

She brushed a lock of hair behind her ear.

'I can give you some eggs.'

'Okay.'

She didn't eat, though, watching him as he shoveled down his food.

'You want something else? Soup?'

She prodded her plate, said nothing.

He left the dishes in the sink.

Without George's ego to fill it, the house felt submerged, isolated, like a space capsule or a Siberian yurt. Jonah promised himself that if the roads cleared they would go to the movies. They tried to play Scrabble but Hannah kept getting distracted. She babbled about the future, a loose goulash of numerology and astrology she'd picked up from a TV show about psychics. He began to worry about her having a major episode. If that happened – in this weather—

They abandoned the game halfway through. He gathered the tiles and Hannah stretched out in the back room, positioned toward the Zenith, as though bowing to the shrine of her mother.

'How you feeling?' he asked. He saw her fighting to subdue the wrong thoughts and let out the right ones. In the end she gave up and shrugged.

He walked to the mantel and removed a photo of Wendy carrying Hannah in a slinglike thing. In the upper-left corner of the frame was George's contribution to the scene: a finger obstructing the lens.

Behind him, Hannah said sleepily, 'I love you.'

He said nothing. He heard her begin to snore.

He braced himself and carried her upstairs.

In her closet was a deep cardboard box, stamped SYLVANIA, in which Hannah had thrown two decades' worth of letters, birthday cards, ticket stubs: the paper trail of youth. Summer camp infatuations, whose mystique and epistolary stamina failed six weeks into the school year. Recruitment offers from softball programs scattered across the United States. Why hadn't she gone to USC, he wondered. Or anyplace warmer than Ann Arbor. A postcard (BRUXELLES) from George that he hadn't seen before.

6–22–71 Dear Wendy Europe is hot, we're staying at a hotel near the train station

Sitting crosslegged, he restacked the box's contents in reverse order on the floor. Hannah turned over in bed, snorted, went still.

At the bottom of the box he found a book.

The Giving Tree

He opened to the inside cover.

> *For my HANNAH on her twentieth birthday. I love you because you are good. Always be this simple.*
> *Your Jonah*

It was dark but he shifted around until he caught a ray of moonlight, and then read the whole thing straight through. The tree, plucked and dismembered and skinned and engraved and, at last, brought low, all in the name of love. He found the story disturbing, not at all the uplifting one of his childhood. When he'd given it to her, he'd meant well, to extoll her selflessness, a point moving along a line.

He sat in the moonlight, remembering her.

Columbus Day, junior year. They spend the weekend alone in a Lake Huron cabin owned by her teammate's parents. The small town with its deserted shops. She enthusiastically peruses second-rate antiques; he plays at being middle-aged. She buys him an old cigar box; he buys her a piece of costume jewelry. They talk to the shopkeeper, who tells them that it is off-season. The fellow who gives walking tours of the forest has that very day decamped for Boca. From the general store they obtain groceries and a pamphlet entitled *Flora and Fauna of the Upper Peninsula*. They take the car inland, passing an unwooded patch purported to be an old Indian cemetery. Hannah derives great pleasure from using the pamphlet to identify trees. Firs and aspens, birch and white cedars. He pulls over and they tramp around in search of wild blueberries. She tells him to watch for poison oak; she used to be a Girl Scout. He hadn't known; he is delighted. Every new detail is a gift.

That night Hannah poaches a salmon, one of the three dishes she knows how to make. They consume half a bottle of cheap white wine. Making love in front of the fireplace sounds romantic but the floor is hard and hasn't been swept in months, and they both start to sneeze. They give up and go to the bedroom instead, returning to the fireside to finish the wine and play Scrabble.

He makes *void;* she makes *mud.* He makes *meaty;* she makes *yarggh.* He points out that that's not a

418

word. She says *It's a sound.* *What sound* he asks. *Yarggh* she says.

They go out on the balcony. It's cloudy but there's so much starlight. He crunches his toes inside his slippers and says *What're you thinking.*

She says *My mom.*

They are quiet.

He says *Do you ever think about getting married?*

She nods.

He says *Well?*

It's so pretty out here she says. *Thank you for taking me here.*

He smiles. *It was your idea.*

She smiles back, and he wonders if that is supposed to answer his question. Then she says *I know.*

They watch the slowly shifting heavens.

People liked to pretend that accidents were choices, and vice versa. To praise your feet for great leaps; to blame your skinned knees on a hastily spinning earth.

SUNDAY, DECEMBER 19, 2004.

Toward the end of his first full day on the job, solitude started to take its toll. He could only watch so much television, read so many pages; look at Hannah for so long. Snow – huge swooping flocks of it – jammed the windowsills, leaving the house murky at midday; what scant daylight squeaked through had started to wane by early afternoon. The heat didn't work well; he walked around in socks and a sweater. Hannah wore a blanket, thrown over her shoulders like a super-hero cape.

The cat scratched at his ankle.

He could hear the air.

He felt, briefly, a pang for ever having said no to George. About anything. This was an anti-life. Although he had to remember that George's loneliness was self-imposed; he was the one who refused to institutionalize Hannah. If he wanted, he could put down the Old Overholt and take up jogging and vegetarianism. The sleeping till noon, the listlessness, all of it had started earlier, with Wendy's death.

It embarrassed Hannah. During breaks and summer vacation, she'd always come to Scarsdale, even though – as Jonah told her a billion times – it took him the same amount of time to drive over to her. *I'll get on the Hutch, I'll be there in an hour.*

No, my dad's not feeling well.

After she got sick, of course, she no longer cared. One of schizophrenia's many contradictions was how it replaced one's normal self-consciousness with an irrational one. The world conspired against you because of your importance – not because you were parading naked up the sidewalk.

By five he was going stir-crazy. A long time seemed to have passed since that morning, and for the sake of hearing his own voice he called

people. First his mother, which he quickly understood as a bad move.

'I'm coming out there right now,' she declared
when he told her that he'd been eating eggs for
twenty-four hours. 'I'll take the two of you to
dinner.'

'We're fine, Mom, I'd rather be alone.'

'But you were just complaining about being alone.'

'That's why I'm calling you,' he said. 'To
complain.'

'But I can come to see you in person, wouldn't
that be better?'

He called Lance at his mother's Amagansett
manse.

'I'm wearing a nine-hundred-dollar shirt.'

Jonah laughed. 'Good for you.'

'It's not mine,' Lance said. 'I left all my clothes
at our place, so I've been borrowing from the
Count. He gave me presents, it's like I'm six. Do
you think it's weird that he bought me herb?'

'No weirder than what you're used to.'

'I get the idea,' Lance said, 'that he was one of
those guys who did a lot of coke in the early
eighties. Dissolved septum, etcetera. He's had a
nosejob, that much I can tell.'

'Your mom must be in heaven.'

'Dude, I think he might pop the question.'

'You're joking.'

'I'm getting that vibe. My mom is having third-
finger seizures. Like she needs something heavy
to hold it down.'

'Congratulations?'

'Can you see me as the fuckin ring boy? And get this: he brought his personal chef. Tonight we're having a formal dinner, black tie and waiters. It's gonna be like this all week. My mom invited all these friends of hers. They're like the fuckin undead, dude, with a capital dead. The materialism makes me want to puke, except they have nice cars. They're all in real estate except for one lady, my mom's oldest friend, who teaches gender studies at Sarah Lawrence and is raising her son to wear thong panties. I pity the fool. Her girlfriend is a producer. I'm going to try and sell her on the selfumentary installments one and two.'

'Good luck.'

'Thanks. That's me, fighting the good fight since 1977. How's life at the asylum?'

'Not bad.'

'Cool. When can we go back to our apartment?'

'I don't know.'

'You sent the cops the clip.'

'They talked to Eve.'

'And?'

'And they won't . . . Tell you the truth, I'm not sure what it'd take. She might have to kill me first.'

'That's not funny. Are you safe?'

'I don't think there's any way she could know where I am,' Jonah said. 'It's one thing to follow somebody around the City. But here, no way.'

'If you say so.'

'Yeah,' he said limply. 'We'll go back after break. We'll put another lock on.'

He called his sister; called Vik, who didn't answer. He and Deanna were probably up in the mountains, their reception hampered by miles of pines. Jonah left a message wishing them a fun time.

The house felt quieter than ever, at once vast and shrinking.

He checked on Hannah, singing to herself as she watched TV. She twirled her hair and tormented her cuticles, and did not answer when he said her name.

Around eight, he stepped onto the front porch. Theirs was the darkest house: lights along the front walk had all burnt out, and they had no decorations up. By comparison, the split-level across the way looked like a funhouse, its gable lit up, Dancing Santa patrolling the lawn. Shivering, Jonah counted stars; hummed carols he didn't know the words to; listened to owls.

He had begun to relax when a loud crash sent him scampering inside. After bringing his nervous system back into line he checked the eyehole.

Nothing.

He fetched a thick glass candlestick. As he opened the door and stepped outside he saw the wind dump a clump of snow into the skeletal shrubs, which sagged and broke under the weight. He chastised himself for being nuts and went back inside.

MONDAY, DECEMBER 20, 2004.

'I can't talk long,' George said. 'It's four dollars a minute. Everything okay?'

'We're all set,' Jonah said. 'Bored, but—'

'Hang on.' The phone dropped away and a woman laughed. Said *stop it. Georgie, stop!* Jonah paced the den, running his fingers along the piano that had been turned into a repository for unreadable books. For someone concerned about the expense, Georgie-Porgie didn't seem averse to a two minute, eight dollar tickle-war.

At least he was having a good time. Jonah goddamn well expected Georgie-Porgie to have the goddamned time of his goddamned life.

'So it's good, everything is good?'

'Listen – what time is the nurse coming on Friday? I'm—'

'Jonah? I need to go.'

'Wait, wait wait wait—'

'I'll call you later. Sorry – I – *Lou!*—'

He continued to say *Hello? George?* as his ear filled up with dial tone. 'Fuck.'

A stair creaked. He turned and saw Hannah in her nightgown.

'That was your dad,' he said. 'He says hi.'

TUESDAY, DECEMBER 21, 2004.

He cut the day into pieces: doing push-ups, running on the treadmill, reading. He fed the cat and cleaned out the litter box. The snow had begun again, healing footprints and rounding off tire marks. The bedroom windows were locked from the inside. The front door was chained and bolted, as were the side doors. The back door he had fortified with a chair.

Strictly speaking, housework wasn't his responsibility but it kept him sane, and the place needed it badly: no way would he let everything go to hell, not on his watch. He realized he was beginning to sound like the embittered sergeants from war movies. *Charlie's everwhere, boys. Turn your back he steals your asscheeks. I run my unit with discipline, that's what separates the dignified from the deadified. Tight ship or we all sink.*

He got out the vacuum.

Snow bricked up the windowpanes.

He could not see out.

WEDNESDAY, DECEMBER 22, 2004.

George had not called in two days. In the Rolodex Jonah found a number for Bernadette, Hannah's usual nurse. It had been disconnected.

(nobody nobody's coming forever and ever)

Hannah watched from the kitchen table as he dealt with the cruise company, trying to get them to patch through a phone call. No, he did not want to send a fax or an e-mail; this was an emergency. Why was it so hard to get through? He already knew the answer: they wanted *George* to call *him* at four dollars a minute.

The ship was docking for several hours that afternoon. When the phone rang at five, he readied his most self-righteous, sermonizing tone.

Hello he said. *Hello*.

The line went dead.

He called Villanueva, who called the Great Neck PD on his behalf, then called back to inform him that a squad car would be by soon.

Great Neck cops were friendly, neighborhood suburban enforcers. They listened to what he had to say and promised to drive by every couple of hours. He wanted to ask them to stay, stay for good, stay the rest of the week.

If anything happens give us a

They wished him a good night and left.

He and Hannah watched several Very Special Episodes of sitcoms that had been off the air for years, their tired jokes made all the more depressing by the knowledge that a high percentage of the child stars delivering those jokes had grown up to become junkies, thieves, or infomercial hosts.

He defrosted an ancient chicken, doused it with teriyaki sauce, and set it in the oven. Within the hour he had produced a kitchen filled with foul, acrid smoke. They made do with microwave mashed potatoes and salad. Tomorrow he would have to go out for supplies.

She dripped raspberry vinaigrette down the front of her T-shirt, a Stüssy logo print that had once belonged to him, and that he'd forgotten about giving her.

He dreamt of a cruise ship. An alarm wailed. The boat was on fire. The cherries jubilee had gone awry; juice gushed from a gash torn in the floor of the ballroom, cresting the smokestacks and drenching the deck. The burning life preservers, passengers screaming, scrumming for lifeboats, skating through hot syrup in untucked tuxedoes and ripped evening gowns. Eve surveyed the scene from the prow, calmly stirring a plate of ice cubes as she smiled at him; he was next to her but unable to reach her, his fingers growing through an infinity, never making contact although she was right there, microns beyond. The ship's frame belched as it tilted, Dixieland tubas of structural grief. The band played on. The band fiddled as Rome sank. They had run aground. The fire alarm sectioned him into rounds. He slid through sweet boiling cherry muck, the floorboards awash in shoes and twitching rodents and drowned bugs, he slid away from her collecting woodgrain under his nails as he scraped, flailed, fell, all of him was on fire, and the pain was incredible, so complete that it surpassed his capacity to feel it, becoming instead a sense of expansion, of flying apart, a trillion jigsaw molecules strewn wild by the hand of God. He slid faster, the cant worsened, splinters piled up beneath his nails and then his nails tore off simultaneously like eight ripping matchbooks, his fingers came off, too, all he had left were thumbs, and he reached for Eve, fixed in space, smiling, stirring. The ship broke apart as the skin of his palms peeled away

hello

The basement was dark. He didn't know what time it was. He didn't remember waking, didn't remember answering his phone but felt it in his hand.

A clipped whisper, *don't wake the baby* – 'Jonah Stem'—

His head still splashed around in fire and melted sugar.

He wanted to hang up but he knew he should not. Keep her on the line. Find out where she is. Call the cops. He had the Great Neck PD's number upstairs on the notepad with the flowers. The notepad was upstairs in the kitchen. The kitchen was across the basement, across the living room, through a door, it – the notepad – the phone number – help – was on the kitchen table. He'd left it there after dinner; he had to get it. He should call 911. It was dark. He had to get the number. He stood up and swayed, disoriented.

He groped his way toward the basement steps. Eve was still talking. He became aware of his heart in his bowels, his bowels bearhugging themselves. He was so drowsy and dizzy and sick, he felt along the wall in the dark, the phone pinned between his hot face and the clammy flesh of his shoulder.

He heard her talking and she seemed to be inside his head, much closer than she should've been, closer than a voice over the phone.

He said, 'Where are you.' He reached the top of the steps and opened the basement door. All the living room lights were off; snow barred the moon. He crossed the room, turned on the kitchen light. A crossword puzzle half-concealed the notepad. He would keep her on the line while he dialed 911 from the house phone. He would induce her to reveal her location. The kitchen clock said four eleven. His mind was clearing. He felt up to the task of deceiving her. He said, 'Tell me where you are.' She said, 'In your heart.'

CHAPTER 33

As he stepped out of the kitchen, he touched the switch near the door, and the living room blazed bright. He cringed. He had to open his eyes. Groggy and achy and dehydrated and stuffed with dread and unwilling but he had to open his eyes.

Then he did open his eyes, and in doing so took in a number of facts at once, like swallowing an entire meal. Wet footprints ran from the back room across the living room's hardwood floor, becoming dark spots in the staircase carpeting. He had missed Eve because she had been upstairs. Now she descended.

'Good morning,' she said.

She stopped on the bottom step: barefoot, her outerwear discarded, probably on the floor of Hannah's room, where she had been. Her lips pale from overexposure. Her hair rigid, like Hannah's when it froze while she hurried out of the shower and across campus without letting it dry. Once some jackass in her Spanish class broke a chunk of it off, laughed, handed it to her, and said *hair you go*, forcing her to get a haircut, despite the fact that she'd gotten a haircut four days earlier, an expensive haircut, the haircut she got for the winter formal. Jonah had been furious on her behalf; but Hannah said *It's just hair, it grows back.*

In her right hand, Eve gripped a knife.

Upon the mantel a digital camcorder hummed.

She said, 'You look like you could use a cup of joe.'

He nodded. He was doing math. The distance to her. The distance to the door. The distance to Hannah. If Train A leaves the station traveling at the speed of fear at the same time Train B leaves its station traveling at the speed of desire while Train C sits upstairs – he had never been good at word problems. He had never been too good at math, in general. He was more of a people person. He was an idiot.

'I'm sorry to wake you so early. I wanted to get a jump on the day.'

In the time it took him to go back into the kitchen and call the police she could easily reach him; could easily get upstairs to Hannah. Assuming she had not done something already. Train C is idling. Train C is bleeding to death.

'This place is hell to get to,' she said. 'The roads are closed. Do you know that? There are no cars out, I doubt if the ambulances are running. I had to walk all the way over. It took me forever. Look.' She held out her hand. It was bluish and trembling. 'I'm still not warm. I feel like a zombie,

431

Jonah Stem. I swear I could break off a limb and not feel a thing. That's funny, isn't it.'

He could use the phone, come in swinging. Who was he kidding, it was a piece of garbage four inches long. The glass candlestick was on the far side of the room. (The crash in the bushes, snow breaking branches; or feet trampling the dead flowerbed; had he *missed* her? had she *been here?*) He could return to the kitchen and get a knife but he did not want to let her out of his sight. If he turned for – how long? Thirty seconds. That would be enough. She could go back upstairs. She could come after him. Although he did not think that she wanted to hurt him. Why would she? She loved him.

'Well,' she said, 'say something.'

The heaviest object within view was a hardcover crossword dictionary, resting on the end table that joined the couch and the loveseat.

'Say something.' She took a step toward him. The skin around her eyes was mottled and puffy, and she shook all over, like the night when she broke the teacup and cut herself. He remembered her blood in the kitchen sink, swirling against the stainless steel, forming fractals and washing away, sucked down into the lead guts of the City, a city feeding on the blood of its residents, and Eve shaking against him. 'If you don't say something I'm going to get angry, say something. *Now.*'

He said her name.

She stopped shaking then. Her posture restored

itself. Her dignity returned. She stepped back, once again blocking the stairs.

'You don't have to whisper,' she said. 'Nobody is asleep.'

He said, 'Where's Hannah.'

'That's all you can think of? I come all the way out here, to this frozen witch-tit hell, and all you can muster is *What's behind door number two?* Surely you jest. Surely you've made a mistake. I'll give you another chance, Jonah Stem. And I'll give you a hint. Say, "Good morning."'

'Good morning,' he said.

'"Good morning, Eve."'

'Good morning, Eve.' He could hit her with a chair.

'"How are you?"'

'How are you.' He could throw the phone but that would break the phone and dent the wall and then he would be phoneless and she angry. It might distract her. He could – shove the, he could throw the cat at her. He could throw the video-camera. He could charge her straightaway, use his bare hands . . . He was unfortunately clear on the unintended consequences of scrapping at close quarters with a knife.

'With a little more pomp, please.'

He could use—

'*Again.*'

'How are you, Eve.'

'Been better. Been better.' Her laughter was warped and high. 'This isn't working the way I planned. To be honest, I'm not sure how we should proceed. As should be evident, I've never been a very good director. My talent is in concept rather than execution. In low light, for example, the auto-focus has trouble. Did you notice that on the DVD?'

He nodded.

'We never had a chance to discuss that, did we. What did you think? Tell me. But please, please don't tell me it was "very interesting." I really shall weep if you resort to that. *Did* you think it was interesting?'

'No.'

'What then.'

'Disgusting.'

'Ah,' she said. 'I suppose that's reasonable. Disgust is one of the basic human emotions. You may be familiar with the work of Paul Ekman.'

He said nothing.

'No? Then take notes. Ekman identified anger, disgust, fear, sadness, surprise, and joy as the six basic expressions common to all humans. That's quite remarkable, don't you think? Of those six, only one is positive. Four are negative. Surprise could go either way, I suppose. What do you think?'

He said, 'I think it could.'

Were he somehow able to get past her and upstairs, they still would not be safe: Hannah's door didn't have a lock. George had removed it as per the recommendation of her psychiatrist.

'But back to topic. The film. Did it surprise you.'

'Yes.'

'Really?'

He nodded.

'Oh good. I was hoping it would. *Suspense*. Film can do that like no other medium. One of its many unique qualities. The written word can never jump out and bite quite the way a picture can. Don't you agree?'

He said, 'Sure.'

'You're not very talkative, Jonah Stem. I'm going to mark you off for participation.'

He said nothing.

'I majored in film. Did I tell you that? I think I told you I majored in theater and literature. I don't remember what I told you, but now I'm telling you the truth. Are you listening? What was I saying. Oh yes.' She had begun to shake again. 'The other aspect of film I find so beguiling is its eternal present tense. Who's to say, for example, that you and Raymond aren't happening, right now, at every instant? Somewhere, on some tape, you are. Over and over again you are killing him, and you will be, forever, until the last copy finds its way to digital dust. And even then it remains in your head. The image lasts forever. That's why it's critical to capture my work, by nature ephemeral. Nobody *really* wants their fifteen minutes to last that long. So I have chosen to work in the medium of memory. Don't do that.'

'What.'

'Move.'

'I thought you wanted me close to you,' he said.

'Not at the moment,' she said.

He stopped moving.

'I have a confession to make,' Eve said. 'I'm a very insecure person.'

He said nothing.

'Were you aware of that?'

'I had an idea.'

'Have you been psychoanalyzing me all this time?'

'No.'

'What else have you come up with?'

'I haven't been psychoanalyzing you.'

'Well, I've been psychoanalyzing *you*,' she said. 'Are you attracted to women with deep insecurities?'

'No.'

'Is Hannah insecure?'

He shook his head.

'It's hard to tell what she's like, looking at her. She's rather different than I expected.'

He said, 'What did you expect.'

'To be honest, I don't know. But not . . . *that*.'

He wanted to beat her, which after all was the whole purpose of this exercise. He could not, of course, on principle. Did that matter now? He believed that if he started hitting her, he would keep on hitting her until something or someone intervened. Maybe she wanted him to. He believed he would. Their interests had finally aligned.

'Love,' Eve called, 'come down and show yourself.'

There was nothing, nothing, silence. And he envisioned the worst of all worlds, Hannah emptied out like a man in a gutter, like a deflated balloon.

'Hannah, love, come here. Don't be afraid.'

She appeared at the top of the stairs. The relief of seeing her alive and untouched was overturned by the horror of her proximity to Eve.

'Hannah,' he said. 'Go back in your room.'

'Come down here, love, we want to see you.'

'Hannah *go back in your room.*'

'Hush, we're old friends, aren't we, love. And old friends aren't unfriendly. They come in times of need. There.' Hannah, mouthbreathing, allowed Eve to take her hand and lead her downstairs. 'There. Look at you. For the love of love, *look at you.* I don't know what I'd imagined she'd be like, but whatever it was, I was *wrong.*'

'Hannah.' He did not sound like an authority figure. 'Come here right now.'

Eve smiled, brushed Hannah's bunched cheek, a gesture that should have caused her to shrink back but did not; she appeared mesmerized.

'Please,' he said. 'Please go.'

'*Stop moving.*'

He stopped.

'*Apologize.*'

'I'm sorry.'

Eve said, 'You interrupted me.'

'I'm sorry.'

'I forgive you. But I'm angry, Jonah Stem. You should have told me sooner. You should have said something sooner, and saved me the trip. Spared my ego.' She drew Hannah into an embrace. 'You're hideous, my love. Shhh, now then, don't be cross. You don't even know what I'm saying, do you.' Over Hannah's shoulder, Eve stared at him. 'You should have told me before. You should have shown me a current photograph. So I could see firsthand what a monstrosity she is. You poor girl. You ugly thing.' Both their bodies shaking; or just one. 'Mercy of heaven, Hannah, are you not but the most repellent creature in Nassau County. A rancid plaster cast. Compared to you I'm a cherub; I am beauty itself. Compared to you I am a thousand feet tall. You should be locked in a cage and dropped to the bottom of the sea.' She laughed, she was crying. 'You're not like me. We're not even the same species. You don't know, do you. How could you. You can't know anything, for you're as stupid as you are ugly. You're not even a person, Hannah. It kills me. *You* kill me. You can't be expected to know what it says, when he chooses you. It says a lot—' She broke their embrace, and the hand with the knife moved *a lot about how* toward the plane where their eyes met; and he saw *a lot about how he* that they were exactly the same height; that *a lot about how he feels* at one point in time, in a kinder world, they might have been taken for *a lot about how he feels about me* sisters.

In his socks he slipped on the hardwood floor, catching himself on the arm of the loveseat with enough time to look up and see the soundless tunnel of Hannah's face, bathing cherry syrup.

EPILOGUE

FAMILY MEDICINE

These days he goes home on weekends. He likes to spend time with his new nephew, whom his mother refers to as *Angel*, as though that was the name on his birth certificate rather than Graham Alexander Hausmann. Kate alternates between (in third person) *The Baby* and (in direct address) *Guh-ram. Guh-raham* she says, prodding his belly until he farts or smiles or both. *Guh-rahahahaham*.

Erich calls his son *Alex*, the name he would have preferred to use, in honor of his maternal grand-father, Alexander Schlierkamp. Throughout the latter half of the pregnancy, Erich campaigned for Kate to move 'Graham' to second place; that is, if anything Erich does can be described with a word as effervescent as *campaign*. What was wrong with Alexander Graham Hausmann? Airily Kate pointed out that Erich had chosen Gretchen's name; by rights, she had dibs. Not to mention that 'Alexander Graham' conjured Alexander Graham Bell, and she didn't want people calling the child 'Baby Bell'; or, for that matter, her 'Mama Bell.'

For the life of him, Jonah's father cannot understand why anyone would name a child one thing and then call it another. He has moreover observed that the baby's eyes are a light, sandy shade that could very well be described as *graham*; the doubled accuracy gives him added pleasure in calling his first grandson by his propers. He tells Jonah that it's intriguing how Kate (brown) and her husband (gray) have produced a child with golden eyes. Then again, genetics aren't what they teach you in high school, when every phenotypic outcome can be plotted on a Punnett square. Any number of complex interactions . . . and besides, everything changes as the baby grows: Jonah, for example, had blue eyes for the first six months of his life, after which new marching orders roused enzymes and proteins that would leave him his legacy of muddy green. Jonah knows all this already but the conversation feels nice.

Gretchen doesn't call her brother anything. She remains in denial, behaving as though the cranky lump that occupies an increasing amount of her parents' energy is a temporary inconvenience rather than a genuine infringement of her sovereignty. She has earnestly suggested that they put It back in Mommy's tummy, a concept Kate finds both delightful and revolting. *Babies don't work that way. And neither does Mommy.*

As for Jonah, he hasn't yet settled. For a while called the baby by his initials, GAH. Graham-Man, elided to Gramman, sounded too much like Gram*ma*. Grambo, Gramcracka, Conan the Grammarian, Jean-Claude Van Graham. For a while he took to speaking to the baby in a Scandinavian accent, à la the Swedish Chef. *Ja de fürden blurden bårdy førdy firk*. Under this schema, Graham became Sven. When Kate threatened to revoke his visitation privileges, he switched over to *G – wassup, G?* – a hopelessly déclassé choice he doubts will last more than a few weeks.

Erich asserts that the child is going to be confused. Out loud, Jonah agrees, though he's not terribly worried. This is a decision worth thinking about. What you call something determines its shape in your heart.

From page forty-two of the *Guide to the Third-year Clerkships*:

> Your third year will be a time of emotional and intellectual growth. Becoming a physician is a gradual process, a forging of knowledge and compassion that comes with experience. Most students learn more about themselves than in any other academic context previously encountered.

From page sixty-seven of the Book:

CONCLUDING THOUGHTS
or

HOW I LEARNED TO STOP WORRYING AND LOVE MEDICAL EDUCATION

Okay, seriously now, you're going to have the time of your life. Third-year can be kind of a whirlwind, but that's what's so much **fun** about it!! Think about all the times in college you put off going to a party so you could prepare for orgo. Think about the girl- or boyfriend who called you a loser and went off to hook up with someone else because you had to stay at home and study. Think about all the **loans** you're going to have to repay. You made those sacrifices **in order to be a doctor**. So now that you have the chance to actually **be** a doctor, take advantage of it. See? Doesn't that make you feel better?

We didn't think so. It makes us want to barf also. But how can you appreciate the good things in life unless you want to barf at least some of the time?

Instead, think of this: fourth year is a breeze, and then internship, and residency . . . in no time you'll be a real doctor, probably no older than fifty. It has to start somewhere, and it may as well be here. Not in college; not during the Boards. Here, on your first day of your first rotation. Welcome to a world of hurt, and a world of healing. We got through it, and so will you.

★   ★   ★

He wasn't through it.

'Christmas break' devolved into a haze of taped statements and tendered sympathies. He felt like he was making the rounds of the talk shows, like he was a celebrity sharing big news: interviewing with the Great Neck PD, the NYPD, three different ADAs. Scottie Vaccaro read the brief item in the *Times* – he was moving up in the world, it seemed – and phoned to ask what had happened. A reporter turned up at his parents' house, where he went to hide out in the immediate aftermath. Friends e-mailed. Vik and Lance came, separately, to visit. And then there was a series of shouting matches with George.

Six months later, all he retains is a sense of displacement and a noxious sort of relief: feeling terrible for feeling better.

His parents – and the HUM administration – believed strongly that it would do him good to take time off. At the time he'd been too shell-shocked to argue. He'd lacked the presence of mind to reply that, if he missed the beginning of second semester, the rotation in question would have to be repeated – during his fourth year, at the expense of vacation time then; and that this arrangement would result in greater misery. Plus he had to make up the psych Shelf. His record was going to look suspiciously lazy. He didn't want to present on paper as someone who'd slid by, not after years of work. And he would recover in a few days, he knew he would, once panic released him, once he could sleep again; Hannah's open mouth, flashbulbed in his memory.

January was bad.

The videotape of that night is in the possession of Detective Luther Van Voorst of the Great Neck PD. Jonah has seen it once, the week following, when he drove over to the station with his parents and Chip Belzer.

Van Voorst wanted to use the tape to guide his questions. *If you're okay seeing it.*

I saw it in person Jonah said.

For five minutes the shot shows the living room. The focus is lousy. Eve passes in and out of the frame, moving furniture around. Always the auteur. Then she disappears upstairs.

Why was she going up there.

To see Hannah.

Do you have any idea why she wanted to see Hannah.

Jonah said *She was jealous of her.*

Over you.

After a while, he said *I don't know how much it had to do with me.*

What the detective wanted to determine was Hannah's state of mind; it bore on whether or not she could be charged with a crime. He paused the tape. *You sure you're okay seeing this again?*

Jonah nodded.

The struggle lasts at most six seconds, and its plainest interpretation is an act of aggression by

Hannah. They both hold the knife. Eve pulling away, although Jonah thought that what she was really doing was pulling Hannah toward her. The blade glints before disappearing into Eve's neck and drawing a huge, wide leer. Hannah's hands on the blade. Eve's hands on Hannah's hands. Or – the other way around. Eve's hands controlling; Hannah, a cover, a proxy, a puppet.

The pressure of moving blood varies throughout the human body. It is highest near the heart. When rent in unison, the vasculature of the neck – the common carotid and the internal jugular, as well as smaller vessels such as the inferior thyroid artery and the vertebral artery – forms a geyser of almost comical force. The carpet and the litho on the wall and the floor, all soaked; Hannah, too, poor Hannah, looking electrocuted, falling in tandem with Eve, swimming in her open throat.

Jonah knew what the detective was thinking; he was thinking the same thing. Could he honestly believe that Hannah had lacked agency, had not provided at least part of the push. Could Eve, could anyone, hate herself enough to cut her own head halfway off.

He overestimated himself; he had to get up and leave the room. He knelt in the hallway. Moments later he felt a hand on his back.

Take as much time as you need.

When he reentered the room with the chair and the table and the lawyer and the detective and the cup of water, the TV had been switched off. Van

Voorst handed him a napkin, which he used to dry his face.

You know, there's a significant time lag before you – I mean, I can see you were dealing with, things.

He'd *dealt with* Hannah by dragging her away from Eve's body, scuffling through pools, she kicking, kneeing him in the groin as he crawled. She was so strong.

When did you go to phone the police?

A few minutes later.

Do you remember how long?

Three or four minutes.

The detective nodded.

It had been more than three or four minutes. Jonah knew, because when he went to the kitchen to phone (he would not recover his cell, which had fallen and slid under the loveseat, until May, when the police mailed it to him in an evidence bag), the microwave clock said four twenty-four.

I was he said. *I was—*

He'd waited in the kitchen, the phone in his hands. Hannah on the floor near the front door, lighting up the house with her shrieks.

The ambulance took a while to get there he said.

Bad weather said the detective.

He'd waited eight minutes. By that time Eve was still. He dialed for help.

The detective said *I forgot to ask: what were you doing at the house in the first place?*

Jonah said *Good question.*

★   ★   ★

448

He does not visit Hannah. The institution where she's sojourning indefinitely is several hours upstate. When he called, he was told that in order to be granted permission to speak with or see her, George had to put his name on a list. This is something Jonah is fairly confident won't happen. George faults him generally, as well as for any legal woes that might accrue to Hannah over the death of Carmen Cove.

By March, the district attorney still hasn't made a decision. By June, Jonah infers that one might not be made for a while. Van Voorst believes that Hannah may have acted of her own volition. The DA tells Jonah that they're juggling several competing truths. There is Hannah's hand on the knife, Eve's hand on the knife. There is the soft focus. Self-defense? Act of will? If so, whose? There is history: Raymond Iniguez and the threats against Jonah, which now seem very relevant. He is asked, in tones of voice that indicate a low opinion of his common sense, why he didn't notify the authorities days or weeks earlier about Eve's behavior. Hannah is mentally ill; are they going to charge her for *criminal* activity when most *sane* people . . . and so on.

Reading the article in the *Times*, one discerns the hovering specter of a civil suit. Carmen Cove's parents are an accountant and a schoolteacher from Lauraville, Maryland. They are puzzled and angered by what became of their Ivy League-educated daughter.

★   ★   ★

Hannah's version of the story remains a mystery; since that night she has not spoken. The last time Jonah heard her voice was as the police put her in an ambulance and took her to Great Neck hospital. She said *No*.

He calls in April, on her birthday, but the nurse will not put her on. He sends a card a few days later. It shows a monkey in a party hat. IT'S YOUR BIRTHDAY, GO APE!!!

George tells Jonah that he has betrayed him. Jonah never found out if George had hired a sub for Christmas.

He has moved out of the east village and found a studio, uptown, in a large building on Third Avenue. Lance understood; he was getting ready to close up shop anyway, having discovered an awesome international-relations program in Amsterdam, the future of worldwide diplomacy, starting in September.

In his new neighborhood – which isn't new, he's been commuting up here for close to three years – Jonah has once again taken up running. He wants to train for the marathon. With four and a half months to go, he might get there.

He runs along the East River promenade, designated John Finley Walk by a black iron sign whose cutout design of a windblown man wearing a bowler shows the Queens waterfront. He runs around Central Park, the whole of it, twice. He runs to the Brooklyn Bridge and back, to the footprint of the

World Trade Center. He gets dehydration headaches that feel great when they go away.

At home he gorges on pasta. Summer, full-throttle, has stripped legs bare, and he looks down from his sixth-floor apartment at people walking north, cars shooting south; listening to the unplaceable low-grade sonic presence that never shuts off in New York City. It's the sound of movement, the sound of speech behind closed doors, the aggregate output of public living and private dying, dramas that he will never watch.

TUESDAY, JUNE 21, 2005.
FAMILY MEDICINE, WEEK ONE.

'Kiddo, long time no speak.'

The clinic, in Jamaica, abuts a half-completed housing development. All around the neighborhood are scrunched, discarded pamphlets inviting people to a sales office in Kew Gardens. *1, 2 & 3 BEDROOM UNITS*. En route from the subway he passes the construction site, where enormous color sketches on posts promise a community of faceless, racially indeterminate folk inhabiting a building that, save its fresh brick, looks pretty much like any other metro-area craphole.

The erection of a retaining wall has turned the alley behind the clinic into a dead end. Someone has taken advantage of the newfound quiet by setting out a suite of plastic furniture: five folding chairs and a table varnished with soot.

He lunches there with his fellow students or, as today, alone.

'You have to take a look at this letter, kiddo. It's unfuckinbelievable. While my client and I remain convinced that our action was and is in the right . . . blah blah to insist blah blah Raymond Iniguez was a blah blah under blah blah *blaaaah* boldface *however*, comma. *However.* Continued pursuance of . . . blah blah . . . quote a source of undue stress to the surviving members of the Iniguez family unquote. "Surviving members," for crissake, like you're a plague of locusts ate their *crops*. This guy is such a bullshit artist he belongs in a *museum*. Give the man a *megaphone*. 'Undue *stress*'? They dropped cause they *can't win*. That, if any, is the source of the Iniguez family's stress: lawyerly incompetence.' Belzer snorts. 'I think I'm going to have this framed. The guy's prose is choice. He manages to sneak in that he believes they would have won, in front of what he says he *expects to have been a biased jury*. I relish that construction. What he *expects to have been*. Insane. Somebody musta called him bad names during childhood. But let's not dwell.'

'. . . I—'

'Sound happy.'

'I'm surprised.'

'There's nothing to be surprised *at*. I told you they'd bend. Now you can get back to more important work. Go save some lives. How's that other thing. They charge her?'

'No,' Jonah says. 'Not yet.'

'They won't. Trust me. Everything'll work out. My love to your folks.'

Jonah hangs up. His appetite is gone. He dumps his sandwich in the trash and heads back inside.

Later, much later, he gets a mailer with a Bronx postmark. Inside is a CD. He puts it in his computer, puts the computer on his knees, feels the optical drive spin. Through his headphones seeps a familiar melody, sly guitar and gentle bass, clutching each other. He remembers its ascending, descending solo.

He puts the song on his MP3 player and adds it to the mix he uses while running. It's not a good choice – too slow to motivate – but he'll leave it on for one day, it can't kill him to think about it for one day.

That afternoon he heads north, past the projects where DeShonna lives. He does this often. His path skirts near the swing set, although he has yet to find her out there. Most likely he won't ever see her. If he does, she might not see him. If she does, she might not recognize him, or might not respond to his wave. It would hurt pretty bad if she didn't. But she also might smile and wave back. He thinks it's worth running there, on the off chance.

ACKNOWLEDGMENTS

Once again I owe an enormous debt of gratitude to those whose expert advice has helped me mask the ignorance that, by and large, defines me. However many errors I may have let slip through, there would be substantially more without the wisdom of Michael Rosen, Michael Strapp, Dr Daniel Stein, Ehud Waldoks, Stephen Provine, Dr Michael Seider, Phil Figueroa, Frank Skrelja, Rabbi John Keefe, Dr Benjamin Galper, Dr Robert Adler, Dr Cathy Ragovan, Dr Derek Polonsky, and Dr Alexander Stein. Thanks also to Debbie Brindley of the late, great Café Repast.

Five people deserve special mention for donating inordinate amounts of their time, and for allowing me to shamelessly plunder their stories. On matters of law: Ben Mantell and Wes Shih, Esqs. On matters of medicine: Dr Jon Kessler, Dr Eli Diamond, and Dr Elena Resnick.

Thanks to my superb agent, Liza Dawson, and my magnificent editor, Christine Pepe, whose cheer and guidance pushed me to the finish line. And then beyond, to the concession stand.

Thanks to Amy Brosey and Eve Adler.
Thanks to my siblings and grandparents.
Thanks to Ema, Abba, Mom, and Dad.
The primary inspiration and source for this book is, of course, my lovely wife, the doctah.